EVE WAS BORN TO RULE IRELAND . . .
BUT FORCED TO MARRY AN INVADER

"I lack a woman's guile and a maiden's tricks," she warned him. "I cannot cook, and a needle is all but useless in my hands, nor do I have the wit to charm a man with my person or my tongue. I'm more honest than most men can tolerate, and more independent than most women can sanction. I've no use for fools or liars." She told it baldly, hoping to put him off. What man would want such a contentious, self-willed woman? The tender, vulnerable part of herself she kept hidden.

Richard de Clare, earl of Pembroke, was unswayed. "If you're as honest and practical as you claim, we'll do well together, Eve MacMurrough," he answered. "I've no need of a starry-eyed wife who is helpless and needy. Are you capable of running an earldom?"

"I'm trained to govern a kingdom," she answered.

She bent down and filled her hands with the rich dark soil of Ireland, then straightened and held it out to him. "There is no place on this earth that burns with an all-consuming passion in your soul. Ireland is my life, my destiny. I *am* Ireland. You can no more conquer this land than you can conquer my heart."

TODAY'S HOTTEST READS
ARE TOMORROW'S SUPERSTARS

VICTORY'S WOMAN   (4484, $4.50)
by Gretchen Genet
Andrew—the carefree soldier who sought glory on the battlefield,
and returned a shattered man . . . Niall—the legandary frontiers-
man and a former Shawnee captive, tormented by his past . . .
Roger—the troubled youth, who would rise up to claim a shocking legacy . . . and Clarice—the passionate beauty bound by one
man, and hopelessly in love with another. Set against the back-
drop of the American revolution, three men fight for their
heritage—and one woman is destined to change all their lives forever!

FORBIDDEN   (4488, $4.99)
by Jo Beverley
While fleeing from her brothers, who are attempting to sell her
into a loveless marriage, Serena Riverton accepts a carriage ride
from a stranger—who is the handsomest man she has ever seen.
Lord Middlethorpe, himself, is actually contemplating marriage
to a dull daughter of the aristocracy, when he encounters the
breathtaking Serena. She arouses him as no woman ever has. And
after a night of thrilling intimacy—a forbidden liaison—Serena
must choose between a lady's place and a woman's passion!

WINDS OF DESTINY   (4489, $4.99)
by Victoria Thompson
Becky Tate is a half-breed outcast—branded by her Comanche
heritage. Then she meets a rugged stranger who awakens her
heart to the magic and mystery of passion. Hiding a desperate
past, Texas Ranger Clint Masterson has ridden into cattle country
to bring peace to a divided land. But a greater battle rages inside
him when he dares to desire the beautiful Becky!

WILDEST HEART   (4456, $4.99)
by Virginia Brown
Maggie Malone had come to cattle country to forge her future as
a healer. Now she was faced by Devon Conrad, an outlaw
wounded body and soul by his shadowy past . . . whose eyes
blazed with fury even as his burning caress sent her spiraling with
desire. They came together in a Texas town about to explode in sin
and scandal. Danger was their destiny—and there was nothing
they wouldn't dare for love!

*Available wherever paperbacks are sold, or order direct from the
Publisher. Send cover price plus 50¢ per copy for mailing and
handling to Penguin USA, P.O. Box 999, c/o Dept. 17109,
Bergenfield, NJ 07621. Residents of New York and Tennessee
must include sales tax. DO NOT SEND CASH.*

The Conquered Heart
Denée Cody

ZEBRA BOOKS
KENSINGTON PUBLISHING CORP.

*This one is for my grandfather, George Gambee, who
taught me the secret of gardens.*

*And special thanks to my fellow word wenches,
Margaret Conlan, Jessica Wulf, Barbara Kidneigh,
and Mary Gillgannon.*

ZEBRA BOOKS are published by

Kensington Publishing Corp.
850 Third Avenue
New York, NY 10022

First Printing: July, 1995

Printed in the United States of America

One

"Look at her, Richard. Have you ever in all your days seen a thing so lovely? It's enough to make a man's soul ache." Morgan sighed, his dark eyes dreamy with admiration.

Richard de Clare, earl of Pembroke, braced himself against the unrelenting rise and fall of his flagship. Morgan, being Welsh, indulged in imaginative excesses, but for once Richard could not fault the younger knight's exuberance. Ireland was indeed fair, a gloriously green island veiled in summer haze that softened the coast into enigmatic shadows and pale light. It was easy to imagine the land sheltered pagan gods laden with mystery.

Richard chided himself for his fanciful thoughts, as wild as any Welshman's. One thing compelled him to gather an army and sail from south Wales to this shrouded place. Land. His pragmatic Norman blood stirred with the same raw land-hunger that drove his Viking ancestors to conquer first Normandy, then England. He wanted the kingdom of Leinster, promised to him by the deposed Irish king Dermot MacMurrough. And he meant to have it.

The forty ships of Richard's invasion fleet sailed through the cold blue-gray Irish Sea toward the walled town of Waterford. The leather sail of his dragon ship caught the wind, and the ship heaved unexpectedly to one side, Richard's stomach lurching with it. God, how he hated boats. He spent most of the long day slung over the side of the gunwale, until only green bile came from his tortured gut. For a man who grew up at the edge of the sea it was a humiliating affliction. It made him feel vulnerable. It was not a feeling he enjoyed. Morgan kept his gaze resolutely on the leafy hills of Ireland until the powerful earl of Pembroke straightened and appeared less bilious. Richard groaned, backhanding the sickness from his mouth. He looked up to see his second in command, flame-haired Redmon FitzWilliam, bearing down on them.

"The captain claims we'll put ashore within the hour," Redmon said, without the preamble of a greeting. He planted his oaklike legs firmly on the rolling deck, as though the ship was as familiar to him as solid ground, or the back of a horse. "Is the princess there with Dermot, do you think?"

Morgan flashed his easy smile at Richard. "My lord of Pembroke prefers not to think on that subject. He fears his bride may prove to be nothing like fair Rosamund."

Richard's gaze shifted to the younger man, who flinched under his icy stare. "Your tongue, Morgan, will get you in trouble one day."

Redmon snorted and clapped Richard on the shoulder. "She can be a half-witted shrew for all it matters. Think of the dowry she brings. Meath and Kildare, Wicklow and Kilkenny and Wexford. And Dublin. Above all, Dublin."

Staring at the land they were preparing to invade, Richard shook his head. "Dublin is mine only if I can take it—and hold on to it. In truth it's not the Irish I'm worried about. It's Henry." Could he take what was promised him by the Irish king without drawing the wrath of Henry Plantagenet down on his head? Irascible, unpredictable Henry, who still bore him a grudge over Rosamund. Why that should be Richard could not comprehend, for it was Henry, as always, who won.

"I, for one, seek more than land. Richard's wife may be a shrew, mayhap we'll be luckier, Redmon." Morgan's eyes held a roguish gleam. "We'll look for sympathetic Irish maids to warm our beds, though I've heard they're all wild, dirty things. A fair-haired maid, with . . . attributes a man can get his hands on to." Morgan made a suggestive motion with his eloquent hands, and cocked a dark brow at Richard, who grinned and turned aside.

"A fey Celtic maid, with sorcery in her fingers, who knows how to play a man until he's insensible with rapture. An imp of a maid, with fire on her tongue to kindle—"

"You're talking nonsense again," Redmon said, scowling at his companion.

Richard fought to control the impulse to laugh. Poor Redmon, he had no poetry in his soul, and little humor. He had known Redmon FitzWilliam since they were squires together. Even then Redmon was larger than anyone else his age. Hell, he had been bigger than boys twice his age. Now he was monumental, towering over other men, broad and powerful, all bulging muscle and with a bearlike stolidness. For faithfulness and integrity he had no equal.

"I've work to do." The big man stalked away.

"Was it something I said?" Morgan raised his dark brows in mock distress.

"You shouldn't tease him. He's a good man."

Morgan smiled, a sweet, mischievous smile. "I've never doubted Redmon's worth, my lord. I may seem frivolous and too quick with my tongue, but I mean no harm. He's so damned serious about everything, I can't resist. I have to see to the horses before we land. Think of it. Tonight we sleep in Ireland."

Richard watched the Welshman walk away with a light step and whistling a ribald tune. Such different men he chose as his commanders: solid, imperturbable Redmon, with his too-careful pride and lack of imagination, and mercurial Morgan, all charm and grace and apparent frivolity. Of the two, Redmon was worth more to him on a battlefield, but it was Morgan he would rather spend his time with.

Turning his attention back to Ireland, he felt a rush of excitement. What waited him in this green and violent land?

Richard's eyes narrowed with resolve. Here, in this extravagant green island, he vowed to win new fiefs and reclaim his pride as well. Pride Henry Plantagenet abused with his greed. He would win the king's good grace by fighting his war for him, but he meant to have the land as well. And Rosamund. Eventually Henry would tire of Rosamund. The unfaithful king, easily bored, regularly found a new woman to pleasure him. Then Richard would claim Rosamund for his own. He wished he could wed her, but the deal he'd struck with the Irish king came with one regrettable detail. He must marry the king's daughter to inherit her lands. When Rosamund became his mistress, he would see to it she was treated with respect. If his wife made a fuss, he'd lock the woman away somewhere. Once she bore him an heir or two, she was no longer useful.

They rounded the outermost crest of land separating the confluence of the Rivers Barrow and Suir from the Irish Sea. Waterford, with her high, looming walls and tall defensive tower lay on the south side of the Suir. Entering the tidal river, the ships' square sails, painted in bright geometric patterns, furled and snapped against the breeze, reluctant to obey the ropes hauling them down. Captains shouted their oarsmen into a steady cadence as the fleet moved in close formation toward an anchorage downriver from Waterford. The ships moved like his knights or archers in one of their intricate maneuvers, with the same economy of motion, each man efficient and competent, so that the whole worked with a smooth elegance. He possessed no patience with disordered, undisciplined men.

Richard had hired the fleet from Irish Ostmen, descendants of Norse adventurers who came as vikings to Ireland in earlier centuries. They had a reputation for the finest ships and sailors in the world. Swift longboats comprised most of the fleet. It was in these the five hundred Anglo-Norman knights and one thousand Welsh archers of Richard's army journeyed to Ireland. His flagship, the *Sea Drake,* was a creature of sinuous dignity, with a high, bold prow carved in the likeness of a dragon, then painted and gilded in exuberant colors. Such a ship could hold as many as three hundred men. For this journey she carried a hundred des-triers, the splendidly trained war horses of his knights.

Richard heard the sound of running feet and turned to see Morgan sprinting toward him.

The Welshman's face contorted in a troubled frown. "Have you seen Tewdr?"

"No. That boy makes himself scarce whenever there's work to be done."

"Who of us didn't, at that age? I thought he'd be with the horses, you know how the lad is, but he's not down there."

"Your squire is more trouble than he's worth. You spend half your time disciplining him and the other half worrying. We should have left him in Wales."

"Tewdr's a free spirit, I'll give you that, but it's better than no spirit. I've no use for a lad who cowers at my every command and resents me for it secretly. I've grown fond of the rogue."

"So have I, truth be told." Richard smiled and clapped Morgan on the shoulder. "Let's look for your truant."

As they walked to the far side of the ship, Morgan pointed. "There he is."

The squires had invented a game of swinging on a rope attached to the mast, arcing out over the side of the ship, and coming safely back to the deck. Richard had forbidden the game. It was dangerous. It seemed Tewdr disobeyed him. The boy swung far out over the side of the ship and began a graceful arc back to the mast. Richard marched toward the boy. The squires watching Tewdr's antics scattered at the earl's approach.

"Tewdr!"

Startled by Richard's shout, the boy loosened his grip. Richard watched with horror as the frisky lad sailed over the edge of the ship, his head barely missing the hard gunwale. Men and boys ran shouting to peer over the ship into the churning waves.

Richard pushed his way through the crowd. A dark head just broke the surface of the waves, and one thin white arm waved frantically.

Stripping off his heavy sword, Richard climbed to the top of the gunwale and flung himself into the water. Though he hated boats, the ocean was no stranger to him. Growing up on the beaches of south Wales, he was a strong swimmer. It did not take him long to reach the boy.

"Christ's blood, what took so long!" Tewdr sputtered a mouthful of water into Richard's face. The boy seemed immensely insulted by his misadventure, as indignant as a cat down a well.

"Serves you right for doing what I warned you not to." He tucked the boy securely under his arm for the swim back. "Mayhap this will teach you some obedience."

"I can swim on my own."

"Stop squirming, damn you, and we'll get there sooner." Richard's powerful stroke brought them quickly within reach of eager hands. He watched as the boy was dragged aboard, then followed.

Standing on deck, shaking the seawater from his hair, Richard watched as Morgan fussed over the boy like a hen with one chick. Tewdr squirmed under the attention, then broke away and came to stand before Richard. He stared down at the child, who must be at least fourteen to be a squire, but who was scrawny for his age.

Tewdr's inky eyes studied Richard for a moment. "I'd not have gone over if you'd not yelled at me like that. My da told me not to trust a Norman further than you can piss."

"Was your father right?"

The boy cocked his head to one side, then smiled, a

quick, bright smile that brought his sharp little face to life. "Not about one Norman. You'll do for me, Richard de Clare." With that the boy turned and swaggered away, to recount his adventure to the waiting, wide-eyed squires. Richard smiled. Ask a Welshman a question, you will get a direct answer. The Welsh were either the most infuriatingly honest people you could ever meet, or the most disingenuous. Morgan came to stand beside Richard.

"I do believe the lad just put me in my place," Richard said.

Morgan, usually so lighthearted, was serious for once. "A Welshman doesn't give his allegiance readily. Once given it's most likely for life. You've won yourself a warrior today."

Did Morgan speak of himself, or the boy? Or both? Loyalty. What was a man without it? There could be no honor, no trust without loyalty.

There it was again, a shimmer on the water, then another, as though the sun splintered on something moving over the waves. Or was it only sunlight diamonding the blue-green sea? Eve reined her mare to a halt, and shading her eyes against the sun, searched the broad estuary.

Since April they waited for the promised help from Wales, her father's army settled like barnacles around the walls of Waterford. They waited as spring rains turned the air redolent of peat bogs, and the ubiquitous oaks flaunted proud new leaves, while impossibly green ferns grew shoulder high beneath the trees. Sheep and cattle fattened, their milk thick with yellow cream, and still they waited. At the solstice they celebrated Midsummer's Night, with bonfires and herbs to ward off evil, and waited through the first harvest at Lammastide. They lingered now in the opulent summer that glowed like a jewel under the August sun, waiting for the English earl and his army.

Eve's mare lowered her delicate head to graze. Ban, her white wolfhound, chased butterflies that fluttered away in the luminous air. She whistled the dog to her side. He came obediently and plopped down into the cool grass. The sun climbed overhead as high, bright clouds drifted in from the west.

Finally she recognized what moved on the water. It was as she feared. Ships. Dozens of them, moving inexorably closer. Gold-and-scarlet banners streamed from the gilded wind vanes, the colors of the long-awaited earl of Pembroke.

The man has come, and brought his filthy mercenaries with him.

Her father, Dermot MacMurrough, bribed the foreigners with pledges of land should they succeed in defeating Rory O'Conor, who drove Dermot from Ireland four years ago. It was one thing for her father to promise fiefdoms to the invaders and quite another to deliver on that pledge. Dermot must regain his kingdom before he could give it away.

Father is a fool, she thought, not for the first time. What could the foreigners be but conquerors? These Anglo-Normans were superior militarily to the Irish, anyone could see that. It was this prowess her father sought to use against his enemies. How could the man be so short-sighted? Once given a toehold in Ireland, who was there to make this army leave? Dermot promised land. These greedy warriors would settle for nothing less. Her father invited the serpent into Eden.

Turning her mare, she rode slowly back toward Waterford. From this day her life would change profoundly, and against her will. Unable to convince her of the necessity of his plan, her father beat her into submission. She still carried the bruises of that battle. She would marry the earl, as her father demanded, in return for that devil's help in regaining Leinster. All for the promise that Richard de Clare, earl of Pembroke would become lord of her inheritance.

That such a man, endowed with vast fiefs and the power

that came with them, felt the need for more land filled her with contempt. That he dared claim her land made him her enemy.

By the time Eve rode into the encampment of her father's steadily dwindling army others had seen the ships row into the river, and chaos threatened. After the months of waiting, in the end they were not prepared. She frowned at the untoward excitement. So that man had arrived. It was not the Second Coming.

Grooms scurried to prepare corrals for the invader's horses; cooks rushed to skewer great haunches of beef and whole sheep on spits over open fires; the petty chieftains in command of her father's army preened and swaggered, bellowing commands to the common soldiers, who yelled at the slaves and laborers; dogs barked, horses stamped and nervously tossed their heads, while over it all the sun shone with indifferent benevolence.

"Is it true? Have the earl's ships reached us at last?" Her cousin Caitlin, avid for news but reluctant to come too near Eve's mare, stood with sunlight shimmering in her honey-colored hair, wringing her hands together in excitement.

Eve slipped from the mare, handing the reins to a trusted groom, and caught Caitlin's hands in her own, stilling them. As ever, she felt protective of her cousin, though Caitlin was only three years younger than Eve's twenty years. "It's the earl and his men, of that I've no doubt. Soon mayhap we'll be in Dublin, where we belong." Having traveled far the last few years, it was Dublin they longed for. Dublin was home.

"This camp life is so dirty." Caitlin brushed an imaginary spot from her immaculate gown. "War is nasty business. I don't see why men can't find a better way to settle their differences."

"Nor do I. It's all glory and honor to them. Father lusts after power and vengeance until it distorts his soul. He's determined to be High King, and no amount of other people's suffering will touch his pride or stubbornness. He'll not back down before Rory O'Conor."

"It's been four years. I wonder if Dublin will be the same."

Nothing is the same, Eve thought. For three years she had wandered throughout England and Normandy, sharing her father's exile and acting as his interpreter, seeking Henry Plantagenet's help against O'Conor. Finally cornered in sunny Aquitaine, the English king unenthusiastically gave permission for any of his vassals who wished to fight for the beleaguered Dermot to do so. A year ago, Richard de Clare pledged himself to the Irish king's cause and spent the time since raising his army of mercenaries. In the back of Eve's mind something nagged her about that. Why would this powerful earl, this kinsman of the English king, turn his loyalty to Dermot? Besides the land he hoped to win, why was de Clare even now disembarking on Irish soil?

Most of her father's men, tired of waiting for the promised army, had long since returned to their fortified duns scattered throughout Leinster. Would they return when word reached them of the earl's arrival?

"Do you think the earl will want to meet you today?" Caitlin's eyes widened with apprehension.

"We need not fear him, Cait. He's bound to be less ferocious than rumor makes him. No man could do all he's credited with."

"It's you I'm fearful for. Look at yourself, you're a fright. When was the last time you wore a clean gown? That one is full of horse sweat and grass stains and who knows what else. And your hair. Holy Saint Brigid, he'll take one look at you and run for Wales."

"What a delightful thought." Eve grudgingly admitted to herself that her cousin did have a point. As always, Caitlin dressed impeccably. Today she wore an overtunic of silk brocade in shades of rose and gold, girdled with twisted gold silk. Her thigh-long hair was parted in the center and braided with gold and purple ribbons into two plaits which ended in gold tips, with small bells around the edge, so that she tinkled merrily when she moved.

Eve looked down at her own serviceable linen gown, originally a deep green, now faded by long use. It did smell of horse, but horse was an honest smell. The grass stains were inevitable, for she rarely remembered to heed how she knelt or sat. She was usually too eager to satisfy her curiosity to care overmuch for her clothes. She touched a hand to her hair. Riding had loosened long silvery strands from the thick braid, and there were bits of grass and flower seeds tangled in it from when she lay in a meadow that morning to listen as larks choired their song. The Irish, men and women alike, prided themselves on having a luxuriant head of hair, but it was a bother. If she possessed the courage she would cut it all off and go about with short hair, like a Norman.

"Don't stand there like an addle-pate. We've work to do before you meet your husband." There was unusual authority in Caitlin's gentle voice. She grabbed Eve by the hand and dragged her toward the tent they shared.

The spareness of the tent furnishings reflected the harshness of camp life. Within there was a single bed, two chests of clothing, a table and two chairs, and an oil lamp. Ban followed them in and took possession of the bed, stretching his long body so that his hairy feet hung over the edge.

"Can't you keep that animal off the bed?" Caitlin eyed the dog warily. "He's full of fleas."

"He is not," Eve said, indignant at such a base insult to her pet. "I wash him once a month. He's cleaner than most people."

Ban, knowing he was the topic of discussion, lifted his large grizzled head, looked from one to the other with eerie gold eyes, yawned mightily, and collapsed again into slumber. Caitlin bent over the clothes chests, both of which she opened, and flung bliauds and mantles and chemises onto the table. "Here it is." She triumphantly held aloft a gown of silk, the deep, vibrant color of emeralds. It matched Eve's eyes.

"That's to be my wedding gown." Eve caressed the wondrous thing. "Something simpler, I think, will do for a first meeting."

Caitlin looked disappointed, but she dove back into the chests, and her muffled curses punctured the warm air. She surfaced with a bliaud of peacock blue, woven of the finest linen, embroidered around the neck in green, purple, and gold.

"That's your best summer gown," Eve said.

"The color will work on you just as well as me."

Eve laughed and shook her head. "It's not the color, Cait, it's the size."

"We're the same size."

"We're the same height. You are much more amply endowed than I."

Caitlin looked down at her breasts, then over at Eve. "I forgot. We could pad you. Men seem to prefer women with large breasts."

"I'll pad myself for no man. Besides, he'd know once the clothes came off that I'd been false with him."

"That won't happen until you're married, and then it will be too late."

"Caitlin, dear, I've no need to woo the man. He's mine, whether I want him or not." She definitely did not want him, and the thought of dressing to please him increased her anger and frustration.

"There's nothing wrong with presenting your best front."

"My front stays the way it is. He'll get exactly what he sees and that will have to do."

"What harm is there in trying to please the man? Surely you don't wish to anger him."

"I don't care what he thinks about me and I'd as soon

he never set foot in Ireland. You know I've been opposed to Father's plan, but to no avail."

Caitlin's blue eyes took on that worried look that made her seem like a vulnerable child, and Eve sighed in resignation. It was not her cousin's fault Eve must wed the degenerate earl, who thought only of the wealth Ireland would bring him. She'd be damned if she would preen for him.

The sound of dozens of horses cantering into camp made Ban lift his head to give a token bark.

"He's here!" Caitlin eyed her with dismay. "At least wear this." She tossed a woolen mantle across the tent.

"It's too hot for that."

"Look at you. What will he think?"

"What does it matter, Caitlin? He'll marry me, no matter what I look like. It's not me he's interested in, but my land. I'm young and healthy enough to bear children. He'll see that and be satisfied."

"How can you be so calm about it?" Tears shimmered in Caitlin's kindly blue eyes. "You're no cow going off to a new master. That damned de Clare is getting a treasure, and I don't mean land."

Eve hugged her cousin close for a moment. Caitlin was too tender-hearted. She expected romance and poetry out of life, and a great, earthshaking love to make her complete. Eve knew such things did not exist. Reality was a marriage, arranged by her father for political reasons, with a man she had never met. If they could learn to live together with mutual tolerance it was enough for her, but Holy Brigid help the fool man if she must choose between him and Ireland.

A bellowing voice, louder than all the others, called her name and Eve recognized her father. He would need her to interpret for him. He trusted no one else with so delicate a task.

"Let's meet what Father and fate have brought me."

Caitlin sniffled one last time, then straightened her dainty

shoulders. Together they marched out of the tent and into
the brilliant August afternoon.

Sweaty, cursing knights swarmed about the place, their
big horses dancing skittishly as Irish grooms and Welsh
squires tried to get the animals into corrals. Eve started
toward the Normans gathered near her father, then stopped
and stared. She could not help herself. He was magnificent.

Letting her gaze slide over the wide, powerful shoulders,
then up the long neck to the refined, intelligent face, her
pulse quickened into a pounding beat of raw excitement
and greedy desire. She must have him. The need was born
in her in an instant. A hunger so strong only possession
could appease her desire. Tall and strongly made, with muscular long legs that promised a fiery grace and great speed,
he stood before her, so proud in his bearing she could believe him born of royalty. His muscular chest, sculpted with
rippling muscles, was broad and deep, and his dark eyes,
full of liquid fire, gazed steadily at her. How would he feel
between her thighs, the hard muscles bunching and stretching beneath her?

He was, without doubt, the most splendid stallion she
had ever seen. Dark bay, almost a blood-brown color, with
black points and not a mark of white. She walked toward
him fearlessly, her hand outstretched, and he bent forward
to softly nip at her fingers with his velvet lips. She laughed
with delight as he tossed his arrogant head. He knew he
was handsome, the rogue. He flirted with her outrageously
as she scratched his whiskered chin.

"I see my destrier meets with your approval."

She looked up into a pair of amused gray eyes, and realized the man seated on the war-horse was quite as handsome as the animal.

Two

Richard watched the woman approach his brawny destrier, Emys. The great lout of a horse grew gentle as a spring lamb under her hand. It was an unnerving thing to see. The Irish were Celts, like the Welsh, and he was accustomed to the occasional fey person. She was so small and delicately boned surely a strong wind would carry her away. A peasant, no doubt, dirty and disheveled, yet she had a glossy mane of silvery hair with small blue flowers stuck in it, not artfully, but as though she had lain in them. If he had first seen her at night, in a secret moon-silvered glade, he would have mistaken her for one of those part-human, part-fairy enchantresses said to live wild in the darkling forests.

The horse, trained to attack anyone who came too near, appeared docile at the moment, and he saw no need to interfere. The animal leaned greedily into the woman's hand as she stroked his round cheek and sleek neck. She must have the gift of animals that Richard's grandmother Isabella so often regaled him with in her fireside stories. One of his fondest childhood memories was of curling onto the hearth fur at his grandmother's feet, along with his considerable contingent of cousins, eating nuts they cracked with their hands, listening to the winter winds howl outside the cold stone keep, as she wove tales that transported them to times and places far away. There he first met Rosamund, when he was a squire under the tutelage of his uncles.

He admired the Irishwoman's courage. Then again, perhaps she was simpleminded. She stared at him out of huge emerald eyes as though he were some sort of loathsome creature. Extraordinary eyes. He surprised himself by the thought. When was the last time he had noticed a woman's eyes?

"Like to get her arm bit off, that one," Redmon said, drawing Richard's attention.

"She seems safe enough." He dismounted in one fluid, graceful movement. "That damned Tewdr has been spoiling the animal." Turning his attention from the dirty Irishwoman, he focused on the man shouting at him in Irish, as though volume could make clear his words. So this was Dermot MacMurrough.

"Don't understand a word the man's saying." Redmon squinted. "Why is he shouting like that?"

"Where's Morgan? He's supposed to interpret for me."

"Last I saw, he was distracted by a red-haired wench down the path a bit."

As they spoke, the ebullient Welshman came running, his dark eyes sparkling with delight. "Have you noticed the women? They're like angels, all of them, so fair and—"

"Enough, Morgan." Richard nodded toward Dermot. "Our host. Find out what he's saying and be quick about it." Richard would have to learn the Irish language, and quickly. He was fluent in Welsh and was surprised to learn Irish was only distantly related, having more in common with the tongue of the Scots. For several months Morgan had tutored him in Irish, but Richard did not trust himself to understand Dermot or communicate with him directly. For now, he trusted the glib-tongued Welshman to decipher the Irish king's speech.

Morgan moderated his wide smile into diplomatic pleasantness and bowed to Dermot. Their chatter gave Richard a chance to take his measure of his new ally, the man who would be King of All Ireland. Of average height and slight build, with a flowing mane of reddish blond hair heavily laden with gray, and a huge bush of a beard, Dermot bounced from one foot to the other. He wore an incredibly gaudy cloak with a vast array of colors woven into a wild Celtic pattern. Dermot's pale-green eyes darted over the knights, yet it was not fear that animated him. Excitement and excess of energy, Richard decided. The Irish king was not likely to be a patient man.

Beside Dermot stood an extraordinarily handsome woman of middle years. Her glossy auburn hair was coiled and braided elaborately about her proud head. She wore an opulent gown of purple velvet brocade, and a jeweled gold torc encircled her slender neck. A cloak of many colors, reserved for Irish nobility, flowed gracefully from her shoulders. Morgan had tried to explain to him the Irish customs involved with the colors the Irish wore. All Richard understood was the higher the rank, the more colors were allowed. He'd heard of Dervorgilla MacLochlain, daughter of the late king of Meath. The tales of her beauty had not been overstated. She had been Dermot's concubine for almost twenty years, since Dermot stole the woman from Tiernan O'Rourke, king of Breifne. With the woman came a claim to fertile Meath, which lay between Dermot's kingdom of Leinster and that of Tiernan to the north and west.

Fixing him with a calm, discerning eye, Dervorgilla quite deliberately took his measure. Apparently approving of what she saw, she gave a slight nod, and a small smile curved her arched lips. Beside her stood a diminutive young woman with hair the gold color of ripe wheat in the sun, and eyes of so pure a blue it gave her a look of untouched innocence. She cowered behind Dermot, and Richard groaned inwardly. So this was his bride, this timid, frightened creature, who, damn her, possessed the same coloring as his beloved Rosamund.

Morgan smiled and said, "You're one lucky devil, Richard. Have you seen the woman? She's a rare beauty."

"And all that land," Redmon said.

Morgan gave the big knight a disapproving glance.

"You've no appreciation of the truly important things in life, Redmon."

"What's more important than land?"

"Enough," Richard said. "Morgan, what did MacMurrough say?"

Morgan cleared his throat and stared at a spot over Richard's right shoulder. "He is glad to see us safely arrived and wishes my Lord of Pembroke good health. He also—"

A rude snort of derision behind his back drew Richard's attention. It was the fey woman, still standing beside his pixied stallion. "What he really said was what the hell took you so bloody long to get here, are there more knights coming, and what are you going to do about Waterford? And when do we march on Dublin?"

Richard turned back to Morgan. "I don't want you to be diplomatic with *me*. Tell me bluntly what he said."

Morgan dug a toe of his boot in the dirt, then his head came up, indignant for Richard's sake. "He showed no respect for you, my lord. He seems to think you're some hired mercenary captain."

"Why shouldn't he?" the woman said. "Dermot is a king in Ireland. Your lord is but an earl."

"The most powerful earl in all England. That petty Irish king should recognize a favor when he sees one."

Richard stared from one to the other. The woman matched Morgan word for word and each grew hotter with the escalating argument. Celts. If this were any indication the Irish would prove as emotional and unpredictable as the Welsh, God preserve him.

"Calm down, Morgan. Your pride is more injured than mine, and I'm the one being maligned."

Dermot began shouting again, and this time it appeared directed at the small, loud Irish woman.

"Holy Mother of God." Morgan crossed himself.

"What is it now?"

"He called her Eve."

"Eve?"

"Eve." Morgan turned mournful eyes on Richard. "My lord, your wife isn't the sweet maid standing near the king. She's that harpy."

Richard turned toward the woman, who smiled at him with a look of triumphant smugness.

"Welcome to Ireland," the dirty little woman said.

A summer sunset burnished the sky with gold as Eve trudged behind her father, the earl, and the dark Welshman, trying to keep pace with their long strides. Morgan busily translated back and forth between her father and the earl.

Dusk settled and the reverberating *quee quee* of curlews sounded less frequently along the river and bay. Lustrous long-tailed swallows swooped and pivoted after insects, and the meadow flowers lifted a fragile perfume into the darkening sky. They came to the crest of a small hill where her father's tent stood, dark against the gold-and-purple sunset flung across the sky. Music rippled from the tent. The sound of a harp and a woman's dulcet voice mingled with the high, delighted laugh of a child.

"What does she sing of?" The earl's voice was low and strangely intimate.

"Of a great warrior, and the lady he left behind," Eve said.

"Why did he leave her?"

Eve's pulse quickened at his nearness, which annoyed her. Just like the barbarian, to not understand the sole leaving an Irish woman was likely to mourn. "He died and left her alone in the world."

"If he died a warrior's death, she can be proud of him."

"Pride doesn't keep a body warm at night, nor protect from the cruelties of the world. Pride is a prize no woman would trade for the man she loved."

He looked at her strangely then, his gray eyes smoky

with some thought she could not fathom. "You speak as though you've known such a love yourself."

She shook her head at the absurdity. There was possession in his tone, as though he had a right to know her past, though there was little enough to tell. "I've listened to the singing. How do you think we Irish maids learn of love, save through our bards and our ballads?"

"She has a lovely voice."

"Dervorgilla does all things well, as I'm sure she'll tell you at every opportunity." She regretted the words as soon as they were out of her mouth. They must make her seem petty and jealous, but Dervorgilla was a standard Eve despaired of living up to. Sophisticated, extravagant Dervorgilla was everything that was strongly feminine and alluring. She drew men to her as naturally as rain to earth, and like the earth was bountiful and charming and mysterious all at once.

"Do you sing, Princess?"

His words were soft, with more than politeness to them, as though he were genuinely curious. Unaccustomed to anyone showing an interest in what she said, or voicing any curiosity about her, Eve wondered how to answer him. "No, my lord, a sweet voice is one of many gifts I've not been blessed with."

"What are some of the other gifts you don't have?"

She thought she heard amusement in his voice, but his eyes were steady and serious. He really did have inviting eyes, gray like a stormy sea, with thick, dark lashes and demonstrative brows. "I lack a woman's guile and a maiden's tricks. I cannot cook, and a needle is all but useless in my hands, nor do I have the gift to charm a man with my person or my tongue. I'm more honest than most men can tolerate, and more independent than most women can sanction. I've no use for fools or liars." She told it baldly, hoping to put him off. What man would want such a contentious, self-willed woman? The tender, vulnerable part of herself she kept hidden.

"If you're as honest and practical as you claim, we'll do well together, Eve MacMurrough. I've no need of a starry-eyed wife who is helpless and needy. Are you capable of running an earldom?"

"I'm trained to govern a kingdom."

The others walked ahead into the tent, but she lingered outside with him. For the first time he aroused her curiosity. What sort of man was Richard de Clare? She told him much about herself, at least on the surface, but he revealed nothing, save that he expected the wild, keening, romantic love of the ballads to disrupt their marriage no more than she did. He was not as handsome as dark-eyed Morgan, but he was pleasant to look at, with his light-brown hair streaked with summer gold, and those changeable gray eyes. They were like mirrors, reflecting all his thoughts and emotions. She wondered if he realized how vulnerable that made him.

Taller than most men, he was lean, with broad shoulders and a narrow waist accentuated by a battered leather sword belt. Strangely, he wore no armor and his clothes were simple, like those a man would wear hunting. In fact, he appeared oddly rumpled, as though he had gone swimming and let the clothes dry again on his body. If she stood close enough, there was a strong fishy odor lingering about him. She sniffed to be sure, taking in a deep breath of the man's malodorous scent. He definitely smelled of fish and ocean.

"Is something wrong?"

She had not meant for him to catch her at it. "I was told this day I smell of horse and that it is a most unladylike scent. I was wondering at the powerful scent of yourself, my lord. Your soap seems made with fish oil."

He looked startled for a moment, then he laughed. "You are honest indeed. It's refreshing in a woman. I've known one other like you in that. Her name was Isabella, and she was the first love of my life."

She stiffened with unexpected jealousy. Who was this Isabella, who captured his young heart, and what was she to him now? She did not ask, only watched as he entered her father's tent.

Standing in the cooling breezes, she realized it was his laughter that disarmed her. When he laughed his face became radiant, with an aching, soft beauty that burned her soul. It was the last thing she wanted from the man, to see him vulnerable and human, rather than the ravening, greedy monster she conjured in her mind all these long months. It was easy to hate the man of her imagination. The reality was much more dangerous. She had few weapons against kindness and decency.

Pushing her unruly hair away from her face, she marched into the tent, prepared to do battle. Inside it was warm and moist, more so than the sultry summer weather alone could make it, and Eve frowned. Then she saw Dervorgilla standing beside a wooden tub, a smile on her face, as she beckoned the earl to indulge in the hot bath scented with heather. It was no more than a customary gesture of hospitality. In fact, its absence would be a serious insult, and the man could certainly use a thorough washing, but something in Dervorgilla's hungry gaze made Eve wary.

Dervorgilla's eight-year-old son Egan stood near the tall knight. The boy's eager, childish voice interrupted Eve's brooding.

"Look at the sword, Mother, is it not beautiful?"

Richard held his weapon for the child's inspection, careful to keep the sharply honed blade beyond the reach of small, curious fingers.

"It is indeed, my son. When you grow to a man's strength, you will have one as marvelous as this."

"Where did you get such a wondrous thing, my lord?" The boy's eyes glowed with visions of future glory.

"It was a gift from my grandmother Isabella de Vermandois, whose father received it from the Conqueror himself."

"The Conqueror? Who is he?"

"William the Bastard, duke of Normandy," Eve told her

half-brother. "He conquered England a little over a hundred years ago, as this man comes now to conquer Ireland." She spoke in Irish, deliberately, so de Clare would not understand. His Welsh lackey could translate for him later.

Though Dermot was ignorant of the Norman-French spoken by the Anglo-Norman lords of England and Wales, Dervorgilla, Egan, and Caitlin were as fluent in it as Eve. It was a strange advantage to have over her future husband, being able to understand whatever he said while she could hide behind words he could not comprehend.

The earl looked at her quizzically but did not press her to explain her words. Egan no longer showed much enthusiasm for the strange knight and went to sit at the table, beside their father. Food soon captured his entire attention.

At least now she knew who Isabella was. His grandmother. It was strange to think of de Clare as a small boy who loved his grandmother. It went against Eve's conception of the man as a ravening beast headed for hell.

Dermot sat with Morgan at the table. Trenchers of roast beef and goat cheese lay untouched near them. Her father plied the unsuspecting Welshman with potent Irish *usquebaugh,* though Dermot drank little of the whiskey himself. Should she join her father before he did the poor Welshman real harm, or should she insist on bathing the earl? What was this strange emotion that threatened to overwhelm her at the sight of Dervorgilla helping the man to disrobe? Could she be jealous? It was a ridiculous thought, and with a toss of her head, she sat to her meal.

She hardly tasted the food. Dervorgilla's throaty, intimate laugh floated in the air. Eve glanced swiftly toward the sound. Her eyes widened in surprise. The earl was naked and just stepping into the hot water. She had seen naked men before. It was unavoidable when you spent four years in a military camp. Seldom had she seen a man's body of such power and grace, with supple muscles rippling under sun-browned skin. He was like his stallion, lean and long

and powerful, as beautiful as any wild animal at the peak
of its virility. She remembered the custom of the ancient,
pagan kings of Ireland. Only a young, unblemished man
could become king. He must be perfect. No lesser man was
allowed to fulfill the sacred marriage rituals which bound
the king to his goddess, Ireland. De Clare was such a man.
His hard, masculine beauty stirred something deep in her.
Something Eve did not want to identity.

"You're not married yet, Eve. Take your eyes off the
man." Dermot's voice was hard and angry.

Blushing, she tore her eyes away, then screwed up her
courage. "I'll be married soon enough, I may as well get
a good look at him. There's no reason to delay the inevitable, now the man is here."

Dermot gulped back a mouthful of whiskey. "You'll wed,
if at all, when I say you do. Not a moment before."

Morgan seemed about to protest, then thought better of
it, and sat back instead, a look of intense concentration on
his face.

*You're right, Welshman. There is something wrong here,
but I don't know what it is any more than you do. Why
would Father want to delay the marriage now? It's all he's
screamed at me for months, the necessity of it.*

Richard stepped from the bath, and Dervorgilla handed
him a velvet robe of dark blue, which he slipped over his
wide shoulders and tied the belt at his narrow waist. He
hurried over to the table. Eve smiled. So Dervorgilla's tender ministrations made the man wary. At least he was not
an utter fool, ruled by that rod between his legs as so many
men were.

His damp hair curled around his ears, making him look
appealingly boyish. With a smile, Eve handed him a cup of
the fiery *usquebaugh*. He took a sip, and his teary eyes
snapped up to stare at her. She felt a twinge of guilt at the
small cruelty. Putting the cup down, he pushed it out of his
reach.

Dervorgilla sat next to de Clare on the cushioned bench. Reaching for a piece of meat, her breast rubbed against his arm. As though by accident, her hand strayed to his once or twice, but he was quick to withdraw it. He put his hand in his lap, thinking to keep it safe. The look of utter shock and disgust on his face when Dervorgilla found it there was fleeting. He was being careful not to let Dermot know what was going on, but Eve could see it all. She barely kept from throwing her sharp eating knife across the table and into that woman's opulent breast.

Why would Dervorgilla dally with the man, with Dermot so near? She was not a slow-witted woman. If she had been unfaithful to Dermot in the past, she was discreet enough not to be caught. Eve clamped down on the anger that clouded her thinking. There was a reason for this seduction. What it was she could not puzzle out. She turned back to her cold food. Richard seemed capable of handling the situation. She felt a warm sense of relief that he found the advances of her father's seductive concubine repulsive rather than inviting. She wondered if any man had ever before denied Dervorgilla what she wanted.

"That murdering bastard Hasculf and his men sit safely in Waterford," Dermot said, leaning forward on his seat. "How do you mean to get them out, de Clare?"

Morgan translated quietly, unobtrusively, fading into the background until it seemed he was no more than a murmurous piece of furniture. Eve felt some admiration for the Welshman, who gave off such an air of happy indifference it was hard to take him seriously. He was good at what he did, and she began to understand why the earl kept him near.

"I seek where an enemy is vulnerable," Richard said. "Find the weakness in a man and exploit it. What is Hasculf without his ships?"

Dermot cocked a bushy eyebrow at the younger man. "You mean to steal them?"

"Burn them. Hasculf will surrender Waterford readily

enough once his transport is destroyed, if I grant him safe conduct. He'll be of little use to O'Conor without his ships."

"Burn the boats? It's Hasculf's head I want, not his boats. That arrogant Norseman murdered my father . . . buried him with a dog's carcass." Dermot's mouth twisted with bitterness. "I agree we burn the ships . . . but let the Norseman go? You ask too much."

"My goal is to garrison Waterford." Richard's voice was hard and controlled. "The port is strategic, being so near Wales. Any enmity you bear Hasculf is unimportant."

Eve crossed her arms and leaned back, letting Morgan do the translating. She was there to correct any mistakes he made. For now she would enjoy watching the earl argue with her father. The earl was not likely to win.

Her father fairly screeched with rage. "Saint Patrick's balls! He thinks to tell me, *me,* Dermot MacMurrough, king of Leinster, what is important? I'll not have it! Tell the earl he misunderstands his position. I am in command of this army."

The look of incredulity on de Clare's face was almost comic. "You have no army, MacMurrough. Less than a hundred Irishmen are camped here. My men have each vowed an oath of fealty to me and no other man, and I have vowed myself to Henry, king of England. No man commands me, save Henry. I will use all the forces at my disposal to restore you to your throne, but not as your vassal. I do it in exchange for the lands you promised, no other reason."

Dermot cocked his head to one side and stared at the earl, then burst out laughing. "If you can do what you claim, I don't care a horse's fart how you do it."

Eve took a sip of mead, to hide her eyes. Why did it hurt to have the conditions of her marriage to this man stated so baldly? Why it should matter puzzled her. The transaction was simple enough: the earl's formidable army for her lands. She was merely the token that sealed the contract. That she was caught in the middle with her life and happiness at stake seemed not to have entered into the equation for either man.

"We agree then about tomorrow," Richard said. "We burn the ships and take the town without bloodshed if possible. I need quick, decisive victories at Waterford and Dublin, so the men I have here can winter safely. We will be vastly outnumbered if Rory has time to gather an army. I mean to spend the rest of this year making his life uncomfortable, but I want to avoid real battle. By spring, the rest of my knights and archers will arrive from Wales. Then I can take on any army Rory raises. There will be time for Hasculf later. It's Waterford I need. If I don't have a secure port close to Pembroke, the rest of my men and equipment cannot be brought into Ireland."

That gave Dermot pause. "How many more men are you planning on?"

"Another five hundred knights and a thousand Welsh archers. They're the best in the world."

"So I've heard, de Clare." The prospect of more men seemed to delight Dermot, while it made Eve slightly sick to her stomach.

"What of Dublin?" Dermot asked. "When we take it from Rory, you'll have your port there."

"Dublin is farther away, and more treacherous to get to. There's no guarantee we can take Dublin, though I plan on trying as soon as Waterford is secure. I mean to station Waterford with the least number of men possible, with Redmon as their commander. A battle in which we kill the townsfolk will make Redmon's task here that much more difficult. It's a situation I hope to avoid."

Dermot sat back, tugging at his beard, the huge garnet of his ring glowing darkly in the lantern light. "It makes sense. We'll do as you say."

Her father was charming, and that made Eve as wary as a high-strung animal before a storm strikes. Everything de Clare proposed appeared well-reasoned, and her father read-

ily agreed to his plans. Too readily. What was her father
planning for tomorrow? Would he let slip an opportunity
to capture Hasculf and hang the Ostman's head from the
walls of Waterford? Dermot lied, of that she was sure.

Hours later, Eve stumbled exhausted toward her tent. The
summer night was cool and she hugged her arms across
her chest. The familiar scents of the ocean and the rivers
blanketed the land like an embrace. Waterford, silent and
dark behind its walls, waited tensely for what tomorrow
would bring. She lingered for a moment in the tranquillity
of the night, under the immense sky with its eloquent stars.
Clouds massed behind the hills. It would probably rain before morning.

Would the earl truly spare Waterford and its folk, as he
promised? What sort of warrior was he, to forego slaughter
and destruction? The internecine feuds that had consumed
her land for five generations were vicious and bloodthirsty
and looked to have no resolution. Thirty years ago, rivals
first disputed her father's right to the kingship of Leinster.
He established his authority by killing or blinding seventeen
of the rebel chieftains. It did not endear him to the people
he ruled. Now, with the overwhelming power of the Earl of
Pembroke's army behind him, Dermot planned a new phase
in the long struggle for the High Kingship. If the Irish were
so merciless with each other, how much more so would
these foreigners be? She stared up at the silent sky, but the
heavens held no revelations.

She hated what de Clare represented. He would bring
more death and suffering to Ireland, despite what he said
about wishing to avoid bloodshed. It was as inevitable as
spring driving winter from the land. In the end, what difference did it make whether the Irish kings and chieftains
tore at each other's throats, or foreigners did it instead? The
result was the same. Her land and people would suffer.

Whatever she expected Richard de Clare to be, the reality left her shaken. There was something about the man that tugged at her. How she longed to believe he was truthful and trustworthy. Such a man could offer her his protection, a safe place in which to grow and mature. She did not know this man, and her heart, while aching to accept him, did not, could not, trust him. She was Dermot's daughter and grew up in a court filled with deadly intrigue, where trust was a luxury of the foolish. Though attracted to the man, it was Ireland that claimed her heart, and for Ireland she must be vigilant.

There was no choice but to marry the man, she understood that. She knew it from the first time her father broached the subject. There was little freedom for a woman of her rank. Men dictated the direction her life would go. Unshed tears stung her eyes. Her childhood had been miserably lonely. Now she was to wed a man she didn't know, a man who wanted only her land. Her father, busy with war and intrigue, immersed in the importance of a man's world, made little time for a daughter. When she was eight, her mother had died, and Eve felt abandoned and alone in the dangerous, unpredictable world of her father's court. From the beginning, Dervorgilla conceived a cold indifference for Eve. There were times she thought the loneliness would surely kill her, but there was one gift in the carelessness. Unsupervised, she ran free, and spent her childhood on horseback. In those journeys she discovered her first and most profound love. Ireland. With the passing years her bond to the land deepened, until she could not imagine herself as anything but an inseparable part of the green and vigorous island that was her home.

Her other consolation was Lorcan, the brother of her long-dead mother. At Lorcan's knee she discovered the world's languages lay bare to her, and found to her surprise that she enjoyed the quiet hours of scholarship, learning Latin and French under his tutorship. From an early age she quickly learned languages. Living in Dublin, with its traders visiting from all over the world, she learned enough Norse and Welsh and English to communicate with men of those worlds.

When her cousin Caitlin arrived in Dublin six years ago, newly orphaned and as neglected and abandoned as Eve was herself, the girls became inseparable. It was then some of Eve's tormenting loneliness quieted. Without Caitlin and Lorcan she would have gone mad long ago.

The realization she could not hate de Clare, as she hated him all the months awaiting his arrival, confused her. She stared at the immense sky, with its numberless cold stars, and felt so small and vulnerable she grew frightened. What was her place in the great scheme of time and fate? What did her future hold, now that this tall, enigmatic man was a part of it?

She pulled her cloak tighter around her shoulders, cold in the damp night, and hurried toward shelter. The oil lamp was still burning when she pulled aside the flap to her tent, and two heads rose from the bed to greet her. Caitlin sat up, wiping sleep from her eyes like a small child, and Ban thumped his tail lazily, then settled back to slumber.

"What are you doing awake?" Eve asked. "The bells for Vigils rang an hour ago."

"I want to hear all about it. Oh, Eve, isn't it exciting."

"You want to hear of the plans to attack Waterford tomorrow?"

"No, silly. What business is that of mine?" Caitlin pulled a blanket around her shoulders and sat at the table. "What is he like?"

"Who?" Eve cut a wedge from a partially eaten wheel of cheese. She ate little of her meal, engrossed instead with the undercurrents that flowed and coiled around her.

"The Holy Father, Pope Callistus, who do you think? Tell me of Richard de Clare, earl of Pembroke. It has a ring to it."

Eve nearly gagged on the cheese, and Caitlin handed her a cup of cool water. "Slow down, you'll choke. He's a formidable-looking man, your earl. Not handsome really, his nose is too big for that, his chin too square. And that short hair, it's so strange, and no beard. Why would men want to cut their hair and shave their faces? He has nice eyes, though."

"I hadn't noticed," Eve lied, remembering how his eyes grew hard and angry, or full of laughter, changeable as the sea, whose color they resembled. "It's late, and tomorrow's likely to be a long day."

Caitlin looked down at her hands shyly. "What think you of the Welshman?"

"Morgan? He speaks tolerable Irish, I'll give him that. And he showed enough sense not to grow drunk on the *usquebaugh* Father was so generous with tonight."

"I found him quite pleasant to talk to. He has laughter in his eyes, did you notice?"

"When did you talk to the Welshman?"

"While you bathed and changed your clothes, before you went to Uncle Dermot's tent. That blue gown is lovely on you."

"Don't change subjects. What did you two talk of"

Caitlin blushed. "Small things, nonsense really. You know how people are when they first meet."

Eve grew speculative. Morgan was an attractive man, and charming, she had to admit. Caitlin was no base-born woman. She bore royal blood while Morgan was a knight-bachelor, with little hope of ever being more. "You'd do well to keep your distance from that one, he has few prospects. Father would never allow a misalliance of that sort, with a base-born foreigner." Caitlin looked at her with such surprise and hurt that Eve was puzzled.

"It's late, as you said." Caitlin climbed back into bed, quiet now, and Eve felt as though she had snuffed some warm little light. She regretted the necessity of it, but her cousin was young and impressionable and needed protection. She crawled in beside Cait, and Ban grunted his indignation at having to shift his position to accommodate them. Try as she might, Eve could not drive the image of a naked Richard de Clare from her tired brain. She finally fell into an exhausted sleep, still thinking of him.

Three

Dervorgilla stretched, luxuriating in the caress of the fur bed-covering against her skin. The inside of the tent glowed with the dim light of a single oil lamp. Beside her, Dermot lay propped on pillows, watching her with his cool, assessing eyes. His hand dropped lazily to one of her breasts and played with the nipple, teasing it in the way she liked. The sex tonight, hard and fast, left them sated and warmly weary. She could not sleep, not yet, not before they settled the problem posed by Eve's imminent marriage. She had no intention of allowing the handsome earl to marry Eve or claim her inheritance.

It was her son, Egan, she meant to see rule Leinster. She'd waited eight years until the time was right to make her move. With de Clare's army, her dream was now possible. Nothing must prevent her. Eve was expendable. It was easy enough to arrange a tragic accident, or poison the bitch, just as she had Eve's mother. Then it would all go to Egan.

Remembering the strong, young body of the earl at his bath, Dervorgilla felt a renewed heat in her loins. It was de Clare she thought of tonight as she lay with Dermot. If the king delighted in her unusual ardor, he seemed unlikely to attribute it to its true cause. Let the old fool think he could arouse her to such a pitch. It served her purpose. Just as it served her purpose to let him believe Egan was his son.

"Do you think de Clare will agree to postponing the wedding?" she asked.

Dermot grunted, and scratched his testicles, rearranging them into a more comfortable position. "Eve will do as I say. She's none too eager to wed the man to begin with. I'll have no trouble convincing her to wait. He gets Eve and her land after I've regained Leinster, not before." The king chuckled and squeezed her nipple harder, smiling at the moan that carved the back of her throat. "Don't worry about it, my dear. De Clare will not be allowed to marry Eve until he has done the job I hired him for. What's to keep him from allying himself with my enemies once he has a firm claim to my land? No, the wedding will wait."

Smiling, she burrowed deeper into the fur. As ever, Dermot was easy to manipulate without his realizing she did so. Once she planted the idea in his brain that the earl couldn't be trusted, that he must win the kingdom before being rewarded, Dermot worried endlessly about the possibility. Eve was no threat to her plans as long as she did not bear de Clare's child. Such a child would have an unquestionable claim to the throne as well as be able to rally English support.

The thought did not occur until tonight, when she first saw Richard de Clare, but after she rid herself of Eve, she could concentrate on the handsome earl. Not for a moment did she doubt Richard would prove a memorable lover. Dermot was old. If need be, she could be rid of him as well. Then she and de Clare would rule Leinster, until Egan came of age. She glanced beneath her lashes at Dermot, who was sliding into sleep.

Her revenge was long in coming. How she hated Dermot. As a princess of Meath, it was humiliating to live as the man's concubine. Bitterness seethed and grew in her with each year. Had she known he would never make her his wife she would have remained with Tiernan, for all his cruelty. At least with Tiernan she was a queen. A slow smile curved her full lips. It would give her great pleasure to place her bastard son on Dermot's throne.

After a few hours of troubled sleep, Eve woke to a day of dark fog. Such a sea-roke was not uncommon near the Irish coasts, but the impatient grumbling of the knights and Welsh archers beyond her tent revealed their displeasure. From within the dry comfort of her bed she listened to the military camp come to life around her. Horses stomped and shook the dewy wet from their backs as squires hurried to bring armor and food to their disgruntled knights, cursing the wet, shape-shifting fog. It would be a miserable day for a battle.

Reluctantly, knowing she could postpone meeting the dreadful day no longer, she lifted the warm blankets and slid from the bed, hoping not to wake Caitlin. She dressed in a wool cloak of dull colors over a sensible gown, then braided her hair into a tight plait and wound it into a crown on her head, covering it with a head-rail of soft linen. Wan light coming through the open tent flap slowly softened the darkness to a dull, tentative gray.

Spread out on the small table were the things she would need for her work. There were herbs and simples in their pouches, cached in a large basket, with rolls of clean linen packed in among them. Sharp knives and needles and stout thread were in her leather scrip, which she tied to the simple girdle at her waist.

Caitlin woke and lay in the bed, hugging the warmth. "I don't understand why you do it."

"It has to be done."

"Why you? There are physicians and priests—"

"Who attend to the warriors, but who ignore the women, children, and old people who are also victims of war and in need of a healing hand."

Eve straightened from lacing her short leather boots. How

could she explain to her cousin that she had no choice in this? It was a duty she had taken upon herself after the first battle she witnessed. The carnage had been horrific, and all she wanted was to turn her head from it, ignore the screams of those in pain, and seek the normalcy of home and hearth. She could not, any more than she could ignore a hungry child, or see an animal in pain, and not try to soothe and heal it.

It was against her nature to turn aside. As a princess of Ireland, with all the privileges and status that brought her, it brought as well obligations to serve the people. They were her blood, and she could not ignore them in their need.

"I want to come with you." Caitlin spoke in a strained voice, and her eyes took on that frightened look they so often held.

"You serve as well here with the other women, with your prayers."

Caitlin climbed out of bed and followed her cousin's example by dressing in her oldest and simplest bliaud and cloak. "They make a great show of piety, Dervorgilla and her women, but it's more fear at losing their men in battle than trust in God that drives them to their knees. It salves their consciences, to pray for the wounded. They go back to their lives without another thought, but it's hard work that is needed at the time of a battle. Not sweet words whispered in God's ear." Caitlin secured a veil over her hair and smoothed the folds of her simple gown. "I'm older than when you began doing such work. It's time I took on some responsibility, though I wish my nature were as adventurous as yours." Caitlin frowned, and nervously toyed with the edge of her veil. "What if I get sick at the sight of blood?"

"You'll be sick. Then you'll do what needs to be done."

The sounds of men shouting, of horses being tacked, of weapons and armor being carried by squires, all the too-familiar preliminaries to war, grew louder and more insistent. An excitement peculiar to battle pervaded the atmosphere, making it thick with anticipation. The two women stepped from their tent, the big white wolfhound following. There was a cold mist and the camp was swarming with confusion. It was like a hive of bees someone had poked a stick into to stir it up, and there was no queen to give it a center.

Slowly a center formed, and Eve watched the magic of it with a keen eye. On his great bay destrier sat Richard de Clare in chain mail, over which he wore a gold-and-scarlet surcote. A shield painted gold, with three scarlet chevrons, rested on his left arm. His presence commanded respect, and an aura of power radiated from the man. He raised his voice no louder than necessary for the men nearest him to hear, and doing so, men quieted to listen.

She had never seen the like of it before. Men who fought under her father's banner showed no such deference to the Leinster king. Fear and greed motivated their reluctant obedience. The respect this man commanded was unmistakable. Then the shouting began, the war cry under which they fought. The name de Clare won for himself on other battlefields.

"Strongbow!"

Men raised their voices and shouted it at the top of their lungs, their fists raised to pierce the air.

"Strongbow!"

It reverberated through the dismal morning, flinging vibrations of excitement down the backs of those who heard it.

"Strongbow!"

The shout rose and crested, and on the wave of that shout they began the march toward Waterford.

Eve found she had eyes for only one man in that crowd, and she watched until he rode out of sight, his broad shoulders carrying a burden of chain mail, and much more. The future of Ireland, and her own destiny, rode with him today. Raising a quick prayer for his safety, she found she could not ask that he be victorious. Neither could she pray for his defeat.

Taking Caitlin's hand, as much for her own comfort as to give the younger woman courage, they climbed the hill where her father's tent stood, to watch the battle. Dervorgilla was there with Egan.

"So, the mighty de Clare goes off to conquer," Dervorgilla said, her throaty voice heavy with sarcasm.

"All he wants today is Waterford, with as little bloodshed as possible." Eve wasn't sure she believed de Clare. She could only hope he told the truth, but she'd not give Dervorgilla the pleasure of seeing her doubts.

"You believe him? Pretty words to make us complacent. No, Eve, it's power and land the man wants, as all men do. He thinks to outmaneuver Dermot, but he'll need be far more clever than he's shown to do that."

"What do you mean?" Eve asked.

Dervorgilla smiled one of her secret smiles and remained silent. What did her father plan for today, and how did it affect de Clare?

Why should I care what happens to that man? Except that as his wife any plot aimed at him is sure to misfire in my direction as well. What is Father up to?

"Mother, when can I ride to battle?" Egan's face turned up to gaze at Dervorgilla. He had the same dark red hair as his mother, and the identical intensity, as though ordinary life was not large enough to contain them. Not for the first time Eve wondered how the boy could have so little of their father about him.

Dervorgilla clucked affectionately, and placed her jeweled hand on the boy's small shoulder. "You shall be a great warrior, Egan, my little fire. The blood of Brian Boru runs in your veins and you will be Ard Ri, King of All of Ireland, in your day as he was in his. Glory will surround your name for centuries to come."

Egan's eyes glowed with the image she drew for him. "I want a stallion like de Clare's."

"You will, one day soon, but you must grow taller."

"How tall?"

She placed her hand at her heart. "When the top of your head reaches here, you may begin your warrior's training. Until then, you learn what I have to teach."

Eve shuddered, and drew her cloak tighter around her shoulders, but it was not the cold fog that chilled her. Why would Dervorgilla fill the boy's head with such visions? He would never be High King, or king of Leinster. Their father disinherited Egan when he promised the kingdom to de Clare.

Vaguely Richard heard the shouts of "Strongbow!" that trailed him. He had earned that name in the wars against the Welsh princes, for his own prowess in battle and the deadly efficiency of his troop of longbowmen. It was a war cry that evoked fear in those who heard it, from Wales to Normandy.

He focused his mind on what lay ahead. Torch the Norse ships and wait for the town's surrender. That was the plot, but battle plans were notorious for going awry. If nothing else, the damned fog could make it difficult to keep track of his men. In reality, he had no idea what the next hours would bring. Outwardly he appeared calm but was, in truth, tense as a bowstring, quivering with expectation. Within, there was invariably doubt, and deep down in the place he long ago learned to hide it, lurked fear.

He galloped with a large group of knights, Morgan and Redmon by his side. There was something reassuring in the familiar sounds and smells of men and horses. Even the nervous anticipation was part of the routine of war.

"Is it wise to let Dermot and his men have their own

wing?" The nosepiece and cheek guards of Redmon's helmet obscured most of his hard, freckled face.

"They're few enough in number they can do no harm," Morgan shouted from the other side of Richard's horse.

Richard glanced to his left, where Dermot and his band of shaggy Irishmen rode at the far left of the battle line. They disappeared in and out of the fog, like ghostly riders out of ancient legend. "Redmon has a right to worry. It's nagged at me, too. We'll have to wait and see how trustworthy Dermot proves to be."

Redmon spat hard. "Just what you need, worrying what that man will do. Doesn't he know we're here to help him?"

Are we? Richard thought. *In truth why am I here? For the land. What happens to Dermot is of little concern to me, except that I've vowed to fight for him. Damn. Whatever the man is planning, I have no way of knowing.*

Richard's archers marched in a tight, well-disciplined formation well behind the mounted knights. They would be of little use today, but Richard wanted a show of force. That as much as anything should ensure the surrender of Waterford without slaughter. Having butchered more men than he cared to remember during Henry Plantagenet's wars, he had little desire to kill.

Hasculf's men watched from atop the town walls, expecting the army to attack the gates. Richard and his men turned aside toward the quay instead. Below Waterford's walls squatted the docks, and anchored there were the swift longships and merchant *knarrs* used by Hasculf to bring riches in silver and goods into Ireland. The ships with which he supplied his friend and ally, Rory O'Conor. Richard's warships lay at anchor farther downriver. It now became clear to the incredulous townsmen why he had done so, and shouts of outraged understanding rose from Waterford. Fire soon engulfed Hasculf's imposing merchant fleet.

The flames were mesmerizing. Sparks lofted skyward and timbers cracked, crashing onto the decks or into the water, where steam roiled. The smell was resinous and bitter. Intense heat drove them back from the riverside. So noisy was the conflagration Richard at first did not notice the shouting upriver. When he finally glanced over his shoulder, what he saw drove a sharp hook of anger into his brain. Waterford was on fire.

The eastern section of the town was going up in a brilliant blaze as a plume of thick black smoke towered into the gray sky. They were too far away for the ships to have sent a spark into the town, but whatever the cause Waterford was too valuable to him to let it be destroyed.

Richard wheeled his horse around and galloped toward the fortified town, his knights thundering after him. Hidden at first by the curtain of fog, what he saw as he drew nearer chilled him with disbelief, then enraged his blood to a white-hot fury.

Dermot and his Irishmen set the town afire, and in the ensuing confusion managed to scale the wall. They flung open the gates of Waterford and poured into the fortress, swords raised for battle.

"Curse the man to hell!" Richard jerked his sword from its battered scabbard, unsure if he meant to back up Dermot's effort, or run the man through.

At the point in the wall nearest the quay stood a tall stone defensive tower, and it was this Dermot fought his way toward.

"He's after Hasculf!" Redmon shouted.

Damn the man, had he listened to nothing? Richard thought Dermot understood his quarrel with Hasculf was secondary to their purpose today, which was to take Waterford intact and without battle. Dermot made that impossible.

Richard's knights surged toward a group of men and women gathered in the street, staring in shocked silence at the invading Anglo-Normans. The people scattered before the massive hooves of the horses and the grim-faced, armored men, seeking the scant shelter of their dwellings.

From the corner of his eye Richard saw someone bearing down on him, weapon raised to strike. With instincts born of years of training and combat experience, he raised his sword and swung his horse around to meet his assailant. Richard's sword sliced downward and to the right in a clean, irrevocable move. He saw his victim too late to deflect the blow, and he cursed as his sword slid into unprotected flesh.

It was a woman, her hair streaming wildly about her furious face. Her only weapon was a crude cudgel that would have done no more than bruise him if she had managed to land a blow. Dismounting, he knew she was dead before he knelt beside her. He had never killed a woman before. Crouching in the mud, he sensed hate-filled Irish eyes staring at him from behind doors.

"Richard? My lord, we need to be after Dermot."

He glanced up to see Redmon mounted on his tall chestnut stallion, his thin mouth drawn down in sympathy and anger. The others had ridden ahead. There was no time to mourn this death, or to sort through his confusion and regret. There never was, in battle.

Rising carefully to his feet, the muscles in Richard's legs shook so he could hardly stand. Before he could remount Emys, a wave of sickness hit him, and leaning over he vomited. *Christ have mercy, I've not done that since I was fourteen and in my first battle.* "God rot you, Dermot MacMurrough," Grimly, Richard remounted and rode with Redmon toward the tower.

It was a well-built round tower, with windows spaced regularly up its four stories, the two windows nearest the ground being ten feet or more above the earth. Such towers were common in Ireland, built in earlier centuries as places of refuge against Viking raids. Here the merchants of Waterford, Norse adventurers after wealth as their ancestors had been, but by commerce rather than conquest, took refuge, pulling their ladders up behind them. At the foot of the impenetrable tower Dermot raged from the back of his horse.

"Where's Morgan?" Richard growled. "I can't understand what he's saying."

"I don't see him."

"Dammit. Find Eve. She can interpret for me."

The big knight rode away and Richard waited, growing more furious with each minute that passed. Dermot continued to shout at a man in the tower, who shouted back with equal fervor.

Richard called up to the blond man in the tower. "Do you speak French?"

Startled, the man turned bright blue eyes on him and slowly smiled. "I do that. Who wants to know?"

"Richard de Clare, earl of Pembroke."

The man's smile faded. "So Dermot has finally found an ally foolish enough to join him. Take care, Richard de Clare, your friend is a treacherous devil."

"What does he want from you?"

The Norseman laughed, but it was a bitter sound. "The idiot wants us to hand over Hasculf. I've been telling him Hasculf escaped Waterford over a month ago. He won't believe me. Seems his pride doesn't want to accept we've made a fool of him. Hasculf is with Rory."

"Where?"

"That, de Clare, I'll not tell you. Call your Irish dog off or I'll put an arrow through his eye for his troubles."

"I can't. I speak little Irish and he no French."

The man laughed, this time with mirth, holding his side. "By God, when Rory hears it, he'll give me a gold arm band for the pleasure it brings him. Dermot cannot talk to his mercenaries. Go back to Wales, de Clare. There's nothing for you here but danger and failure." The man was serious now, and paid no heed to Dermot, as though the Irish king was nothing more than an irritating gnat swarming near his ears. "There are seventy men in this tower with me. What do you plan to do with us?"

"Nothing. I'll grant you safe conduct out of Waterford. I strongly advise you to leave as quickly as possible."

The man shook his head and hooked a thumb in Dermot's direction. "Even if I believed you, which I don't, what's to keep him and his men from attacking?"

Richard raised his longbow, with an arrow nocked in place, then slowly lowered it until it pointed directly at Dermot. "Me."

Dermot was silent at last, his eyes darting from Richard to the Norseman. It was then Redmon returned, with Eve riding pillion.

She slid from the horse in an indignant haste and marched to Richard's side. "How dare you? I'm a princess of Ireland, and by God and Holy Brigid, you'd do well to learn to treat me like one."

"Be quiet, woman." Anger made his words harsher than he intended. "Tell your father to call off his men."

"Do it yourself."

Richard pointed the arrow at her, holding it inches from her chest. She did not flinch. "This is the language your father and I share. I'd prefer not to use it on him if I can help it. Tell him to call his men off and let the seventy Norsemen go. I've given them my safe conduct out of Waterford."

Her brilliant green eyes fixed on him, and he saw there a mixture of fury and curiosity. "Do you mean that?"

"I wouldn't say it otherwise." He lowered his weapon, and slipped the arrow back into the quiver at his thigh.

Dermot was shouting again, this time at his daughter. She turned to answer him. By the look of disbelief that came to his face, she translated Richard's message accurately.

"What's he saying?" Richard asked.

"He thinks you're a fool to let these men go. They'll run

straight to Rory and tell him how strong a force you've brought with you."

"That is precisely what I intend to have them do. I want a chance to negotiate with O'Conor. If we can come to some agreement, we may avoid battle."

She looked startled. "My father won't back down on this. He's determined."

"So am I."

Dermot rode over to where his daughter stood, his horse close enough Richard could reach out and grab the reins. Dermot shouted something in a tone that left no doubt in Richard's mind that it was a command.

Eve was pale as she translated. "He says to do what he wants or you will never set foot on Leinster land, nor possess any piece of it."

Dermot sat with a look of smug composure on his ruddy face. It was all Richard could do to keep from backhanding the fool. "Remind your father he's vowed those lands to me and I'll not tolerate his threats. I'll sail for Wales on the first tide if he breaks his part of the bargain, and take my men with me. Without me and my army he'll never again be king of Leinster. He'd do well to learn that now, and remember it."

She translated. It was like setting fire to tinder, so quickly did Dermot take offense, so hot did his temper flare. Richard could not believe the man's foolishness as Dermot raised his sword and came toward him.

In one quick, practiced move, Richard pulled his sword from its scabbard. With an almost casual strength, graceful in his precision, he disarmed the older man. A dozen of his knights drew weapons and surrounded Dermot, the determination in their faces leaving no doubt that they would obey any command Richard gave them. "Redmon, get fifty knights down here with an equal number of archers to guard Dermot and his men. I don't want them to move a finger until the Norsemen are well out of town."

"If the Irish resist?"

Richard did not hesitate. "Kill them. And start with Dermot."

The big knight smiled, an unpleasant expression on his hard, ugly face, and herded the Irish into a well-guarded mass of outrage.

Where was that woman? Richard could not trust the father, of that he was abundantly sure. Had the daughter run off to some mischief?

Then he saw her, a crumpled heap lying in the road. She must have been caught between the horses when Dermot attacked. He cursed under his breath. Dismounting, he knelt by her. She lay on one side and gently he turned her onto her back. A large bruise marred her cheek. Pulling the mail gauntlet from his hand, he pushed a strand of silvery hair back from her face. The softness of her pale cheek surprised him.

"Eve," he whispered, and shook her gently. She looked like a hurt child, so small and vulnerable. Her eyelids fluttered, then slowly opened, and he found himself snared in the emerald intensity of her eyes.

"You great bloody oaf, you could have killed me," she said, but softly.

"Can you sit up?"

"I've a bump on my head, nothing more. I think I'll live." She sat up, then leaned over, clutched her head and moaned.

He scooped her up in his arms. She was as light as a child, but those weren't a child's eyes, sparkling with passion and indignation.

"Put me down."

"You're in no condition to walk. I'll take—"

"Damn you, you arrogant Norman, I said put me down! I have a headache, there's naught wrong with my legs. I have work to do."

"What work is so urgent?"

"Are you going to put me down?"

Except for her sharp voice and obvious displeasure, he found holding her a rewarding experience. As she squirmed in his arms, he was discovering all sorts of soft curves. His fingers stroked one breast, and she grew instantly still, a new look of outrage on her face. Reluctantly, he put her on her feet, but he kept hold of her shoulders. "What work?"

"Somebody has to clean up the mess you've made. There are wounded I need to tend to."

He puzzled over her words, and the conviction behind them.

"Look at what you've done this day, de Clare," Eve said, her arm sweeping wide to encompass the town. "You swore you would take Waterford without bloodshed. You lied. The least you can do now is let me attend the people your men have hurt."

For the first time he looked about him. The people of Waterford peered out of their houses at him, their eyes round with fear, and with something more dangerous. Hatred. Damn Dermot to eternal perfidious hell! How could he garrison the town when the people were now hostile to him and his men? In the distance he heard shouting and the sounds of the fire that still burned along the town wall. How could they not resent him, these Irish folk, and blame him for the destruction of half their town? He could not explain that none of it had been in his plan, that Dermot was the culprit. They would not believe him. He was a foreigner, an invader. He cursed softly.

It did not need to be like this. He did not want to kill the Irish commoners, or burn their towns. Irish warriors under Rory O'Conor and his allies were his target, not these simple folk. "Are there many injured?"

"A dozen or so townspeople."

"What of my men?"

"I don't know. I've left them to your physicians. They're not my concern. Oh, but I did find that Welshman of yours. Morgan. He's been wounded. I was on my way to find one of your men to care for him when that great ugly knight of yours caught me up and brought me here. I've left my cousin Caitlin with your Welshman, but she's young and frightened and doesn't know what to do. She may do more harm than good."

"Where is he?"

"In St. Olav's Church."

"Are you skilled in healing?"

"Of course. Why else would I take on such a task? Otherwise, I'd be more useful at my prayers."

Richard began to walk toward the church, pushing her along ahead of him.

"Others can look after your man, de Clare. The common folk have only me."

"I'll send my physician to treat them. Morgan is important to me."

"As my people are to me."

"No more, woman." Perhaps it was the weariness in his voice, but for once she refrained from arguing with him, and marched resolutely beside him, her teeth clenched against the pain in her head.

She was a brave woman, he would give her that. Never would Rosamund be found on a battle site, helping others, nor his mother or sister. None of the women he knew would subject themselves to such danger and unpleasantness. He had never known a woman who was so forthright. No, that was not true. His grandmother Isabella, granddaughter of the French king, Countess of Vermandois, Vexin and Valois by birth, of Leicester and Warenne by auspicious marriages, had been the same, allowing no man to rule her. Remarkably, it made her seem more womanly rather than less in his young, adoring eyes.

Raised by an unbending code of chivalry to believe it his duty to protect women from unpleasant realities, he puzzled over the dilemma of Eve. She appeared perfectly capable of taking care of herself. If she was afraid of anything, he had yet to discover what. For the first time he worried that his marriage to the Irishwoman might not be as simple as he had assumed. Above all, Eve did not seem the type of woman who would allow him to keep a beloved mistress without causing problems. He frowned. He'd allow no insignificant woman, especially his wife, to keep him from Rosamund.

They found Morgan and Caitlin just within the church door. "How is he?" Richard asked.

Caitlin looked up at him with tear-filled eyes. "I fear he's dead."

Kneeling beside the Welshman, Eve pressed her fingers against his throat. "He's alive."

"Where is he wounded?" Richard squatted down beside her.

"His arm. The wound isn't deep and he's not bleeding too heavily, but he needs to be stitched up. I'm more worried that he's still unconscious. He may have suffered a blow to the head."

Richard placed his arms under Morgan, then lifted his friend. "It'll be easier for you to work on him in my tent." He stalked away without another word. Eve had no choice but to follow.

Four

Eve tied the last bandages into place and straightened. She pressed her fists into the small of her back, and rubbed at the dull ache. How long did she bend over to clean, stitch, salve, and bind the Welshman's wound? It was a long sword cut, from shoulder to elbow, complicated to stitch together. Luckily it wasn't deep. If she could keep it from putrefying, Morgan had a chance of keeping both the arm and his life.

"Well?"

She looked up at de Clare, his face tight with worry. Tewdr's frightened face peeked from around the earl's back.

"Dammit, woman, will he live or not?" Richard demanded.

"I've done what I can, the rest is in God's hands. In the next few days we'll know if the arm will rot. He's young and strong and didn't lose too much blood, that's in his favor, but I can't tell you whether he'll live or die."

A stifled sob drew their attention. Caitlin, her eyes wide and frightened, stood with a fist over her mouth.

"Come away, Cait." Eve held her hand out, but her cousin shook her head, and backed away a step. "You need your sleep, and there's nothing more we can do here."

"No, I must stay. He needs someone near when he wakes."

Richard took a step toward Caitlin. "You've been brave and kind, Lady, and he's sure to know it, but I'll be here all night, and Tewdr. If he wakes and needs help, we'll send for you."

"I'll escort the lady to her tent," Redmon said. Caitlin hesitated a moment, then placed her hand on the knight's outstretched arm and left with him.

Eve turned abruptly to confront de Clare. "Caitlin spoke in Irish. How did you understand her?" She tried to remember everything she'd said in front of the man.

Richard smiled and shook his head. "Morgan has been teaching me the language, but my vocabulary is limited. I understood most of what your cousin said, though you'll notice I answered her in French."

"You've been dishonest."

"How? No one asked if I spoke your language, and in truth I understand little. There are more important things we need to talk of. How long will it be before Morgan can ride again?"

Eve squinted at the injured man, where he lay naked on a cot, a woolen cloth covering him from the waist down. "If he recovers, he can probably ride in a few weeks."

Richard lifted the tent flap, then followed her out. "I'll walk with you. There's more we need to discuss."

The air was soft only as Irish air can be, saturated with moisture, heavy and fragrant, drenched with the scents of rain and grass and the wild roses that grew in profusion near the tent. He stood beside her, quiet for the moment, and seemed to be taking in the same sensations with wonder and pleasure. If he fell in love with Ireland, with the land, perhaps he would treat her people with dignity. Eve sighed, knowing it was an empty dream. He might well love the land and still despise the people, treat them as little more than serfs, as his traditions trained him to do. His people and hers were too different.

Eve was incredibly weary and longed to wash the blood from her hands and arms, then collapse into obliviating sleep. She tried to ignore the sensation de Clare's nearness caused, but found it impossible. Something she could not explain drew her to the man. *It is because I am tired that I am so vulnerable.* If only he were the arrogant, blood-thirsty warrior she expected him to be. If only she did not see compassion and integrity in his words and his actions. If only he were not so overwhelmingly male.

He walked toward the river. Wearily, she gathered her skirts up out of the wet grass and followed. Whatever it was he wanted to talk about, he seemed in no hurry to broach the subject.

They stopped upwind of the ruined ships, the acrid smell of destruction borne away from them on the breeze. Only the moist night scents intruded. The sound of the river was soothing. She loved water in all its variations, and never tired of listening to its music; the small sound of quiet misty rain, the heart-wrenching wonder of a thundering storm, the varying rhythm of the ocean, from gentle to raging extrava-gance, and rivers and lakes and trilling streams that trans-formed Ireland into a tapestry of green and silver.

She stared at the river, no longer trusting herself to look at him so confused were her thoughts. The sun was low in the sky, but there was enough light to see. "What is that?"

"Where?"

"In the water, there, near that large rock at the bend." Eve walked toward the riverbank and he followed. When she was close enough to see clearly, she gasped, then turned on him in anger. "You bastard, you lied to me!"

"What are you shouting about? Speak French, not Irish."

She pointed, and he went down to the river's edge, where he squatted. With a curse, he pulled the object toward him. It was a man with his hands tied behind his back and his ankles bound together. Once thrown into the river he'd had no chance of survival.

Eve scanned the river. There were dozens of bodies, all tied in the same manner. "My God, what have you done?" she whispered, too appalled to challenge him.

"Look at me, Eve." He grabbed her by the shoulders and turned her when she did not move, too shocked by what she saw to respond to him. He shook her, hard, and her anger soared.

"You lied! You filthy bastard, you lied to me. You didn't let the merchants go, you killed them and in a coward's way. You're a monster."

Wrenching the long, sharp knife from the scabbard at his belt, she was not quick enough to use it. He held her wrist, not so hard as to be painful, but enough to render her powerless. The knife glittered between them.

"You wouldn't use that on me, would you?" He sounded like a hurt boy. She almost laughed, that he could be so brutal and so vulnerable. Who was this man?

She loosened her grip, feeling defeated. The anger drained from her to be replaced by despair. Like a fool she'd hoped to come to some workable arrangement with the man.

He slipped the knife back into its scabbard. "Listen to me, Eve, and listen carefully. I did not lie to you. I let the merchants go. I didn't kill them nor order them killed. If any of my men disobeyed my command, they will pay with their lives."

"Then who?"

Richard stared at the carnage in the river. "Dermot wanted them dead."

The look he gave her was one of disgust and anger, but it could not silence her. Even when her father beat her, she spoke her mind and took the punishment rather than cower and become nothing, as was expected of women. It was in her blood, this boldness she would not tame. Not for her father, not for de Clare, not for any man.

"You're lying."

"I don't lie. Ever. I'm told it's my greatest fault." His voice was low, but there was an edge to it she knew better than to ignore.

Had her father murdered these men? Though her mind

tried to deny it, her heart knew the dreadful truth. She stared again at the river. Dermot did not hesitate to break a pledge if it was to his advantage, and counted the man who trusted him a fool to manipulate. She'd seen his treachery at work more than once and there were tales of atrocities she prayed were not true. Her father hated Hasculf, but why such extravagant vengeance? What demons drove her father to acts that put his very soul in jeopardy? She felt as though her legs would give out and was grateful de Clare still held her by the shoulders. "What will you do to my father?"

"What can I do? I'd like to kill the man, he deserves no better for his perfidy. But he's no use to me dead." His voice was calm and cold. "Your father proved today his word means nothing. He attacked Waterford after swearing not to and killed these men after I promised them safe conduct. Then he threatened not to give me the lands he pledged. I can't trust the man." He scowled at her. "I want the land he's promised me, damn him. I mean to secure that vow, before I do anything else."

"How do you propose to do that?"

"We'll marry tonight. There are priests enough in Waterford, we're sure to find one to say the words. When you're safely my wife, I'll have an unquestionable claim to your lands."

"You can't be serious?"

Anger hardened his features. "Ireland is in chaos, one petty king battling the other until it's such a muddle of feuds, no one can keep them straight. I've no interest in fighting Dermot's dirty little war if there is nothing at the end for me to own. I was hired to do a job at a certain price and expect to be paid what I was promised."

His words proved to Eve beyond doubt that the only reason the man was in Ireland was to seize her inheritance. His arrogance roused her defiance, even as disgust for her father made her want to weep. "You're as bad as my father, de Clare. You'll kill just as he does, not caring how the people suffer so long as you get what you want." The anger building in her made her shake. Were all men so? Their ambition above all else?

"I don't care what you think you've been promised, de Clare, you can't command me to marry you. No one can. I want peace in Ireland. There are too many dead and crippled men, too many widows and orphans. For thirty years my father has failed miserably, unable to end the fighting. In truth I fear he has no interest in doing so. He follows only his desire for vengeance and power. By his actions this day he has destroyed whatever faith I had left in him. I know now he will never bring peace to my people. I would do anything to end the fear and misery, even marry you. But I look at you and see only war."

Richard stood with his arms crossed over his chest and eyed her intently. "Believe what you will, woman, but I've no desire to see the Irish peasants killed or made homeless. What good is the land with no one to work it? I'm a hard man. I do what I must, but only a fool destroys what is his. A land at war cannot prosper. It is peace I want for Ireland, not war."

How could she make him understand the burning passion Ireland was in her soul? "You hold a barony in Normandy and an English earldom, yet neither England nor Normandy are home to you. Born in Wales, you have no Welsh blood. How deep can your loyalty to that land be? Now you come greedy to Ireland, lusting for my land and the power it can give you."

She bent down and filled her hands with the rich dark soil of Ireland, then straightened and held it out to him. "There is no place on this earth that burns with an all-consuming passion in your soul. Ireland to you is what you can get from her. Ireland is my life, my destiny. I *am* Ireland. You can no more conquer this land than you can conquer my heart."

Dirt drifted between her fingers in a fragile shower as the silence lengthened between them. His large hands covered hers. The earth she held grew warm between them. "Ireland does not claim so fierce a loyalty from me, Princess. How can it? I'll not lie to you, I want the wealth the land harbors. To do that Ireland must be calm so it can be farmed, so I can keep Dublin open to trade. You want peace to end the suffering of your people, I want it so the land prospers. What difference does it make why I want an end to the wars, if in the end I bring order?"

There was something compelling about him when he spoke, a passion behind the words that made her wish she could believe him. What Leinster needed was a strong leader, who honored the principles of justice and fairness, who held compassion in his heart as well as the strength of character to rule wisely. Her father was not such a man. Perhaps de Clare was. Where was the truth? Unthinkable as it was to her, would it be best for Ireland to marry the arrogant earl, no matter the personal sacrifice she must make of her happiness? Or would she bring disaster to her people?

"What if I refuse to marry you, de Clare? How will you get your land then?"

"You can't refuse, your father and I have agreed to it. You have no say in the matter."

"Your arrogance is matched only by your ignorance. There are eight different kinds of marriage in Ireland. Unlike your English laws, Irishwomen are free to choose whom they marry. I have every right to refuse you. I see no advantage in this agreement you've made with my father."

"Save that I can bring peace to Ireland, and your father cannot."

He smiled at her, but it was a weary, almost sad smile. For some reason, that touched her. He was as caught in this mess as she was.

She looked away. All the months spent fighting her father, refusing to marry de Clare, refusing to believe a foreigner could be a better ruler for Ireland than a native prince, seemed meaningless now. Damn the man for his arrogance, but it seemed he was the best hope she had. The idea took shape in her mind, and became a clear and pragmatic decision. If she used Richard de Clare to protect her land and people, if she could bring peace to Leinster through him, she would marry the man. But he must be made to understand her terms.

"If I agree to marry you—"

"You've no choice, woman. It's not for you to decide."

Hadn't he heard a word of what she said? It was all she could do to keep from walking away from him, but Ireland was more important than her pride. "If you keep your mouth shut long enough to hear what I have to say, you may be surprised."

He looked as though no one had ever told him to shut up before. "Have your say then, and be quick about it." He folded his arms across his broad chest and towered over her. She refused to be intimidated.

"I will agree to marry you, if you make certain promises."

His eyes narrowed with suspicion. "What promises?"

"The absence of war is not peace. I need your promise you will rule Leinster with justice, and use the laws my people know."

"I can't do that. It's English law I'll use."

"Then it's in England you'll do it. You'll have no say here, de Clare, because I'll not marry you without the promise."

His lips narrowed in anger. "If I promise to use Irish law for the Irish people and English law for my men, will that suffice?"

"Aye. Further, you must promise you will allow me a say in governing Leinster. I am your equal in status and wealth. Under Irish law it is my right."

He looked at her as though she had gone mad. "Women don't rule over men."

"They do in Ireland. Besides, you'll need me, de Clare. You'll need a liaison the people can trust to mediate between you and them. They trust me."

He plowed his fingers through his short hair in exasperation. "Jesu, woman, what you ask is unnatural."

"What I ask is customary and practical."

"Dammit, you ask too much. And don't tell me again about Irish law. For all I know you've made up every word of it. I'll not be forced into vows I can't keep."

"Your arrogance is remarkable, de Clare. Is it to be all your way? Am I to have no say in the governing of my lands because I'm a woman? In Ireland women can be all things, save a priest. I'm not some meek, obedient lady from your English court. If you think I'll marry you then be silent, you're badly mistaken."

"My men will never allow themselves to be ruled by a woman."

She cocked her head to one side. "Wasn't your father one of the Empress Matilda's most ardent warriors when she claimed the English throne? Hasn't her son, your king Henry FitzEmpress, rewarded the families who supported her lavishly? Yet you tell me your men will not consider a woman as their ruler."

"If you know your history, you'll remember England was torn by war for many years over whether Matilda or Stephen should reign. All it proved in the end is that men are better able to govern." He held a hand up as she opened her mouth to argue. "Enough. I propose a compromise. I agree to consult you in the rule of Leinster. In truth, it does make some sense, since you know the people and customs. But I'll not have my men know of this arrangement."

Eve turned her back on him and directed her frustration at the darkening sky. *Lord, give me patience. The man's an arrogant, stubborn pigheaded fool. He may also be the only chance I have of seeing peace in my life. If I didn't know better, Lord, I'd believe you have a perverse sense of humor.* When she turned back, she forced herself to speak calmly. "I can agree to that."

There was a spark of humor in his eyes. "The women I

know are quiet, feminine things, gentle and pretty, and in need of a man's protection. You're none of those, but you may well be what I need in this strange land. A strong, outspoken wife who will tell me honestly what I must know to rule here is an invaluable help. Is there aught else you'd have from me?"

He was less than gracious in accepting her terms, but accept them he did. "Swear to me you will be true to your word and I'll marry you. But remember, under Irish law I have the right to divorce you. If I do, all my wealth reverts to me."

The smile disappeared from his face. "You can't be serious. A woman can't divorce her husband, except for being too closely related. No such laws exist in any Christian land."

"They do in Ireland. Those are my terms. Accept them or not, as you see fit."

He paced back and forth, glancing now and then in her direction and shaking his head. She waited. It was he who wanted the land. If he wanted it badly enough, he'd agree to anything. He came to stand before her and placed his large, warm hands on her shoulders. The touch sent an odd shiver through her body.

"I swear to you, Eve MacMurrough, and I do not lie. Unlike your father I am a man of my word, though God's truth I begin to wonder what I have gotten myself into. But I would secure a promise from you as well."

Clever man. "What would you have of me?"

"Your loyalty. You must place me above your father, above any other claim to your honor. I'll have nothing less from my wife. I must be able to trust you."

"My deepest loyalty will ever be to Ireland. I'll not vow that away."

He lowered his head and sighed. Finally, he looked up. "If we agree we both want the same thing for Ireland, that we want her at peace, and prosperous, I'll never ask that sacrifice of you."

"You understand the only reason I agree to marry you is the hope you will end the suffering of my people."

He quirked a crooked smile at her. "That is the only reason?"

"Aye, de Clare. What else could there be? We understand each other then. I'll marry you for your promise to bring peace to Ireland and rule the people with Irish law. You'll also grant me a say in the governing of my lands. In return you get my inheritance and my sons."

"The things you say, woman. I must be mad to agree to any of this, but if it will get you to marry me, I'll do so. You'll voice no objection to our being wed tonight?"

"Now? Look at me. I'm covered with blood, and I'm bone tired. Who would witness it? No, de Clare, this can wait."

He looked at her as though seeing her for the first time. "God won't care what you look like, and I want your vow tonight."

"My vow you have, the marriage can wait. I'll not go to my bride-ale looking like a peasant you've dragged from the field. I'm a princess of Ireland, at least allow me the dignity the occasion normally demands."

He thought for a moment, then nodded. "Tomorrow then. Noon, at St. Olav's Church."

"Tomorrow!"

"No more arguing. It'll take a day or two to garrison Waterford, then we march on Dublin. I'd have us wed by then."

"You're an infuriating man. Do you never ask?"

He looked puzzled for a moment, then broke into a wide grin. "In truth, rarely. It comes with wielding power from a young age, I suppose. One grows accustomed to it and never gives it a thought. But you're right, it's not something to demand of a woman. Tomorrow, at noon, will you meet me at St. Olav's Church, and there become my wife?"

He was charming when he smiled, and her belly did a funny flop. She lifted her chin and looked up into his gray eyes. "That I will."

She watched him walk away, calling for his men to retrieve the bodies of Hasculf's dead followers. *God help you, Richard de Clare, if you are false with me. Ireland is first in my heart. If you betray her, I'll not hesitate to leave you and deny you any claim to my lands.*

Five

Eve woke with a start. Something tickled her. A cold, wet nose snuffled in her ear, followed by a warm tongue on her cheek. "Ban, no." The wolfhound beside her grunted and rolled onto his back, his feet sticking up in the air. Caitlin was right. She never should have allowed the dog to sleep with them, but when he had been small and frightened, she could not resist the warm little body cuddled close to her own. Now he was big and indolent and spoiled.

"Caitlin, are you awake?" There was no reply. Her cousin had been sleeping when she returned to their tent the night before, so Eve had yet to tell her that she was to marry the earl today. *My wedding day,* she thought, and her head started to pound. She scratched Ban's belly, and he grunted with pleasure. The tent was dark, and she lay quietly, reluctant to leave the warm, safe place.

Her father's strange remark at dinner the night before, forbidding her to marry de Clare until Dermot deemed it time to do so, made Eve reluctant to tell her father of the imminent ceremony. Whatever Dermot had in mind, from this day she would determine her own destiny. She no longer trusted her father to look to her interests. At times she wished she were the daughter of a simple man, who had no blood on his hands and did not make decisions of life and death for so many. She knew it to be a specious dream. Not all men who ruled did so cruelly. Not all men became so blinded by ambition they were able to justify to themselves the most reprehensible acts. Even so there was a corner of mournful regret in her heart that she could not admire her father.

Richard, for all he was a stranger to her, a foreigner come to conquer her land, appeared to be an honorable man. Every instinct in her cried out against de Clare, cried for an Irishman to rule an Irish kingdom. Fate brought her no such man. Instead, she must trust her destiny and that of her people to the tall, gray-eyed, dangerous man she expected to hate, and could not.

She would do what was best for her land and her people. At the moment, marriage to de Clare seemed more likely to bring stability in Leinster than any other course open to her. It could be the biggest mistake she ever made.

"Caitlin?" Again, there was no answer. Eve leaned over the dog to check, but the other side of the bed was empty. It was just beginning to grow light outside. Where could her cousin have gone so early in the day?

She pushed the covers aside and dressed quickly in the semidarkness. Her first duty was to check on Morgan and change the dressing on his wound. Then she would think about finding her cousin and preparing for her nuptials.

She squished her way through the mud toward de Clare's tent, past knights and archers beginning to stir for the day. Men hacked and coughed and spat, casually relieving themselves onto the grass. The scratching and grunting and low growly voices created so masculine an atmosphere that she felt like an alien moving through them. A few called polite greetings, some stared, most ignored her. That a woman could walk through their camp unmolested, with her dignity intact, spoke much of the discipline expected of the earl's troops.

The glow of a lantern lighted the entrance to Richard's tent, and pushing aside the flap, she went in.

Caitlin swooped down upon her like a raptor after a

mouse. "Thank God you're finally here. You must do something, Morgan is raging with fever."

Alarmed, Eve moved quickly to the Welshman's bed and placed her hand against his brow and cheek. He was warm, but not hot. He groaned, and his eyes opened for a moment, then he fell again into a fitful sleep. It was a good sign. He would be fully conscious soon.

"What's wrong, you must tell me. Is the arm poisoning him?"

"Caitlin, calm yourself. He has a slight fever, no more than expected with such a wound. Now help me change the bandage." She spoke calmly, as she would to a nervous horse, and Caitlin grew quieter, her eyes less filled with apprehension. Eve glanced to where Richard and Tewdr stood, and saw the relief in their eyes as well.

"Tewdr, come help." She held a wooden dish out to him. "Hold this."

"Yes, m'lady."

Cutting away the bandages, she dropped the soiled linen into the bowl, then leaned over to inspect the wound. The lantern was moved closer so she could see more clearly. Glancing up, she saw de Clare leaning toward her, curious and concerned. She bent back to her task. The wound looked clean, no sign of puss, and little bleeding. She bent closer and sniffed. No putrid smell. No discoloration. Straightening, she saw three tense, anxious faces. "The wound is clean, which is a good sign. A very good sign." There were sighs of relief all around.

"Has he awakened yet?" Eve asked.

"Three times through the night," Tewdr answered. "He asked for water last time. I gave him some. Did I do wrong?"

"Nay, lad, it's good he has sense enough to ask for water. Sleep now is the best healer."

Taking a jar of garlic and oak bark salve out of her leather scrip, she handed it to Caitlin. "Spread this on the wound thickly. It will help in the healing. Do you think you can do the bandaging?"

Caitlin nodded and bent to her task, careful and gentle. Eve watched her closely. Her cousin was strangely disheveled. She had not even pulled a comb through her hair, which was unlike her. Why did she come running to this tent, to this man, as soon as she woke, ministering to him now as though her very heart were in the task?

Eve looked at Morgan with cold, appraising eyes. He was a handsome man, there was no denying it, with his chiseled, symmetrical features, sensuous mouth, and fine straight dark hair. He was not tall or large, but well proportioned and strong for his size, with the lean, hard muscles of a fine wolfhound, not the bulking strength of Redmon, who looked like an ox. It was his eyes, dark and liquid and filled with mirth, the low melodious voice, and the smile that charmed, that made him beguiling.

Could Caitlin be falling in love with the man? The idea was ridiculous. Surely she had more sense than to give her heart to such a man. *You're setting yourself up for heartbreak, Cousin, and if it's in my power to prevent it, I will.*

Caitlin stood back from her work and Eve checked it, nodding in satisfaction. "You learn quickly, and your touch is gentle. It's a good skill to have, some healing in your hands." Caitlin beamed at her.

"He will recover then?" de Clare asked. His voice was unexpectedly close, and Eve shivered at the sound of it, so low and masculine. It rumbled through her.

"His chances are better today than they were yesterday. The longer he goes without infection the more likely he is to recover."

"Thank you for your care of him."

"I'd do the same for anyone who needed me."

"I believe you would, but you still have my gratitude. Morgan is special to me."

"So you've said before. Why?"

"He was my squire, until two years ago, when I knighted him on the battlefield for valor. He's like the younger brother I never had, or a well-loved cousin. Morgan makes life bearable. I'd have little laughter or whimsy in my life without him."

She knew it to be true, so sincere was de Clare's voice. Had he been so serious all his life, burdened with the cares of his high station? He would have need of someone like fun-loving Morgan in his life, to help him be human. She suspected the powerful earl hid his true self carefully. Was the real man hidden behind layers of dignity and responsibility? Morgan would know the man behind the facade, and was probably one of the few people in Richard's life who he allowed near enough to know him intimately.

Just because the tall earl found Morgan so indispensable did not make him any more appropriate for Caitlin. Eve decided it was time to put some distance between her cousin and this too appealing Welshman. "Caitlin, I have need of you today. Tewdr can watch Morgan—"

"He's only a boy."

"He'll know where to find us, should there be a need. We've done all we can for Morgan until he wakes. You must come with me, I can't dress myself for my wedding."

Caitlin looked at her wide-eyed, then glanced at the earl, then back to her. "You're not serious."

"I'm afraid she is," Richard said. "But she insisted it be today, no matter how I protested."

"I did not." He was smiling at her, and Eve blushed, unused to being teased.

"Well, then, we've work to do." Caitlin smiled. "This is wonderful. I'm so happy for you, Eve."

The pounding in Eve's head intensified. She was going to have to endure Caitlin's enthusiasm, and God alone knew how her father would react. With luck, she would be done with the nasty deed before he heard a word about it.

"I'll see you at noon," de Clare said.

If she did not know better, she would have thought he winked at her.

The air was dense with unshed rain and smelled like a lush rose just past its prime. Summer was moving toward autumn in its usual slow, sweet pattern. By noon, a few rays of sunlight broke through the clouds. Richard paced back and forth before the altar in St. Olav's Church, the nervous Irish priest glancing from him to Redmon and back again.

"She won't be late," Redmon said.

"How can you be sure? She wasn't keen on showing up at all. Damn the woman, I need her vow freely given so there can be no question of its validity. Nothing else will protect me from Dermot going back on his promise."

Redmon rubbed his chin, where a week's worth of red stubble grew. "I'd not thought of that. She's a woman, she'll do as she's told. Once married, you're her master, there's no arguing that."

"You haven't experienced the pleasure of an education in the finer points of Irish law. I doubt anyone has *told* that wench what to do."

Redmon grunted and hooked his thumbs in his sword belt. "Get your lands and your sons from her, and lock her in a tower somewhere if you must. That's what you do with a woman who won't obey."

Richard shrank from Redmon's cold pragmatism. His parents had suffered the hell of a disastrous marriage, the hatred between them a livid thing. He did not want his own marriage to be the same. His mood changed from nervous to gloomy. The woman must see reason, must see her loyalty was with him now, not her father. To cut herself off from her family and cleave to him, as the wedding vows said, were more than words. They were promises he meant to see her keep.

The mud-muffled thud of hooves on the road drew his attention, and he turned toward the door. A brave shaft of sunlight slanted in through the arched windows behind the altar, reaching its pale light halfway down the aisle. Two women entered the church, but until they reached the patch of sun he saw no detail. When he did, he sucked in his breath in surprise.

Caitlin was there, delicate and lovely as ever, but it was Eve who riveted his attention. This was his bride? Where was the rough-and-tumble hellion he had come to expect? In her place walked a creature of ethereal beauty. Her hair haloed her face and shoulders like silver gossamer, and fell freely in luxuriant waves past her hips. Tiny braids were plaited here and there, and at the end of each a delicate gold bell was tied, so that she sang with elf music as she walked. The gown of shimmering green silk was the color of the richest summer fields, but the style was unlike any he knew. It left her arms bare from the elbows down, and on her wrists she wore massive Celtic arm rings. The gown was square-necked, and about her delicate throat she wore a splendid golden torc, set with emeralds and amethysts. She was crowned with a diadem of gold set with stones to match the torc, and hugging her slim waist, accenting the very womanly curve of her hips, she wore a girdle of twisted gold filigree, so delicate it moved with a suppleness that matched her grace. Around her shoulders and trailing like a waterfall behind her was a mantle of lustrous silk, woven in an intricate Celtic pattern of fanciful beasts. Every color of Irish royalty gleamed proudly in the mantle. She looked like a fairy creature come from the deepest mists of the forests. She was every inch a princess, her bearing proud and unhesitant as she moved toward him.

"God's toes, she's wearing a fortune in gold." Redmon's voice quivered with admiration.

Richard nearly laughed. Leave it to Redmon to see only

the trapments instead of the regal and spirited young woman.

As he took her hand, Richard leaned forward so only she could hear, and whispered, "You are lovely, Princess, and glad am I that you will soon be mine." Her hand trembled in his, and the green eyes she turned to him were proud, yet held a vulnerability in their depths that made him feel unexpectedly protective. He tucked her arm securely around his and together they walked to the altar rail, where they knelt.

Redmon eased his bulk down beside him, and on Eve's far side he heard Caitlin go to her knees in a cloud of silk soft as a whisper. The priest opened the elaborate manuscript that held the prayers of the wedding service, and they bowed their heads as the sonorous Latin, tinted with the lilt of Ireland, washed over them.

The priest finished the ceremony, naming them man and wife until death, when the sound of galloping horses racketed into the churchyard.

"Bloody Christ, now what?" Redmon sprang to his feet.

Richard looked at Eve, and the surprise in her eyes told him she knew no more of what was going on than he did. The shouting from outside was in Irish, and he recognized one voice above the others. Dermot.

"You did tell your father you were getting married today, didn't you?"

Her chin tilted up at that defiant angle he was beginning to recognize. "I thought it better to wait until after the fact."

He helped her to her feet. "When there's time I must ask you why you thought that particular precaution necessary. For now, let's receive your father's benediction."

Dermot surged into the church, his cloak billowing around him. He marched straight to Eve, and grabbing her roughly by the upper arm, forced her to his side. Redmon stepped toward the Irish king but Richard restrained him.

"Hold. I'm curious to see why the man's angry. Eve, what is your father saying?"

Her voice quivered. "He says it's not in the bargain for us to marry so soon. You haven't yet fulfilled your terms by defeating O'Conor and restoring my father to his throne. What is to keep you from coming to terms with O'Conor, now that you have a claim on the land?"

"Tell him I have vowed to help him. I'll not go back on my word."

"That's all you have to say?"

"What more could there be?"

"Nothing, my lord. You marry me, you get the land. It was foolish of me to think it more complex than that. You'll need more to convince my father. He seems to think now that you have me, you'll abandon him."

"What do you think, Eve?"

She gave him a long look, then lowered her lashes over her angry eyes. "I believe you to be a man of your word. My father says the marriage is invalid as long as it isn't consummated, and he'll be keeping me in his tent where he can keep an eye on me."

"No he won't, I'll not allow it. The marriage is valid. We exchanged our vows freely, without coercion, and that makes them true, not the priest's words, not a physical act between us, but the truth in our hearts, before God. If you tell me now you lied at this altar, lied to me and to God, I'll let you go back with your father, for in truth, no matter the land or the wealth I'll have no such woman to wife."

Her head came back up, proud and indignant. "My vows are true, as God is my witness. For better or worse I have cast my future with you. There is no turning back now, de Clare. We're in this together."

Turning, she said to her father, "I've wed the man in God's house, with a priest as my witness. There is nothing you can say that will undo our vows."

Richard should have seen it coming, but it happened so

quickly. The sound of Dermot's fist hitting Eve's cheek reverberated through the church. As he pulled his arm back for another blow, Richard leapt forward.

"You cowardly whoreson!" He pushed the older man away from Eve. Dermot stood, trembling with rage. "Hit me, you ugly excuse of a man. Hit me and see what it gets you."

Dermot could not understand the words, but he knew the intent well enough, and though his anger did not cool, he backed off. He looked from Richard to Eve, then a slow, ugly smile split his face. Without another word he stalked from the church.

Richard went to Eve, who stood quietly. Caitlin hovered near her, murmuring softly, her voice tearful with sympathy.

"Are you hurt?" Richard asked.

"Don't make a fuss, I'm accustomed to it." Her voice was flat, and he hated to hear it. It was as though Dermot destroyed that bright, argumentative spirit that made Eve so different from the other women he knew.

"Does he do this often?" Richard asked.

"Only when I talk back to him, or displease him in some way." There was humor in her voice now. "In other words, yes, many times, from when I was very young."

She looked so small and fragile he wanted to gather her into his arms, but the brittle way she stood told him she would not welcome a man's touch. "I swear to you, Eve, you'll never know such treatment at my hand." He spoke softly, and the effect, instead of comforting her, seemed to undo her careful facade. Her face crumpled and tears slid down her cheek, where the mark of her father's fist was plain to see.

"Would to God I could believe you," she whispered. It was the most heart-wrenching thing he had ever heard, her voice so full of hopelessness.

Richard turned to face the priest and Redmon. "Get the reliquary from the altar and bring it here."

"Eh, what do you want with the Saint's bones?" Redmon asked.

"Just do it, man."

The big knight brought the ornate golden cask, followed by the priest babbling in nervous Irish.

"Eve, tell the good father no harm will come to his precious relics."

She did as he asked, her face now animated with curiosity.

Holding the sacred relics, he knelt before her.

"What game is this, Pembroke?"

"Give me your hand, Wife."

Slowly she placed her hand in his. Her fingers were cold, and she still trembled. Leaning forward, he turned her hand over and placed a gentle kiss on the palm. "I swear to you on these holy relics, in this house of God, before these witnesses, that never will I be violent with you."

Her mouth twitched at a corner, then both sides turned up into a smile. "That's not good enough, de Clare."

Good Lord, was she now going to take advantage of his good nature and extract more promises from him, promises sanctified by the relics he held? "I've promised to rule the Irish folk by Irish law, I've promised to have you rule with me. What more do you want of me, woman?"

She was solemn again. "God be willing, I will bear you children. I want the same promise for them."

"That I won't beat them? My God! How can you believe I would do such a thing? I swear by everything I hold holy, and on my honor, that I will protect and cherish any children of mine, and the woman who bears them." That she asked such a thing of him told him a great deal about the miserable childhood she must have suffered under Dermot's heavy hand.

She knelt before him, and her hand covered his on the relic box. "I do believe you, God help me. But if you betray me, or my children, be forewarned there is no wrath like that of an Irishwoman."

The pact between them was a fragile and tenuous thing, but one armatured with sacred vows. It was the land Richard wanted, the land that would be Eve's. That he found his protective instincts roused by her surprised him a bit. He had not thought to feel much of anything for the woman he wed. She was the means of obtaining what he wanted. After all, she was not Rosamund, and there was no woman in the world who would claim his heart as that fair cousin did. But Eve was his wife, and would be the mother of his sons. As such she deserved respect, and he would ensure she was treated with all the dignity the title countess of Pembroke brought with it. That she was intelligent and brave spoke in her favor. That she was pleasing to look upon he found disconcerting somehow.

They rose together and walked out into the delicate sunlight. Redmon handed the precious case back to the nervous priest, and with a grunt, offered his arm to Caitlin, who, her eyes so full of happy tears, could hardly see where she walked.

Six

Riding through the town gate, the wedding party started across the wide field toward the army encampment. As they rode into camp, squires hurried forward to take their horses. Eve dismounted and noticed the fifty or so men of Richard's *mesnie,* the most powerful and loyal of his knights who made up his household troop, were gathered nearby. They seemed strangely animated, most with wide grins on their clean-shaven faces. Tewdr was there, looking like a cat who had been into the cream. Of course. Tewdr knew of their plans, he had been in the tent that morning when she tended to Morgan. No doubt Tewdr spread the word of the earl's marriage as quickly as any old woman at her gossip fence.

The boy came forward with Ban close on his heels. The dog was spending much of his time with the scrawny Welsh squire, and Eve knew it was because the boy enticed the animal with scraps of meat and large bones. She could not fault either of them. The boy was likely to be lonely, and the dog needed to run and play.

The knights followed Tewdr and closed around her and Richard. Their ribald shouts made Richard grin good-naturedly. Eve blushed and wished she could hide, embarrassed by the suggestive remarks. Tewdr pulled an armful of heather from behind his back, and with an awkward bow presented it to Eve. "M'lady," he mumbled, before scurrying back to the safety of masculine company. She held the flowers to her face to hide her smile at Tewdr's shy gallantry.

She wouldn't want to embarrass the boy by making a fuss, but it really was very sweet of him.

One of Richard's knights came forward. "My lord, I've been asked to speak for all of us. We wish you happiness in your marriage." He turned then and smiled at Eve. "Lady Pembroke, may I be the first to vow you my loyalty?"

Before she could speak, the man was kneeling before her, head bowed. She glanced at Richard, her eyes silently beseeching him to tell her what to do next. He leaned in and whispered, "Touch him on the head or shoulder to signal your acceptance."

She hit the burly knight smartly on the top of his head with the heather. He looked startled, then smiled broadly. Small purple flowers crowned him as he rose. Another man took his place, then another. Richard introduced each man to her, but after a dozen the names became a blur. She did notice an abundance of men named Beaumont or Montfort, all cousins of Richard's.

Within the hour, Richard's elite guard wore Irish heather in their short hair. She had not thought of it before, but the men who pledged their fealty to Richard would now include her in that loyalty. Even so, she knew most of them would not hesitate to kill her should she do anything to dishonor her husband. Their sense of duty bound them to him, not to her.

Born a princess of Ireland, she was now countess of Pembroke in Wales, countess of Striguil in England, and baroness of Longuevill in Normandy. Places she would likely never see. Ironically, in the eyes of these Anglo-Norman knights, each of those titles was more impressive than the one she was born with. They probably did not realize the insult. Any Anglo-Norman title was superior to an Irish one. Even a royal one.

By the time Richard's knights all became victims of her strange dubbing ritual, she was exhausted. It was the strain of the last few days that made her want to collapse. The gold and jewels she wore made her head throb. Who would have thought a crown could weigh so heavily? She was tempted to remove it, but Richard's men were about and her pride would not allow her to show discomfort in front of them. While she wore the Irish regalia, she would wear it proudly.

Richard finally stepped forward, and the knights gathered grew quiet. "Lady Pembroke and I thank you. We can ask for no better men than those gathered here today." A happy cheer interrupted him.

"Kiss yer bride, ye great fool," someone shouted from the back of the crowd, and the men roared with laughter.

He wouldn't, not here in front of all these men? She looked up to see him smiling at her, and knew she could not escape. He gathered her into his arms, crushing the flowers she still held between them. Leaning down, he kissed her gently on the lips and she quickly pulled away.

"I'm not done yet, Wife." He held her closer, his large, strong hands fanning out over her back, pulling her hips up against him. Once more he leaned down, and this time the kiss was slow and demanding. A surge of warmth spread through her, and instead of pulling away, she moaned and leaned closer. Her lips opened beneath his and the tip of his tongue played along her startled mouth. When he finally stepped back, she felt dizzy. The smell of warm, crushed heather surrounded her. She would forever think of his kisses when she smelled that flower.

Another cheer, louder this time, from the joyous knights. They began to disperse, with an air of revelry clinging to them.

The early morning rain had cleared to an August afternoon bright with sunlight, with a few high clouds scudding before a southwesterly wind. A tiny wren, his tail cock-up, shouted his song to the gods of summer. Eve's heart was surprisingly light, as though the beauty of the day and the kiss lifted the dread and fear that had dogged her for months. For better or worse she was wed to the foreigner, and she was determined that he look favorably upon her people. That he was to rule in Leinster, after her father died, was inevitable. It was up to her to see he did so with compassion and understanding. How to accomplish so daunting a task? How to transform a man of war into a wise and peaceful ruler?

"You are deep in thought, Lady." His voice held a low timbre that made it melodious. She wondered if his singing voice held the same resonant depth.

"I'm thinking of our future. There is much we need to discuss."

He raised an eyebrow at her, and a small smile lifted the corners of his mouth. A very pleasant mouth, she thought, and remembering what it was like to kiss those lips, she blushed and looked away.

"We have a lifetime together to know one another, and to discuss the things that occupy your mind. For today I must see Redmon and his men garrisoned in Waterford. We leave for Dublin in the morning." He frowned as he gazed over the camp of men and horses, spread out in loose array around them. "I won't have time to see you again until this evening, but I will come to your tent then, Wife. Be sure your cousin sleeps elsewhere tonight."

With that, he turned aside, trailing Redmon in his wake, leaving Eve and Caitlin standing in a field of wildflowers, not far from their tent.

"The arrogance of that man." Eve dug the toe of her leather shoe into the ground.

"What did he say to anger you so, Coz?"

Eve stared after him, even in her irritation noticing the broad, strong shoulders tapering to a narrow waist, the long, graceful stride. A dangerous, tightly controlled power cloaked the man. Why was she angry? Not married a day, she found herself abandoned. What woman would not be furious at that? If she were honest with herself, it was a profound disappointment she masked with temper. There would not be the traditional wedding feast, just as there were no guests to witness the deed. She thought she would prefer it this way, without fuss, just get the unpleasant necessity over with. Now there was a strange hollowness, and she realized she regretted the plain ceremony. Such a momentous step in a woman's life was best celebrated elaborately, and with joy. Then the impact of his last words sank into her brain, past the hurt pride. "He means to make me his true wife tonight."

Caitlin smiled, and her blue eyes grew misty. "Surely that is something to be thankful for. He could have married you for your land alone, with no intention of being a husband in more than word, or locked you away like some men do. I can think of worse fates than to lie in Richard de Clare's arms."

"He'll bed me until he gets me with child, of that I'm sure." Only now did that become a reality to her. There would be children, and with them another dilemma. "Caitlin, what am I to do? How can I bear his sons? They'll be neither Irish nor Norman. Where will their loyalties lie?"

Caitlin stood silently, chewing at her lower lip as she did whenever she was deep in thought. Finally, she looked at Eve. "It would be folly to try to fight de Clare. He would win in the end and destroy you in the process, and what good would you be to Ireland then? If you raise your sons to be more Irish than Brian Boru himself, they will rule as Irishmen."

Shaking her head, Eve squinted as she gazed at the knights and Welsh men-at-arms of her husband's army. "Look at them, Caitlin. Over a thousand men, and they're just the beginning. Richard means to bring more soldiers over before spring. What chance does Rory have against them? The Irish are brave, but they don't have the equipment or the training of these men. Richard will win Leinster back for my father, of that I have no doubt, and our children will inherit the kingdom. But as Irishmen? Do you really think de Clare will allow that?"

"You speak as though you think this army is here to stay,

but they will leave, once Uncle Dermot is king again, and go back to their homes in Wales and England. Except your husband. Oh, Eve, he won't want you to live with him in Wales?"

"They won't be going anywhere." Surprise at her cousin's naiveté made her voice hard, but Eve did not regret that. Caitlin must see what the future of Ireland would be. "They mean to have Irish land. Even if I can convince de Clare to rule as an Irish king, what of the others who will follow. Do you not see it coming?"

"Surely your father thought of such things before he asked the English for help?"

Eve made a rude gesture of dismissal. "More like he begged. You didn't see him with King Henry. I was ashamed, an Irish king debasing himself like that. My father will do anything to regain his throne, including selling Ireland to the highest bidder."

They stood near their tent but were reluctant to go in, where the heat of the summer day was concentrated and dull. "I have a marvelous idea." There was a gleam in Caitlin's blue eyes, and Eve grew instantly wary. "You must make your husband fall in love with you. So in love that he would give you the moon and the stars were it in his power to do so. He's not an unreasonable man, surely he can be made to see the folly of imposing foreign ways on us."

Eve laughed, and shook her head. "You were ever the romantic, but you've been listening to too many tales of love and valor. They are stories, Caitlin. I cannot force de Clare to love me."

"Did I say to use force? Gentleness wins this war."

"I wouldn't know how to go about it."

"You could begin by opening your heart to the man instead of closing yourself off behind a wall of distrust and hostility. It may take more courage than anything you've ever done, but I've never known you to falter because a task was challenging."

"This is absurd. I don't want or need to have my husband

love me. If he keeps from beating me, as he promised, I'll be content."

"It's not for yourself you wage this war, it's for the welfare of Ireland." Caitlin placed her fists on her round hips and squinted hard at her cousin. "Just what is it you're afraid of, that Richard de Clare will love you? Or that he won't?"

Eve looked in the direction in which her husband had disappeared and sighed. "I'll admit your idea has merit. It may well be the best way for me to help my people, having a husband so besotted with me he'll do whatever I ask. How difficult can it be to please a man? They're simple enough creatures."

Her cousin stamped her delicate foot. "I do despair of you ever understanding anything of love."

"What do *you* know of it?"

The younger woman blushed furiously and looked away.

"Caitlin, answer me. You haven't done anything foolish, have you? Father would be so angry if you've compromised yourself."

"I've never known a man, Eve. Do keep your voice down."

"If I didn't know better, I'd say you're besotted with that Welshman, but you've hardly talked to him. You can't be so foolish, Father will never allow it. Morgan has nothing of value and you are a dowered heiress. The whole idea is unsuitable."

"Is it any less suitable than you marrying a man you don't care for? I admit I'm attracted to Morgan, but as you've said, the man barely knows me. I'm not such a fool as to think he cares for me, but neither am I such a cynic that I think the idea isn't worth pursuing. I'm going to Morgan now, to tend to his wounds. You asked how to make a man love you? I intend to start by showing concern and affection for him. His response will show whether further pursuit is justified."

Eve watched openmouthed as Caitlin marched away from

her, her dainty shoulders set in firm defiance. What was happening to her meek cousin? Closing her mouth with a sharp click of teeth, Eve turned toward her tent. Her head felt ready to split. In the course of a few hours her world had changed beyond recognition. Richard's men vowed a loyalty she was not sure she wanted the burden of accepting, she argued with Caitlin, and her father's inexplicable rage worried at the edges of her brain. Why was Dermot so angry at her marriage?

What she needed was to get out of her uncomfortable clothes and go for a long, hard ride. That invariably cleared her thoughts. Walking into the tent, she removed the heavy gold arm rings and placed them carefully on the small table. The jeweled coronet followed, and she rubbed her temples, where the crown had rested. They were beautiful, these symbols of rank and privilege. As with many grand things, they were not easy to live with.

Finally, she removed the heavy gold torc, with its emeralds and amethysts, and laid it on the table beside the other pieces. Her fingers lingered on it for a moment. The gold was warm from her skin, and the exquisite beauty of the workmanship as ever inspired a reverent admiration. That human hands wrought such intricate beauty invariably humbled her. The neckpiece was over a hundred years old, originally a gift from Brian Boru to wild, beautiful Gormflaith. Since then, it had passed from mother to daughter until it came into her hands. It was a tangible symbol of her link to her past, to the proud, strong ancestors whose blood still sang rich and loud in her veins. Proud Brian and untamed Gormflaith. She carried something of them both in her heart. The torc, so distinctively Irish with its pagan beauty, was her most prized possession, not because of the value of the gold and the jewels, but because of its link with those who had gone before, who laid their lives down for this green and haunted island.

Seven

Eve changed from her wedding finery to a loose gown and cloak. She needed time to think and solitude to do it in. Having married the arrogant man, she must now decide what to do with him. What a mess her father's obsession with the high kingship and Richard's lust for land made of her life. "Damn all ambitious men to hell! They're nothing but a plague on the earth."

She stomped from the tent, muttering to herself, drawing the attention of soldiers lounging around camp. Glaring at them, they were the first to look aside. Let them think her an ill-tempered bitch. What did she care? They were men, too. A plague on them all.

There was a wide curve of beach south of Waterford that she often rode to when she needed time alone. She headed toward where the horses were corralled. Her gray mare was there, small among the immense war-horses. In his own paddock was the earl's stallion, Emys. She walked over to the fence and placed one foot on the lowest rail. He was a beautiful brute. Everything about him cried speed, strength, and intelligence.

He stared back at her out of dark, fiery eyes. Holding out her hand, she whispered to him, enticing him nearer. Placing his soft lips along her arm, he nibbled it with surprising delicacy. Beside her, Ban whined and looked at her with worried, mobile brow, his black nose quivering with apprehension. "Go back to the tent if you're afraid."

The horse wore a halter but no other tack. How she itched to ride him, but how? Richard would be furious. That made her smile. Really, she shouldn't. The horse was valuable. Years of intensive training made the stallion an indispensable aid to a warrior. He was not meant for pleasure. She knew she could handle the animal, she rode as well as any man she knew and better than most. All that speed and fire waiting for her to capture it was too great a temptation.

Her mare was much smaller, and Eve had no trouble tacking her. With the stallion, even if she could lift the massive, high-cantled saddle a knight used, she was not tall enough to get it onto the animal's back. That was if Emys would allow her near enough to try.

Spying Tewdr heading toward her, she stood as tall as she could and spoke in her most imperious voice. "You there, boy, I want this horse bridled."

"That one, m'lady? But that be the earl's own horse, no one else ever rides him."

"Did I ask your opinion? Just do as I say and do it now."

He eyed her warily, but her tone left no room for argument, and, mumbling, he went to do as she bid. He returned bowlegged under the weight of the saddle he carried.

"I don't need the saddle, just the bridle."

"No saddle? I've not heard such a thing. How will you stay on him? He'll slip you off his back soon as he feels the weight of you, and then the earl will blame me for your injuries. M'lady, please, 'tis dangerous what you be after."

She wondered if all de Clare's men were so forward with their opinions, or if it was the boy's burgeoning manhood that made it so easy for him to argue with her, a mere woman, though she was royal born and from this day his countess as well. "Give me the damned bridle. I'll do it myself."

"Nay, mistress, I'll do it for you. Stand back, this horse can be vicious." He quickly and efficiently did the job, then stood holding the reins, a small, smug smile on his lips. " 'Tis done then, but I don't see how you'll get onto his back with no saddle to help you up. He won't stand for ye mounting him from a fence."

"Just hold him. I'll manage." When she was a young child, she had learned how to mount any horse unassisted. As long as she could reach as high as the animal's withers and gather a good handful of mane in her hand, she could vault onto the horse's back. She was relieved to be able to reach far enough on Emys, and with a swift, graceful movement she was soon seated securely on his back. Tewdr eyed her with undisguised admiration, then with a wide smile handed her the reins.

"Now open the gate."

The horse was quivering beneath her, unsure of this stranger on his back, but she held the reins with a sure hand and applied a steady pressure with her strong thighs. The stallion danced nervously under her.

The gate opened, and she walked Emys through at a sedate pace, to let him know who was in control, and though he broke out in a nervous sweat, he obeyed her. She walked him through the camp, ignoring the startled men around her, and only when they were clear did she touch her heels to his flanks.

He flew forward and she bent low over his neck. The earth tore away under his hooves. His gait was so fluid she sank into its rhythm as naturally as if she were part of the creature. He jumped small obstacles with a deft elegance, and she laughed with joy at the freedom and power that thrilled through her. They pounded down the green hillsides and onto the sandy beach that curved away to the south, far from prying eyes. In the distance she heard Ban as he ran after them, his occasional bark letting her know he followed. He would catch up. She did not intend to go far, though she wished she could go forever and be free, just her and the animals, and never have to deal with another man as long as she lived.

* * *

"That's my horse!"

Redmon squinted and nodded agreement. "So it is. Who's fool enough to take him under hand?"

Who indeed? Richard thought. He saw clearly the tiny form with the wild silvery hair streaming behind her. "It's my wife."

"That animal is worth six good serfs. Doesn't the girl have more sense than to run him wild like that?"

They hurried toward the corrals. "Actually, Redmon, it's my wife I'm worried about. That horse is willful and needs a strong hand."

"So, it seems, does the woman."

If Richard did not know the big man as well as he did, he might think Redmon was teasing him. He would miss Redmon's solid practicality, once they moved on to Dublin, but Redmon was the best man to command the garrison at Waterford. Richard grabbed the nearest horse and slapped a bridle onto the nervous beast.

"You'll never catch up to her. She has too much of a lead."

"Watch me."

Vaulting onto the animal's back, and clenching his thighs tightly to keep his seat, he turned in the direction Eve had disappeared. Richard thundered through camp, men shouting curses and encouragement as they scattered out of his way.

Redmon was right. He needed to handle Eve with a strong hand or she would run wild. He did not worry too much about her or his stallion, though if the little hellion broke her neck it would be no more than she deserved. She had not asked his permission to ride the animal. Richard chuckled. There were very few men he knew who would take such liberties with his good nature, and no women.

This wild Irishwoman intrigued him as much as she exasperated him. She was as different from Rosamund as any woman he knew, and because of that Eve was no threat to the love he bore Rose. Eve was his wife. His heart belonged to Rosamund.

They had been betrothed when Richard was fourteen and Rosamund seven. Sweet, gentle Rosamund, who thought him handsome and valiant and wonderful. Delicate Rosamund, in need of a man's protection and guidance. Compliant, obedient Rosamund, gently bred, with the manners of a lady and the face of an angel. It was the summer Rosamund turned sixteen, and her father finally deemed her old enough to marry, that Henry Plantagenet first saw her and he claimed her as his own. Henry, who could command any woman in England, Normandy, or Aquitaine, and who, over the years, kept several mistresses, was unusually faithful to Rosamund. Enough so that for once Queen Eleanor's formidable jealousy was roused.

It was then the rivalry with Henry began. Nothing Richard did seemed to please the man. Henry made sure Richard was sent to fight far from England, far from Rosamund. Richard served with honor, giving no excuse for rebuke or censure, but he vowed by all he held holy that Rosamund would be his again. Henry would tire of her eventually. He always tired of his women.

Though Richard knew other women over the years, none touched his heart, nor did he seek a replacement for his first love. The women he used were there to appease his appetites, not burn his soul. He never grew close to them, any more than he expected to be intimate with his wife save in a physical sense. He certainly did not expect, or want, any sort of emotional entanglement with Eve. Their marriage was a convenient arrangement and would suit him well, as soon as he tamed that stubborn Irishwoman.

Urging more speed out of his horse, he struggled to catch a glimpse of his wayward wife. He marked the trail her passage left in the long grass, and hoped she would not

ride far. He had more important things to do today than
chase after an errant woman. Rosamund never caused him
such trouble.

Coming to rest in a sheltered cove of sand south of Waterford, Eve dismounted and gave the stallion his freedom.
He pranced for a minute, uncertain what was expected of
him. Lowering his head, he gently butted her on the shoulder. "Go, you're free for a bit." Tossing his head, he turned
and trotted away from the beach with its sparse grass toward
the lush hillside beyond.

Sunset was a few hours away, and the afternoon glowed
under a lazy amber light. The ride released some of the
nervous tension, and her head hammered less fiercely,
though between the bump she had from yesterday and the
bruise on her cheek from her father this morning, she was
not surprised at having a pounding headache. Why was she
so angry? She had not been forced to marry that man, but
she could not trust him. She was angry because she was
afraid. What if she made the biggest mistake of her life that
morning in St. Olav's Church?

Walking along the beach, she tried to bring some order
to her chaotic thoughts. The sea was tame today, the waves
whispering over the cambered sand. Plovers ran in and out
with the tide on their stilty orange legs. Across the waters
she could see the misty lumps that were England and Wales.
There was a world that thought of Ireland as uncivilized
and primitive, its people uncultured and heathen. The earl
and his mercenaries probably felt justified in their invasion
because they assumed the Irish were inferior.

*That's true of any victor, in all the wars throughout his-
tory, past and to come. They think winning makes them superior, when all it means is they are better at slaughter,
and are more ruthless.*

"God cast you into the deepest pit of hell, Dermot

MacMurrough, and may you spend eternity with that devil you brought into our land!"

"Such a potent curse."

Whirling around, she saw de Clare grinning down at her from the rock he stood on. Her wolfhound was licking the man's hand with a revolting show of obsequiousness.

"You can take that disloyal animal with you as well, de Clare. I've no use for any of you."

Turning her back on them, she stormed down the beach, scattering startled birds at her approach. The last thing she wanted was to confront that man when her emotions were in such turmoil.

She stopped and stood for a long moment staring out at the vast sea. How many tragedies had that ocean witnessed only to continue its eternal flow, back and forth? Her troubles were small in the great weft of history, but they were significant enough and must be dealt with. Clenching her fists at her side, she turned and marched resolutely back the way she had come. She never in her life ran from anything, she did not intend to start now.

De Clare was where she left him, sitting and scratching Ban's ears. The dog wore a look of stupefaction on his face. "Traitor," she growled at the dog, then glared up at the man. "Why did you follow me?"

"You stole my horse."

"I did not steal him. I borrowed him."

His mouth twitched, but he displayed enough intelligence not to smile. "I stand corrected. Next time ask first. I wouldn't want you or the animal to come to harm, and I don't like the idea of you riding alone. Too much can happen."

"I've never been hurt on a horse."

"It's not your riding ability I worry about. I can't protect you if I don't know where you are."

"I've never asked for your protection. I can take care of myself."

"You're my wife. That makes you a target for my enemies."

She knew he spoke the truth, even as a stubborn defiance held her tongue. No matter how reasonable his request might be, she was unaccustomed to answer to a man for her every move. Glancing over his shoulder to where the stallion grazed in the tall, flower-quilted grass, she sighed and admitted defeat, at least to herself. "I'll not ride again without telling someone where I'm going."

"That's not enough. I want an armed guard with you whenever you're outside the town walls or beyond the military camp."

"What more do you want from me? You will have my lands, my sons will be your heirs, now you take my freedom. There is nothing else of value for you to seize."

"There you are very much mistaken, Princess." His voice was gentle. "You know this land and these people in ways I never shall. That is invaluable to me."

"Why? So I can reveal to you all our weaknesses, all our follies, so you can rule us more harshly?"

He jumped down from the rock and walked over to her. His height forced her to crane her neck back to look him in the eye.

"I've borne great responsibility from a young age, and I take those burdens seriously. Ask any of my people, from the lowliest serf to my richest barons, and they will tell you I am a fair man. I am not the cruel monster you seem to have made in your imagination."

"I don't know why you think I should trust you, de Clare, or believe a word you say. You may be playing me for a fool, hoping I'll confide in you so you can use me to your own purposes."

"You confuse me, woman. Last night we agreed to the terms of our marriage. I will rule the Irish by their laws, as you ask. God have mercy, I've promised to let you rule with me. You came willingly to the priest this morning. Why do you suddenly doubt all I've told you? What has changed?"

"You're an ambitious man, de Clare. That alone makes you untrustworthy."

"I was ambitious yesterday, yet you vowed to work with me."

"I've seen what unrestrained ambition does to a man, and to a country. My father is obsessed with his desire for the high kingship and he'll use anyone to gain his ends, or destroy anyone who stands in his way. It's like a fire in his belly that devours him."

"I'm not your father. When I give my word, I will die before breaking it. How can we accomplish a damned thing if we can't trust one another? Why isn't my word enough for you when it is for kings and emperors? Dammit, Eve, you must decide if you are with me or not. I'll not have you going back and forth, perpetually wondering if today is the day you betray me."

Reaching out, he took her by the shoulders. His touch made her uncomfortably aware of him as a man and she tried to pull away, but he held her firmly. He was close enough she could smell him, a heady odor of man and horse and heather. "I don't ask you to like me, only to believe me. I don't know what more I can do. I've made promises to you before God and on holy relics. If my word isn't good enough, surely you must know I'd not endanger my eternal soul by swearing falsely."

The sincerity in his voice was unmistakable. He either meant what he said or he was a proficient liar. "I'm not sure why, and Holy Brigid help me if I'm wrong, but I believe you when you say you'd die before breaking your word." Pausing, she looked into his eyes, hoping to read his will. She could not. "It's difficult for me to trust, there have been so few people in my life who haven't lied to me, or used me to their own ends. You're right, we've agreed to work together to bring peace. If that means I must quiet my fears and doubts to trust you, I will. I want you to love Ireland and her people. I want you to bring peace to the land because it tears your soul apart to see her bleeding and helpless."

Cocking his head to one side, he removed his hands from her shoulders. "You ask a great deal of me. I won't lie to you, I don't share the passion for Ireland you do, I don't know that I ever will. It's the land I want."

"That puzzles me, de Clare. You've more land and wealth than any one man needs. Why are you here, why do you want my land?"

He smiled. "There are those who say a man can never have enough wealth. But you're right, gaining Leinster is not my sole objective. I'm here to do Henry's dirty work."

"Go on." She tried to keep the fear from her voice.

He began to walk down the beach, and she followed. "When Pope Adrian decreed Henry Lord of Ireland, he gave the king a mandate to invade this island and force the inhabitants to a truer conformity to Holy Church. Henry thinks of Ireland as his. Subduing the people to that reality is a formality he would as soon see me accomplish for him as bother with himself."

"That papal decree is twenty years old, and Adrian long dead. Surely your English king doesn't hold great store in that old charter. We Irish have never taken it seriously. We were Christian long before your Norse ancestors, or Adrian's either for that matter."

"Powerful men make their own realities of the world. They have the wealth and the armies to make the truth whatever they deem it should be. It concerns kings and popes little what the Irish think in this matter. The Irish church is far too independent and wealthy for Rome to ignore it. Adrian needed but a slight excuse to give his good friend the king a gift as large and rich as Ireland." A small smile softened Richard's face. "It seems the pope and his bishops are most dismayed at the tolerant attitude of the Irish prelates toward marriage and divorce and the freedoms you allow women."

She placed a forefinger in the middle of his chest and gave it a hard poke. It was like a gnat attacking a rock. "They are the laws you have vowed to keep."

"It's more than the marriage laws. Rome cannot sanction your custom of lay abbots ruling Irish monasteries."

"Our monasteries have always passed from father to son. How else is the wealth to stay within the family who founded the monastery? The abbots have great power."

"That is precisely the problem in the pope's mind. The Church loses land and wealth when the monasteries are treated as family possessions instead of Church lands."

"And this is why Henry of England feels justified in sending you and your men here? To reform the Irish Church?"

"Henry is not so pious. Few kings, or popes, can afford to be. It serves admirably as an excuse for Henry's ambition. He's been watching Ireland and knows she is divided by wars. That makes her vulnerable. The Norse trading towns along the east coast are wealthy, and they take trade away from England. Henry wants that wealth."

"Including Dublin?"

"Most especially Dublin. It's not your father only I must please, but Henry as well."

"Why do you serve Henry so faithfully? From what you've said, you don't like the man."

"Henry was my friend once. My argument with him is private. He is my Liege Lord and has my vow of fealty. I have no choice but to obey him."

"What happens when the promises you have made to me and my father run counter to this immutable loyalty you owe your king?"

Richard sighed and closed his eyes. When he opened them he looked weary. "Henry's coming is inevitable. If I were not here, some other baron would be. I mean to rule Leinster by law. I fear other of Henry's barons will see Ireland as a rich prize to be looted."

She turned from him, her heart pounding with fear. It was worse than she had imagined. It wasn't Richard who posed a threat to Ireland. It was Henry Plantagenet with his huge army. Henry would divide Ireland into pieces and distribute them to his men as rewards for their service. Even as her father had promised Leinster to de Clare. Why did Richard tell her? Could it be he was the honest and honorable man he claimed to be, and saw no reason to lie?

"You said I must earn your trust, well, Norman, so must you earn mine. Why didn't you tell me sooner about Henry?"

He seemed genuinely surprised. "I thought it obvious. I haven't come to Ireland on my own, in rebellion against Henry. I'm here with his blessing. I've pledged to help your father regain Leinster because he has promised it to me. But in truth it is Henry who will decide if I rule there."

"I see. By marrying me you thought not just to secure your claim to Leinster with the Irish lords, but with Henry as well. How clever of you. How dare you call yourself an honest man."

He seemed startled by her anger. "Woman, the way your thoughts fly from one to another, you make me dizzy. Will you find fault with everything I do? I married you to get Leinster, what do I care which king grants it? No one can undo our vows."

"Are you always so practical a man? Does emotion never move you?"

"I'm not an unfeeling brute. Would I want peace if I were?"

They walked silently across the sand. Ban splashed clumsily through the water chasing birds.

"Tell me, de Clare, if you and Henry dislike each other, why does he trust you to do his will in Ireland? Why did he chose you? Surely others were willing to conquer Ireland for him."

"Mayhap I was the only one foolish enough to try."

"I don't believe that. Surely there are others as foolish as you."

He laughed. "You surprise me, Princess. I'm a warrior. I go where my king sends me, but there is more to it. Henry took something that was mine, that he had no right to. I was young and impulsive. I recklessly rebelled against him. He squashed me like a flea between his fingers. My lands in Wales are heavily fined to this day. Not that I can blame him, but Henry does not completely trust me, though I've been loyal to him since. No matter how well I serve him, I cannot earn back his respect. If I lose my life in Ireland, he'll not be heartbroken. It would rid him of a troublesome baron."

This man was more complex than she imagined. For the first time she felt a tentative compassion for her husband. She reached out to touch him, then drew her hand back. Why did she think to comfort that man? "This thing Henry took from you, is it something you can have again once you have land in Ireland?"

He shook his head, and the pain in his eyes clutched at her heart. "I fear Henry will never give her up. If I must wait a lifetime, Rosamund will be mine. I swear it."

All the tenuous hope of the day lay shattered at her feet. "You bastard, why did you marry me if you want this other woman?"

"What does Rosamund have to do with us? When I make her my mistress I'll not expect you to live in the same place. You're my wife. You'll be treated with dignity."

Biting back tears, she turned and walked to the edge of the waves. He loved a woman named Rosamund. Why it hurt so she could not understand, but it did, deeply. It was like the pain when her mother died and there was no longer anyone to show her affection, no one to hold her or comfort her. She'd built defensive walls around her heart, thinking to keep from being hurt again. It didn't work. Instead of making her impenetrable, she was like an open wound that never healed. Did she secretly hope her husband would love her, would relieve the unbearable loneliness?

He placed his hand on her shoulder and the rush of longing, the need to have him hold her made her weep silently. She stepped away from him.

"Come, Wife, enough for today. It'll take both of us time to adjust to this marriage. I've work to do in Waterford, we need to return."

His voice was calm, and she turned to watch as he called his stallion. She wiped the tears away. Just as her father could not break her with force, she would not allow this man to torment her with his indifference.

Eight

"Where is the fool man?" Dervorgilla pulled the hood of her voluminous cloak closer around her face. The sun had gone down an hour ago. Her irritation at being kept waiting turned quickly to anger. Must she do everything herself? The oak tree she sheltered under kept her from view, though she saw no one else as she waited. The gates of Waterford would close for the night soon. She did not wish to explain why she was beyond the walls after dark and alone.

She heard someone coming toward her and her displeasure grew. The clumsy oaf made enough noise to frighten away every creature within a half mile. When she saw it was indeed the man she expected, she stepped from the deep shadows into the moonlit meadow. "Where have you been?" she hissed.

"I could'na get away so soon as I thought. Where's the harm?"

"I expect you to be reliable. I can find someone else for this work."

He quirked a bushy eyebrow at her and crossed his massive arms over his chest. "Can ye now? And are ye sure they'd be as discreet as I've always been for ye?"

"I've paid you enough over the years to buy your silence. If I thought otherwise, you'd be dead."

"I've na doubt that be truth. We understand each other then. Have ye me pay?"

She held the ring in her gloved hand. It had been simple enough to steal the bauble from Dermot's chamber. He'd never miss the gaudy thing, he had so many others, but he'd worn it enough for it to be easily recognized. If anything went wrong with her plot, she wanted Dermot to have the blame. She dropped the ring into the man's outstretched hand. "Here's the first part. You'll get the rest when I know the task is done."

"In coin, like ye promised."

"In gold, if you do what I want."

The man nodded and slipped the massive ring onto his finger. "Don't wear that near Dublin, you fool, unless you want to be hanged as a thief."

His eyes turned hard and angry. "Do na call me a fool, woman. I'm many things, but niver that. I'm doon with Dublin once I have me gold. It's back to Scotland I'll be heading."

She watched until he was well away, then pulled the hood forward again to hide her face and began the walk back to Waterford. The man was good at what he did. Several times before he'd proved himself deadly, circumspect, and with not a shred of conscience. When he accomplished his task, there would be no gold waiting. This time she needed to be rid of him. She could not risk him talking.

Something pushed tenaciously at his shoulder. Richard grunted and turned over in his narrow bed. The intruder prodded more firmly. He cracked open one eye to see Tewdr hovering over him with a lantern. "You wished to be awaked at dawn, m'lord."

Richard moaned and looked toward the tent flap. Dawn? It was dark as night out there still. Then he heard the rain, steady and hard. Damn! The last thing they needed was rain. If it did not delay their march to Dublin, it would make the trip decidedly uncomfortable. He was beginning to wonder if it did anything but rain on this soggy island.

He had spent all night with Redmon, discussing what was necessary to keep Waterford safe, and slipped exhausted into his bed an hour or two ago. Sitting up, he wiped the grit from his stinging eyes. He needed more sleep, but he was not likely to get it anytime soon. Then he remembered Eve, and his promise to visit her last night. She'd likely be in a foul mood today. He cursed his stupidity, and, groaning, rose from the bed.

"Your usual cheerful self, I see," Morgan said from the other side of the tent.

"It does my heart good to see you awake." Richard crossed the tent to stand by the Welshman's cot. "You gave us a scare. Can you tell me what happened, how you came by the wound?"

Morgan's dark eyes clouded with remembrance. "It was one of Dermot's men. I approached him with my sword still in its scabbard, never thinking the bastard would turn on me. I'm ashamed to say I was woefully unprepared. It won't happen again, that I vow."

"I've told you before you're too quick to trust. A little more cynicism will keep you alive longer."

Morgan stretched, and grimaced as his injured arm bumped the side of the tent.

"Does it pain you overmuch?" Richard helped his friend to a sitting position, careful not to touch the injured limb. "We're leaving for Dublin today, and I thought to have you go by ship if you're up to it, or you can stay in Waterford until you're stronger."

"I'm sore as hell, but I am strong otherwise. I'll go to Dublin with you, Richard. Can you just see me stuck here with Redmon for weeks at a time? I know you find merit in the man, but I'd go mad from his dullness if you leave me here. Who will translate for you if I stay behind?"

Tewdr was busy laying a meal of bread, cheese, and ale,

but he skipped over to Morgan's bed to accost him with his news. "My lord of Pembroke's wife will be riding with him to Dublin. She speaks Welsh and Norman-French tolerably well."

"Your wife? My congratulations, Richard." He quirked a crooked smile at the other man. "She'll lead you a merry chase, that one, if I'm not mistaken. But riding to Dublin, do you think that wise? It'll take four days at least, and that through hostile territory. By ship would be safer."

Richard began to dress, and kept his back to Morgan, who could read his face too well and was quick to voice an opinion. He did not want to admit he much preferred a four-day ride, no matter the danger, to another minute aboard a rocking boat. "You worry overmuch. It's easier to take the bulk of men and horses by land. I want to see this place we've come to claim, though I'm beginning to think the whole thing is a grand misadventure."

"Regrets, Richard? I wouldn't have thought it of you."

"Mayhap I shouldn't have married the woman so quickly," Richard said. "I thought it needed doing to secure Dermot's promise about the succession to Leinster."

"I don't follow your reasoning. Now you've married the woman, there's naught Dermot can do about it. It was a wise move. You've greatly strengthened your claim by doing so. What bothers you about it?"

"The suspicion that Dermot never intended me to inherit a pinch of Irish land. It's the only reason I can find for his rage when we married."

"If you believe that, you could be in mortal danger. What if the princess is conspiring with her father?"

"There may be danger from Dermot, but Eve won't hurt me."

"How do you know that? Are you so sure you'd stake your life on it?"

Tying the laces of the quilted gambeson he wore under his harness of chain, Richard frowned. Why did he trust

Eve with his life? There was something about the woman that convinced him he was safe with her, but what was it? His mind teased at it as Tewdr helped him into his chain hauberk. It was her honor, he decided, which she wore like an aegis of gold. An honor that would not compromise, would not bend, just as it would never betray or murder, for that would violate the essence of who she was.

Turning to Morgan, he said, "Strangely enough, I do trust her. The problem is her lack of belief in me, and to tell you the truth I don't know how to begin to break down the walls she's erected. It seems commitment comes hard for her, and with Dermot for a father I can see why. The sooner I can get her to accept me, the easier this whole affair will be. Without her I can't hope to win the fealty of the Irish people, and without that I have no hope of ruling peacefully."

Morgan chewed on a hunk of dark bread. Tewdr sat beside him, chomping noisily on his own food. "You've wed the woman, but have you wooed her yet?"

Swallowing a mouthful of cold ale, Richard put his tankard down on the small table. "What is the sense of that?"

Morgan heaved a heel of hard bread at him, hitting Richard on the shoulder.

"What the hell did you do that for? That wound has festered your brain."

"It's you who are thickheaded. Redmon is impervious to romance, but I thought you were made of better stuff, Richard. Any woman is more yielding if you shower her with affection and attention. Eve's your wife, but if you want her as a partner you'll have to make her your lover as well, in every sense of the word."

"How do I go about such a task? Believe me, she'd rather spend time with my horse than with me."

"Emys is better tempered than you. The solution is easy enough. She'll fall in love with you, all you need do is fall in love with her."

"Damn your unruly tongue, you go too far."

Morgan's smile faded and he lost his jocular tone. "I'm serious about this, and you'd best listen, or you'll make your marriage a living hell. Rosamund is of the past, you no longer have any claim to her. Henry will never give her up, he's made that abundantly clear. Rosamund is a sickness in your blood, and like any illness must be purged."

"You forget your place."

"I thought my place was as your friend. If I've been mistaken, my lord, I do beg your pardon. It won't happen again."

Richard felt the ice in the other man's voice, and it cooled his temper. "It's I who wrong you. The one thing I most value is your honesty. You tell me what I need to hear, no matter how I fight you. In truth, Eve didn't seem pleased when I told her of Rosamund. It—"

Morgan nearly choked on the ale he was drinking. "You told her about Rosamund? I despair for you, Richard, I truly do. How can you know so little about women?"

Wide-eyed, Tewdr listened with big ears, enjoying every moment of their argument.

"We're here to conquer a kingdom and you tell me I must spend my time winning my wife instead?"

"Win that battle, Richard, and the war will be simple."

By midmorning the fleet of forty sleek ships, loaded with most of the supplies Richard's army would need in the coming months, as well as those passengers who preferred to travel by sea, set sail for Dublin. With luck they would reach that port, one hundred miles north of Waterford, before nightfall the next day. The sea was gray and rough, the white froth of the wave tops breaking high on the sides of the ships. Rain continued to fall, and the dense, dark clouds showed no signs of diminishing.

Richard watched from the stout walls of Waterford as the ships rowed out of the bay. Dermot and many of his men were aboard, as well as the few women and children willing to follow their men. Once on the open sea, the sails were unfurled and the graceful vessels headed north. Climbing down from the walls, he joined Eve and his army waiting at the gate.

"I still think you should have gone by ship," Redmon said. "It's dangerous overland. You're too easy a target."

"We'll be safe enough." Richard took the reins of his horse from the big man, and mounted Emys. "Keep Waterford safe for me, Redmon. Without a port close to Wales and England we're too isolated here, and too vulnerable."

"I'll do that."

Richard took one last look at Waterford. If anyone could keep the town secure, it was Redmon FitzWilliam. Having done all he could to ensure the port stayed accessible to his ships, he rode through the gate with Eve on her gray mare at his side and Ban following behind. His elite troop of knights, the fifty men who made up his household *mesnie,* rode behind them. Spread out in an orderly line were the rest of his knights and Welsh men-at-arms, trudging resolutely through the mud. They would travel north and west to cross the Suir, before turning north again for the march to Dublin.

The rain continued through the day, and by afternoon Eve was ready to call a halt to the forced pace Richard set. This miserable overland journey would take four, perhaps five days, and there was the constant threat of attack by Rory's troops, though they could not be sure the Irish king knew yet of their position or their strength. She glanced from beneath her woolen hood at the man riding beside her. He seemed impervious to the weather, unaware of the discomfort. *If he can bear it, so can I,* she thought stubbornly, and squared her shoulders.

"Does it rain often?" he asked, glancing down at her.

She almost laughed. The one constant, predictable thing about the Irish weather was the rain. "Look about you, my lord. What is the first thing you notice about Ireland?"

They were passing through an oak wood where the ferns grew luxuriantly, some taller than a man. It was like a dark-green tunnel, the trees overhanging, the grass and ferns and heaths thick beneath their feet; even the water riling through the small steams reflected the green of summer, dark today because of the cloud cover. He shook his head, puzzled.

"It is the green, de Clare. Look around you and you'll see every shade imaginable, from the palest new buds of spring to the rich dark grasses of summer. Even in the heart of winter there is green in the landscape. Ireland is a fertile land, and it is the rain that makes it so."

"Do you mean to tell me it does this most of the time? Our armor will rust off our backs."

She suppressed a smile at that delightful thought. "Waxed cloth will protect the chain of your armor. I'll see to it when we reach Dublin, though enough for all your knights may take a few weeks."

"With all this wet, how do you keep the wheat and barley from rotting in the fields?"

"There isn't much grown on this island in the way of grains. It's the grass that feeds us by giving excellent grazing to our stock. You may not find much bread in Ireland, but you'll never lack for meat and milk and cheeses."

He scanned the landscape, as though seeing it for the first time. "There is much for me to learn about this land, and you'll have to be my teacher. I need to learn Irish, I'm too vulnerable without knowing it."

She glanced at Richard, startled. Never had she heard her father admit to a weakness, nor ask for help. It put Dermot in the position of being unable to admit any wrongdoing, until he no longer acknowledged he was as fallible as all men. Power corrupted her father. He was a man people feared and obeyed—and resented. In the four years since

Rory O'Conor drove him from Leinster, Dermot had grown fanatical in his demand for unquestioning loyalty. Where he suspected betrayal, he reacted with a hot fury that left destruction in its wake. If her father was restored to his throne, how far would his obsession for revenge reach? How many more of his countrymen would he slaughter?

Again the shocking idea came to her that Leinster would do better under de Clare's rule than under her father's. She glanced through her lashes at the tall, wet knight who rode beside her. There was something appealing about the man. He was strong and determined. Well, arrogant actually. He was honorable, or so he said, over and over. At least he seemed true to his own code of honor, which apparently included fidelity to his mistress but not his wife. Handsome, in a rough, warrior way. If one was attracted to that sort of man. She preferred poets. So much more refined. In truth, she cared naught for the man. She was indifferent to him, just as he was to her. Then why did she have the incomprehensible feeling she had known de Clare for a lifetime? She felt a peculiar surge of warmth toward him. He admitted to vulnerability, and in her mind it did not make him weak but simply more human. If she admitted it to herself, in spite of her best intentions the man fascinated her.

They rode in silence, beneath the dripping canopy of overhanging oaks, with the occasional cheerful song of a finch rattling between the trees. The forest, usually so teeming with life, seemed deserted, but it was no surprise considering the appalling racket made by de Clare's army. If any of Rory's men were within a few miles, they knew of the army's presence. De Clare seemed unconcerned by the possibility, which meant he was either very sure of himself, or an utter idiot. She knew this man was no fool.

Rain dripped from the end of her nose and tickled her upper lip. She sneezed.

"Are you unwell? Do we need to stop?" His tone implied he would be most displeased if she interfered with the progress of their march. It also implied he assumed she would not have the stamina to keep up with him.

"I'm fine, de Clare. Don't worry about me, I'm accustomed to being in the saddle. I'm young and healthy, and except for the rain, the ride is pleasant enough. Take us as far as you deem necessary, I'll not interfere."

He seemed amused but did not bother her again. Four hours later, when he finally called a halt for the night, she was relieved, not because she was overly tired but because she was ravenously hungry. Their small meal of bread and cheese at noon, which they ate while riding, had not been nearly enough.

They dismounted, and a squire came to take the horses. "I'll have a tent set up so you'll have a dry place," Richard said. He left her under the low-hanging branch of a beech tree where there was some shelter from the rain, and went to see that his men were settled. Watching, she realized with dismay that their camp would be primitive. There were no fires because of the rain, which meant whatever they ate would be cold.

She hoped it was not more of the hard, dark bread the Normans seemed so fond of, nor of their smelly, wormy cheese. What she wanted was a hot roast of beef, or a mutton stew savory with onions and cabbage, or a salmon from one of the bright rivers, smothered in a creamy herbed sauce. A simple apple would be welcomed, with its sweet juices running down her chin. What she was going to get, she knew, was campaign food. Her stomach growled, and Ban lifted his head from where he lay at her feet and stared at her as though insulted. "You're not likely to get anything different from what I eat, unless you go into the woods and catch yourself a fat hare, so don't look at me like that." Ban grunted and lowered his head.

The rain came harder, and she pulled her cloak closer over her shoulders and head. The wool was so tightly woven, water did not penetrate, but the moisture made the garment heavy, and as night descended in the shady forest she grew cold. She was always cold. Richard promised her a tent. She could have a brazier for warmth there, and blankets. If she could not eat well tonight she could at least be warm. She began to look around, to see if a tent had been erected anywhere near. The only one she saw was Richard's, blazoned with the gold and scarlet of the de Clares, and the realization hit her like a fist in her gut. *He means to have me spend the night in his tent.*

Last night had been an unexpected reprieve, when he did not come to her, though she felt an absurd disappointment before falling asleep. Like any man, he would expect her to fulfill her marital duties. This was the first time they would have privacy for the act, if you could call encampment in the middle of more than a thousand men privacy. She chewed on her lower lip, worrying out a solution to her predicament. It was not that she disliked the idea of what would happen between them. In a way she was eager to satisfy her curiosity. Would he be rough with her? When Eve was a child, Dervorgilla frightened her with horror stories of the sexual cruelty some men inflicted on their wives. Then the concubine smiled that wicked, knowing smile of hers, and said it was not inevitably unpleasant. The strange sensations that man roused whenever he touched her bewildered Eve.

Perhaps she could persuade him to leave her alone until after they reached Dublin. "Not likely." She scratched so vigorously between Ban's ears that the dog shook his head and lumbered to his feet. Still, the tent was there and she was growing colder by the moment. She sighed and stood, squaring her shoulders resolutely. She would at least be out of the rain.

Richard watched her walk toward the tent, the big white wolfhound who was her devoted companion close on her heel. The lack of sleep on the crossing from Wales, the battle, the night tending to and worrying about Morgan, the long hours seeing that Waterford was garrisoned and the ride today all added to his exhaustion. He wanted nothing more than to stuff his belly and fall into bed. But there was Eve to consider. She would expect him to fulfill his duty, to consummate the marriage. He had never shirked a duty and did not intend to start now.

He had simply been too busy to give the matter much thought, but he could not avoid it any longer. She was a pretty thing, it would be no great hardship for him. Then he frowned. If he were lucky she would make him forget Rosamund. He seriously doubted he would be *that* lucky. There were likely to be three of them in that bed. *Damn you, Henry for taking the one thing I ever truly loved.*

All around him men were settling for the night, knowing the next several days were likely to be as miserable for travel as this one. They were disciplined enough not to grumble too much. He made sure guards were set at adequate intervals, and that the horses were well hobbled, before gathering a sack of food and trudging through the sodden forest undergrowth to his waiting wife.

She looked up with startled eyes as he pulled aside the tent flap. "I've brought food." He held aloft the sack he bore.

"Thank the Lord. I thought I'd starve. I don't see how your men can survive on the rations you give them."

"Their rations are more than generous, lady. They don't find the food as repulsive as you do, and so eat more of it." She blushed at the rebuke, and he was sorry he spoke harshly. What had Morgan said, woo the woman? He wasn't doing a very good job of it. She looked frightened as a deer brought to bay by the hounds. The tent held a pile of padding and blankets to serve as a bed, and no table or chairs. She had lighted the lantern, and the small peat-filled brazier was beginning to glow, but the tent was not yet warm.

Crossing to the makeshift bed, he sat down on the precarious pile of blankets. "Come sit with me, Eve. I've brought something I think you'll like."

Like a curious child she came and stood nervously, one foot over the other, then puffed up her courage and sat beside him. When he pulled a wheel of creamy sheep cheese out of the pouch, her eyes widened with pleasure, and she gasped when a whole roast capon followed from the depths of the bag.

"It's cold, but it's meat."

She attacked the food greedily, and he sat back to watch. Every few bites she handed some of the capon or cheese to the dog, who waited patiently for his share. She was so different from the cosseted ladies he knew, women who would be whining unmercifully if they found themselves in the same primitive condition his wife seemed to take for granted.

"Don't I get any?" he asked.

"I thought you ate with your men. Good Lord, de Clare, why didn't you say something sooner?" Leaning toward him, she held a piece of capon in her fingers. He leaned toward her and took the meat into his mouth, his lips touching the tips of her fingers. She snatched her hand away and threw the rest of the bird into his lap. The dog eyed the bouncing fowl with keen interest.

It was obvious his touch disconcerted her. He leaned a little closer, and watched her squirm away so their thighs no longer touched. She smelled sweet and clean and her face was flushed a most becoming shade. Suddenly the idea of bedding her was immensely appealing. "I have some wine, do you want any?" he asked, trying not to smile.

She nodded, and he took the skin from his belt. He watched as she tilted her head back to squirt the liquid into her mouth. Her hood fell back with the motion and her beautiful hair, glimmering like pale moonbeams, caught the light from the lantern. He could see the pulse at the base of her long delicate neck, and desire, hot and undeniable, surged through his tired limbs.

Reaching out to touch the curve of her pink cheek, a low warning growl stayed his hand.

"Ban, no, bad dog." Eve scolded, handing the wineskin back. "I don't know why he did that. Usually he only growls if he thinks someone is going to hurt me."

"Perhaps the dog should sleep outside tonight."

"Outside? In the rain?"

He tried not to grin at her outrage. "My men are sleeping in the rain. It won't hurt the dog."

"No, but he won't be happy. He'll sit outside that tent flap and howl all night long, until nobody within miles gets a wink of sleep. Ban's not used to being outside."

"So I gather. He'll have to learn I'm no threat to you."

"How will he know that, de Clare, when I'm not sure of it myself?" There was a look of deep sadness in her emerald eyes.

They finished every crumb of food, and the dog was lying in the middle of the bed, grooming himself. The tent began to warm. Richard slid down to the floor, bracing his back against the pile of bedding, and stretched his long legs out in front of him. Leaning his head back, he closed his eyes. He would rest for just a minute. He was so tired. The ungodly noise the dog was making would surely keep him from sleep.

He woke with a start. The lantern still burned, but the brazier was long since cold. Sitting up, he rubbed the ache in his neck. Eve had tossed a blanket over him, but he still wore his wet cloak and his armor. Glancing behind him, he saw Eve cuddled into a tiny ball in the middle of the bed, the dog on the far side of her. Ban lifted his head and stared at Richard, his tail giving one or two desultory thumps.

"God's teeth, she sleeps with the beast." The tail thumped

more enthusiastically. "Stop that, you'll wake her," Richard
hissed. The dog's tail pounded ferociously.

Groaning at the cramps in his legs, back, and neck, Richard stripped out of his cold armor and sodden clothes. Holding the lantern high, he looked down at the sleeping woman.
His wife. Her face was as peaceful and innocent as a babe,
all pink and white. Her lashes cast soft shadows on her
smooth cheeks, and her mouth had lost its customary firm-
ness. She looked tender and delightful. He could see her
teeth between her slightly parted lips, and the steady cadence of her breath was a peaceful sound. Tendrils of hair
escaped her braid and lay in soft curls around her shoulders.
Leaning forward, he gently moved a strand of hair from her
forehead. She sighed, and a small frown puckered her brow.
Ban cocked his head to one side but no longer seemed to
think Richard was a threat and kept silent.

Sighing, he blew out the lantern, then crawled under the
covers. He lay with his back to her, bone tired, but found
he could not sleep. She curled up against him, instinctively
seeking warmth. She had removed her wet cloak, but still
wore her clothing, except her shoes. He flinched as her icy
toes snuggled greedily against his legs. Worse, he could
feel her breasts pressed against him, and the curve of her
hips fitted perfectly along his back. Growing hard, he cursed
under his breath but dared not move. Desire began to war
with common sense. Now was not the time. They were both
tired, and Eve was a virgin. She deserved comfort and gentleness the first time. He would wait until they reached Dublin. He groaned again. It would be a long three days indeed
before they arrived.

Nine

Eve tried to push away the cold, wet nose snuffling so tenaciously in her ear, but Ban persisted. She woke reluctantly. The makeshift nest of blankets was warm, and from the sounds outside the tent she knew it was still raining. Drawing herself closer to the warm, broad back she lay curled against, she slipped her arm around the man's waist.

Man! Coming fully awake, she jerked upright and scrambled out of the warm snare of the bed. Ban bounded after her, stretching and yawning. Eager to put as much space as possible between her and that man, she crossed to the tent flap and let the dog out. The rain was lighter than yesterday, but the clouds were thick and low and showed no signs of clearing. It looked to be an hour or so before dawn. Letting the flap fall back into place, she glanced at Richard. He still slept and was naked, with one arm thrown out over the edge of the bed. She was fascinated by his hands, large, with calloused palms, and long, elegant fingers. What would it be like to be fondled by those hands, to have them brush against her throat, caress her breasts, find ever more intimate places to stroke? An unmistakable tingling sensation blossomed between her legs. He was her husband. There was no shame in such thoughts, but so far the man showed little interest in her as a woman.

Richard made a soft sound in his sleep, drawing her attention. The blankets fell away and he lay exposed to her in all his masculine glory. He was beautiful, all muscle and lean, long grace. In repose his face held a peacefulness she had not seen on him before.

Richard's ambition made him eager to claim Leinster, but what would make him as fervent about possessing her? No doubt his heart was still with this Rosamund he spoke of, and so she could not hope to win his love. Stiffening with pride, she tried to beat back the sadness the prospect of a lifetime spent in a loveless marriage evoked. Foolish jealousy made her react with anger when Richard told her of Rosamund. Foolish because though she was now his wife she really held no claim to his fidelity. Few married men were faithful to their wives. Love had little to do with marriage, especially among people of their class, who married to form alliances and consolidate wealth and power, not from personal preference.

Though another woman laid claim to Richard's heart, Eve was the only one who could provide him with legitimate heirs. What good was his wealth if there was not another generation of de Clares to pass it on to? The idea took hold firmly in her brain. Provide an heir, and quickly. Not only would it bind Richard to her, it would ensure the succession to Leinster. A ruler without an heir inevitably attracted a great number of ambitious men eager to fill the void, by force if necessary.

She would do what she must, but it was more than that. She was attracted to the man, for all her best efforts to see him as the enemy. But he was not that. Perhaps he never had been, except in her imagination. Richard de Clare was the best hope for peace and security in Leinster. If they fought each other, nothing good could come of their union.

The sensations he roused in her whenever he was near, the fire that rushed through her at his touch, the quivering in the pit of her stomach at sound of his voice, all puzzled her. His maleness intrigued her. That he was her husband emboldened her. She wanted to satisfy her curiosity about this mysterious thing that happened between men and women, that people spoke of but would not explain to her. She was not totally ignorant of the act. She had seen animals mate, even occasionally come across a couple copulating feverishly behind bushes or in a dark corner. It looked outlandish to her. Since it was the only way to ensure an heir, she would have to endure whatever unpleasantness went with it. To breed an heir love was not necessary.

Slowly, with shaking fingers, she unlaced the sides of her gown and pulled the garment over her head. She carefully folded the heavy wool into a neat pile, her leather girdle placed on top. Next came the linen chemise and men's braies she wore while riding. Shivering, she stood naked in the dimly lighted tent. What if he laughed at her, or found her repulsive in some way? Could she risk making a fool of herself? Perhaps it was unseemly for her to be the one to initiate such a move, but she did not know for sure. There had been no one to tell her how these things were done. She gathered her fleeing courage and tried to quiet the unnaturally rapid breathing that made her slightly dizzy.

Her hair was nearly unbraided, and she pulled the ribbons from it, then raked her fingers through to untangle the mess. Digging in the scrip attached to her girdle, she pulled out an ivory-and-silver comb. The methodical strokes as she combed out her thigh-length hair were calming. Her hair was the one undeniably beautiful thing about her, and so she combed it until the waves and curls lay like a silken veil about her face and down her back. She was putting the comb away when Ban bounded into the tent, shaking the rain from his fur. The cold droplets spattered her thighs and belly and she reached out to swat the dog away. "Stop that. No, not the bed, you'll wake that man."

"I'm awake."

She whirled around to stare at him. How long had he been watching her? Even from this distance she saw hunger, hot and eager in his eyes. Her heart was beating against her ribs so hard she could hardly draw a full breath, but she forced herself to walk across the tent, as though appearing naked before a man was something she did every day. It would seem he did not find her offensive.

He stood up as she approached, and at the sight of his splendid body, fire poured through her, heady as the best *usquebaugh,* sweet as autumn honey. He was glorious, all muscle and sinew, hard angular male contrasting with her soft woman's curves. Golden skinned, long of leg, broad-shouldered and lean, his chest was covered with brown hair, and she longed to touch it, to see if it was as soft as it looked. She avoided looking lower, to that part of a man that was still unknown and incomprehensible to her. That part so full of extravagant legend she was not sure where the truth lay, but knew she would soon find out.

He held his hand out to her, and she placed her own in it. A strange peacefulness filled her at his touch. It was like coming home to a place you endlessly longed for, but did not know even existed until you arrived. It seemed as natural as breathing to go into his arms and be enfolded by their gentle strength. For the first time in her precarious and unpredictable life, she felt completely safe, and where there had been fear, a strong, riotous hope sprang to life.

"Are you sure that this is what you want?" he whispered.

She pressed against him, her head barely coming to his chest, her breasts crushed against his hot skin. Into her belly pressed that large and still enigmatic part of him that seemed most urgent of all to know her. "I'm very sure."

He trembled, and she marveled that she held such power over him. When she raised a hand to stroke his face, he leaned into it, then caught her hand in his own, and turning her palm up, placed a hot, quick kiss there.

His eyes were full of need, and a strange sound escaped from the back of his throat. "My God, Eve, you don't know what you're doing."

"Nay, my lord, I know exactly what I'm doing. I want

you, Husband, here and now." Her voice shook with eagerness, and held no fear.

Groaning, he scooped her into his powerful arms, then laid her on the pile of blankets. "You deserve better than this, Princess, especially the first time."

"I don't need anything but you, Richard." She spoke his name softly, and it felt natural to her, as though she had known it all her life. She ached for him in a way she had never known or imagined. Ached to have him kiss her, touch her, to come into her and fill her with his maleness. She wanted to know the feel of this man, the taste of him. There was an unbearable urgency building in her, setting her blood rioting. Wanting—she knew not what exactly—but with such a powerful longing she feared she would die if he did not fulfill that fiery craving. Could he be experiencing the same?

Lying down beside her, Richard turned her to face him. She moved closer trying to wrap her leg around his hip. "No, Eve, not yet. You're not ready for me, and I fear I am more than ready for you. Lie quietly. A virgin's first time should be slow and gentle, but I can't do that if you're too eager." His voice was low, and held a note, almost of pain, she had never heard before.

Not ready for him? What could he mean? She felt she would burst if he did not do something immediately. Reluctantly she obeyed him, trusting that he knew more about what was happening between them, trusting that he would show her the way.

He touched his lips to her forehead, her eyelids, the tip of her nose, and the kisses were gentle and light. It burned her, and made her ache, deep in her belly. His mouth found hers and he nipped delicately, the tip of his tongue playing against her lips, until she opened her mouth to him, and their tongues danced with each other in a delightful little jig. She decided she liked his mouth, firm yet soft, and the things it did to her.

His breathing was as ragged as her own now, and he lowered his head to her throat, to kiss the pulse beating wildly there. His hands cupped her breasts, and he lowered his mouth to one of her nipples and suckled there, first easy and gentle, then taking the hard bud between his teeth. Arching against him, she thought she would die of pleasure. How much more could there be?

Reaching blindly she found his wide shoulders and pulled him closer, her nails raking across his back. Now it was Richard who burned with demanding need. She saw it in the turbulent eyes he turned on her as he laid her on her back and moved between her thighs. She spread her legs wide, greedy for him. His hard maleness probed her soft woman's place, and she reached out to guide him. He groaned at the touch.

"Now, Richard," she whispered hot against his ear, pleading, commanding. He slid into her slowly, filling her a little at a time. The throbbing ache increased in intensity. There was a small, sharp pain, then a feeling of fullness. It felt exactly right.

"Did I hurt you?" His voice was ragged, and he held himself still waiting for her reply.

"No, Richard. Please, don't stop."

He began to move rhythmically, slowly at first, until she met the strange new dance with her own thrusts, then he moved more quickly, more deeply. Their movements were perfectly coordinated, as though they had always been together. Passion grew until nothing existed in the world but the two of them, together for the first time, as though they were the first man and woman still in Eden, unaware of anything but each other.

The throbbing, expectant need finally burst and left her gasping with awe. Richard shuddered, plunging deeper into her, until a primitive cry tore through his large body. Gradually his movements slowed, until with a sigh he pulled her once more to his side and lay beside her. The throbbing of her body was matched by his, slowly quieting into faint spasms as they lay entwined, reluctant to separate.

It was no longer a mystery to her, what happened between a man and a woman. Except that it was more enigmatic than ever, now that she knew the wonder of it. She could not believe such an extraordinary thing had been so long unknown to her. Somewhere deep within she knew it was Richard alone who would bring her to such heights of passion. There would be no other man for her.

He stroked her hair with a trembling hand, and whispered in the fading darkness, "What have you done to me, Princess?"

her body was attacked by his, slowly quieting into faint spasms as they ebbed....

Ten

The rain stopped just after dawn, and though the clouds were low in the morning, by noon they began to lift. Rays of sunlight penetrated here and there through the mist and the dense canopy of forest. Richard threw his scarlet mantle back over his shoulders, welcoming the warmth after days of cold and rain. Beside him Eve rode on her small mare. She was unusually quiet all day, and he'd had little to say as well. They were both, he suspected, thinking about their lovemaking.

He realized he would need to bed his wife and get sons from her to secure his claim to Leinster. Being a healthy man in his prime he even expected to enjoy the sport of it. What happened that morning, in the darkness of his rough tent, he had not anticipated. His wife, stubborn, quick-tongued, brave, was also the most exciting woman he had ever bedded. Whenever he glanced at her, a burning need hit him such as he had not known in years. Even Rosamund had not roused so lusty a response from him. Their love had been chaste and young, unconsummated, the love of innocents.

Eve, while untouched by a man until this morning, was no innocent. She had seen too much of the evil underside of the world to walk through life with unrealistic expectations or romanticized ideals. It gave her a hard, clean strength of character he found appealing, and wondered why. Women were supposed to be quiet malleable creatures. Those who were shrewish or too independent were dealt with harshly, their spirits broken until they conformed to the ideal of a meek and helpless woman in need of the protection and guidance of a father or husband. Eve was no such woman. He did not think she ever would be, and he had no desire to break that clear and uncompromising spirit. There was intelligence in the quick tongue, and an independence of thought and action that reminded him of himself. She would no more follow orders meekly than he would. Life with this woman would never bore him.

As seductive as Eve might be, it was Rosamund who was the great love of his life. Or so he had thought, until today. Rosamund was a pain that throbbed and would not heal, because he kept picking at the scabs around his heart. Morgan said she was a sickness in his blood. Richard glanced again at Eve. Was it possible the tiny, sharp-tongued Irishwoman was what he needed to finally purge Rosamund from his soul? The idea settled into his brain, and he found it intriguing. For the first time in a very long time, thought of Rosamund did not bring pain.

How was it possible Eve affected him so strongly? She was different from all other women he had known, and passionate beyond his wildest hopes. That was what he found appealing. But he still did not trust her. There was something she was keeping from him, and it probably had to do with Dermot. Thought of that treacherous ally turned his mood instantly sour.

He came to Ireland fully prepared to help Dermot win back his throne, only to find a proud and dangerously ambitious ally. Vengeful, cruel, rapacious, the things he now knew about Dermot were enough to rank him with the worst rulers Richard ever heard of. Nothing stood in the way of Dermot's ambition, or his revenge. The thought of having vowed himself to help such a man made Richard uneasy, but he gave his word. Eve was his real means to obtaining

Leinster. Without her, Dermot could easily renege on his promise. Richard would then be forced to fight him as well.

"At this pace we'll reach Dublin by midday tomorrow." Eve glanced at the sky to calculate the time.

Startled out of his reverie, he realized he had not been paying much attention to their surroundings for the last hour or more. He had rarely done so foolish a thing. The quickest way to get killed in enemy territory was to relax one's guard.

They made good time, in spite of the rain, and he was eager to see this journey end. Once they reached Dublin safely, he could begin the serious work of conquering Leinster. "Dublin will provide the strong center I need to carry on this campaign."

"Do you mean to go after Rory O'Conor?"

He nodded, and his jaw took on the hard line of determination that made him seem older than his thirty-two years. "It's dangerous to wait. That gives Rory time to gather an army. He can call many thousands of men into the field and so overwhelm my forces we have no chance of winning. It is that I must avoid. Rory must not have time to build an army. I'll take the offensive, and if all goes well we can come to terms with O'Conor before winter."

"Terms? You mean to secure a peace with the man?"

His eyes narrowed on her. "Peace is preferable to war and the unnecessary loss of lives. I mean to live peacefully in Ireland, and to leave a tranquil kingdom for our sons to rule. What man would not wish the same?"

"My father, for one." Her mouth set in a line of bitter resignation and disgust. "My father wants revenge, not victory."

Richard was encouraged by the harshness of her tone. Could her loyalty to her father be wavering? "There can be no peace under those circumstances. One act of vengeance rouses another, until the circle of retaliation becomes endless, and feeds upon itself. At some point the urge to avenge old wrongs must come to an end."

She shook her head, and a sad smile played on her lips. "It isn't just my father. Rory and Tiernan will not be happy until Ireland is in ruins, to avenge their pride. Of them all Rory is the most honorable. In truth, he has been a fair enough ruler, but his ambition is boundless. He wants all of Ireland for himself and means to crush the traditional kingdoms to do it. I want an independent Leinster. We have our own traditions, our old loyalties. The kingdoms have feuded among themselves for so long, *Septs* warring for the elusive honor of the High Kingship, that half of Ireland bears a deadly grudge against the other. I see no end to it."

Chaos is what she described, or something near to it. While it divided his opponents and made them weak, it also hurt the country. War disrupted the regular planting and harvesting of crops, the regulation of trade, which was the one source of outside wealth for this island. Worse, it wasted whole generations of men to incalculable suffering, lost to battle, or crippled, embittered, and useless. A land of widows and orphans could not be a land of wealth or prosperity, no matter the bounty of the earth itself—Ireland, marvelously fertile, held a treasure of richness in her wet, generous bosom. It needed but a strong, sure hand to guide her, to bring all that potential to fruition.

"You speak as though you know O'Conor."

She looked at him with a crooked smile on her lips. "I was to wed Rory, when his first wife died. It was an excellent plan. It would have bound the two kingdoms together. Our sons would have ruled both Leinster and Connacht."

He felt a spur of jealousy, and dismissed it as unmanly. "What prevented the marriage?"

"My father, of course. Even for peace he wouldn't relinquish his ambition. It wasn't enough that his grandsons might rule a united Ireland. He wants the High Kingship for himself. He will never be content with less."

"Were you disappointed?"

"It would have been a workable arrangement. Rory is a good man. I came to know him the summer I spent in Belangare."

Jealousy rushed through him at her words. "You spent time with the man?"

She looked up at his tone, her eyes startled. Then she laughed, softly and easily. "I was eight years old, de Clare. Nothing happened between us, if that's what you're worried about. It's customary when a girl is betrothed to spend time with her husband's kin, to learn their ways. It builds loyalty in the girl."

He felt foolish, but only scowled down at her. "We do the same. It's how Rosamund came to spend time at my uncle's court, when I was a squire there." She seemed to withdraw when he said that. His mention of Rosamund apparently disturbed her. He smiled realizing this jealousy he was so unused to dogged at her as well.

"For all I could have been content with him, it seems Rory was not my destiny." She shifted in her saddle, rearranging her buttocks to a new position. "It would have been much less complicated than this alliance my father has bargained with you."

He grunted, but did not answer. Destiny. Was there such a thing? The Celts still clung to the pagan notion that a man's life was written in the heavens, immutably scribed, so that each person acted out exactly what was preordained for them. It went against Christianity, which said man possessed free will, and could choose his own actions, and with them, suffer the consequences. He saw the appeal in the older belief. It relieved a man of responsibility. Whatever he did was ordained and unchangeable. While he rejected the idea, he could not help but wonder if he was not part of a larger plan. By his actions he could determine his fate, at least to a certain extent. It was that part of each man's life that lay beyond his control, the external events to which he must respond, the unexpected decisions he was called upon to make, that held the mystery of his destiny.

Henry Plantagenet claimed God, through the pope, decreed that Ireland be conquered and brought into conformity with the Roman church. Richard had serious doubts about the bishop of Rome's ability to hear the voice of God so clearly. A doubt he judiciously kept to himself. The idea of his fate, woven into an eternal tapestry, intrigued him. He had been content in Wales, until the lure of Ireland called. Though he came with the idea of acquiring land, and the wealth and power that went with it, there was something about the land itself that was compelling.

It was true, what Eve accused him of that day on the beach. There was nowhere on earth he thought of as home, no place that demanded his loyalty above all others. Perhaps it was because there was no territory he had won on his own, no land he struggled to possess. It had all been given to him, an accident of birth. There was no merit in that, no proof of his superiority as a warrior or his worth as a man.

Then there was Eve. As mysterious and unpredictable as the land, stormy and generous, and with a sense of place so rooted it was unbreachable. Ireland was Eve's destiny, of that he had no doubt. Was it now his as well, and with the land the woman?

He felt foolish. Such ideas were alien to his practical mind. Ireland was a job that needed doing, while Eve was his means of ruling Leinster, and would be the mother of his sons. Nothing more. Why then could he not stop thinking of her soft skin, and the cloud of silvery hair that caressed him in the darkness? Of her hands eager for him, her lips, warm, soft, and so new to the joys of exploration and discovery?

He scowled down at his wife, and was surprised to see a worried frown on her face. She kept looking over her shoulder, as though expecting something, and Richard's first thought was of treachery. Was she due to meet someone? Were they riding into an ambush? "What do you look for?" he demanded, his hand ready at the bow slung across his back.

She looked at him with wide, startled eyes. "It's a feeling. Silly, I'm sure."

He tensed. He had spent too many years listening in the dark for the approach of an enemy not to take her seriously. Sometimes it was intuition that kept a man, or an army, alive. "What sort of feeling?"

Shaking her head, she glanced again over her shoulder. "Something isn't right. It's as though we're being watched. My spine keeps crawling."

He searched the trees around them. They rode through a forest of beech and oak, a thick tangle of old trees and tall, lush underbrush. An army could hide in such cover and not be seen. If the Irish were anything like the Welsh, and he had every reason to think they were, then ambush and sudden swift attack by hidden bowmen would not be unusual.

Raising his hand in a silent signal, his men grew quiet and watchful, hands twitching at sword hilts, archers fingering arrows in the quivers at their hips. Several knights moved forward to surround Eve, seeking to protect her with their massive horses and heavy shields. Before they could reach her, an arrow whined through the air. It glanced off the leather of Eve's saddle, and her mare reared at the impact. She struggled to control the startled animal.

Richard searched for the hidden archer. Another arrow whistled into the confusion of rearing horses and shouting men. The second arrow struck Richard in the shoulder, but the chain he wore protected him from injury. He saw where the shaft came from.

Spurring his stallion around Eve, he pulled bow and arrow into position as he rode. Not for nothing did men call him Strongbow. His eye was as sure as any man's, and the

Welsh bow he used was deadly accurate within its range. The attacker was well within range, and a grim smile crossed Richard's lips as he aimed and let fly the arrow, all in one smooth, facile movement.

Hit squarely in the chest, the man toppled heavily from the nervous horse he rode. Keeping a keen eye open for any others, Richard soon determined the man acted alone, which puzzled him. It made little sense, a lone archer stalking a well-armed troop of cavalry. Unless the man had a single target in mind, and hoped to hit his mark and be gone before anyone saw him. Richard stared down at the Irishman, who was dead, the arrow deep in his heart.

Having regained control of her mount, Eve rode to Richard's side.

"Are you hurt?" He slung his bow over his shoulder and dismounted.

She shook her head, staring at the Irishman. "The saddle leather deflected the blow."

"Why would he shoot you?"

Her green eyes moved to his face, then back to the dead man. "It seems more likely you were the target, de Clare. I was in the way."

There was something strange in her voice, more than the fright she had just experienced. But what? He walked over to the corpse, and, dismounting, Eve followed. "Do you recognize him?" Richard asked.

"Of course not. Why should I?" Her voice was fierce with indignation. "Surely you don't think I had anything to do with this?"

His men gathered near. One of the knights whistled low, and pointed at the dead man's hand with the point of his sword. "Bloody Christ, even the peasants wear jewels."

Richard squatted. On the middle finger of the dead man's left hand a ring glittered. Removing it from the cooling finger, Richard held it up for closer inspection. It was a man's ring, massive and gold, set with a large garnet with rubies in the band. It was worth a small fortune and could not have been come by honestly by the simply clad archer. Either the man purposely wore clothes beneath his station, to deceive them, or he acquired the ring in one of two ways. He had either stolen it, or been given it. If given to him, was it a gift, or a payment?

A sharp gasp from Eve made him turn back to her, and what he saw turned his blood cold. Her face blanched and she swayed, as though she would faint.

Slowly he stood, and held the jewel out to her. "Whose ring is this?" His voice was quiet. A few of his men heard the question and grew silent, waiting for her answer.

Eve shook her head and turned away. The fear and shock in her eyes made him doubly sure she recognized the ring. He grabbed her by the shoulder and turned her to look at him. "It is Dermot's, isn't it? Isn't it!"

She nodded, muted by the betrayal, reluctant to acknowledge the irrefutable evidence he held in his hand. His voice, low and quiet, cracked with anger. "Your father lost little time coming after me." She stared at him mutely, and he marched her away from his men. "Now, Eve. You must decide between me and your father." The ultimatum was necessary. Why then the sudden chill at the thought that she might choose Dermot?

Her voice was strangled with disbelief. "Father wouldn't do this."

Richard held the ring up. "How do you explain this?"

She sighed, and rubbed her eyes with thumb and forefinger. "We don't know if it's my father's doing. The man could have come by that ring by a different route."

"Such as?"

"I don't know."

Richard turned from her and paced angrily beneath an oak tree. Was Dermot behind the plot? He found it hard not to believe so. But why now? As long as Richard and his army were useful, they should be safe from the Irish king. He turned and stared at his wife, who looked so miserable a wave of compassion washed over him. The outrageous thought stormed suddenly through his brain. What if Eve were the target? It would be a more subtle way of undermining his claim to Leinster. He could hope for no heirs from a dead wife, and what was to keep Dermot from killing him after the task of winning Leinster was completed? Would Dermot kill his own daughter?

A cold anger grew in him. He realized, to his surprise, it was because of the damage this did to Eve. She stood motionless, all the spirit drained from her, and though she did not cry, she appeared on the verge of collapse.

She looked so fragile, as though she would break at a touch, her arms folded across her chest, her green eyes glazed with a look that reminded him of men in battle, who sustaining a mortal wound had yet to die. He gathered her into his arms, where she trembled like a tiny, frightened kitten. Gradually she grew less tense, and melded herself into the hard contours of his body, her head resting on his chest. Finally, he turned her to face him and lifted her chin with a finger. "I swear to you, Eve, I will protect you with my life."

"You would be paying too high a price. I've put you in danger by marrying you. Perhaps an annulment would be best."

"It's too late for an annulment. You may already be carrying my child. Even if that isn't true, I would not give you over to the care of your father. If you are with me I can protect you. Until we know who is behind this, neither of us is safe. We are stronger together than apart. Besides, I am done with other men taking what is mine. They will have to kill me before I will let you go, Princess."

She shook her head and stepped back from him. "No one has said such things to me. There must be something you want in return."

"There is. You must choose, Eve. Me or your father. It's no longer possible for you to divide your loyalties."

There was a strange look in her green eyes, something he could not read, then she bowed her head. "God help me, but I know that. Do you think I have thought of anything else since we found the men my father murdered? How can I support him and not endanger my own soul?" She looked up at him and her eyes were bright with unshed tears. "My father cannot bring peace to Ireland. In the thirty years he's been king, he has gone from one act of vengeance or cruelty to another."

"Then you are with me?"

She chewed on her lower lip as she stared at him. "Give me your sword."

Puzzled, he pulled the long sword from its scabbard and handed it to her. She held it up between them. The pommel of the grip was in the shape of a cross, and embedded in it was a relic. He knew then what she wanted. Solemnly, he kneeled in front of her, his hand covering hers on the sword.

"Swear to me, Richard de Clare, that you will rule Leinster with a strong hand and with fairness."

"I do swear it."

She leaned forward and said in a strong, clear voice, "Then hear my vow. You are now my life. You and Ireland share my loyalty. As long as you keep your promise to rule this land well, you can trust me with your life."

"You make it conditional. What if you decide I am not good for Ireland. Where is your heart then?"

She hesitated, and her hand trembled beneath his. "Don't make me choose between you and Ireland. You ask too much of me."

It was more than he hoped for. He knew she would no longer support her father against him, but he wanted it all. All of her loyalty and trust, all of her fierce heart and passion. As much as he wanted it, he would not force her. "It will do for now, Princess. But some day you will have to make that choice as well."

They stood for a while, and something new and fragile came to life between them. From that moment they became man and wife, lover and friend. Trust, new and ephemeral, took root and began to grow tentative tendrils around their hearts. Their mingled destiny began to weave together like a great tapestry.

Eleven

Dervorgilla watched the king of Leinster struggle. Dermot's eyes were closed, his face pinched with the intensity of the moment. His arms shook as he supported himself above her, working vigorously between her legs, pumping and pounding and pushing. She made a desultory try at helping him.

When had Dermot grown old? There was more gray than red in his hair and beard, and his face was lined with deep creases. The once bulging muscles had slackened and lost strength. The worst change was that in his virility. He no longer grew as hard as he once had, nor maintained it as long. Despite her best efforts he was in decline. She used him, twenty years ago, to rescue her from the cruelty of her husband Tiernan O'Rourke. It had been such an adventure, the abduction, the resulting long war with Tiernan. She felt like Helen at the gates of Troy. Then Tiernan allied himself with Rory O'Conor and Hasculf and four years ago drove Dermot out of Leinster. Four years of exile and hardship were not part of her plans. But they were home, in Dublin, at last.

Closing her eyes, she allowed her mind to wander. She conjured Richard de Clare, powerful, with the deadly grace of a wild animal. Remembering him naked at his bath, and the caress of her fingers on his soap-slicked back, the texture of the smooth skin and bulging muscles beneath her hands, her desire climbed. Like a mare in heat, with a stallion within sight but out of reach, wanting, aching, until she thought she would scream, knowing it was Richard she wanted in her bed, his young, hard tool between her legs, she thrust harder against Dermot, writhing in a frenzy of lust.

Groaning, she shoved her hips up, hard. Dermot redoubled his efforts, until with a satisfied grunt he fell on top of her, gasping, the sweat rolling from his head to her breasts. Unfulfilled, still aching for a climax, she resisted the urge to push him away.

She lay with her hand, palm upturned, over her eyes. Dermot was old and could not live long. A small smile curved her lips as she thought again of Richard de Clare. It would be easy to be rid of Dermot, once he was no longer useful to her. Just as she'd been rid of that damned wife of his. It still possessed power to infuriate her, that even after that simpering woman's death Dermot would not marry her, would not make her his queen. She thought a child would move him to do so, but Egan's birth wrought no change in her status. It was all Eve's fault. But for Eve it would have all been hers.

She was the daughter of the king of Meath. She deserved a higher status than Dermot MacMurrough's concubine. Now, with de Clare and his army, her desires could finally be realized. She could be rid of Dermot and Eve. Then her son would rule Leinster and she with him, the true power behind the boy king's throne. For that she was willing to be patient a while longer. With luck, the young, virile earl of Pembroke would be at her side.

"Magnificent." Dermot fondled her breast with his sword-roughened hand.

"When will Richard reach Dublin?"

"Richard is it?" He sat to look at her, rubbing his chest. "If all goes as planned, he'll arrive tomorrow. Piss on de Clare. It's his army I need."

Carefully, she kept the surprise from her face. "What do

you mean? The army is useless without its leader. If aught happens to the earl, his troops will leave Ireland on the first tide."

"Aye, woman, I know all that. In truth, the man surprises me. He seems a man of honor, can you believe so ludicrous a thing in this age? It may be the first time in my life I've an ally I don't need to worry will slip a knife in my back. I mean to use him and his army, I'm not fool enough to think they owe me any loyalty. When Eve took it into her head to marry the man, she complicated matters. I may need to change my strategy a bit. I'll never understand what got into the girl. She's been loud enough for months about not wanting the union. Bah. Who understands women? Their minds are feeble and flighty."

"But is that not what you intended all along? That the earl marry Eve?"

He looked at her with cunning, secretive eyes. "It's what I wanted him to believe. I meant to keep him hungry, assure his loyalty to me by delaying the marriage. His claim was weak without it. Promises can be broken. Eve's given de Clare reason to fight for his own gain now, rather than mine. What's to keep him from seeking the High Kingship for himself, now he has a strong claim to her land? Still, I'll manage de Clare. I can make it work to my advantage."

She could have slapped him for his stupidity. Dermot was no longer angry with Eve, despite Dervorgilla's best efforts to drive a wedge between them. He'd never agree his daughter must be eliminated, or that she was a threat to his ambition. Why had he always favored that girl over Egan? It was unnatural. A son should take pride of place in his father's heart. Dermot did not know Egan was not his. She watched as he pulled a tunic over his head. If he suspected Egan was bastard born, it would explain much of what Dermot did. But why would he suspect anything? She had been so careful all these years as she planned and waited for her revenge. How could Dermot know?

A sudden thrill of fear made her shiver and pull the furs up around her breasts. If Dermot truly harbored such doubts, it was more important than ever that she set her scheme into motion. Nothing must stand in her way of seeing Egan on the throne. The idea of eliminating Dermot as well as Eve took on new urgency. With de Clare to fight for Leinster, Dermot was no longer necessary. If he truly did suspect Egan was not his son, she must do something to protect herself.

Eve must be dealt with now, before there was any possibility she could bear the earl a child. A child who could claim Egan's throne. A child whose pretension the English king could use as an excuse to invade Ireland. With luck the stupid girl was dead. The man she hired had never failed her before. Climbing from the warm bed, she stood behind Dermot, wrapping her arms around his waist, her breasts flattened against his back.

"Don't you get enough, woman?" He chuckled.

She cooed and ran her tongue around his ear. "Never, love." She must be clever in manipulating Dermot to achieve her aims. He was not a stupid man. She ran her hands up and down the king's arms. She needed to know what was in his mind. "Come back to bed," she murmured, making her voice thick as though with desire.

Where the hell was Dermot? Richard saw no sign of the Irish king and the men who sailed with him from Waterford. Why weren't they camped to the west of Dublin, as had been agreed to?

He stopped and raised his arm, and the long way back along his line of knights and archers went the cry "halt"! Something was wrong. This empty countryside was not what he expected to find. It was then the gate opened and a single rider cantered toward them.

"Jesu, is that Morgan?" Richard could not believe his

eyes. He spurred his stallion forward to meet his commander.

"What took you so long?" Morgan asked. "We expected
you a day gone. How went the journey?"

"We can speak of that later. Where is Rory's garrison?"

Morgan smiled widely. "When your fleet arrived in Dublin Bay, O'Conor's Ostmen took one look at the warships
and ran for the hills. They've sought refuge with O'Conor
in Connaught."

"There was no battle?" Richard was puzzled. "Why did
O'Conor leave Dublin so undermanned?"

Morgan shook his head. "I can't credit it. First Waterford
and now Dublin. Rory didn't have troops in either place.
Those who fled Dublin seem to be richest of the townsmen
and merchants."

"No doubt the very men who've allied themselves with
O'Conor over the years and fear retaliation from Dermot."
Richard wound the bridle reins tightly in his fingers. "I've
need of the merchants and traders to make this work. Dublin
is useless to me without them."

"They'll be back, my lord. Dublin is too rich for them
to stay away. Nary a man impoverishes himself over principles."

Richard cocked an eyebrow at his friend. "You've become a cynic, Morgan."

The younger man laughed. "Just more realistic. There
was one bit of good news. From what I've been able to
gather, Hasculf was not here. He's been with O'Conor for
a month or more."

"That's luck on our part. Hasculf wouldn't have run. Did
O'Conor expect merchants to fight?"

Eve joined them, stopping her gray mare next to Richard.
"Rory levied a tax of four thousand cows on Ireland, a huge
sum, to purchase the loyalty of the Dublin Ostmen. It would
appear men who sell their honor so cheaply are not willing
to risk their lives for their lord."

"At least that explains their cowardice. They weren't warriors." Richard studied the walled town critically, assessing its strengths and weaknesses. Ireland's countryside was a rich bounty waiting to be exploited; her monasteries lay undefended, like fat geese for the plucking. But it was Dublin that inflamed men's greed.

They approached from the west, along the south shore of the River Liffey, which formed the northern border of the town. Earthen ramparts surrounded Dublin, and stone walls, five feet thick and ten feet tall, topped with a wooden palisade, crowned the ramparts. With her strong walls Dublin was the perfect site from which to base his military assault on Rory O'Conor.

Richard hoped to negotiate with Rory rather than fight the man. If the mere threat of his knights and archers forced the Ostmen out of Dublin, could the same fear bring Rory to a treaty? He sighed. It was highly unlikely this would end without bloodshed, on both sides. "Dermot is in residence?"

"Aye, that he is." Morgan's mouth twisted with disgust. "He swaggered into Dublin and promptly took up residence in the royal palace as though he's not been gone the last four years."

"He *is* the king."

"We all know who the better man is." Morgan smiled, and bowed his head slightly, careful to cradle his wounded arm against his chest. "Welcome, Lady de Clare. It is good to see you healthy and safely arrived."

Richard glanced at Eve and saw tears brimming in her eyes. "You are sad, Princess?"

"No, my lord, happy. I am home."

Home. Looking around, he saw nothing more than he had before. A prosperous, strongly walled merchant town. For Eve it held a lifetime of memories.

"There, to the northeast," she said, pointing, "is Clontarf, where Brian Boru died. He was the first High King. It all started with Brian, the wars, the pride in the hearts of men who would be as he was, King of All Ireland. Yet none since then have held the land in peace."

Bloody field at Clontarf. Richard knew of that battle, and that king. Eve had the blood of Boru in her veins. She shared that great monarch's devotion for the land and the people. He felt a rush of envy that he knew no such passion. The duty he owed to Henry of England, and now to Dermot of Leinster, was that. Duty. A job to be done. His word to keep. But his heart was not in it. He was weary of war.

Word spread quickly through his men that there would be no battle to win Dublin. Rough cheering followed them up the last hill and through Westgate into the town. They rode on unpaved narrow streets bordered by walkways of wood. The streets were lined with hundreds of single-story mud and wattle houses, each of which stood on a tiny lot enclosed within a fence. They were unlike the Irish dwellings he had seen in the countryside, or the cottages of the Welsh or English folk. These buildings, with their steeply pitched thatch roofs, reminded him of York in the north of England. York, like Dublin, had been settled by Norsemen. With sudden recognition Richard realized he was looking at a Norse town, not an Irish one.

He studied the faces of the people of Dublin. Not only were the rulers of Dublin Norse, so seemed most of the common folk. They were a strange mix, revealing the pattern of invasion and settlement over the tumultuous centuries. Here was the fiery red hair of the Norse, there the darker Danes, along with Irish blonds, a collection of faces freckled and fair, eyes pale and wary. A handsome people, some curious, some cautious, more than a few openly hostile. None turned aside as he passed, and he felt their assessing eyes on his back.

They rode through the street where the wine merchants traded, and the Street of the Weavers. Boys ran before them shouting, their young voices high with excitement, to tell folk of the newest invasion of Dublin.

It was the people Richard must win if he were to rule here in peace, and leave order for his sons and his grandsons. He meant to sire a dynasty in this fertile land. In his mind he saw the generations of descendants who would prosper and carry his name through the centuries. What man did not dream of such glory?

He noticed then the quiet that the noise of his men covered. Squinting, he looked more closely at the streets of Dublin. The town appeared nearly empty. Where had the people gone? Did they follow their Norse leaders into the hills, to the protection of Rory O'Conor? Damn, the Irish would be difficult enough, how was he to win the trust of these Norse merchants? Without them Dublin could not trade efficiently. It was the port, with ships visiting from around the world, that made Dublin rich.

To the left of High Street, near the river, sat an imposing wooden church with its monastery. "What church is that?" Richard turned to Eve when she did not answer.

Her eyes were fixed on something beyond him, and turning in the direction she stared, was at a loss to know what caught her attention so strongly. Then he saw a tall, fair, elegant man, smiling and calling her name, striding toward them from the oak-shadowed church.

With a cry of undisguised joy, Eve slid from her mare and ran toward the man. He swept her into his powerful arms and twirled her around and around, until her cloak and skirts billowed like the petals of a windblown flower.

Biting down on his sudden, inexplicable anger, Richard rode toward the pair. Mounted on Emys, he towered over them. Most men had the sense to be intimidated. This man looked at him and smiled, so open and honest and cheerful a smile, Richard wondered if he could be simple-minded. The man held Eve tightly, as though reluctant to let her go.

"Unhand my wife." His voice was low and steely.

The man's eyes shifted uneasily from him to Eve. He had green eyes of an unusual deep color. Something stirred in

Richard at sight of those eyes, and tried to penetrate the fog of anger that clouded his vision.

"How dare you speak in such a tone to Lorcan." Eve's indignant anger was bright and hot.

"Lorcan? And who is Lorcan that I should watch without protest as he mauls and kisses my wife?"

"Lorcan O'Toole. Archbishop of Dublin. My uncle."

He saw it then. The man's eyes were the same clear summer green as Eve's, and his hair was near as fair as hers. Lorcan was so obviously related, only a fool would not see it. Now he saw, too, not a bald spot, but a monk's tonsure on the back of the man's head. This robust, handsome man looked no more a priest than Richard.

"You are married then?" Lorcan looked from one to the other, the smile wavering a bit. "I thought Dermot would wait until you arrived here. I hoped to perform the ceremony myself."

"Don't worry yourself." Eve smiled at Lorcan and wrapped her arm around his. "I married the man willingly enough, though God's truth he's a difficult person. You've never seen so short a temper on a man."

Richard, who prided himself on his patience and his cool, detached assessment of any situation, could not believe the words coming from his wife's dainty mouth. Then he saw the spark of mischief in her eyes. Angry one moment, teasing him the next, she was as unpredictable as the passing clouds, and as hard to grasp. He relaxed a bit and smiled. It would take a lifetime to get to know this woman. He thought he would rather enjoy the adventure.

"Your journey was uneventful?" Lorcan shaded his brilliant eyes from the sun with his free hand, and looked up at Richard, still mounted on the tall war-horse.

Richard wondered if the man's words were as innocent as they appeared. Until he knew Lorcan better, he would not offer more information than necessary. "The rain slowed us the first two days." He warned Eve with a glance to say nothing of the ambush. Her mouth set in a stubborn line, but she kept quiet.

If Lorcan noticed the sudden tenseness, he gave no sign of it. Richard stared into the archbishop's cool green eyes, and saw there no malice, only a watchful concern.

Turning to Morgan, Richard said, "Where's Dermot? We need to plan our march against Rory."

Morgan's face twisted with loathing. "He's spent most of the day mustering your men, or trying to. Why he thinks they'll obey him I can't fathom."

"It would seem our ally needs a few reminders." There was still the matter of the ambush he wished to discuss with the Leinster king. Dermot must be made to understand who he was dealing with. Richard turned his attention once more to Eve and Lorcan. "There are things I must see to, Father. Would you escort my wife?"

"That I will, and gladly. It's been four long years since I've talked to my favorite niece. She has much to tell me, of that I'm sure."

There was that smile again, as innocent as an angel, but Richard would swear there was not a naive drop of blood in the man. Guileless perhaps, and that was remarkable, especially in a man of God. Lorcan was not inconsequential, that much Richard already knew of the man. The archbishop could be a powerful ally. Or a dangerous enemy.

Richard turned and spurred his stallion into a canter, Morgan at his side. He was eager to get his hands around Dermot MacMurrough's scrawny, treacherous throat.

"Child, will you not tell me what disturbs you so?" Lorcan asked. "Is it the earl? Do you fear him?"

"No, Uncle, strange as it seems. Richard de Clare is a man of compelling honor, and though no Irishman, I trust him with my life."

"I've known you since my sister carried you in her womb.

I baptized you and taught you your letters and all the languages I know. I've watched you grow from a wild, stubborn child into a woman of strength and integrity." Lorcan stopped and turned her toward him. "I cannot help you now if you don't talk to me."

Eve hesitated. This man would never divulge what she said, nor be judgmental, yet she was reluctant to tell him what was in her heart. How to explain the confusion she felt? How was it that Richard, still virtually a stranger to her, roused so strong and deep a loyalty? Above all, how to tell she suspected her father of wanting Richard dead.

Lorcan sighed, and with his thumb traced a cross firmly on her forehead. "When you are ready, Eve, I will listen."

She watched as he walked into the wooden church, his long stride graceful and purposeful. His simple blessing calmed her. Lorcan was the rock, the anchor she had been missing these several years. Lorcan could invariably help her sort through her confusion or anger. Why then had she failed to confide in him?

Lorcan disappeared through the cathedral doors. Eve smiled. Christ Church Cathedral of the Holy Trinity was a singularly unprepossessing cathedral compared to those she had seen at Canterbury, Rouen, and Paris. It seemed a lifetime ago she had been in those distant lands. The cathedral was a simple wooden building, founded by a Norse king of Dublin and built in the Norse style, with a steeply pitched thatched roof. The one thing to mark it as an Irish church was the wonderfully carved free-standing cross in the green yard. A huge oak tree, said to be hundreds of years old, bent protective arms over the building, shading it to a dark, cool emerald.

Eve led her gray mare away from the church and decided to walk about Dublin first, before going into the palace precincts with its stifling atmosphere of intrigue and corruption. Now that she knew someone meant Richard harm, how was she to live here, as though nothing had happened?

She no longer knew whom to trust. It still did not make sense to her that Dermot wanted Richard dead. Her father was short-tempered, often cruel to his enemies, dangerously ambitious, but he was not stupid. He had nothing to gain by killing Richard. But if it was not her father, who wanted Richard dead?

Dublin was green and gold with late-August sun filtering through the oaks. The traditional seat of the Leinster kings was farther south, at the monastery of Ferns, but Dermot made Dublin, with her wealth, his main residence until forced out by O'Conor. It was Hasculf who ruled the town the years Dermot was in exile. The town of her childhood was familiar to her, but an absence of four years wrought subtle changes. A house had burned and not been rebuilt. A tree had died and been cut down and tenacious saplings sprang up in a circle around the old root. It was time for the afternoon prayer of Nones, and the bells of Dublin rang like liquid silver in their towers. *Ath Cliath na cloc.* Dublin, rich in bells. The parish churches mingled their music with those of Christ Church and the Nuns' Abbey of Saint Brigid. North beyond the river the austere Cistercian Abbey of Saint Mary added a melancholic tone. It came back to her, listening to the tolling, that she knew each church by the sound of its bells.

Ban followed her, sniffing busily at any intriguing scent he could find. Children ran through the rutted streets, though there seemed far fewer of them than she remembered. The weavers still sat over their looms, the rhythmic clack of their shuttles punctuating their lively conversation. Mothers yelled at children, masters yelled at slaves, slaves yelled at dogs. Some things never changed.

It did not take her long to realize Dublin was deserted by more than half its people. She saw very few of the Norse families that had been so common. It was the poorer Irish merchants and craftsmen who remained. How was Dublin to prosper without her people? How was Richard to win the loyalty of those vital Ostmen? Walking past a green field set aside for the grazing of the town geese, she finally approached the gate to the royal enclave. The enclosure was a walled fortress within the larger walls of the town. Reaching the gate, she found her way barred by two young guards wearing the scarlet-and-gold livery of Richard's men-at-arms. They looked Welsh to her, with their dark hair, and she spoke to them in that tongue.

"Move aside." She expected them to do as she commanded, and was shocked to find a large hand holding her none too gently by the upper arm. Ban growled deep in his throat, and the man quickly released her arm, but still barred her way. Ban relaxed, sitting beside her, and looked with wary curiosity from one man to the other.

"Hold there, sweetling, we can't let just anyone into the earl's compound. State your business and mayhap we'll check with the steward to see if you merit admittance." The man was young, with a round, pink face and twinkling eyes. His companion, tall and silent, smiled at her with a lecherous grin.

They did not know who she was, and Eve cursed under her breath at her lack of foresight. She wore her oldest gown and a serviceable cloak of a single color, both of which were coated with dust and dried mud from the long ride. She wore no jewels, and there was nothing in her dress that spoke of her rank. The absurdity of it hit her. She was a princess of Ireland and countess of Pembroke, married to their liege lord, yet her appearance made her seem a simple country woman, and they treated her accordingly. Rank had its privileges, but only when one's rank was recognized. It seemed a little dirt made everyone equal.

Drawing herself up straight, she put as much dignity and authority as she could into her voice. "I am the countess of Pembroke. Let me pass."

The men laughed, great loud peals of laughter, until people within the enclosure began to stare, wondering at the source of their amusement.

She could see the humor of it herself, through her frustration. Had she been one of the guards she probably would have reacted the same way. How was she going to get in?

The guards' loud laughter drew the attention of one of Richard's knights, who approached the gate to see what the commotion was about. Eve sighed with relief. Surely this man would know who she was.

"What's going on here?" He spoke Welsh but with a heavy French accent. His blue eyes assessed Eve coldly.

"This one claims to be de Clare's countess. Can ye credit it? Her all dirty and wild looking."

The knight looked her up and down, slowly. "Get away, you Irish slut. You'll not get in with such a tale as that."

She would not budge. "Fetch one of the Irish guards. He'll know who I am." How dare he call her such a thing?

"You're beginning to try my patience. I told you to move on." The contempt on the knight's face was unmistakable. Was he by nature insensitive, or was it a hatred of the Irish folk that sharpened his tongue?

"Don't be so hard on her, Sir Gui," one of the guards said. "She may be able to bribe us."

Her anger flared at his words. It was their duty to guard this gate, and since they truly were unaware of who she was, the idea they would allow a stranger to bribe her way in was appalling. She could be a spy from Rory's camp for all they knew.

"Don't be a fool." The knight's voice held a strong note of anger. "We've strict orders from Morgan himself. No strangers admitted."

"I meant no harm by it, Sir Gui. A kiss or two was all I be after. I'd not have let her in."

The knight grunted and spat into the dirt, barely missing the hem of her gown. "You think too much with that cock of yours, and not enough with the brain God gave you. No quick tumble with some dirty Irish peasant is worth Morgan's wrath. Or, God forfend, that of Richard himself."

"Ach, enough. It was but a jest. Still, the girl looks a satisfactory piece. A bit on the scrawny side, but clean enough."

Eve looked from one to the other, discussing her as though she did not stand three feet from them, in full view and able to hear each word. Men! The arrogance of them, as though they had the right. If she'd had a weapon at hand she would have attacked them both. As it was, she stood impotent and ineffective. Then, across the yard, near the bake house, she saw Tewdr as he snatched a loaf of bread and ran from a screaming cook.

"Tewdr." She yelled as loudly as she could. The boy did not hear her. She placed her hand on the wolfhound's white head and knelt beside him. "Ban, find Tewdr." His ears perked up, and his eyes darted back and forth. "Tewdr. Find Tewdr."

The dog bounded past the startled men. She watched with horror as one of the guards whipped an arrow from the quiver at his thigh and nocked it to his bow, aiming at Ban's retreating form.

"No!" She dove for the man, barreling into him as hard as she could. They went sprawling into the dirt, her last shred of dignity gone.

"God's blood. Get her off me."

The knight grabbed her from behind, and roughly hauled her kicking and screaming to her feet. He held her against his broad chest, laughing softly at her struggles. When he squeezed one of her breasts, hard, she knew it was deliberate. The clatter of hooves drew their attention. Eve stared up, past Emys's proud face, into Richard's incredulous one.

His gray eyes were cold as ice, and his voice held a definite chill. "There had better be a damned good reason why you are mauling my wife, Gui Beaumont."

"Wife?"

The knight let her go so suddenly, she nearly fell on her

face, only saving herself by bracing against Emys's wide chest with her hand. The stallion lifted his head nervously, then lowered it to nibble at her hair.

"My lord, we didn't know, in truth," Gui said.

"Aye, Lord Pembroke, we thought her a peasant lass."

"Where is your sense?" Richard looked from one to the other with growing anger. "How many peasants do you know have horses?" Richard dismounted and came to stand beside Eve, and for once she was profoundly grateful for his big, solid presence. The guards could not apologize quickly or profusely enough, stumbling over each other in their haste.

Noticing the slight twitch at the corner of Richard's mouth, she hissed, "Don't you dare laugh."

"I wouldn't think of it."

It was then she glanced at Sir Gui, and the hard anger in his eyes startled her. There was something about the man that awakened all her caution, something more than the small cruelty he'd inflicted on her. He was a handsome man, with dark curly hair and blue eyes, but there was a coldness about him that was disconcerting. Named Beaumont, she knew he must be some sort of cousin to Richard, though there was little resemblance to each other.

Richard placed his hand firmly at the small of her back and gently pushed her through the gate. With his other hand, he held Emys's reins and that of her mare, and the horses followed docilely. Just then Tewdr appeared, with Ban trotting alertly at his side, the dog's greedy eyes fixed on the partially eaten bread in the boy's hand.

"M'lady, I knew you must be near when the dog found me. Did you mean for me to come to you?"

"Yes." She nodded her head wearily, relieved both dog and boy were unharmed.

"Well, I wasn't sure, you see. He was all eager at first for me to follow him till he saw the bread, that is, then it's like he forgot what he was about. Have ye seen the king yet, m'lord? He's all in a dither, eager to be off after Rory and that Norseman he hates so much, but Morgan keeps telling him he needs wait for you. The man has no more sense in him than this great beast of a dog." The boy tore a piece from his loaf and tossed it to Ban, who gulped it without chewing and immediately begged for more.

They walked toward the stables and barracks which lay well beyond the great hall of the king. Tewdr took the horses' reins from Richard.

Eve glanced up at Richard, a frown puckering her brow. "Did you see my father? Was he at the docks?"

Richard shook his head. "No. Morgan is trying to find him."

"How is Morgan? Has the arm given him trouble?" Eve asked, turning toward Tewdr.

"The arm heals well, m'lady. It's his head I'm worried after."

"His head?" The frown deepened between her brows.

The boy made a wry face. "I swear he's fairy-touched. He goes about the place mewling and sighing and making a great silly fool of himself. Love. I tell ye, I'll have none of it, it makes a man soft in the head, it does. I'll stable the horses for ye, m'lord. Your bower's ready and you'll be wanting to bathe and eat after your journey. I'll have hot water sent from the kitchens. Will you be needing me to attend you tonight?"

"No, not tonight," Richard said.

Eve tried not to smile at the boy's new maturity. Where was the Tewdr who ran from work to play at his harping or challenged the other squires to games of chance?

They watched as the boy led the horses away, Ban still following after the remaining loaf. "That dog has no loyalty," Eve said.

"What did he mean, Morgan in love?"

"I was afraid this would happen. I tried to warn her. It's inappropriate, Morgan's no more than a landless knight."

"Morgan's one of the best men I know. He'll not be landless long, not if things go as I plan. But who did you warn? What wench has finally snared his heart?"

"My cousin is no wench."

"Caitlin?" He chuckled, his eyes bright with mirth.

"I fail to see the humor in the situation. It's a disaster."

"It seems eminently suitable to me. She'll bring him wealth and bear sons with royal blood. Morgan's no mercenary. He'll marry where his heart dictates. As good to fall in love with an heiress as a peasant."

"Marry? Never. I won't allow it."

He stopped then and stared down at her. "Allow it? You'll have naught to say in the matter, woman. Morgan is my man, he'll marry with my permission and my blessing. It's exactly what I want to have happen here, my men marrying Irishwomen."

"Why, so you can more easily conquer us?" She thought he would grow angry at her words, but his voice was gentle.

"You do not understand me yet, Eve. You call me Norman, but am I? I've been to Normandy, to my fiefs there, and on the king's business. I speak the Norman-French of my ancestors, the tongue still spoken in England by the aristocracy. But we speak English now as well, unlike the Conqueror and his companions who kept themselves separate from the Saxons they conquered. Slowly, in England, we are becoming one people, no longer Norman or Saxon, but Englishmen. So it will be here if my men marry native women. In a few generations there will be no more Norman or Welsh, but only Irish."

"I wish I could believe in your vision, but I see the future differently. If you are successful here, if you establish a stronghold in Ireland, won't more of your kind come? Men who owe their loyalty to King Henry, not to you. Men who do not share your vision, who will not deign to marry native women. Men who will hold my people in contempt, as your ancestors did the Saxons of England, reducing free men to serfs, and serfs to slaves."

"If you believe that, what keeps you from putting a knife in my back when I sleep?"

She trembled at his words, spoken so softly. His eyes, gentle and filled with sadness, made her ache to touch him, to reassure him, yet she held her hand back. Why did she no longer see him as the enemy? She knew the answer, and knew it was her undoing. Her desires made her weak, but she could not stop the rush of them, overwhelming her. She was falling in love with this man. Never in her life had she felt more vulnerable.

"I've told you before that you have my loyalty, but not above what I owe Ireland. Nothing comes before that, de Clare. Ireland is my first love."

"You sound like your father when you say that."

"I am nothing like my father. How can you say such a thing?"

"You don't have his cruelty, but you are as adamant as he in what you want. You are as rigid as he, as unwilling to see another side, unwilling to compromise."

She was silent, fighting the anger and hurt his words evoked. There was truth in them, she recognized that, but who was he to say such things to her? The passion she carried close to her heart for Ireland at times had been the one thing that comforted her or gave her life meaning. Now he wanted her to make room for another loyalty and it frightened her. To question what she held as true, to see the world as he saw it, to modify her vision of what things could be, none of what he asked was easy. He asked too much when he asked for her complete and undivided loyalty. That she could not give. "What of you? Am I the only one who must compromise? Is that fair?"

He sighed, and, reaching out, traced the curve of her cheek gently with his thumb. His touch sent a shiver through her, as it always did. "Do you not see it, Eve? I've already changed. I came here with the idea of conquering Ireland for the power and wealth it would bring me. Now

I want more. Much more." He leaned down and, lifting her chin, kissed her firmly, possessively.

She leaned into him, and his arm came around her back to pull her closer. All argument went out of her head, all thought of battling him. In his arms she believed he could do as he said. She believed he could bring peace to Ireland, when no one else before him, save Brian Boru for a short time, had accomplished such a thing.

When she finally pulled herself away from him, there was shouting and laughter from the squires and soldiers who had witnessed the kiss. She ducked her head to hide the flame of embarrassment.

"Little wife, you'll see, together we can do great things. Together we can create a new Ireland."

"We can try."

He chuckled. "It's a start. I need to meet Morgan. Where is this bower Tewdr spoke of?"

"He must mean my old cottage. It's the third one to the west, behind the stables."

"I'll join you there within the hour."

"I'll be waiting." He walked away, and she watched, delighting in the loose, long grace of him, the strength and gentleness that made him so seductive.

It was dangerous what this man did to her. Could Ireland be as he envisioned it? Could it be that good? She had to keep a cool head if she were to think clearly, but his kisses made all coherent thought flee, as though she were some silly dairy maid instead of a woman with serious responsibilities. Like any wanton, she was beginning to hunger for his kisses and for his touch at night as they lay together. She could not let herself be blinded by pretty tales, and dreams built of desire. Loving the man could well be her downfall. Richard de Clare must still prove himself to her. If only she could find someone who would explain to her how to keep her heart safe from him until then.

Twelve

The barracks was a long, low building of rough-hewn wood and smelled ripe with too many men and hounds. Richard paused in the doorway, amused by the cacophony of Celtic voices shouting and singing in two languages, the lilt of Irish contending against vigorous Welsh. The motley guard of a hundred or so Irishmen who made up Dermot's household troop were the remnant of a much larger army he had lost over the years. If those men of Leinster did not reappear in the next few weeks Richard would find it difficult to meet O'Conor's superior numbers.

Even if the Leinstermen did return, it was a risk trying to put together so disparate an army; part garrulous Welsh, part intransigent feuding Irish, part covetous Anglo-Norman. Each man had his own loyalties and reasons for being here. Some of those reasons were sure to cause conflict among the corps.

Richard's knights were quartered more comfortably in bowers within the enclosure, or crowded into dwellings nearby. It provoked animosity among the native Dubliners having his troops quartered among them. More military housing was desperately needed. He walked away from the noisome building toward the sound of hammering. He found Morgan where they had agreed to meet, near the new buildings.

Richard placed his hand on the knight's shoulder and gave

it an affectionate squeeze. He pointed to the new barracks going up. "The work goes well."

"They tell me the rainy season is coming, though how it can get wetter than it has been I fear to see," Morgan said. "We need shelter for the men, and the safest place is here, inside the royal enclosure. The people of Dublin tolerate us, but barely. They've heard of the massacre at Waterford and most lay the blame for that at your feet."

"Did you find Dermöt?"

"He's in his hall, there, that large building with the stream behind it."

"We'll see to him later."

They walked toward the stables, where Tewdr and the other squires brushed or washed or exercised the great warhorses of their knights. Most of the boys would rather be there than anywhere else on earth, with the beautiful, strong animals, hoping one day to be able to afford such a mount themselves. Richard and Morgan watched the boys and the horses for a while, smiling at the young but entirely masculine voices raised in delight as they raced and argued and bragged among themselves.

"How was the journey? Any sight of O'Conor?" Morgan cut a quizzical glance in his direction. "Was there trouble?"

"Not from O'Conor."

"Who then?"

"I don't know. Yet. Someone sent a killer. The maddening thing is, I'm not sure if I was the target, or if his arrow was meant for Eve."

Anger and concern darkened the Welshman's eyes. "Was the countess hurt?"

"She's fine, at least physically. I think Dermot is behind it. My wife disagrees."

"Jesu, what a muddle. Dermot's ambitious, what king isn't, but why would he beg your help then turn against you once you're here?"

Richard placed a foot on the lowest rail of the corral fence and was silent for a long moment. "I've been wondering the same, and can make little sense of it. What if he never meant to keep his promise to make me his heir? It would explain why he was furious when we married. What I don't understand is, why, if I'm his target, he would try to be rid of me now, before I've won Leinster back from O'Conor? He needs my army. Why would he risk losing it?"

Morgan pushed the fingers of his good hand through his dark hair and shook his head. "He seems to have it in his mind that your men are his to command. If he had managed to get provisions together quickly enough, he would have marched against O'Conor before you arrived. I made sure his orders were ignored. I'm afraid I've not endeared myself to our host."

Richard chuckled. Leave it to Morgan to be subversive in a quiet and efficient way. "I've explained to Dermot that my men are loyal to me alone. Their oaths don't extend to him. Why doesn't he believe me?"

Morgan's dark eyes held a hint of amusement. "You talk as though Dermot is an honorable man. The more I'm near the man, the more wary of him I grow. He runs down his own crooked path of reality and doesn't hesitate to do whatever is expedient to get what he wants. Honor means nothing to him. Dermot takes what he wants, and he wants your army."

Richard smiled grimly. "Well, he can't have it."

"I have an uneasy feeling about this. Is it worth the risk? With Dermot untrustworthy how can you be expected to fight O'Conor? And if we win, what then? When you're no longer of use to Dermot, what is to keep you safe? I'm beginning to think it would be better if we returned to Wales."

On his left hand Richard wore the ring he had taken from the unknown archer. His thumb worried the stone, back and forth. If Eve was in danger he must know who sent the archer if there was any hope of protecting her. He couldn't keep her caged like an animal, even for her safety.

Should he leave Ireland, as Morgan suggested. He knew his pride would never allow him to run to Wales, but it was arrogance to risk good men if there was no hope for victory. There was another nagging worry Richard did not know how to explain to Morgan. He coveted this land more than ever, but for different reasons than he originally held. A dream was carving itself in his mind, a vision of what he could do here, with Eve by his side. With each day it became stronger, more persuasive, more real. He felt foolish, though, trying to give it words. He couldn't explain it to himself yet, let alone someone else. "It past time we called on Dermot."

"A show of force wouldn't be amiss."

Richard looked about and saw four of his knights lounging against a corral fence. He recognized them and smiled. The Beaumont brothers, William, Thomas, Gui, and Alexander. All were large, heavily muscled men with intense, dark faces. They were a formidable clan. "Alexander, get over here and bring those curs you call kin with you."

"It's a relief you've arrived, Richard. That damn foolish Irishman has been raving at us for days now. Luckily, not a man of us speaks Irish." Alexander smiled, displaying several broken teeth, and his brothers nodded their agreement.

"I've a message for Dermot and could use an escort." Richard gazed at the huge long swords hanging at their sides. "Keep your hands near your weapons but don't use them without my command."

Grunts of approval sounded at his back as Richard marched at the head of the small but formidable band, Morgan beside him.

Gui walked on Richard's other side. "I do apologize for not recognizing your wife, Richard. She wore the cloak of a peasant. If she'd been wearing one of those gaudy royal cloaks, I'd mayhap have known who she was."

Richard glanced at the knight. He had never much liked Gui Beaumont, though his brothers were good men. Gui had unfailingly been more impressed with himself than reality warranted. Even his apology was arrogant, as though Eve were at fault for his stupidity. "You know her now. No such mistake will happen again." Richard spoke coldly, but Gui did not understand he had been dismissed.

"You're a lucky devil, Richard," Gui said. "You've a pair of creamy Irish thighs to disport between while in this barbarous place. The rest of us will have little luck, I'm afraid. There don't seem to be many women left in Dublin."

Richard nearly backhanded the man. "You'll show my wife the respect owed her as your countess, or you'll keep your mouth shut. Is that plain enough for you?"

Gui flushed angrily at the reprimand, but nodded his assent.

"There'll be whores in Dublin," Alexander said from behind them. "Have no fear, Gui, you'll find what you need."

"I hate whores. They stink." Gui fell back to be with his brothers.

Richard had disliked Gui before. Now he found him repellent. Beaumont was exactly the sort of man Richard did not want under his command. Gui was not alone in assuming all the Irish were uncivilized barbarians and therefore could be treated with contempt. Such men would do more harm than good and Richard wished he had a way of knowing who among his knights thought so. He shook his head, and the anger built along with his frustration. He'd have to be rid of most of his men, if truth be told. All he could hope to do was restrain them from acting on their bigotries.

He forced his thoughts back to Dermot. The Irish king's hall was an immense wooden structure, two stories high, with few windows and a single entrance. The thatch of the pitched roof was colorful with summer wildflowers and grass, and the moss that grew in abundance in this wet country. A colony of yellow-petaled herb bennet grew in the shade a huge oak cast on the thatch. The herb was said to ward off evil. Richard thought the king of Leinster had special need of such a shield above his head.

The lone guard at the door started to unsheath his sword at their advance, then thought better of it and stood aside as Richard and his men pushed their way through the narrow doorway.

They marched down the long central aisle of the hall toward the dais at the far end. Richard noticed the wooden pillars supporting the second story were carved and painted with that exuberant, vivid playfulness he was beginning to think of as peculiarly Irish. In his wake trailed Morgan and four implacable Beaumont knights. Slaves stopped their work to stare at them. Dermot's men came instantly alert, hands aching for swords, but watching first before committing to battle. The bustling noise of the hall quieted until the only sound was the purposeful footsteps of Richard and his men, and the dangerous soft resonance of their scabbards rubbing against their thighs.

On a throne of carved oak sat Dermot, his eyes wide with surprise.

By the time Richard reached the foot of the dais, Dermot had schooled his expression into one of ingenuous charm. Richard wanted to wipe the insipid grin off the king's face with a fist. Instead, he removed the ring from his finger, holding it so the light of nearby torches caught in the large garnet. He circled it slowly this way and that, all the while watching the Irish king's secretive eyes.

Dermot gazed at him quizzically. "How came you by that, de Clare?"

"You recognize it?"

"Of course, I had it from my father. I keep it under lock in my bower. I demand to know how you came by it."

"I took it from the man you sent to kill me."

As Morgan translated, Richard watched Dermot's face carefully. The man seemed genuinely bewildered.

"What a ridiculous accusation. Why would I do such a thing?" Dermot sat tall in his chair, flushed with indignation.

"You've been known to do worse."

"Mayhap, but I don't rid myself of men who are useful to me. The last few days have made it abundantly clear your men will obey your command only, de Clare. I have no argument with that, so long as you fight for me and not against me."

"We need to understand each other, MacMurrough."

"Aye, seems we're off to a bad start if you can accuse me of so foolish a thing. I'm a hard man. I do what I must, but I'm not completely without honor."

"There is still this." Richard held the ring before Dermot's face. Was that anger he detected in Dermot's eyes? He had thought to see fear or guilt. Why would the man be angry?

"So there is. You were ambushed you say? Where? When?"

"That matters not. The man had nothing to identify him, save the ring. Eve recognized it as yours. You do understand it may have been Eve who was the target."

For the first time fear fleeted across the other man's face. "I expect you to keep her safe, de Clare."

"And I expect not to have to watch my back while in service to you. I can't fight O'Conor and treachery here as well. I'm a wealthy man, as well you know. I can easily take Eve to England or Wales and live comfortably on my demesne lands. I'd not hesitate to leave you to fight your disagreeable little war, if I thought you betrayed me."

Dermot leaned forward on his throne, his hands gripping the arms so tightly his knuckles were white. "I have no reason to see you dead, and no matter how ill you think of me, I'd not kill my own child. I had nothing to do with this."

"You expect me to believe that, after seeing how you treat your daughter?"

Dermot's lips pressed together in a firm line. "My temper's ever been my bane, but there's no harm in hitting a woman. It's how they learn. I was angry. It was not in my plan to have you marry Eve so soon."

Richard did not hide his disgust. "So I gathered. Would you care to explain why? It was the promise of marriage to your heir that brought me here."

"Nay, be honest with yourself, man. It was her land and the wealth and power that go with it you lusted for. Eve is merely the most convenient way of getting it. Now that you have my daughter and her claim to Leinster, what's to keep you from fighting for your own gain instead of mine? What's to keep you from siding with my enemies against me, if they promise you Leinster when I'm defeated?"

"You have my oath of honor." Richard glared down at the man. "Strange as it may seem to you, that means something to most men."

The king was quiet, his eyes squinted in appraisal. When he finally spoke, it was with a small smile on his thin lips. "I'm almost tempted to believe you, de Clare."

"I have the army you need to regain your throne. You've promised me land, should I win it for you. That was our original bargain. I fail to see how anything has changed."

"Nor do I," Dermot said. "As long as we understand each other, we can work together well enough."

"I'm not convinced you didn't send that killer." If not Dermot, who was behind the treachery? Richard flung the ring into the king's lap. "I'm going to tell you this once, MacMurrough, so listen carefully. If anything happens to me, if I die by any hand save that of an enemy on a field of battle, I have ordered my men to kill you, and slaughter all of your folk, women and children included." The lie rolled easily off his tongue, and with a slight hesitation Morgan repeated it.

"If any harm should find my wife, I will kill you myself, very slowly." This time he did not lie.

"And I tell you this, I did not send an assassin. If I had,

be assured you would be dead now. I can ill afford to lose you before you've done what I hired you for."

"Then we understand each other?"

"Perfectly." Dermot stood and held his hand out to Richard.

He hesitated, then clasped the man by the arm. "I still don't trust you, MacMurrough."

"Nor I you."

A smile tried to turn Richard's lips, and an answering quirk showed on Dermot's face. They both turned away, before they could betray themselves. God rot the man, but Richard believed him. It was not Dermot who was his enemy. He would not rest until he knew who was.

Turning on his heel, Richard left the hall, his grim-faced guard marching with controlled but no less deadly menace, behind him. Even Dermot could not misunderstand the message he delivered.

Eve paced from the table with its small feast, to the bed, to the steaming bath made fragrant with heather, then back again. Where was the man?

Ban lifted his massive head from the wolfskin rug he had commandeered as his own and watched her pace, picking up her raw energy, twitching now and then with sympathetic nerves. The bower was small, an outer chamber with hearth, a table and several chairs, and an inner bedchamber. Small but pleasant, with a window in each room and a thatch roof tight against the rain. Eve and two servants had worked for hours to clean the place, sweeping dust and mice out the door, hauling ashes out of the hearth, folding clothes into the huge chest in the bedchamber. It was perfect now, with fresh rushes on the floor, clean, crisp linens on the bed, a hot meal, growing colder by the moment, on the table. If Richard did not arrive soon, she would have to call the slaves for more hot water for the bath. She trailed her fingers in the water, testing the temperature. It was still wonderfully warm.

Memories of Richard naked flooded her thoughts, and she felt her face burning. She had many such thoughts lately. A few days of marriage had turned her into a wanton, hot as any mare at stud. The things he did to her with his practiced hands, with his hot mouth, with that big, marvelous staff between his strong thighs, overran her thoughts and dreams. What on earth was keeping the man? It had gone dark an hour ago. Did he never stop? Surely he must eat.

She felt foolish, waiting so eagerly, and was beginning to fear she was making an ass of herself. Her wanting was too obvious and unsophisticated. Having thrown herself at him initially, she found it impossible to act the coy maiden, too hungry and eager for the magic they made together to play at games now.

Looking down at the diaphanous bed gown she wore, its loose folds hanging gracefully around her, she wished she had not allowed Caitlin to convince her to wear the thing. What would he think when he saw her?

Holy Mary, what's wrong with me? She plopped down on the bed and lowered her head into her hands. *I've no dignity left, not where that man is concerned. If he crooked his little finger and told me to jump off a cliff, I'd do it with a bemused grin on my face and count myself lucky to be asked.*

She knew then that the worst had happened, the thing she dreaded most in the world. She had betrayed all her loyalties, to Ireland, to her own sense of self, to her people, whom she wished to protect from these rough invaders, by falling in love with her husband.

He mustn't know. It gives him too much power over me. It makes me weak. And it hurts, knowing how he cares about that woman, that Rosamund, knowing he doesn't, can't, care the same for me. How do I protect myself? How do I fight him?

The door flew open. Richard stood there, in all his strong, masculine grandeur, and a groan escaped her before she could call it back.

She looked like a fearful young girl perched on the edge of the bed, her feet not touching the ground, pink toes peeking out from under the edge of her thin gown. Her hair was still damp from her bath, curling around her face, falling in a veil over her shoulders and down her back. Such glorious hair. He had never seen anything like it, the color caught between gold and silver. She stared at him with huge green eyes, her mouth open just enough for him to see her small, white teeth. A generous, full-lipped mouth, sensuous even when she was angry. He longed to kiss that luscious mouth.

If he were not so filthy he would stride across the room and take her now, until that mouth called out in the passion he knew was there, waiting for him.

Instead, he unbuckled his sword belt and laid the heavy scabbard and weapon on the table, where he could get to it quickly if need be. Someone had tried to kill once. Most likely he would try again. He was scowling, and as he glanced up, he saw Eve flinch and look away. *Dear God, I frightened her. Why would she act like a flighty, timid woman?*

Where was that adamant, stubborn spirit he was accustomed to battling? Why did she look so damned vulnerable and appealing? Eve fighting him he knew how to handle. This quiet, watchful Eve made him nervous.

"Are you going to help me undress, or do I need to send for my squire?"

With no quick rejoinder, no spark of anger, she came silently, solemnly, and began to unlace the awkward mail hauberk. It felt good to be out of the armor and the hot, padded gambeson he wore beneath it, though the stench of sweat and dirt that clung to his shirt disgusted him. Pulling the sark over his head, he tossed it across the room.

He saw her nose wrinkle at the odor. "Burn the thing, it's beyond cleaning. You've married a warrior, Eve, not a courtier. I'm sorry for the smell."

A smile curved her lips. "In truth, my lord, it's a stench honestly earned. I've smelled worse."

He sat on the bench near the fire as she removed his leather boots, and was startled to notice the hole in his stock, with his big toe sticking out. He had never given such things much thought before, but wondered now if it offended her. She was unlacing the leather cross garters that held the stocks up, and he felt her fingers tremble slightly, as she worked her way up his leg, past his knee, to his thigh. That small quivering sent a fierce vibration through him and he grew firm with wanting her. It was all he could do not to crush her beneath him, there on the floor in the sweet new rushes. She was clean and rosy from her bath, smelling of lavender and heather, he could not bring himself to lay a dirty finger to her cheek.

Women. How they complicate a man's life. For years he had been perfectly content with his dirt and his sweat.

Finally, only his linen braies remained. He stood so she could untie the cord that held them. With shaking hands, Eve gently pulled them down his hips and legs, until the braies fell to the floor. His arousal sprang forward between them, and a mischievous smile played over her lips. With the tip of a finger she tapped his penis playfully, and her smile widened as it sprang back to attention.

"Stop that." Groaning, he turned toward the waiting bath. His tiny, surprising wife was half shy, half wanton, and all irresistible temptation. It was going to be the longest bath of his life.

The fragrant water felt wonderful, hot and soothing, as he slid down into it. He had never had flower petals in his bath water before, and wondered what his men would say if they saw it. Redmon would be embarrassed by such feminine frippery. Morgan probably bathed in rose petals on a regular basis, and rarely alone. Richard wondered if what Eve told him was true, about Morgan and Caitlin. He had forgotten to ask earlier.

The wooden tub was not large enough for him to stretch out, but it was deep, and soon only his head and shoulders and knees poked up above the surface of the water. He let the heat work its way into his weary muscles.

"Lean forward, so I can scrub your back."

He did as she said. The soap was heather scented, not the harsh lye and ash stuff he was accustomed to. After lathering the rough cloth, she scrubbed vigorously, working on the knots between his shoulders. There was one spot that was usually sore, and he grunted with pleasure as she found it. His squires were never this attentive. He could grow accustomed to having a wife. She poured a bucket of warm water over his head, and began to wash his hair.

"Why do you wear it in such an unattractive style?" She ruffled his hair, tugging at it.

"You don't like it?"

"I'm not used to a man without a mane of hair. It's strange to me. And no hair on your face, except now you have that terrible rough stubble. It hurts my face when you kiss me."

"Then I'll grow a beard, to save your sweet face."

"You wouldn't. No Norman I've seen has a beard. Do you mean a full, thick Irish beard? You'll never do it, Richard."

He had meant it as a jest. Then he wondered what it would be like not to have to scrap the hair off his face all the time. Probably be warm in the winter. He would give it a try. Besides, she had challenged him.

"Just finish your scrubbing." He was rewarded with another bucket, this time of cold water, thrown over his head. He sputtered and spit and looked around at her accusingly.

"Oh, was that too cold?"

"You know it was."

"Here, clean your front yourself." She thrust the cloth and dish of soap at him.

"I'd rather you did it for me, sweetling. That way you can't sneak up on me with more cold water."

She hesitated, then lifted his arm, and beginning with his hand she soaped and rubbed the limb vigorously, then did the other arm. She leaned over the edge of the tub to reach his chest. Cupping a handful of water in his hands, he splashed it across the front of her gown and grinned as her breasts were revealed to him through the flimsy material.

"Keep your hands to yourself."

"I never touched you," he said, a mask of innocence on his face.

"Do you want me to finish this?"

"Oh, yes, Eve, I do want that." His voice was low and husky, and he knew he was not going to be able to tolerate much more of her attention. Her touch roused desire in him like none he had known, desire she alone could satisfy. Innocent and wild, that was what she had been since their first lovemaking. A combination that excited him unbearably.

The women he had known before were whores, or an occasional married noblewoman, angry at her husband or bored with her life, who took his coin and his seed and gave nothing in return. They had been proficient bed partners, but there was no innocence in them, no freshness, no sense of his being any sort of instructor in the arts of loving. How he would enjoy that role with Eve. Already she was learning to use her raw passion to give them both pleasure.

She finished washing his chest and his legs, then stood, and stared down at him. "You wash . . . that," she said, pointing between his thighs.

"Nay, Wife, I'd have you do it." His voice was gentle, but there was a raw note in it. "There's nothing to fear, it'll not bite."

"But he does have a bite, that little man of yours. He comes hungry and greedy into me. He devours me."

"Does he not give you pleasure?"

She blushed but did not look away. The pink spread across her chest, and he saw that she was breathing quickly, as he was. He could see the pulse pounding at the base of her throat. Taking her hand, he pulled her down beside the tub. He guided her hand down into the water and her resistance melted away. Her fingers closed around him and slowly, with exquisite torment, she caressed that throbbing, impatient part of him that would no longer be denied.

He rose from the bath, water sluicing off his powerful body, and stepped from the tub. He gathered her into his arms, and crushed her against his wet chest. "Never play there, Eve, unless you mean to fulfill the craving you rouse."

Her head tilted back, exposing her white, vulnerable throat. Her eyes were full of some emotion he could not read. "Never, my lord, will I begin what I cannot end," she whispered.

His mouth lowered onto hers. Warm, soft lips responded to him with growing eagerness as her arms came up around his neck. Her body, sweet, lithe, needy, pressed into him, her hips swayed against him, until he clasped her hard against his thighs and chest. He lowered her to the floor. Too eager, too close to completion to bother removing her gown, he pushed it up over her hips.

Filled with overwhelming need, without hesitancy or uncertainty, they came together, hunger against hunger. Writhing passionately beneath him, she clawed at his back and wrapped her strong legs around his waist.

Her breath tore ragged from her throat. "Richard." Her neck arched, her eyes closed. "Richard."

He buried his face against her neck, and whispered in a desperate voice, "God, how I need you."

Pounding into her, she matched each thrust. Moans crowded the back of her throat, until her cries escaped and grew louder. Incoherent, frenzied cries of pleasure and need, spurring his desire to almost unendurable limits. His passion mounted, higher and harder, and they reached fulfillment together in a torment of pleasure.

They lay together like one creature, sweat-glistened bodies entwined, their breath harsh and ragged, clinging with strong hands. Now it was gentle, the afterward, holding each other, waiting for their hearts to slow. He shifted position until he was beneath her and gathered her to him, cradling her against his chest, reluctant to withdraw from that warm, secret place made for him.

She stroked his cheek with a trembling hand. "I never knew it could be like this. No one ever told me."

Nor me, he thought, and took her hand in his own. "I wish it could last."

"What do you mean?" Her eyes were large, fear bright in them.

"I can stay long enough to get my men ready to march, then we must go after O'Conor." He held her close again and felt her whole body quivering against him as she clung to him. "Would to God I could stay here with you." He heard the naked longing in his voice and it surprised him, but it was true. Given a choice he would never leave her arms. Duty was a harsh mistress and he had ever been obedient to her call.

What had she done to him, this tiny stubborn woman? She was working her way into his heart, where he thought none but Rosamund would ever dwell. Rosamund. He could hardly remember her face. The thought gave him pleasure.

"When do you leave?"

"A fortnight, three weeks at the longest."

"So soon." She kissed him at the base of his throat, tenderly, then up his neck to his chin, finally claiming his mouth.

Her kisses grew more eager, more insistent, and he answered with greedy desire of his own. He nibbled her ear, kissed her soft neck, twined his hands in her luxurious hair, caressed her breasts with his tongue and mouth, and grew hard again inside her. This time he was slow and gentle; and there was no one in the world for him but Eve.

Thirteen

"They'll be safe." Caitlin slipped her hand into Eve's and held it tightly. The two women stood on the rampart that ran the perimeter of Dublin. They could see for miles, but all they cared to watch was Richard's army.

Few of Dermot's supporters had gathered at Dublin in the three weeks since Richard arrived. The army that rode today from the walled town consisted mainly of Anglo-Norman knights and Welsh archers. It appeared there were few Irishmen willing to fight under a foreign banner. Fewer still allied themselves with Dermot, they knew him too well. Richard's army was not so formidable a force that victory over O'Conor was a sure thing.

Is Richard riding from my life? So much can happen. What if I never see him again? The thoughts swirled in Eve's head, making her stomach queasy with fear. Her calm, composed face revealed none of the emotion besieging her.

"Morgan shouldn't be going," Eve said. "He's not completely healed."

"What choice did he have? Richard needs him."

Eve glanced at her cousin. "You don't resent the necessity?"

Caitlin was silent. When she spoke, it was with sadness. "I hate it more than I can say. I want him safe and with me, not fighting some battle. Are we hopelessly naive, to think the world should be safe to raise our children in?"

"You love Morgan." It was a statement, not a question.

There was no hesitancy this time in the answer. "More than my own life. Does that shock you? Will you lecture me again on how inappropriately I'm behaving?"

Eve regretted those harsh words. "Forgive me, Cousin, I didn't know what I was saying. I understand better now. You don't necessarily find love where you seek it. Love finds you, and once it does your life, your destiny, changes. If you truly love Morgan, don't waste a moment you can have together."

Caitlin threw her arms around Eve and gave her a quick, hard hug. "Only a woman in love says such things. It saddened me to think your marriage was no more than a political alliance, with no affection between you and Richard. That's changed. There's a peace and happiness about you, sweet Cousin, that I've never seen before. You are lucky indeed to be so in love with your husband."

That was the worst of it, Eve thought, the one-sided love she bore. Not once had Richard said he loved her. His days the past hectic weeks were spent in organizing his army and planning an autumn campaign. But the nights were theirs. Glorious, passionate nights, with never a word from him of loving her, only of need, of desire, of hunger. Did his mind and heart still belong to Rosamund Clifford? What if Eve never heard such words from him? She did not think she could bear the humiliation, to lose her heart to a man who could not love her. It was not a thing she could force from him, and never, never would she beg.

Her life was unalterably changed by this unexpected, complicated love. It came like a whirlwind, catching her up in its strong force. Only now could she once more touch ground, now that Richard was gone and she could put some distance between her feelings and him.

Watching him ride away, she felt a hollow emptiness. If he did not return, she feared that hollowness would become a permanent part of her being, and she dreaded the thought of enduring such anguish. That love could make her so vulnerable she found one of its most unexpected features.

The indulgent September sun warmed their backs as they watched the last of the foot soldiers disappear along the road leading into O'Conor's kingdom of Connaught. Richard could not tell her how long the campaign would last. He hoped to return by Christmas.

"I'll go mad if I do nothing but wait." Eve turned away from the wall and began the climb down the steep earthen stairway. The two knights who would serve as her bodyguard followed at a discreet distance.

"What do you mean to do?" Caitlin followed her down the stairs.

"I'm not going to sit all day and embroider shirt cuffs, of that I'm sure. I've been trained as a healer. I'm good at it." Eve swung her arm wide to encompass the town spread before them. "Look at the Dublin folk. Most of those with wealth have fled, but the poorer people have no place to go. They get sick, they have babies, they need care as much as any. I've been thinking there must be something I can do to help. Lorcan will know what is needed." She hurried toward Christ Church, sure to find her uncle there.

Caitlin caught up and pulled at Eve's elbow to slow her down. "You mean to mingle with the peasants? Richard likely will not approve."

Eve stopped, hands on hips. "He's my husband, that doesn't mean he controls my life. Scripture tells us to care for the poor, to nurse the sick. What objection could he have?"

"He'd not argue with the scriptures, but I've yet to meet a nobleman who wants his wife endangering herself with exposure to poor folks' diseases. Some are truly disgusting."

"All the more reason to care for them, if no one else will."

"What of the monasteries? Such foul work should be left to the nuns and monks."

"Holy Mother of God, Caitlin, listen to yourself. They are people, just like us. They know pain and fear. I've more time than I know what to do with. It would be selfish of me, sinful even, to withhold my help. They are my people. I was born with obligations and commitments, and I mean to live by them."

Caitlin looked aside and chewed vigorously on her lower lip. "You make me ashamed."

"That's not my intent. I've not asked you to join me."

"Still the shame is there, and deserved. It's that I've never had much to do with common folk. I've not given them much thought."

"No doubt you've been told they are dirty, ignorant, vulgar, and violent. It is common among nobles to believe so, and to teach their children their hatreds and fears."

"But why?"

Eve shook her head and placed her arm around Caitlin's shoulder, giving her cousin a small, comforting squeeze. "I've wondered the same. I think it is so their consciences don't bother them when the commoners suffer. No one cares if a peasant dies during a famine. If the richer folk allowed themselves to be troubled, they would have to do something."

"Not all people feel so."

"No, thank God. Though I fear most of Richard's men believe all Irish, from common to noble, are ignorant savages."

"That's ridiculous. Surely they can see for themselves it isn't true."

"They have no desire to see us as we truly are. They can't afford to. How do you go about conquering a people you admire?"

"Richard is not like that."

"No, he isn't." *That is why I cannot hate him. He offers me hope. Mayhap under his sure hand Leinster will prosper again. It is this painful love that complicates matters. God help me, I do so love Richard.*

The oak trees of Dublin shaded the path as they walked toward Christ Church. Bees wallowed drunkenly from one flower to the next, and the sharp scent of the nearby ocean felt warm, teeming with life. It was so peaceful, so beautiful, Eve's heart contracted with grief. This was as Ireland was meant to be. Five generations of war over the High Kingship must come to an end if her land and people were to survive. *God keep you strong, Richard de Clare, and give you victory.*

They found Lorcan in the monastery garden, putting in a planting of late cabbages. Eve knelt in the dirt beside her uncle and helped him put the tender young plants into the rich Irish soil. Lorcan grunted and smiled, but neither spoke until the row of cabbages was in.

Lorcan stood and stretched, his hands to the small of his back. "Glad I am to see you both. Caitlin, you're looking happy and well. Eve, you look—well, there's the dirt on your hands and gown, but I probably wouldn't recognize you otherwise. I doubt you came to help with the cabbages. Come sit with me and we can talk."

He led them to a stone bench in the cemetery behind the church. One of the canons came from the kitchen with a pitcher of cold mead and three cups. "Ah, thank you, Brother. I've a strong thirst, and I'm sure the ladies could use some refreshment."

"Let me know if you need aught else, Father." The man quietly returned to his kitchen work.

"Now, Niece, tell me what has you so excited you can barely control your tongue."

Eve laughed and told of her desire to be useful, to do something with her healing skills. Lorcan listened intently, now and then taking a sip of mead.

When she was silent, Lorcan sat a few minutes longer, thinking. "The idea has merit. There is a definite need, especially among the women and children. The good sisters at St. Brigid's are few in number and lack anyone skilled in healing. Sister Walburga tries, bless her, but she hasn't the training you do. I should think the lady abbess would be glad to accommodate you. Her infirmary could easily be made to serve your patients."

Eve jumped up and kissed the startled man on his cheek. "You are brilliant, Uncle. Of course the abbess will have me."

Lorcan's eyes gleamed with amusement. "Then I suggest you ask her permission straight away. There's no reason to postpone putting you to work. I was afraid you'd grown lazy and spoiled in the years you've been away. I see now I need have no such fears." He stood and thumbed a cross on Eve's forehead. "God's blessing on your work."

Caitlin stood before Lorcan. Eve thought she looked ready to cry.

"I'm so ashamed, Father. I've ever thought the common folk lesser than myself. I want to assist with Eve's work, though I fear I don't know enough yet to be of real help."

Lorcan traced a cross on Caitlin's forehead and pulled her against him, gently. "Bless you, child, you're not capable of an uncharitable thought. You but think you dislike the common folk when it's only that you've never known them. Your own goodness ensures you'll see the truth of it. Do this work, with Eve, but not as a penance for what you imagine to be past sins. Do it with a joyful heart and as a gift."

Eve and Caitlin waited in the small room they had been shown to in St. Brigid's Abbey. It was an austere room, with no furniture of any kind and no window. A single wall lamp lighted the darkness. On the same wall a huge crucifix hung in gory detail. Eve wondered what sort of person sought to live like this. The desires that drove women to become nuns were a mystery to Eve.

"I'm glad you want to work with me, Cait. It would be lonely without you there."

"I'm still not sure how much good I'll do."

"Have a little patience. You'll learn quickly enough."

A large, ruddy-faced nun barged into the room and stood solidly before them, her fists on her wide hips. "They told me Lorcan sent you. I've never known the man to be a fool, so there must be a reason you're here. Well? I'm a busy woman, tell me what you want."

"Are you Abbess Ancilla?" Eve asked. The rough, loud woman seemed more fitted to be the abbey cook or laundress, mayhap even one of the simple sisters who worked in the fields and barns.

"Of course I'm the abbess. Don't waste my time with absurd questions. Who are you and what do you want?"

Eve tried not to let her anger rise at the woman's curtness. "I am Eve, the daughter of Dermot MacMurrough, and this is my cousin, Caitlin."

"Well? Get on with it."

"I'm skilled in healing. Caitlin and I wish to use your infirmary to treat the people of Dublin."

The nun crossed her arms over her ample bosom. "Why?"

Jesu, was the woman always this rude? "Because it needs doing and I can do it."

A dark eyebrow quirked, causing the white coif and black veil the abbess wore to rise slightly. "You've married that man, haven't you?"

Eve was startled by the sudden shift in conversation. "If you mean Richard de Clare, yes."

"Why? Because your father told you to?"

"No, not entirely."

"Good. I dislike women who don't have the strength of character to make their own decisions. But why marry the foreigner if not forced to it?"

What any of this had to do with working in the infirmary Eve could not understand, but it appeared she would not get the permission or help she needed until she answered all the questions so rudely posed to her. "My father is an ambitious man. He knows only that he wants to be High King, wants revenge on Hasculf, wants power and recognition. The needs of the land and people are not foremost in his heart. I fear at times they find no place at all there."

"You've just described most of the kings of Ireland. Ambition is much the same no matter where it burns, or in whom. Do you have some reason to believe this de Clare is made of better stuff?"

"I have reason to hope he is. He's promised to rule the Irish by our laws instead of the English laws. He's recognized our tradition that a wife of equal status with her husband has an equal say in all matters."

"Has he now?" The abbess stepped closer, until her face was inches from Eve's, and squinted bright blue eyes to see more clearly. She stepped back again. "Ach, you're in love with the man. No one thinks clearly while in the throes of that disordered passion. But who am I to say you're wrong. God alone knows how faithful this man will be to his word. Show me your hands, woman."

Another unexpected change in subject, but Eve obediently placed her hands in Abbess Ancilla's large outstretched palms. She doubted there were many people courageous enough to refuse this woman.

The abbess studied Eve's hands intently. "You've dirt under your nails."

"I was helping Lorcan with the cabbages."

"You'll need to keep them clean, working with people, for your sake as well as theirs. There's never too much soap and water."

Eve was beginning to enjoy this game the abbess played so well. The gruffness was tempered by intelligence, and if she were not mistaken, a large, compassionate heart. She pursed her lips to keep from smiling.

"Wipe that smirk off your face." The abbess turned Eve's

hands over and studied the palms. Her large thumbs rubbed across the calluses caused by bridle reins. "You've good, strong hands, not afraid of work or dirt." She turned her attention to Caitlin. "Your hands."

It was an unmistakable command and for the first time Eve glanced at her cousin. Poor Cait. Her eyes were wide with shock, and she looked as guilty as a small child caught stealing sweets. Instead of holding her hands out to the abbess, Caitlin hid them behind her back.

"Don't be stubborn, child. I want to see your hands, there's no harm in that."

This time Eve did smile. Mother Ancilla's voice was full of maternal warmth and humor when she spoke to Caitlin. Slowly, the younger woman held her hands out for inspection.

"Just as I feared. Look at this." The abbess held one of Caitlin's dainty hands aloft. "As soft as a newborn's buns. I fear, child, you may not be suited to the work you ask me to allow you."

Eve knew Caitlin was frightened by the large, brusque woman, and was surprised when her cousin spoke.

"I've not done hard work with my hands, 'tis true. I'm willing to try."

"She has a gentle heart," Eve said. "She'll bring comfort to the sick."

Mother Ancilla released Caitlin's hands and turned to face Eve. "I've no doubt she will give her heart to the work, but I fear that heart may be too gentle. It takes a measure of toughness to watch people suffer, especially when there is naught you can do to ease the pain. Watching children die is gut-wrenching, no matter how many you've seen die before. So many young women die in childbirth, with nothing one can do to prevent it. It's hard to believe in God's mercy while you watch someone howl in agony like a dog and beg for death."

Eve reached out and placed her hand on the older woman's arm. "You're not going to scare me off, Lady Ancilla."

"Nor me," Caitlin said.

The abbess patted Eve's hand and sighed. "I was afraid you'd say that. Very well. I'll let Sister Walburga know to expect you. She'll show you about the infirmary and help when she can. When would you like to start?"

"Tomorrow, if it's not too soon."

"Tomorrow then." The abbess turned and hurried from the room.

"What a tyrant," Caitlin said.

"I rather doubt that." Eve smiled as she led her bewildered cousin into the bright sunlight.

The first day, a woman came to have her finger stitched. Eve had more than enough time to inventory the few herbs kept in the infirmary, explaining their use to Caitlin. On the afternoon of the second day a woman brought her son. The boy had a cough, but didn't appear to be seriously ill. Eve gave the woman a tisane of flax seed mixed with honey and told her to bring the child back if he developed a fever. By the third day, a dozen people dropped by. On the morning of the fourth day, Eve and Caitlin rose early, broke their fast, and hurried toward St. Brigid's. The sight that greeted them brought them both to a sudden stop. People, dozens of them, waiting.

"Merciful heavens." Caitlin nervously raised her hand to straighten her veil.

Eve smiled. "It's working, Cait. I knew they'd come."

"How are we going to care for so many?"

"They've been without good care for years now. Once we've seen to the immediate problems, I doubt there will be so many."

"More like the word has spread you don't charge for your services. Do you realize, Eve, that those Cistercian monks in

St. Mary's Abbey have a physician? An actual physician, trained in Italy and Byzantium. But they expect a *donation* of a penny for his ministrations."

"A penny is too much for these folk."

Caitlin crossed her arms and glared at Eve. "Makes one wonder if those Norman monks don't care to dirty their hands serving poor Irish savages."

Eve laughed. "That sounds dangerously close to righteous indignation, Cait."

"Does it? About time, I'd say." Caitlin grabbed Eve's hand, and together they hurried toward the infirmary.

Sister Walburga greeted them at the doorway and pulled them into the building, slamming the door on the waiting crowd. "Lord have mercy, what are we to do? The abbess will be most displeased. We never expected so many."

Eve's head began to pound. In the calmest voice she could manage she tried to allay the nun's fears. "First, I decide who is in most urgent need of attention. We see to——"

"I don't know what to do. Some of those people are truly sick." Sister Walburga lowered her voice and her eyes rounded with horror. "Some of those people are *men*. Surely Mother Abbess did not mean to have you treat men."

"I'm a married woman. Men hold no mystery for me. If they're sick I'll do what I can to help them."

"Oh, I don't know about this. I'll have to tell Mother Ancilla."

Caitlin put her arm around the nun's shoulders and turned her away from Eve. "Sister Walburga, be an angel and help me roll the bandages. I know you showed me before, but you are so good at it. Could you show me again?"

Eve smiled. Where did Caitlin learn such shameless manipulation? Opening the door, she stepped outside to see who needed her help.

Fourteen

September degenerated into a rainy October, turning the roads of Dublin to sucking mud. Day after relentless day the sky was a leaden shroud weeping over the patient earth. The ancient oak trees leaned down under the burden of heavy, wet leaves, and the cries of the gulls echoed mournfully in the thick, dull air.

It was midday, but so dark in Eve's bower they had lighted lanterns to see by as they rolled bandages. Caitlin sniffed occasionally, the remnant of a lung fever that had afflicted her a few weeks earlier. Eve listened, satisfied that the rough cough had gone and that her cousin would be fully recovered in a few more days. The damp weather and chill of autumn usually brought such afflictions, and they were kept busy ministering to folk who were miserably uncomfortable but seldom seriously ill. It kept her occupied, as she hoped it would. She had little time to dwell on what would become of her if Richard did not return.

Eve sat with the linen strips she had been rolling rumpled in her lap, forgotten in her idle hands. What she feared the last few weeks was true. There were too many signs to pretend otherwise. The fatigue, the soreness, the sickness that came and went, all confirmed her suspicions.

Her cousin lived with her again, sharing a bower so that neither would be alone with their men gone. They were as devoted as the closest of sisters, yet she did not tell Caitlin. Her left hand covered her lower abdomen protectively.

Spreading her fingers, she caressed the soft mound that was growing there, familiar already to her sensitive hands. For now she was safe. It was not noticeable to anyone else.

Eve knew she could not keep her pregnancy secret. It was still unknown who had tried to kill Richard, or why. If someone wished him dead, the baby, who was his heir, was not safe. Looking up, she caught Caitlin staring at her.

"How long have you known?" Caitlin asked.

Eve was not surprised by the question. They lived too close and Caitlin knew her too well. "I've suspected for almost a month. I've only been sure the last several days."

"A summer-born babe." Caitlin smiled, then the smile froze and fear, naked and raw, filled her blue eyes.

"Yes, I've thought of that, too. Someone may not want this child to see life." She had told Caitlin of the attempt on Richard's life. How could she not tell Caitlin? She had to tell someone or go mad. Even Lorcan she had not trusted with it. Not that he would have breathed a word of what she said, but he would take it upon himself to right a wrong, and so expose himself to danger.

"Whoever it is wouldn't dare lift a finger against you if Richard were here."

"But he isn't here, and I'm pregnant. We are the only guardians this child has, for now."

Crossing the warm room, Caitlin sat on the floor at her cousin's feet, leaning against Eve's knee for support. Eve stroked the younger woman's soft hair, giving and receiving comfort in the simple act of touching. "How I envy you," Caitlin said quietly.

"How so?"

"Oh, not the situation, never that, and I will die to protect you and the child. But Eve, how I long to carry Morgan's child. What greater gift can we have from the men we love?"

A gift. She had been too consumed with worry over its safety, too angry at the timing of it, trying not to feel abandoned, trying to adjust to all the unusual things happening to her body, to think of the blessing that had come to her so unexpectedly. A baby. Richard's child. *Dear God, I am going to be a mother. I haven't yet learned to be a wife.* It seemed overwhelming, yet it was a gift, as Caitlin said, to be cherished and nurtured. Already it roused in her a passionate protectiveness. This tiny thing, less than two months in existence, changed her life.

Her child was heir to a kingdom, and that was why it was in jeopardy. Not for the first time she wished she were a simple woman, with no more than the care of fields and animals and cottage, devoted to her husband, with a house overflowing with dirty, happy children. If only she knew when Richard would return. If it was to be soon, she could wait and manage her fear. The pregnancy could be kept secret another few months, especially with colder weather when everyone wore cloaks indoors and out. If Richard was gone past Christmas, she and the baby could be in greater danger. How could she travel at that time of year, where would she go? Who could she trust?

The unexpected knock at the door startled them. Ban, asleep near the fire, erupted into watchfulness, hackles raised, a growl deep in his throat. "Oh, be quiet, you silly beast." Eve crossed the bower to open the door. A blast of wet wind gusted in. A small slave girl stood shivering in the cold, her thin, short gown little protection from the elements. Eve felt a flash of anger. Dervorgilla was notorious for the abysmal conditions of her slave quarters, too greedy for her own comfort to see to the necessities of others.

"Come in, child, and warm yourself by the fire."

Eyes round with disbelief, the girl hesitated. Her short hair was plastered to her delicate skull by the rain. She was dirty, skinny, and frightened. It wrenched Eve's heart to see her. A hard, short life of labor and snatched pleasures awaited the child as a member of Dervorgilla's household. With a sigh, Eve took the girl's fragile hand and drew her gently into the warmth of the cozy room. The priests taught it was God's will that some were slave, some were noble, with the many common freemen in between, but Eve had ever been uneasy with such merciless dogma. What had this child done to deserve her wretched life?

The girl stood trembling before the fire, her bare feet crossed one over the other. Ban came and sat next to the child, his tail wagging lazily as he gazed at this potential playmate, unaware that his size intimidated the girl.

"Now, tell me why you're here." Eve squatted next to the child, to be more on her level, and spoke softly.

"The mistress says ye must come. Her son be terrible ill." The child spoke in a small, frightened voice, so quietly Eve and Caitlin had to lean close to hear.

"You can't go there." Caitlin's voice sharpened with indignation. "Dervorgilla has been nothing but cruel to you since your mother died. You owe that woman nothing. Let her call the royal physician."

Eve straightened and looked at her cousin. "Egan's a child and needs my help."

"Don't be so damned noble. He probably has no more than a sniffle, and will be fine in a week whether you minister to him or not."

"He's my brother."

"He's no better than a stranger to you, so seldom has Dervorgilla allowed you to see him. I know that look on your face. Nothing I can say will sway you." With an exasperated sigh, Caitlin pulled her cloak, and one for Eve, from the wall pegs near the door. "If you insist on doing this I'm going with you, so don't try to talk me out of it."

Eve did not intend to try. She accepted the cloak gratefully, wrapping its heavy woolen warmth around her shoulders, pulling the hood up to cover her head against the rain. She glanced at the slave, standing greedily close to the fire. The child looked pitiably small and frail. "Stay until you've warmed yourself, and take as much of the bread and milk and cheese as you want from the table." The girl stared blankly. "Do you understand?"

"Yes, m'lady."

"Ban, come."

They hurried toward Dervorgilla's bower, seeking what shelter they could find under the narrow eaves of the buildings they passed. The guard at the door to the bower expected them, and they passed through without question.

The outer chamber was stifling hot, with a dozen or more braziers set about the room. Dervorgilla's serving women were gathered in knots of whispering anxiety.

"God's teeth, what took you so long." Dervorgilla pounced on her, grabbing Eve hard by the upper arm.

Forcing the other woman to release her, Eve resisted the urge to rub her arm, sure she would sport a bruise there. "Calm yourself, Dervorgilla. You'll do Egan no good with your hysterics. Where is the boy?"

The older woman was too distraught to take notice of Eve's reprimand. "He's in my bed. You must help him, he burns with fever."

"How long has he been sick?" Eve asked.

"It started last evening. By this morning he couldn't rise from his stupor."

Eve did not like the sound of that. A child who sickened so quickly was vulnerable, but children often had an amazing capacity to recuperate as well. They walked into the inner chamber, and as always Eve found the extravagant luxury repugnant. Like everything about Dervorgilla it was too bright, too rich, too much. Eve's own chamber was colorful and comfortable, with a subdued elegance. Here all was shimmering silk, and opulent velvet brocade in sumptuous scarlet and purple, heavy and dark. It was suffocating.

In the midst of the overwhelming room was a large bed, and in the center of the bed a small boy. Egan tossed restlessly with fever, his red hair plastered to his skull with sweat, and Eve's heart leapt to her throat at sight of him.

Ignoring Dervorgilla's wailing, she sat on the edge of the bed and leaned over to examine her brother. His fever was dangerously high. She pulled the covers away from his naked body. A rash of pinkish brown spots covered his face, neck, and shoulders. If it progressed as she thought it would, within a day the rash would cover his body, in another day his limbs. What brought on the disease she did not know, but if it was what she thought, he would recover in a week to ten days. That is, if it did not settle into a lung ague, which could be very serious indeed. For now the fever must be brought down before it caused convulsions.

"I need cold water and clean cloths."

"That's it? You're going to bathe him?" Dervorgilla screeched in disbelief.

"The sickness itself is not serious, but this fever is. Cool water is the best way to bring it down. I can't dose him with anything until he's conscious enough to take it without choking."

Dervorgilla's eyes flitted from her son to Eve, and back again. When she spoke, it was with eerie calm. "If he dies, do not count yourself long for this world."

The warning sent a chill of fear over Eve's skin, followed by a burst of heated anger. "Do not think to threaten me. I will do what I can for Egan, not because you command it, but because he is my brother."

"You dare speak so to me?"

Rising from her seat on the bed, Eve pulled the hood of her cloak back over her head. "You obviously don't want me here, Dervorgilla. I can't help Egan if you fight me. Get the fever down, keep him comfortable. When he wakes, feed him broth when he's hungry and force as much clean water down him as you can. For now your prayers would not be amiss. With God's grace he'll recover in a week." She turned to go, disgusted beyond words that even now Dervorgilla wanted to manipulate, to exercise her power over others.

"No, wait. They say you have healing in your hands." The husky voice men found so irresistible held a note of pleading in it that astonished Eve. "Do what you must, I'll not interfere."

Eve glanced at Egan and knew she could not abandon her brother. "Caitlin and I will stay, as long as Egan needs us."

No word of thanks came, but Eve had not expected any. Instead, Dervorgilla descended on the women in the outer chamber, demanding basins of water and the softest of linen cloths.

"Holy Mary, in her a mother's love is a terrible thing," Caitlin said, laying her cloak over the back of a chair piled with velvet cushions.

Eve placed her cloak beside Cait's while Ban settled near the foot of the bed. She had never doubted Dervorgilla's love for her son. This nascent love she felt for Richard's child was already so strong a compulsion, she could understand the ferocious protectiveness that drove Dervorgilla.

The bedchamber was as stifling as the outer room, and sweat trickled between Eve's breasts. She walked to the window and threw back the heavy wooden shutters. "This stale air can't be good for Egan."

"Do you truly think he'll recover? Dervorgilla would be a madwoman if he died."

"This illness is rarely fatal in children, though it can be severe in adults. It's the fever that has me worried. The sooner we can break it, the better."

Rolling the sleeves of her gown back past her elbows, Eve prepared for a long night of hard work. With the shutters open, wonderfully cool air surged into the room. The heat made her nauseated and she was glad for the relief. The last thing she wanted was to rouse any suspicion by being sick.

Water was brought, and carefully, to avoid irritating his raw, blistered skin, Eve pressed the cooling rags against her brother's body. Caitlin joined her on the other side of the bed. Dervorgilla watched, her hands nervously clutching and pulling at the edge of her wide sleeves.

"Christ, but you're rough with that." Dervorgilla pushed Caitlin aside and took the cloth in her own hand. Caitlin had been as gentle as any angel in her touch, but she stepped back without a word.

In complete silence Eve and Dervorgilla worked against the illness that reached out for Egan. So many children, healthy one day, were dead the next. Eve had seen it too many times to count. But not Egan. Not if she could help it.

It took three hours for his body to cool to a more normal temperature, though he was still warm. They piled blankets on him against the chills that now wracked him, setting his teeth chattering. Sometime after midnight the fever again peaked, and once more they bathed him, but this time it took only an hour to bring it back down, and the chills when they came were milder. An hour later, he woke and demanded food.

Dervorgilla laughed and said she would call for roast hare and cheese, as much as he could eat. Eve told her to feed him a strong, clear broth of beef and a little bread, to save the meat for tomorrow or the day after. Dervorgilla stared at her across the room, her eyes as hard and distant as the stars. Finally, she called for broth, and turning her back on Eve, gave all her attention to her son.

Eve was exhausted. It was the baby in her. She was tired all the time lately and in constant need of the privy. Gathering her cloak around her shoulders, she went out into the cold night air, Ban and Caitlin at her side.

The rain had stopped for the first time in days, and a pale line of light curved behind the eastern horizon. It would be dawn in another hour. Ban pushed insistently against her thigh until Eve paid him some attention, scratching behind his ear.

"Not a word of thanks." Caitlin's voice was quiet with disbelief.

Something had nagged at Eve all night. Something about Dervorgilla. She knew the woman disliked her, but there had been unmistakable hatred in Dervorgilla's eyes. Eve stopped and turned around in the street, staring at the bower. "She'll never forgive me for this."

"What do you mean?" Caitlin yawned, unable to stifle it.

"Dervorgilla will never forgive me for saving her son. Any normal mother would be grateful and wish me well, but that woman hates me. Because I've helped her, she'll feel guilty, and guilt will twist her hatred."

"That's insane."

"That doesn't make it less true."

Fifteen

"Eve, you haven't heard a word I've said." Caitlin set the pitcher of warm ale down on the table between them. "You've hardly eaten. Is something wrong?"

"I'm tired, but it will pass." She pulled at the neck of her gown, uncomfortable in the stuffy warmth of the bower.

It was a week since Egan began to recover from his fever, but several more children were ill. For days she had rushed from the opulent bowers in the royal enclosure to the simpler cottages of Dublin, where she reassured worried mothers and left potions and advice, before she hurried to the next sickbed. So far none of the children had died and for that she was immensely grateful.

There was a sharp chill in the autumn air, and the peat fire in the small hearth had been built up, the fragrant smoke spiraling lazily toward the louver in the roof.

"It's too hot in here." Eve's gown stuck to her body where the sweat touched it, along her ribs, and down her back.

"Is it? I find it comfortable."

Eve rose to open the door to let in fresh air, but was instantly dizzy, and grabbed at the edge of the table. Caitlin was quickly by her side and helped her back into her chair.

"This is more than fatigue. Sit still and let me look at you." She placed a cool hand on Eve's brow. "Sweet Mother of God, it's not the bower that's hot, it's you. You're burning with fever."

No. That cannot be, Eve thought. What passed lightly in

Egan would manifest itself more severely in her, and what it might do to the child she carried she did not want to imagine. "I'm tired. Help me to bed, I'll be fine in the morning."

Leaning on Caitlin, she made her way slowly to the bed, with its haven of cool linen and blankets of soft, cream-colored wool. She wanted nothing more than to slip naked into bed and sleep. First she must be rid of her clothing, which seemed to weigh a great deal more than usual, and whose laces she could not untie with her aching fingers. Caitlin helped her out of the garments, then into the bed. The linen felt cool on her hot skin, and she sank into the depths of the feather bed, filled with the finest eider and soft as a mother's embrace.

The wind increased in the trees overhanging the bower, lamenting through the heavy branches. Rain whispered in the thatch, running in muddy rivulets across the ground, gathering in puddles in streets and yards. She dreamed of standing naked in the rain. Rain slacked the heat of her body. Cool and sweet, it soaked into her fevered brain. Waking in the middle of the night, with one small lamp to light the darkness, she moaned at the sharp pain in her head. Thirst made her tongue swell in her mouth, and the aching soreness in her joints made the slightest movement difficult. Caitlin was beside her, wiping her brow with cool cloths, helping her drink, soothing her with voice and touch. She slept again.

For days the fever stormed through her body and mind. In her few lucid moments she began to fear she would die. The thought was unendurable. How could she leave without seeing Richard again? Was her child destined to die with her, before it ever had a chance at life? She struggled against the dark, implacable death angel, who sat in the corner of the room and waited with the patience of eternity. "You won't have me, not yet," she hissed at him. He settled more comfortably on his haunches to wait.

Wish You Were Here?

You can be, every month, with Zebra Historical Romance Novels.

YOU'RE GOING TO LOVE GETTING
4 FREE BOOKS

These books worth almost $20, are yours without cost or obligation when you fill out and mail this certificate.
(If the certificate is missing below, write to: Zebra Home Subscription Service, Inc., 120 Brighton Road, P.O. Box 5214, Clifton, New Jersey 07015-5214

Complete and mail this card to receive 4 Free books!

Yes! Please send me 4 Zebra Historical Romances without cost or obligation. I understand that each month thereafter I will be able to preview 4 new Zebra Historical Romances FREE for 10 days. Then, if I should decide to keep them, I will pay the money-saving preferred publisher's price of just $4.00 each...a total of $16. That's almost $4 less than the publisher's price, and there is no additional charge for shipping and handling. I may return any shipment within 10 days and owe nothing, and I may cancel this subscription at any time. The 4 FREE books will be mine to keep in any case.

Name _____

Address _____ Apt. _____

City _____ State _____ Zip _____

Telephone ( ) _____

Signature _____ LF0795
(If under 18, parent or guardian must sign.)

Terms, offer and prices subject to change without notice. Subscription subject to acceptance by Zebra Books. Zebra Books reserves the right to reject any order or cancel any subscription.

TREAT YOURSELF TO 4 FREE BOOKS.

A $19.96
value.
FREE!

No obligation
to buy
anything, ever.

AFFIX
STAMP
HERE

ZEBRA HOME SUBSCRIPTION SERVICE, INC.

120 BRIGHTON ROAD

P.O. BOX 5214

CLIFTON, NEW JERSEY 07015-5214

lll..l...llll....llll.l.l.l..l.l..l.l....llll.l.l..ll.l..lll..l

Lorcan came. Or did she imagine it? Beloved Lorcan, who invariably had time for her when she was a child, when she was so lonely she thought her heart would break with it. Lorcan, who thought her worthy, who cherished her. Why did he look so solemn and sad? He leaned over her and whispered something she could not quite hear. Then she felt his thumb on her eyelids, marking the sign of the cross, and again at her nostrils and her mouth, on her burning hands and hot feet. The touch was gentle. She should not be soothed by it, something deep inside her screamed. Fight the greedy, devouring angel. Fight Lorcan's touch. It is the touch of death.

It was the middle of the night when Richard rode into Dublin, Morgan and Tewdr close on his heels. Just the three of them, riding straight from Drogheda where O'Conor had his camp. Lorcan's message had reached him that morning, but he could not believe it. Eve could not be dying.

He jerked his stallion to a slithering stop in the muddy yard, and was out of the saddle while the animal still moved. As he rushed into the bower, his sword clanged against the chain mail of his leg armor and his spurs sounded sharply on the floor. Morgan and Tewdr followed.

"Richard? Morgan? Thank God you've come." Caitlin emerged from the inner chamber, and rushed into Morgan's arms. He held her gently, stroking her disheveled hair.

"How is Eve?" Richard asked.

She looked at him with eyes swollen from weeping, and shook her head. "She's in God's hands."

"But she is alive?"

"Yes."

"Then there's hope."

He went into the dark inner chamber. Beside the bed sat Lorcan, holding one of Eve's fragile hands, his fair head bowed in prayer. He looked up at Richard with weary, pain-filled eyes, then bowed again to his task. The room smelled of sickness, hot and fetid and sour. Richard looked at the woman in the bed. Covered by a virulent, oozing rash, her features were swollen almost beyond recognition. Her hair, once so shiny, was dull and limp in its braid. The blanket that covered her barely rose with her shallow breathing. He went to the opposite side of the bed from Lorcan, and stood, unsure what he should do now that he was here.

"I was afraid you wouldn't get my message, or wouldn't be able to come." Lorcan pressed thumb and forefinger to his eyes and rubbed at the weariness there.

"Is she dying?"

The archbishop sighed, and there was such sadness in the sound, Richard's hope wavered. "I've given her last rites, but she wasn't aware of it. She moves in and out of dark dreams. The fever is eating her alive. Caitlin and Mother Ancilla take turns bathing her in cool water, and the fever abates for a while, but always comes back. They can't get it to break. It's surprising she hasn't lost the baby."

"Dear God, she's with child?"

Lorcan looked up at him. "Forgive me, I thought Caitlin told you."

"You've been here all this time, you and Caitlin?"

Lorcan lifted his hand as though to brush aside any comment on that. "Mother Ancilla comes every day as well. I've been shouting in God's ear, but I don't know if He hears me."

"If He won't listen to you, Lorcan, what chance do I have of getting His attention?"

A small smile quirked one side of the priest's mouth. "Do you love her?"

Richard glanced down at the frail woman who bore no resemblance to the vital, vibrant maid he had married, and his heart nearly broke with the painful love he felt. "More than I ever would have thought possible."

"Then the Lord hears you, and heeds what is in your heart. But it is not Eve's recovery I pray for."

"What then?"

"That we accept His will, whatever happens. It is all we can ever ask."

Richard's heart and mind rebelled against that idea. A man of action, accustomed to storming whatever resistance he met and taking what he wanted, he wanted Eve and his child to live. The helplessness made him want to rage at God, but he could not bargain or intimidate the Deity into submission.

In her weakness Eve had need of Richard's strength. He leaned over and brushed her cheek gently with his fingers. The heat there frightened him, more than any battle. Here was an enemy he did not understand and could not fight. All he could do was wait.

"Tewdr!" Richard shouted. The boy's solemn face appeared around the doorway. "Get in here and help me out of my armor."

The squire came silently, unprecedented for him. After undressing Richard, burdened with the chain mail and sword, Tewdr stood for a moment, as though unsure if he should speak. "Is there aught I can do for m'lady?"

Richard was about to tell him no, then knew such an answer would make it appear hopeless. "See that the fire in the hearth is well stoked." The boy seemed relieved to have something to do, and left quickly.

Lorcan rose. "I'll leave you alone with her." The priest walked slowly from the room, his shoulders stooped with fatigue.

Clad in his shirt and braies, Richard climbed into bed beside Eve and gently pulled her into his strong embrace. She reclined against his chest, cushioned there and shielded. How hot she was, and damp with sweat. All excess flesh had been burned from her and he could touch each delicate rib through the cloth of her gown. She weighed no more than a child in his arms.

He leaned down and kissed the top of her head. "Don't you die on me, Eve. Not now. Not when I've come to love you more than life itself. How will I live without your laughter, without your sharp tongue to keep me humble?" The soft murmur of his voice was the only sound in the chamber. The light of the single lantern cast dancing shadows on the walls where bright tapestries hung.

He talked to relieve the dangerous quiet, hoping she could hear. "Who would have thought I'd so deeply love my little Irish wife? I want you with me, by my side for a lifetime, Eve. I want to hold our child, and the children that follow."

The hours passed toward dawn and still he talked to her, until his voice grew raspy. Methodically, he wiped her body with cloths soaked in cool water. He wept at sight of her beautiful body ravaged by disease, and was as tender as any mother with a one-day babe when he touched her. He sent Caitlin away to sleep when she offered to relieve him. Morgan tried to make him eat but Richard growled at him, and the man left him alone. Lorcan came and went, a silent, comforting presence. Richard stayed and talked, pouring the need and hurt and loneliness he had carefully kept hidden into his words.

The voices in the outer room quieted and finally were silent. Ban, gaunt and worried, slept uneasily at the foot of the bed, waking often to come to Richard for reassurance. He would rub the big dog's broad head and send him back to his sleep, wishing he could comfort himself as easily.

Through the long hours he kept talking, as though sound alone would keep her from slipping away. "I need your strength and your compassion, Eve. They make me human. Knowing you, loving you, has made life worth living again, when I thought there would never be pleasure or purpose to it. Do you bring me all these gifts only to take them from me now?" He whispered to her, softly, holding her close. He knew she could hear him, knew it with a conviction he could not begin to explain in any rational manner.

He could not plead with God, but he could damn well plead with Eve. She must hear him, hear his need, and live.

Dawn came and with it a day of late-October sun in a sky so clear and blue it made the heart ache. The soft Irish hills were gilded amber, and under the oak trees where a few ferns still unfurled green leaves, rain shimmered in jeweled droplets at the tips of delicate fronds. Richard opened the door and window and breathed deeply of the freshness. It swept the noisomeness of the sickroom away, leaving in its stead sweetness and the smell of rain in the earth. The bower was bathed in semidarkness until, in the afternoon, a shaft of sunlight pierced the dimness. It burst through the open window and lighted the dust motes as they drifted and swirled, and spilled in a golden shower over the bed. Night came fast and cold. Once more the shutters were fixed and the fire blazed hotly on the hearth.

He slept off and on, cradling Eve in his arms. When he woke, he talked to her. At times nonsense filled his mouth, but he kept talking through that long night. He revealed all the secrets of his soul, all the things he had kept to himself and shared with no one. Those shameful, vulnerable needs that ached in him, that she had touched with her love. They were a quivering, living thing inside him, now that he had given voice to them and made them real. Above all he feared his aloneness in the world, now that she had shared herself with him. How could he go back to that adamant self-possession he had armatured himself with?

He looked up once to see a large nun in the doorway. She nodded and turned around without a word, leaving him alone with Eve.

The night deepened toward midnight, the sound of the bells in the churches and monasteries long silent and not yet ringing the monks and nuns to the office of Vigils. Then he heard the noises, faint at first, like a sough of wind pleading at the windows. The sounds strengthened, became shouts, and cries, and singing, and screams. They were not the noises of battle or of attack. He recognized it as the bright, happy sounds of festival and celebration. "What is that?" he asked Caitlin.

"Samhain. I'd forgotten."

The Celtic festival of the dead, when spirits roam the earth and the doorway between the living and the dead is thrust open. It was celebrated in Wales, too, at the end of October, with dancing around huge bonfires, and drinking of new cider, and lusty, wild trysts under the bushes. It was said a child born on this night would be gifted with the Sight, and that the future could be read in nutshell ashes and in apples cut crosswise and in witches' mirrors. In spite of all the priests could think to do to eradicate the pagan festival, the people gathered and the old beliefs prevailed.

Fear crept down his spine. The night of the dead. It was as though this night, of all nights, Eve was most vulnerable. Tonight the battle would be lost or won.

He lighted candles, as many as he could find, badgering Lorcan to bring more from the cathedral chandlery. The light was comforting on this ghostly night, and he set the candles about in the room until it glowed with immaculate radiance and smelled of wax and honey. Darkness would not prevail here. He settled again into the bed, Eve held in the warm cove of his chest, his arms wrapped around her slight form. Was it his imagination, or was the rash less red, the swelling of her eyes and lips less pronounced, her breathing stronger? Or did wanting it make it seem so?

He crooned to her now, in a singsong voice, as a parent would to a restive child. The candles burned low, a few sputtered in their dishes and went out. The sounds of idolatrous revelry continued through the Devil's Hours of the night. He grew sleepy, and against his will nodded off, holding her as though the strength of his arms could keep away all harm.

"Richard?"

It was soft, a sigh against his chest, a trick in his ear. He smiled in his sleep, then woke suddenly, his heart pounding. Had she truly spoken, or had he dreamt it?

He brushed the back of his fingers against her cheek. She was warm to his touch, but no more than any sleepy person would be. The fever was gone.

"Richard." She whispered his name, her breath as delicate as butterfly wings against his chest. "I knew you would come for me." She snuggled against him, and with a sigh, fell asleep.

Eve gorged herself on roast mutton, sucking at the bones to get the rich marrow. It seemed she had done nothing but eat and sleep the last three days. She could have done little else if she had wanted to, since Richard refused to let her out of bed except to take care of necessities. She found herself content to do as he ordered, too weak to protest and welcoming his overprotective hovering.

"I must look a fright." She ran a hand over her hair. How long had it been since she bathed?

"You were dreadful enough to shock the dead a few days ago." Tewdr stood at the foot of the bed, where he scratched Ban behind the ears. The wolfhound grinned with pleasure.

"He lacks a diplomat's wit." Morgan cut a sharp glance at his blunt-tongued squire, who ignored him.

"You look much better now," Caitlin said. "The rash and swelling are nearly gone. In a few days I'll help you bathe and wash your hair, and you'll feel human again."

Eve smiled and shook her head. What an honest bunch they were. A little flattery would not be amiss, but she would find none of that from these three.

Chewing on mutton sopped in a warm sauce of cider and

onions, she glanced at Richard, sitting in a chair next to the bed. Strange, it seemed as though he had talked incessantly while she was sick, but she was not sure if that were true. Could he really have said the things she remembered hearing? For now he seemed content enough to be near and say little.

Caitlin and Morgan shared their meal. Their heads, one fair the other dark, bowed together in so intimate a gesture it left little doubt as to where their hearts lay. She must speak to Caitlin about it the next time they were alone. Sighing with a vast sense of contentment, Eve spread more thick butter on dark bread and stuffed it into her mouth. The people she loved were in this room, and the child was safe in its womb. She would see to it that Morgan and Caitlin could be together, in spite of any protest her father might voice.

Life was too short to let love slip by. That was one thing she would never again question if she lived to be an ancient crone surrounded by her grandchildren's children. Love was life, it was living.

Eve placed her hand in Richard's. "How soon do you leave? You've been gone too long from your army."

"I don't want to leave you."

She smiled, his words warming her like sunshine in summer. They also strengthened her to say what she knew she must. "I'm well enough and I'll be safe with the guard you leave. Your duty is elsewhere now."

"In truth, I don't trust your father. There's no telling what he might do, and I don't like the idea of him in the field, trying to command my men. God knows what foolishness he'll lead them into. We have Rory surrounded, and with winter coming it shouldn't take too long a siege to get him to capitulate to treaty terms. All we must do is wait him out."

It was then they heard shouting and the clatter of many hooves. The bells began to ring in the church towers. "What

the hell?" Richard strode from the bedchamber and threw
open the door, staring out into the royal enclosure.

"What is it?" Eve stood beside him, but could not see
what had caught his attention.

"Damn that whoreson to deepest hell!"

"Richard, whatever is the matter?" Then she saw, and
could not believe her eyes. Her father had returned and
brought with him every knight and man-at-arms of Richard's army. "He's lifted the siege?"

"So it would appear. God alone knows at what terms."

She watched as he marched across the yard, Morgan
close beside him. What foolhardy thing had her father done
now?

Sixteen

Rumors flew from mouth to ear, each more fantastic than the last.

"Rory has surrendered, and agreed to make Dermot his heir."

"Are ye daft? Why would the High King do so fool a thing? No, Dermot's run back to Dublin to avoid battle with O'Conor."

Richard listened as he and Morgan hurried toward the king's hall, but none of what he heard made sense. He could get no reliable information from any of his commanders, except that Dermot met with Rory privately for several hours a few days earlier. What the two kings talked about, or why Dermot returned so hastily to Dublin, they could not explain.

Pushing through the crowds near the palace, Richard and Morgan made their way into the hall. Dermot had called a hasty meeting of his councilors. Men impatient to hear the king filled the cavernous room, their voices loud with speculation. At the far end of the building, Dermot stood with Dervorgilla and Egan beside him. The woman, pale and shaken, looked as though she could not believe what she heard. Her long, elegant hands gripped so tightly on Egan's shoulders that the boy squirmed beneath them.

The area around Dermot was hushed as an empty church. His white-bearded elders, stiff with dignity and age, stood as stunned as Dervorgilla, their eyes betraying their disbelief.

"You cannot mean to do this. It is madness!" Dervorgilla broke the silence into brittle shards, the fear in her voice palpable.

Morgan stood beside Richard, effortlessly translating into his ear.

"Keep your tongue civil, woman. Do you forget who you are speaking to?" With a smile, Dermot gestured toward Egan. "Come here, boy. You understand what I've done, don't you? It'll be a great adventure for you. You'd like that, wouldn't you, Egan, to be part of my treaty plans?"

How could Egan be involved? What had Dermot done? Richard feared whatever it was, he was not likely to be pleased.

Pushing past the preoccupied guard at the foot of the dais, Richard climbed to where Dermot stood. He towered over the king. He did not try to conceal the anger in his voice, and beside him Morgan translated with equal fervor. "You bring my army here against my explicit orders, Dermot. You had better have a damned good reason."

Cold triumph lighted the king's eyes. "I've done what you could not, de Clare, with all your army and strength of arms. I've signed a treaty with O'Conor. He's agreed to leave us in peace."

"At what terms? What did you concede?" Richard dreaded what the answer would be. It was too easy. Whatever Dermot had agreed to could not have accomplished Richard's goals.

"I've granted Rory nothing. That's the beauty of it." Dermot gave a chuckle, then ruffled Egan's bright hair.

"If you have given nothing to O'Conor, then what have you won from him? What do you hope to gain?"

"Time, of course. We'll have all winter to supply ourselves and await the reinforcements from England and Wales. You've promised more knights, and until they arrive I'm not willing to risk open battle with Rory. Victory will be easy in the spring, when the rest of your army is in place." A strange smile deformed Dermot's face. "Ireland will be mine."

Richard's hands fisted at his sides, but it was the only sign of anger he allowed himself. He must stay calm with this unpredictable man. "You believe O'Conor will leave us in peace while we gather this army? What possible pledge could he give to convince you?"

Dermot drew his hauteur around him like a cloak and pulled Egan to his side. The boy looked up at him with fervent, adoring eyes, unused to being the focus of his father's attention. "Rory has agreed to exchange hostages. He will send us his son."

Richard was afraid he knew the answer to his question before he asked it, but he wanted the words from Dermot's mouth. "What have you promised in return?"

He pulled the boy closer. "My son, Egan, in exchange for Rory's son."

Morgan finished with the translation. A deep silence filled the hall, the quiet spreading like ripples in water, then an incredulous whispering began along the edges of the crowd, toward the back. The whispers grew more adamant, anger edging the voices.

Richard could not believe the idiocy of it. What puzzled him most was why O'Conor agreed to such terms, knowing Dermot's poor record when it came to the treatment of hostages. More than one had died while under Dermot's protection over the years.

Dervorgilla, livid with fear and anger, advanced on Dermot. "You fool! What is to keep Rory from killing my son, once he learns of your treachery?"

"Your son?" Dermot asked. "Careful, Dervorgilla, or I'll send you back to that one-eyed husband of yours. Do you think I haven't ensured Egan's welfare? The boys will be exchanged again at Eastertide. When Egan is safely back, I can deploy my army against Rory. Egan will go as my representative, as I've promised. I'll not hear another word from you on the subject."

Dervorgilla looked around her as though seeing the crowd for the first time, her eyes wide with confusion. "I'll never forgive you if you do this." Her voice was low and quivering. Dermot gave her a long, speculative look, then deliberately turned his back. With impotent fury, she stalked from the hall, her nervous women following in a silent trail behind her.

"When does this exchange take place?" Richard asked.

"In a week. We meet Rory at Tara."

"I don't like it, Dermot. Not any of it." Richard's voice carried to the far ends of the hushed hall. "It puts the boy in too much danger, and we gain little by it. If you had remained at Drogheda as we agreed, we could have brought Rory to favorable terms in a few weeks. We could have overwhelmed him if it came to battle. Now you give him time to regroup, to gather more men, to plan his strategy."

One of Dermot's eyes twitched. "I did what had to be done, while you came running back to Dublin on some ridiculous pretext."

"Lorcan sent word my wife was dying. I find that more than sufficient reason to return."

"Lorcan is a weakling. Like all clerics he's so frightened of death he sees it everywhere. My daughter lives, thank God, but she would have lived or died whether you returned or not. Your duty is with me and my army. Do you dare question my decision, when you were not there to discuss it?"

"Never again will I make the mistake of leaving my men under your command, MacMurrough. My absence was merely an excuse to put this extraordinarily foolhardy plan into action." What he could do to prevent handing Egan over to the enemy Richard could not see. Dermot could not refuse without seeming the worst of cowards. *The duplicity men resort to in the name of pride.*

He wanted to be with Eve, surrounded by the warmth and peace she brought to his life. He was unaccustomed to the changes working in him, this desire for a quiet life with children gathered at his knee, where before the companionship of warriors had been his one requirement.

"I pray to God your foolishness doesn't endanger Egan." Richard's voice was cold and steely. "I swear to you, if anything happens to the boy, it's me you'll answer to."

He turned and walked from the hall, Morgan following. In the yard, slaves hurried through the mud, and soggy dogs napped uncomfortably on porches. Richard drew a deep breath into his lungs.

"Too much can go wrong. Too much is beyond our control," Morgan said quietly, frowning. "Damn that fool. Rory now has the winter without having to worry about how to feed and shelter an army. He has time to gather more men before launching a full-scale campaign."

"Exactly. I expect another one hundred knights before Christmas and more in the spring, but I'd hoped to win Leinster before then. My plans rested on bringing Rory to battle before he gathered an army. Dermot now makes that impossible. Why Dermot doesn't see the threat puzzles me. He's relying too heavily on my knights. If Rory can outnumber us forty to one, our cause is all but hopeless."

"Do you think Egan will be safe?" Morgan's voice was edged with concern.

Richard shrugged. "I don't know. From what I've heard, Rory is a man of honor, a man of his word."

"But Dermot is not."

"No. Why do you suppose Dermot would risk his son so foolishly?

"Why does Dermot do anything? He has the enviable capacity to convince himself a thing will be as he envisions it, and no doubts assail him once his mind is set. It's as though he thinks fate would not dare contradict his wishes."

"Then he's worse than a fool." Richard stood in the rain

and frowned. Something puzzled him. "Morgan, did you translate all that was said, word for word?"

"Of course, what good am I to you if I don't?"

"Then I didn't misunderstand, Dervorgilla called Egan her son?"

"Is that odd? He is her son."

"Dermot seemed to think it strange. She has every right to be fearful for her son, what mother wouldn't be. It's her words I keep coming back to. Her son, not our son, not your son. Dermot noticed it."

"I don't follow. What difference does it make?"

"I dislike where my thoughts are leading. Even Dermot must have a limit to his cruelty."

"Christ's blood, Richard, what are you thinking?"

"What if Egan isn't Dermot's son? Would he use the boy to buy time, with no intention of seeing to his safety later?"

"If that be true we have no way to know what Dermot plans."

Richard cursed and marched toward the barracks. It was raining again, a cold, miserable day. If autumn was like this, what waited them in winter? The rain pelted him with its cold, cleansing water, and for once Richard was glad of it. He felt unclean, as though Dermot's idiocy contaminated him.

They walked toward the bowers, clustered like a small village to the east of the king's hall. Here the Irish nobles lived when they were in Dublin. The snug timber cottages were more solidly built than those of the townsfolk. The farthest one from the hall, and nearest where the new barracks for Richard's men was now completed, was the cottage he shared with Eve. It drew him like a beacon.

Richard glanced at Morgan, who walked with his dark head bent against the rain. Though the Welshman's wound was healed, he was still unable to use his sword arm with any effectiveness. He never complained, but the anger must be there, beneath the calm exterior. Such a limitation would drive Richard insane. What was he if not a warrior?

From the moment he was born and known to be male, Richard's life was directed toward one thing. To be a knight, a fighting man. That he was the scion of a powerful family also meant he was born to rule and hold the fate of others in his hands. Morgan's life was less complicated, with no great estates to keep, no army to feed, no king to appease. Richard felt a twinge of envy for the younger man.

"What are your intentions concerning Lady Caitlin?" He had not meant to blurt it out like that, with no preliminary.

Morgan looked up at him with startled dark eyes. "Am I allowed to have intentions?"

"Only honorable ones, I'm afraid."

"I'm a simple knight-bachelor, dependent on you for the very food I eat. What can I possibly hope to give to a woman of royal blood?" There was a note of bitterness in his voice.

Richard frowned. "Do you love the woman?"

"Since when did such a thing matter? Weren't you the one who insisted marriages are meant to enhance a family's prestige, to secure land or wealth or power? When did love come into the balance?"

Was that amusement he saw in the Welshman's eyes? Damn if the man wasn't teasing him, even now. "This is serious, Morgan. If you don't mean to marry the woman, I want you to stop seeing her."

Morgan stopped in the pouring rain. "I love her with all my heart, but where does that get us? I've still no land, nothing with which to support her and a family. It's a hopeless situation."

"Mayhap not."

"What do you mean? If I can win lands for myself here, there's hope. Until then, I must wait."

"I have a small manor in Wales, a hundred acres, but enough to support a keep. Enough for a man and his family. Dermot is not likely to give up Caitlin's dower lands, he's too greedy a bastard for that. If I give the manor to Caitlin as her dowry, you could marry, then no matter what may happen to you, she will have land of her own. The lands you will have from me in Ireland, if we are successful against O'Conor, will make you a man of some wealth."

For once Morgan was speechless.

"Well, what say you?"

"You would do that for me?"

"Could you give up Caitlin if I ordered it?"

"No."

"I didn't think so. Rather than have you dishonor your oaths to me, or make you an enemy, it seems a practical solution."

"Yes, I see. Eminently sensible. Good business."

"Yes."

Morgan laughed, the rich, melodious laugh that made even Richard's mouth turn up. "Then you'll marry the woman?"

"Yes, my lord. If you insist."

Mud sucked at their leather boots and rain cascaded from their heavy cloaks. As they came within sight of the bower, Ban leaped off the wooden porch and splashed through the rain and mud toward them, barking playfully. The door opened, and Eve and Caitlin stood framed there with smiles on their faces.

"It seems we're expected," Morgan said, reaching down to give the wet, muddy dog an affectionate rubbing around his neck and shoulders.

Richard smiled. It was good knowing she waited for him, his mysterious, passionate Eve. How had she worked her way so completely into his heart? If not for her he would leave this place, with its intrigues and its half-mad kings with their ancient grudges. Leave the wild, unpredictable people for the familiarity of Wales or his huge fief of Striguil. His English earldom covered over one hundred square miles along the Wye Estuary, with the castle of

Chepstow at its center. He could make a home there, with Eve and their children, far from all this. But she would never consent to leave. Ireland was in her blood. Ireland was her soul. And he was bound to her, forever.

Eve was in the bower, Ban, stretched before the fire, her only companion. She heard clearly the sounds of Richard's troops at their drills. Even in the rain and muck he insisted on the discipline of daily practice with sword and bow. He would not allow his men to grow flabby with inactivity, or have their skills degenerate from lack of use. The Irish looked askance at the constant marching. Autumn and winter were times to feast and be lazy. War was a spring and summer diversion.

Soon Richard would travel to Tara to exchange Egan for Rory O'Conor's son. Her brother showed a brave front, but she saw the fear lurking in his young eyes. How could their father be so selfish? So much could go wrong. It was unfair to use Egan as a pawn in Dermot's ambitious scheme. She had been his pawn as well, maneuvered and manipulated to his self-seeking ends. Inadvertently she had thwarted her father by marrying Richard. The irony of it did not escape her. She married reluctantly only to find her life would be hollow and incomplete without Richard.

Pulling her cloak closer around her shoulders, she bent toward the hearth. Despite the fire, the bower was cold and damp. Richard had told her tales of countries far away, where it was rarely cold and rain was a luxury. When her father was first forced out of Ireland, they had traveled to Aquitaine in search of the English king's help. It was summer, and Eve reveled in the hot, languid days, so unlike an Irish summer. Lands where every season was warm were beyond her experience. She was not sure if she believed Richard, and would like to see for herself such hot, dry lands. Even so, she knew it was Ireland that would claim her loyalty, no matter how beautiful or exotic another land might be.

"Move, you ugly beast." She gave Ban a gentle nudge with her toe. The big dog grunted but did not move. "You're useless. You know that, don't you?"

He opened an eye to look at her, then closed it again, settling his head resolutely on his forelegs. She shoved him more firmly this time, until he moved to a nearby rug of bear fur, then circled a few times and settled back to his nap.

Crouching, she placed some peat on the fire and watched as the blaze flared and tickled the new turves. Would Egan be warm this winter? Would Rory treat him unkindly, perhaps throw him into some dark, unheated cell, with moldy bread for his food? While it was dishonorable to treat hostages in such a manner, she knew it happened. How were they to know if Egan was treated roughly? Rory was a good man. She remembered that about him above all else. He was strong enough to show compassion.

Eve hardly knew her half-brother. They had been kept apart by Dervorgilla, and she could only guess at the lies his mother might have told the boy. Still, she was fond of her brother. How she wished she could be with Egan, to keep him safe, but she knew it to be a futile hope. She rose slowly. Mayhap there was a small thing she could do to give the boy some courage.

She crossed to the bedchamber and opened the largest of the clothes chests that sat against the wall. Within was a smaller wooden casket. Inside were the few pieces of jewelry she owned. She drew out a soft leather pouch, and, opening it, poured the contents into her outstretched palm. A gold cross on a chain gleamed in her hand. The cross was not overly large, but it was exquisitely made. So intricate and precise was the art of it, that it was hard to believe human hands had wrought the object. There were no jewels to mar the perfection of its gold surface, which only added to the refinement of its design.

Lorcan gave it to her last year. It had belonged to Gormflaith, one of Brian Boru's wives. It was said she had it from Brian himself. Fire-haired, half-Viking, half-pagan Gormflaith had been Brian's passion and his bane. She was too wild, too independent to be happy as any man's wife, even Brian's. He tamed an island and a people, becoming the first and most powerful Irish High King, but he never tamed Gormflaith. It was Gormflaith and Brian who were Eve's ancestors. A proud heritage, manifest in the gold that came untarnished through the centuries to lay in her hand.

Slipping the cross back into the bag of red leather, she attached it to her girdle. She locked the small chest and placed it in the bottom of the larger chest, then removed the light wool cloak that she wore while in the bower and put on a heavy outdoor mantle. "Ban, come. We have a message to deliver."

The dog came to her side, his tail wagging with anticipation, glad for any excuse to go on an adventure. She scratched his head. "Too bad I can't send you along with Egan. You'd keep him safe."

She looked down at the wolfhound, seeing him as others must. He was huge. His shoulders stood at her waist and his head came nearly to her chest. Though he was a friendly animal, a spoiled pet really, never used for the hunting of wolves, he was intimidating. And he was loyal. He would defend her to the death if anyone threatened her. Could that loyalty be transferred to Egan?

The rain fell in a steady drizzle as Eve made her way through the muddy streets, past the royal kitchen, through wet oak leaves, dodging horse and dog droppings, trying to keep the hem of her gown out of the mud. Dublin needed cobbled streets, like those she had seen in London and Rouen. A pile of waste lay rotting malodorously beside the kitchen, and pigs rooted in its reeky depths. The wet inevitably intensified the smell from the rows of privies. She had forgotten the stink of Dublin. The freshness of living in an army tent in the green fields was preferable in many ways, though a tent was no place to be in the winter.

There was a guard at Egan's door, but she was allowed in without an argument. Lorcan and Egan were bowed over a chess board before the fire. They looked up as she entered. Beside her, Ban shook vigorously, spraying everything within five feet with rain water. The odor of the wet dog was powerful in the small, warm room.

"Come here, boy," Egan said, smiling, and leaned forward, patting the side of his chair. Ban came to him for a thorough thumping of his chest and back, and made small, happy noises in the back of his throat. Eve watched them, and decided her plan might just work.

Pulling the wet hood of her cloak away from her face, she leaned down to place an affectionate kiss on Lorcan's cheek. "Why the guard?"

Lorcan glanced to where Egan and the dog played, then said in a low voice, "Dermot doesn't want Dervorgilla near the boy."

How odd, Eve thought, but refrained from saying more in front of Egan. She pointed to the chess board. "Who's winning?"

"Egan, as usual. I rarely beat him at chess, though his Latin grammar could use some work."

Egan made a face.

"My Latin was never good enough, either," Eve said, laughing at the memories. How patient Lorcan had been. Eventually she became proficient in Latin, as she had in the other languages he drilled into her, and learned to read in those languages as well. Removing her cloak, she laid it near the hearth to dry. "Egan, I've brought you something." She removed the leather pouch from her girdle.

Egan's eyes lighted with boyish delight. He made room for her on his chair, and Lorcan sat back to watch. She pulled the cross from its pouch, letting it hang from its chain. It caught light from the hearth fire and seemed to glow with a light of its own as it twisted slowly back and forth. Egan reached out to touch it, then drew his hand back.

"Take it. It's yours now."

He reached for it again, and this time held it in his small, sturdy hands, turning it this way and that to examine it more closely.

"It was a gift from Brian Boru to our ancestress Gorm-flaith."

"From Brian? And I'm to have it?" The boy's voice was filled with a reverent awe. The great Boru was held up as the best and brightest example of Irish manhood. Every boy dreamed of duplicating Brian's adventures, and his great-ness. Egan happily slipped the chain over his head. The cross lay on his chest, like a badge of honor.

"I've brought you something else as well, so you won't be alone when you stay with Rory."

She saw the quickly suppressed fear in his eyes. How could he not be afraid? He was about to be given over to the care of hostile strangers.

"What have you brought?" Egan asked.

"I'm sending Ban with you, to protect you and keep you from being lonely."

The boy scratched the dog sitting beside him with his big head leaning against Egan's shoulder. "But he's your dog, Eve. He won't come with me."

"We have six days before you leave for Tara. We're going to work together until Ban's comfortable obeying you. He'll go with you, when the time comes." She felt the back of her throat tighten. Ban had been her constant companion for five years. He knew all her secrets. Now she must send him away.

Egan hid the tears in his eyes by burying his face in Ban's shoulder and hugging the wet dog closer.

"It's a kind thing you do." Lorcan's voice was gentle and soothing. The look on his face told her he understood how difficult this would be for her, and she turned away from such warm sympathy.

"We have work to do. Egan, get your cloak."

Seventeen

Teamhair na Riogh. Tara of the Kings. Such a melancholy place, Richard thought, with the abandoned ring fort and halls slowly decaying back into the earth. Once the home of pagan kings, now crusted with memories of past glory, Tara was the dwelling of feral creatures, cursed by the Irish saints. It was almost two hundred years since a High King sat on Tara's throne. A tawny-eyed fox ran low along the base of a hill, sneaking into the cover of tall gorse. In an abandoned building a rookery was in turbulent residence, the raucous birds ragged and unfinished looking in comparison to their larger, sleeker cousins the ravens.

They had arrived yesterday, and today expected Rory O'Conor to appear with his son. The sky was still gray, and the sun, just below the horizon, tinted the edges of the clouds pink and gold as he walked toward the highest part of the ancient settlement. He felt tremendously alone in this eerie world, waiting. Waiting for what he could not express. Something more than Rory and their encounter this day. He had been restless for weeks now, with a vague, unnamed longing.

Eve wanted to come with him but he forbade it. She was still too recently risen from her sickbed and he could not guarantee her safety here. He did not know if either Rory or Dermot meant some treachery, and so spent a sleepless night, tossing in the dark in an abandoned barn. For once there was no rain, which was fortunate, since the roof of the barn was partly rotted, and what was left of the thatch infested with spiders and mice. He spent most of the night staring at the stars, waiting for dawn.

Ban followed as Richard climbed toward the summit. The wolfhound chased some small creature through the damp grasses. Richard recognized the sacrifice Eve made in sending the dog, though she never said a word. That was typical of her, to do what had to be done without fuss.

Richard reached the crest of Tara Hill, and his heart filled with wonder. Ireland spread her gifts before him like a wanton, careless with her extravagant beauty. This wet island, dreaming under her shroud of autumn rain and mist, with silver rivers embroidering green valleys, opened her secrets to him, laying herself bare and vulnerable beneath his gaze. The proud blue hills were oddly ethereal, like a mirage shimmering around him. Ireland enticed him with a siren call that roused in him a hunger as strong as any he had known, save that which he felt for Eve.

In some mysterious way he could not explain, which he had stopped fighting or trying to understand on any rational level, Ireland was growing in his soul. A profound peace filled him. At last he knew where the strange restlessness of the past weeks originated. It was the tune Ireland sang to his soul. On the mystery that was Tara he gave in to the seduction. He knew his destiny. Eve—and Ireland.

Ban raised his head and barked. Richard glanced over his shoulder to see sleepy-eyed Morgan making his way up the hill toward them. He turned back to watch the brightening horizon. Morgan soon stood beside him, and was silent for several minutes, watching with him as the sun gilded the edge of the world with glory.

"You're up early," the Welshman said. "Are you as worried about this as I?"

Richard clasped his hands behind his back and stood with one knee slightly bent, his weight more on the other leg. He let out a long, frustrated sigh. "I never know what to expect with Dermot. He may plan to slaughter O'Conor, and what O'Conor means to do I can only guess."

"No one can approach Tara without being seen. Dermot has five men with him, including us. Even if he wanted to ambush Rory, he doesn't have the manpower."

"All he needs is one strategically placed archer."

"Then we had better be sure Rory is well guarded when he is out in the open."

Richard laughed, a short, sarcastic sound. "As usual, we must protect Dermot from himself. He is quick-tempered and vengeful, and as ambitious and selfish a man as I've ever had the displeasure of knowing. How did he manage to breed a daughter of such passionate courage? God, Morgan, Eve should have been born a man, to rule after Dermot. She would make a damned fine king."

"Richard, I do believe you've fallen in love with your wife."

The earl looked down at the shorter man, whose dark eyes were alight with barely suppressed mirth. "That I have, my friend, just as you told me I should." He loved Eve more than he thought possible. It frightened him. He had never had so much to lose.

Ban barked, head and hackles up. From the direction of the River Boyne rode a small party of men. Richard scanned the countryside uneasily, but could see no one else in the clear dawn.

The sky grew steadily lighter as they waited. The bird chorus, always at its loudest just before dawn, hushed into quieter melody. Ban ceased barking and sat beside Richard and Morgan, waiting with them as the horsemen drew nearer and finally began the ascent up Tara. There were six in all. At their head rode a man of middle years, with pale hair and cold, clear eyes. His beard was braided with gold bells and filigree balls, as was his flowing hair, and he wore the ornate cloak of Irish royalty. The scarlet bridle of his white stallion was hung with bells of silver.

So this is Rory O'Conor, High King of Ireland. Richard could not help but compare him to the kings, emperors, and dukes he had met while fighting King Henry's wars. While O'Conor had a commanding presence, he was not as majestic as those other princes. Perhaps it was because Richard was accustomed to knights, fully armed and armored, on their large war-horses, that the Irish seemed so insignificant.

These Celts wore no armor except an occasional hauberk of boiled hide. Their horses were small, shaggy beasts compared to the large destriers of Richard's knights. The Irish used short bows and swords, while Richard's men used the superior weapon, the longbow, with deadly efficiency. It would help compensate for their fewer numbers in the inevitable battle with O'Conor. As a mark of bravery, Irish warriors fought from the backs of wicker chariots, and took pride in their considerable skill with those awkward vehicles. The chariots were no match for Richard's mounted knights, just as no army could match the skill of his longbowmen. The Irish would fall in glory, but they would fall.

Richard was not so arrogant he thought the Irish were not a formidable foe. Any man fighting for his own land was not to be underestimated. The sheer numbers Rory could call to his banner was enough to make any man with sense more than a little nervous. It was why Richard had besieged Drogheda when he first arrived, hoping to force Rory into surrender before the Irish king had time to gather thousands of disaffected Irishmen. Now the man had all winter to recruit an army, thanks to Dermot. Richard preferred negotiation to battle. There was no glory in the loss of good men, on either side of an argument. If this truce could effect a real treaty, then Dermot's rash plan could be made to work to their good.

Beside Rory rode a boy of perhaps fourteen years, as fair as his father. The youth's mouth was set in an angry, rebellious line. It would seem he came grudgingly to fill his father's pledge, and Richard knew there would be trouble with the lad if he approached this with defiance in his heart and contempt in his mind.

Richard turned to Morgan and said, "We'd better wake Dermot. His guests have arrived."

The fire in the hearth lighted the bower with a ruddy glow. Moving her chair closer to the warmth, Eve stretched her bare toes toward the heat. Caitlin leaned back lazily in her chair, staring at the fire with a dreamy look on her face. The flagon of wine on the small table between them was nearly empty. Eve held her silver goblet in both hands, warming the wine that tasted of the sunshine of France. With the steady beat of the rain on the thatch, she dreamed of those long, hot days of summer in Aquitaine, when she accompanied her father on his search for King Henry. Richard and Morgan were at Tara and would not return until tomorrow. She was content to sit before the small fire and drink the good wine.

At Christmas, Caitlin was to wed Morgan, and Eve had never seen her cousin so happy, with an almost delirious joy. She was going to enjoy the busy nuptial preparations. It would keep her from thinking too much about Egan. Try as she might, there was a sharp edge of worry in a corner of her heart that the wine could only dull.

"What is it like?" Caitlin asked.

"What is what like?" Eve took a small sip of wine, enjoying the way it slipped down her throat and warmed her blood.

Caitlin glanced at Eve through fluttering eyelashes. Placing a hand to her breast, she said in a low, husky voice, "The loss of one's virginity."

Eve giggled, then sobered at the indignant look on her cousin's face. She blushed and looked into the fire. "It's nice."

"Nice? Is that all you can say? I want details, woman.

I've seen the way you look at Richard, the way he caresses you when he thinks no one is near. It's more than nice and I want to know about it. I don't want to come to Morgan frightened and ignorant."

"The unfamiliarity is part of the fun. Morgan will teach you so many wonderful things. It's like when you touch yourself, only better. Much better. It's wonderful and a little frightening."

"I knew it. What all the old women say is true, it's painful, isn't it?"

Eve shook her head and took a larger sip of wine. "A little, at first. If the man is gentle and takes his time with you, the pain is quick. There's so much more than just bedding, if you love the man. It's frightening what it does to your heart."

The fire flared as it rose to consume an untouched turf of peat. Their passion for each other was like that, Eve thought, like peat consumed by fire, reduced to ash, transfigured by the flame. "Love complicates everything. I'm vulnerable now in a way I never was before."

"You were lonely before," Caitlin said.

"So lonely I thought I would die. This is a different pain. I don't think I could survive without Richard. I fear most things worth having come with a measure of pain and sorrow."

They were silent, watching the fire, listening to the soft flame and the sound of the wind outside, mourning in the night. Eve felt stronger every day. Now all she needed was to convince Richard it was safe for him to come back to their bed. Since her illness he'd slept in the barracks with his men. He apparently feared she was too weak for his lovemaking, so he treated her like a piece of delicate glass, set upon a shelf to look at and enjoy but too fragile to use. She would put an end to that nonsense, and soon.

Eve noticed a cold draft, and, glancing over her shoulder, saw Richard and Morgan standing in the open doorway.

Caitlin jumped from her seat and rushed into Morgan's eager arms.

"We didn't think to see you until tomorrow." Eve placed her goblet on the table beside her chair.

Richard closed the door and came into the room. He smelled of wet wool, and Eve went to take his damp cloak from him. "We decided to come ahead of Dermot. There was no reason to linger at Tara. O'Conor has gone back to Tiernan's stronghold at Drogheda. I don't like that he's a one day march from Dublin, but this truce should keep him from mischief."

"How did Egan look to you when he left?" Eve asked.

"He's a brave boy. You'd have been proud of him." Richard wrapped an arm around her shoulder and drew her near, dropping a kiss on the top of her head. "Ban went with him as though they were litter mates."

"What of Rory's son?" Caitlin asked. She stood with her back against Morgan's chest, his arms crossed in front of her.

"A sullen, disagreeable lad," Morgan said. "We'll give him some honest hard work to do. That'll keep his mind off his troubles."

Caitlin yawned, a huge, face-breaking yawn. "Oh, it's late. We should be going."

Eve could hardly keep from laughing. When had her ingenuous cousin learned such things? Caitlin was no more tired now than she had been a few minutes ago, when she was bubbling with enthusiasm and fun. She wanted to be alone with Morgan. Eve knew just how she felt. "Yes, it's very late. Now, where did you leave your cloak?"

"There, near my chair."

Eve retrieved the cloak and watched as Morgan gently settled it around Caitlin's shoulders. They left quickly, both eager to be gone. The fire had burned down to embers, and Eve carefully gathered the glowing peat into a small pile on the hearth and covered it with the clay fire keeper. Standing, she turned to Richard and held out her hand. "Come to bed. It grows cold in here." He looked at her with those beautiful gray eyes, the dark lashes framing them like wings, and she saw longing in their depths.

"Are you sure?"

"Very sure."

The bedchamber was dark, and she lighted the oil lamp that stood on the shelf beside the bed. It was colder in here, though the window was tightly shuttered. Stripping out of her gown and the thin chemise beneath, she heard him undressing behind her. Such masculine sounds, the chink of his sword as he unbuckled the belt from his slim waist, the soft jingle of chain mail. She climbed into bed and snuggled the wool blankets over her naked shoulders.

Richard yanked his linen shirt over his head. She enjoyed watching the muscles in his back move as he undressed. When he turned toward her, she saw the soft mat of brown hair on his chest and where it plunged to a single line down his belly, until it flared again around his sex, which stood proud and eager in the faint light of the lamp. Such an adamant appendage, almost with a mind of its own, and such wonderful things it could do.

Then he was striding toward the bed, a crooked, licentious grin on his lips. He loomed over her like some hulking beast, his shoulders hunched forward and his arms stretched over her. With a growl of pure pleasure, he jumped into bed, rolling her into his arms, blankets and all, until they were hopelessly tangled together. She shrieked at his silliness, and laughed until tears sprang from her eyes.

She found herself perched on top of him, with her hair like a veil around them. His hand smoothed her hair back, and rounded on her shoulder, stroking slowly in hot circles, sliding down her arm, her back, to her thighs.

The laughter left his eyes as he reached up and pulled her closer. "God, how I missed you." He kissed her throat, leaving desire in his wake.

"I missed you." She traced a finger down his chin, then reared back and stared at him. "Are you growing a beard?"

His laugh was a rumble, deep in his chest. "Don't you like it? You badgered me about it long enough."

"I did no such thing."

"What a fickle wife you are. Don't look so shocked, it's only hair."

Laying her head on his chest, she snuggled closer. A Norman with a beard. She never thought to see the day. Smiling, she slowly moved her hand lower on his body, teasing as she went. His breathing quickened as her hand closed over his hard, soft-skinned penis. He trembled at her touch, and his hands, calloused but incredibly gentle, fanned out on her buttocks and pulled her close against his body. *What a wonder this man is. Hard muscle and soft skin, strength and tenderness. He is needy and vulnerable and generous all at once.*

She straddled him and guided his eager rod into that warm place that wanted him with a burning urgency. Slowly, he pushed her up and down the long hard length of him until she throbbed with desire.

How cleverly her body was made to receive other people in it. First the man, then the child, in a cycle no less miraculous for being universal. She reveled in the earthiness of it, voluptuous and hot with their unruly loving.

She breathed in the odor of him, all man, lusty and primal. Greedy for him, wanting more, she thrust against him until she was filled with his largeness. It was so good, him deep inside her, as close as they could get to each other, until they were one creature made of fire.

"Eve." It was a hoarse whisper against her ear. "Ah, love. My sweet love." He spilled his seed in her with a trembling gasping urgency.

The extraordinary passion he excited in her crested and broke, leaving her in awe at the magic they conjured. She collapsed on top of him, her heart beating hard, matching his as their life blood pounded against each other. Gradually their breathing slowed to normal. When the air grew cold against their glistening bodies, Richard pulled the warm blankets over their nakedness. She folded herself against him, her head on his chest, one leg thrown over his waist, heavy with sleep.

What did he call her? His sweet love. She burrowed more securely against him as a tear of joy slipped from her eye.

Eighteen

"I've work to do, Husband." Eve tried to push Richard's eager hands away from her breasts. After laying together the night before and twice this morning, desire flared anew in her at his touch. "You're insatiable."

"And you're not?" He pulled her close to his chest.

"Have mercy, Richard. We don't have time."

He kissed her throat.

"Richard, I'm serious. It's near noon. There are people waiting for me at the infirmary."

He swept her up and carried her to the bedchamber.

"I swear if you don't let me go, I'll—"

"You'll what, sweet wife? Refuse to come to my bed?"

He lowered her gently to the bed, then lay beside her. His hands roamed up her legs, teasing. His tongue trailed flame down her throat. She relaxed under his touch, her body opening to him as inevitably as a flower to the sun. Richard chuckled and began to unlace her gown.

"You think you're so clever." She undid the buckle of his belt.

"Nay, I'm not at fault. It is you who have ensnared me, you're to blame, woman."

"And will you punish me?"

He pulled his linen shirt over his head and leered down at her. "That I will. You're going to be in this bed another hour or more. That will teach you not to flaunt yourself before me."

"Flaunt? I was fully dressed and on my way out the door. You do seem to see things in a—"

"Be quiet, woman." He stopped her words with a kiss.

"Where have you been?" Caitlin barely glanced up from the boy she was examining as Eve rushed into the infirmary. A woman in the simple dress of a peasant sat silently near the boy.

"I was detained."

Caitlin straightened and looked at her more closely then grinned. "I see."

"It's not what you think."

"No, of course not. You had much to discuss with your husband this morning, no doubt."

Eve slipped out of her cloak and adjusted a clean apron over her gown, ignoring her cousin. "What do we have here?" She squatted next to the boy. "What's your name?"

The boy kept his mouth shut, his blue eyes full of uncertainty.

"His name be Bryan. Answer the lady when she speaks at ye." The woman gave a small tap to the boy's head.

"Are you Bryan's mother?"

"Aye, who else would take the time to bring 'im? What he's got I don't want him to be givin' to the others. Have ye ever had eight snot-nosed boys to care for all atta same time?"

Eve shook her head and tried not to smile. "No, I can't say that I have. Can you tell me what's wrong with Bryan?"

"He's been puking all night." The woman picked at a scab on her thumb. "Aye, well, he's less trouble than most his brothers. Bryan's me youngest. I always hoped for a girl, to help with the work, but all I get is boys. Bryan's the best of 'em."

"When was the last time he vomited?" Eve placed her

hand on the boy's forehead, then on the back of his neck. He was a bit warm but nothing serious.

"Eh? What's 'at mean, vom—vomi—"

"When did he last puke?"

"Why did'na ye say so, lass? Tossed his guts up less than an hour gone. Been doin' it all night."

"How old are you, Bryan?" Eve asked.

He held up six fingers. "Really, that old? I don't believe it. Prove to me how strong you are." She held her hands before him, palms toward the child. "Go on, push as hard as you can."

The boy pushed with all his small strength, and Eve was satisfied. Whatever was wrong, it had not weakened him. "My, you are strong. I would think you were eight at least."

Bryan beamed up at her, revealing the gap where his front teeth would soon grow in.

"Has he eaten the same things as everybody else in the family?"

"Far as I know. Where else would he be gettin' food? The boy don't thief, if that's what ye be after."

Bryan had his head tucked so far down against his chest, and he blushed so furious a red, Eve knew he was suffering some sort of guilt. She stood and placed a hand on the mother's shoulder. "Why don't you wait outside while I examine the child?"

Suspicion jumped to life in her eyes. "What ye goin' to do to me boy?"

"I won't hurt him, I promise. If you go to the abbey kitchen, I'm sure there will be a cup of mead for you."

The mother ruffled her son's hair affectionately. "Aye, well, then, I'll not be gone long." The woman closed the door with a bang as she left.

"Caitlin, will you please prepare a small pouch of crushed basil?"

"Is that a cure for the vomiting?" Caitlin searched

through the shelves that held Eve's simples until she found the correct jar.

"If the affliction is a light one, it can help. It's more for the boy's mother than for Bryan."

"You want his mother to eat it?"

Eve laughed. "No. She's to make a weak tisane and give it to Bryan for the next few days. It can't hurt the boy and it will give her a reason to pamper him. That will be better for the child than any dose I give." She squatted down beside the boy again. He had a thumb firmly in residence in his mouth. "Do you need to puke now?"

He shook his head and looked down at his feet. Eve placed a finger under his chin and lifted his head. "Bryan, your mother isn't here and I promise not to tell her anything you say to me. Do you understand?"

He nodded his head once.

"You must tell me what you ate yesterday that your mother doesn't know of."

His mouth opened and incredulous blue eyes looked up at her with disbelief. "How'd ye know?"

"Just tell me so I'll know how serious your sickness is."

"Apples."

"But the apples are just beginning to ripen. Do you mean you ate green apples?"

"Aye, Dolan made me do it, he said he'd hit me if I didna."

"Who is this bully?" Eve imagined some loutish child, much older than Bryan, terrorizing the boy. No wonder he didn't want his mother to know.

"Dolan's no bully, he's me brother."

"I see. Is he much larger than you?"

"Aye, he's nine."

"Now you know what happens when you eat too many green apples. You'll not do that again, will you, Bryan?"

"God's guts, no. I don't like the pukin'."

The boy's mother returned, and Eve gave her instructions

on what to do with the basil. She watched as they left, the little boy holding his mother's strong hand while she scolded him affectionately. There was one person waiting on the bench in the small hallway outside the infirmary, a young woman with rosy cheeks and wide gray eyes. She was dressed in the colors of an Irish noble, and Eve was surprised to see someone of her rank. Most of her patients were among the poorest folk of Dublin. Eve smiled and signaled the woman to follow her into the abbey.

The woman was tall and slim and walked with a winsome grace. Her light-brown hair framed a delicate face and flowed in heavy braids down to her thighs. "I'm Maeve, wife of Brendan O'Rourke." She looked as though she expected Eve to be offended by the name. Her husband must be some sort of kin to Tiernan O'Rourke. All Eve cared about was what brought Maeve here.

"Welcome, Lady O'Rourke. What may we help you with?"

Maeve looked from Caitlin to Eve, and seeing no rejection or judgment in either of them, visibly relaxed. "I need to know if I'm pregnant."

Eve gestured for her to sit on the edge of a nearby bed and pulled up a chair to sit beside her. "Do you want to be pregnant?"

"Oh, yes. More than anything."

Eve smiled. More often than not, she had women in who dreaded another pregnancy and wished nothing so much as to end it. "Tell me why you think you may be carrying a child."

The woman listed a litany of symptoms common to early pregnancy. Eve had her strip down to her linen undertunic and lie on the bed. "I'm going to examine you, Maeve, but in truth I will be very surprised to find you are not expecting." The area around Maeve's nipples had darkened and her breasts were tender. Eve very gently spread Maeve's thighs so she could look at the woman's private parts. They, too, had darkened to the unmistakable color of a woman with child. Eve had her sit up. "You are pregnant, there is no doubt in my mind. When were your last courses?"

Maeve grinned happily, her eyes bright with tears. "Seven or eight weeks, I'm not altogether sure."

"Then I would guess you'll have this child sometime between late April and early June."

"I will pray for you." Caitlin smiled and placed a hand on Maeve's shoulder. "You are blessed. I hope my husband and I will soon know the same happiness."

"My child can have no greater gift than good folks' prayers. I thank you."

"Get dressed and go tell your husband the happy news." Eve stood just as the door to the infirmary was roughly pushed open. She whirled to see Gui Beaumont clutching one arm, blood seeping between his fingers.

"I've had an accident on the drill field. I need stitches."

"If you're not bleeding to death, wait outside." Eve tried to keep the anger from her voice.

Gui smiled and closed the door with his foot. "I rather think not."

"I have someone here. You must wait until I'm done." Eve tried to shield Maeve from Gui's eyes. The poor woman was still clad in her thin undertunic.

Gui stretched to look over Eve's shoulder. "The peasant can wait. My arm needs attention now." He walked across the room, and his smile grew as he saw more of Maeve. "The wench is a beauty, I'll give her that. Ask how much she charges."

They spoke in French, since Gui had no understanding of Irish. Luckily Maeve could not understand a word of it. Eve clamped down hard on her anger and sudden fear. The man was predatory in a cold, calculated way, so arrogant it never occurred to him Maeve was anything but what his bigotry perceived her to be. Eve turned to Caitlin and Maeve and spoke as calmly as she could, in Irish so Gui would not know what was said. "I fear this man may be dangerous. Cait, I want you and Maeve to leave by the far door. Even such as he will not follow you into the abbey cloister. Don't bother to dress. Take your things and go, quickly."

"I don't want to leave you alone," Caitlin protested.

"I'm Richard's wife. Gui would not dare hurt me. Go quickly, before he knows what you intend."

Caitlin grabbed Maeve's hand and hurried toward the heavy door that led into the nuns' cloister. No man was allowed within, not even the pope, without Abbess Ancilla's permission.

Gui lunged after the two women. When he reached the door he found it was locked. He turned furiously on Eve. "You meddlesome Irish slut, how dare you defy me! I want that woman and you know it."

"The woman is married to an Irish noble. She doesn't have a price. She isn't available to you."

"Don't be tiresome, woman. You're de Clare's wife and I'll do nothing to displease him where you are concerned, but no such restraint holds true for any other Irish peasant I want. Do you understand me?" He towered over her, his handsome face distorted by anger.

Eve feared she understood him only too well. In Gui's mind all Irishwomen were lowly and unimportant, to be used as he pleased. "You cannot frighten me," she lied, holding her hands tightly together to keep them from shaking. "You'll curb your appetites while in my land, or I'll send you back to Wales."

He laughed. "Do not think to threaten me. You forget I am your husband's cousin. He'll not raise a hand against his kin."

"And I am his wife. Who do you think he will believe, you or me?"

"Why, me, of course. What an absurd question. Save for the land and the heirs you'll bring to Richard, you're of no consequence. He'd mate with a sow if he thought it would bring him land. All of us in the family know how deeply devoted Richard is to his fair Rosamund. No woman, most especially no Irishwoman, can ever take her place in Richard's heart."

He is lying. I don't believe him. Gui's cruel words sent a sliver of doubt through Eve's heart. "Get out."

"My wound still needs tending." Gui rolled back the arm of his tunic as he approached her.

She hated to touch him, but it seemed he would not leave until she looked at the wound. The cut was not deep, and the bleeding had all but stopped. It didn't need stitching. If he kept it tightly bandaged for two or three weeks, it would heal well enough. She looked up to see his face distorted with lust.

Eve took a step back. He grabbed her and pulled her up roughly against his chest. As his face lowered toward her, she struggled to free herself. He held her head still and forced her lips apart. His tongue invaded her mouth, and Eve feared she would be sick. How dare he assault her?

"Enough. Get your filthy hands off the princess!"

Gui jerked away at the unexpected shout, and Eve quickly retreated to Mother Ancilla's side.

Gui smiled as he ignored the nun and spoke to Eve. "You enjoyed that as much as I."

Eve wiped the back of her hand across her mouth, her voice full of loathing. "You're mad to think so. I find you repulsive."

"Woman, you do lie badly."

"Enough, both of you," the abbess said, pushing Eve behind the protective bulk of her body. "You will leave. Now."

The tall knight looked at the nun with unconcealed contempt. "I've come to have my arm stitched. I'm staying until it is done."

The abbess turned to Eve and asked in Irish, "Does his arm need to be sewn?"

"No. It should heal if well bandaged."

"We'll see about that." Abbess Ancilla lumbered over to the knight and none too gently took his injured arm in her large hands. She turned the arm this way and that, poking and prodding. Gui squirmed but made no sound at the pain she caused.

With a look of pious innocence, the nun smiled at Gui. "I fear you do indeed need stitches. Twenty, mayhap thirty or more. It's a terrible nasty cut you have. Eve, bring me thread and a needle."

Nineteen

"Eve, my love." Richard's hard body lay curled along her back, one hand resting on her belly, protectively.

She snuggled closer and sighed as he planted tender kisses on her shoulder and the back of her neck. As usual, she was sleepy in the aftermath of their loving, and the warm comfort of the bed added to her languor. She had grown accustomed to this small ritual of Richard holding her in his arms as they fell asleep. She dreaded when he would next go to battle and she must sleep alone. The bed would seem large and lonely without him.

They bolted upright, startled by the loud pounding on the door of the outer chamber. "Jesu, they're loud enough to wake the dead." Richard crawled out of bed and threw a cloak over his nakedness before stalking to the door. The pounding continued. "Stop that racket!" Richard shouted as he pulled the door open.

From the bedchamber Eve could not see who stood at the door, nor hear the words they spoke, but she knew it was a man and that he spoke Irish. She slipped into her chemise and pulled on a cloak as she hurried into the outer chamber.

No anger showed on Richard's face. Instead, he looked concerned and frustrated. "I can't understand what he's saying, but they need help. It's you they've come for."

Puzzled, Eve pushed past Richard. On the porch stood a young man with an unconscious woman in his arms. "Bring her in, quickly. Richard, pull the blankets from the bed and light a lamp. I must have light to see her injuries."

Richard hurried to do her bidding as the man followed on her heels. "Lay her on the bed, gently now," Eve said.

A moan escaped the woman. She was alive. "Richard, bring that lamp closer."

Richard held the lamp so that the woman's features were illuminated, and Eve snapped upright with a startled gasp.

"Do you know her?" Richard asked.

"She came to me three days gone to have me confirm her pregnancy. Good God, look at her Richard. She's been beaten, and savagely." Eve turned her attention to the man who stood on the opposite side of the bed, clinging to one of Maeve's hands. "Are you Brendan O'Rourke?"

He looked at her with anguished eyes. "That I am. Will you help my sweet Maeve? Merciful Christ, don't let her die."

"I'll do what I can. I need to undress her to examine her."

Brendan cast suspicious eyes at Richard.

"This is no time for false modesty, O'Rourke. Help me get your lady out of her clothes."

Bruises covered most of Maeve's delicate body, one arm was broken, her face was swollen almost beyond recognition, and there were cuts on her mouth where a fist had slammed into her lips. Eve had never seen so savage a beating. Then she saw the bite marks, unmistakably human, on Maeve's breasts and her anger leaped higher. From Maeve's harsh, painful breathing Eve feared there was internal damage, broken ribs, perhaps a punctured lung, what else she could not be sure. But she did know Maeve was dying.

"Give the lamp to Brendan." When Richard had done so, she moved to examine Maeve's battered body more closely. "Hold it close, Brendan, and keep it steady if you can." The man nodded, his mouth set in a grim line. Eve gently pulled Maeve's thighs apart. Blood flowed from between Maeve's legs. The miscarriage was unmistakable, but that wasn't what she looked for.

"Was she raped?" Brendan's voice was low and vicious.

Eve nodded. Brutally, fiercely raped, until she was torn and raw. What sort of animal did this? She covered Maeve's bruised body with a blanket.

"There is naught I can do for her, Brendan O'Rourke." The words as she spoke them tore her heart with anger and despair.

Brendan bent over his wife, holding her hand to his cheek. "She is dying? My sweet Maeve?"

Eve nodded her head, not trusting herself to speak.

Richard placed a hand on Eve's shoulder. "God in heaven, who would do such a monstrous thing?"

Eve could only shake her head and lean against his chest, seeking comfort there. This was the worst of it, when people died and she could do nothing to prevent it, nothing to ease the pain.

Brendan whispered to his wife, words full of anguished pleading. "Don't leave me, love . . . can't live without you. You're my life, my heart." He sobbed through the words, and brushed the hair back from his wife's face. Tears coursed down Maeve's cheeks, to mingle with Brendan's. "I love you." The words were torn from her injured throat and mouth.

Standing beside the dying woman, Eve bent down and spoke softly. "Who did this to you, Maeve?"

At first Eve could not understand the word forced painfully from Maeve's battered mouth. Then it was clear. "Gui," Maeve whispered.

"I'll send for a priest," Richard said. He left the chamber quietly.

Eve settled on her knees to pray. It was all she could do to help Maeve now, but her anger climbed with each labored breath the young woman dragged into her lungs. Gui Beaumont would hang for this.

Brendan's sobs had quieted to silent tears of misery.

The priest came but offered little comfort. Maeve was unable to give a confession, so did not receive the Church's final sacrament of grace to ease her into heaven. Richard joined them in prayer, his closeness a comfort to Eve. Maeve's breathing became more labored, there was more time between each painful episode. Finally, the terrible struggle stopped. Looking up, Eve saw Brendan staring at her with eyes so full of suffering it tore anew at her heart.

"Who is this Gui?" Brendan asked.

"The earl's cousin, Gui Beaumont," Eve said, wearily. They spoke Irish, but Richard could not mistake the name.

"What of Gui? What does he have to do with this?" Richard asked.

She rose slowly and waited until Richard stood beside her. "Gui Beaumont must be executed." Her voice was flat and hard. "That animal you call cousin raped and killed Maeve and the child she carried."

Richard frowned and was silent for a moment. "What makes you think it was Gui?"

"Brendan and I heard it from her mouth. What more could you want?"

"The woman was in pain and could easily have been confused. There's no proof it was Gui. God, Eve, he's my cousin. I've never much liked the man, but I can't believe him capable of such viciousness."

Why was Richard arguing with her? She tried to still the flutter of apprehension in the pit of her stomach. "What will you do to punish Gui?"

Richard plowed his hands through his hair. "I can't punish him, not without more evidence. Maeve's word doesn't convict Gui."

"Why not? Because she's a woman, because she is Irish? Or both?"

"I can't hang one of my men over something I can't prove. I need the loyalty of my knights. All of them. If I punish one over his treatment of an Irishwoman, I risk alienating the others."

Eve could not believe the words coming from his mouth. Her fear turned icy, the pain of his betrayal so deep she could not bear to examine it. "Do you hear yourself, Richard? Hanging Beaumont will not compensate Brendan O'Rourke for the loss of his wife and child, nothing can, but it would be justice. The man must be executed. Irish Law of the Innocents demands his death."

"Dammit, Eve, my knights are not subject to Irish law. That was not in our agreement."

"You will do nothing?"

"There is naught I can do without angering my men."

"What of the Irish people? Do you think if Gui goes unpunished you win their favor? You promised to rule Ireland by Irish law. You promised to bring peace. What you do now breaks both of those promises."

Richard's voice was angry. "God's blood, Eve, you put me in an impossible position. I promised to rule the Irish people by Irish law. Gui doesn't come under that promise."

"Have you no compassion? Look what your cousin has done." She stepped aside so Richard had a better view of Maeve. "Does this woman's life mean nothing to you? Is she no more than a dog in your sight?"

"Of course not, you know me better than that."

"I thought I did. What if someone did that to me, Richard? Would you be satisfied to see him go free?"

Richard's mouth set in a grim line. He looked at Maeve and slowly, sadly shook his head. "No. I'd kill the bastard with my own hands, no matter what the law said. But I can't allow my emotions to dictate how I rule. That is what law is for, to keep people from acting out their hatreds. I will do all I can to punish Gui, but it will be under English law."

Brendan stood at the foot of the bed, without tears, his

face angry and determined. "When will de Clare hang the man? I want to be there."

She and Richard spoke in French, and Brendan had not understood a word of their argument. Eve confronted Richard, who had retreated to the shadows beyond the lantern light. "He wants to know when Gui will hang."

Richard turned tortured eyes on her. "I can't."

"That is the answer I give this man?"

Richard nodded and turned aside.

When Eve spoke to Brendan, the bitterness and anger in her voice were unmistakable. "Under English law the earl cannot punish Gui Beaumont for his crime without more evidence. Maeve's word means nothing."

Brendan stared at her, the muscles in his jaw clenching around his anger. "I don't know what English law has to do with this, but Gui Beaumont is a dead man."

She stood silently as Brendan stormed from the chamber, was silent after the outer door slammed shut. Finally, with immense weariness she turned back to Richard. "If you fail to do justice in this, I will divorce you." Her heart felt as though it had been ripped from her body.

His eyes filled with disbelief. "You don't mean that. Do your claims of love mean nothing? Were you deceiving me all this time?"

She could not look at him, his voice was so full of pain. "Love has naught to do with this. You've broken your word. The one thing I asked of you, to rule my people by Irish law, you fail to do. That renders our vows to each other meaningless." Walking to the bed, Eve placed a gentle hand over Maeve's eyelids and closed them for a final time. "I'll have the nuns from St. Brigid's collect Maeve's body. For now I need water and cloths to clean her."

"Eve, you must listen to me. We can't—"

"No. There is nothing you can say. When I am finished here, I will be leaving you."

"This is madness! Where will you go?"

"To the nuns' abbey for now. In a few days I'll choose a more distant monastery. One thing more. I will undergo an honor fast until you see justice done."

Richard looked so stricken she felt her resolve weakening. How was she to live without this man? She turned her back on him.

"I'll send the abbess to you." He left the bower without another word.

When she heard the door close, Eve collapsed to her knees and buried her face in her hands, trying to close her heart against the overwhelming pain. Why had she trusted Richard to keep his word? He was the same as any man, quick to promise whatever he thought could get him what he wanted. The idea of leaving him made her sick. God help her, she loved the man so much she wasn't sure she could endure without him. Why was he more concerned about retaining the loyalty of his men than seeing justice done? Such a man was not an acceptable ruler for Leinster. She was still sobbing when the abbess and five nuns walked in.

Richard sat in the dark before the cold hearth. He had no wish to sleep in the empty bed. He was by turns angry and frightened. Angry that Eve was so uncompromising, so stubborn. Frightened that she might leave him, as she threatened. He could not bring himself to believe it. His life would be meaningless without her. But damn the woman, he could not do other than what he told her.

Richard groaned and buried his face in his hands. *It's an impossible judgment. Rule by English law and I lose my wife. Punish by Irish law and my men will hate me. Damn Gui to hell. I'd kill him myself given the chance. The man is a fiend and deserves death. I've no doubt he did as Maeve accused him, I know the man too well not to believe her. Without proof what can I do? I can't let Maeve's murder go unpunished. Eve is right. Justice must be done. But where is justice?*

He sat for hours, going over and over in his mind what he should do. He wouldn't lose Eve, but neither would he cave in to her demands. She was being unreasonable. How could he reconcile English and Irish law and do justice to either? There had to be some middle ground, some agreement they could both live with.

Near dawn there was a knock at his door. When Richard opened it, he found Morgan. By the look of the younger man, something disturbing had happened.

"What?" Richard asked

"Your cousin, Gui Beaumont, is dead."

"Did they catch the man who did it?"

"Jesu, Richard, how do you know it was murder? Gui was killed sometime last night, and his brothers found him only minutes ago. The killer is an Irishman. He's asked for sanctuary at Christ Church and Lorcan has granted it."

Richard was not surprised. He should have known Brendan would exact his own justice, and in truth he could not blame the man. He would have done the same, if Eve died so horribly. Unfortunately, though Brendan's action was understandable, it could not be ignored. Richard's men would expect him to execute Brendan, and that he did not wish to do. What an ungodly mess. What was he to do now?

"The Beaumont brothers and many of your knights have gathered before the church. They are demanding the man's release."

Richard cinched the sword belt around his waist. "We'd best calm the fools, before someone is hurt."

Richard and Morgan pushed through the crowd gathered near the church. The mood was ugly, armed knights shouting their rage. There were no Irish folk in sight.

"I demand you release my brother's killer." Alexander Beaumont towered over Archbishop Lorcan, shouting at the priest on the threshold of the cathedral.

"The man has sought and been given sanctuary. I'll not give him over to you and your bloodthirsty comrades until his case has been heard."

"What case, old man? By seeking sanctuary, he proves his guilt. Hanging is too good for him."

Richard and Morgan climbed the steps, and the crowd quieted.

"Bloody hell, Richard, it's time you got here. Talk sense into this dithering Irish priest," Alexander demanded. His brothers stood at his back, their faces distorted by rage.

Lorcan stepped out of the shadows of the church. "Richard, do—"

"We'll talk later. Trust me. Go back to the altar and keep him safe."

Lorcan nodded and reentered the church, closing the door firmly behind him.

"Sheath your sword, Beaumont. There will be no blood here today." Richard waited while the incredulous knight looked about him, checking if he had enough support to defy his order. With a curse, Alexander slipped the weapon into its scabbard. Richard heard the slide of other swords as they were resheathed. Climbing the stairs to the church entrance, he turned to address his men. "If you don't hang that stinking peasant, what's to keep any of us safe from them?" Alexander shouted.

Shouts of outrage rose all around. Richard raised a fist and waited until the angry cries quieted. "The man is in sanctuary. Until this matter is settled he will remain there. No one is to come armed into the cathedral. I will not hesitate to order killed any man who disobeys me."

Men cursed and shouted at him.

"Silence!" Richard's furious voice thundered over the mob. "This is not the forum for arguing this case. At noon, Dermot MacMurrough and I will hold a court of justice at the king's hall. Anyone, including the Irish, who have any statement or opinion to express will do so there, in an orderly fashion. I will rule by law in Ireland." Men grumbled and cast angry glances back over their shoulders, but most began to disperse.

"We're not leaving," Alexander said. "Two of us will be here at all times, one to watch the altar, the other here at the door. We'll not violate sanctuary, that I vow, but if that murderer takes one step away from the altar, he's a dead man."

"So is any man who harms him," Richard warned. "Remember that, Alexander. I do not make idle threats." He turned to Morgan. "I want a troop of Irish soldiers stationed at this door. No one is to enter or leave without the archbishop's consent."

A dozen or so knights milled about in the churchyard. One came forward. "Lord Pembroke, we would be honored to help guard the sanctuary."

"You do not believe as the others, that this man deserves death?"

"Whether he does or not I'll trust you and the Irish king to decide. Sanctuary is important. None of us knows when we may be called upon to seek shelter from an enemy."

"God's feet, what if they decide to let the dog go free?" Alexander shouted.

The knight turned to confront Alexander. "If the earl and the king make a mistake in their judgment, God will punish rightly in the end. What of your own soul, Beaumont, if you kill an innocent man?"

Richard placed a firm hand on the knight's shoulder. "You are welcome to join the Irish guard, and you have my thanks. I've need of more men like you."

"You have them, my lord, more than you know. 'Tis grief makes Gui's brothers so hotheaded. They will calm eventually."

"See to it then that you guard your prisoner well. Morgan, we've work to do." Richard hurried away from the church.

"Do you believe Gui's brothers will see reason?" Morgan asked.

"I very seriously doubt it. Especially after I let Brendan O'Rourke escape."

"You can't be serious."

"I've never been more so. I want to talk to a woman. I'll need some help to make my plan work."

"Are you going to tell Dermot of your intentions?"

"I'll have to. I don't want to risk him making some sort of dramatic gesture and without realizing thwart my strategy."

"Can you trust him?"

"Do I have a choice?"

Twenty

Richard and Morgan walked to the far side of Dublin and rang the bell at the entrance to St. Brigid's Abbey. A rosy-cheeked nun let them in and silently led them to a small, immaculate room. They did not wait long before Abbess Ancilla marched in.

"Greetings, lady. I've come for your help." Richard spoke in Irish, though he knew the words were badly accented. Morgan quirked an eyebrow at him but remained silent.

The nun pursed her lips and squinted at him. "No need for you to mangle an admirable language. I speak French. Your wife told me what happened. I don't agree with the conclusions she has drawn, but she's broken-hearted at what she calls your betrayal."

Whatever Richard had expected to find it was not this calm, pragmatic woman. His shoulders slumped with relief. He carefully explained to the abbess what he hoped to do and what part he wanted her to play in it. She was silent for a long time, chewing the inside of her cheek as she studied him intently.

"Your plan is dangerous. For myself I have no fear and will gladly join in your madness, but I hesitate to ask my fellow sisters."

"I'd not ask you if I could think of another way."

"I know that, de Clare. I'll go to Lorcan, as you ask, and see if he is willing. You may have a problem there. Lorcan has an infuriating habit of letting his conscience dictate his actions. He won't agree if he believes it is immoral."

"What is immoral about trying to save a man's life?"

"If that were your true motive, he'd not hesitate. But it's your marriage you want to save. Be honest with yourself, if not with me. Speaking of which, do you know your wife is not here?"

Fear pierced Richard. Had Eve left Dublin, as she threatened? Would he never see her again? "Where is she?"

Mother Ancilla crossed her arms and sighed heavily. "The mess you two have made of it. You're both proud as they come, though I must say of the two of you, it's Eve who is stubborn as an ox. You at least have come up with a way of resolving this. Your plan is convoluted and risky, but it will probably work, if we're careful."

"Please, Mother, where is my wife?"

"She's with Lorcan. She's taken her honor fast to his altar. The sooner we put your plan into action, the better our chances of it working. Let's get this over with."

As she turned to go, Richard placed a hand on her arm. The abbess looked over her shoulder at him. "I've one question for you. What is this honor fast you and Eve speak of?"

"Did the woman not explain herself to you?" Mother Ancilla turned to look at him directly and shook her head in exasperation. "It's an ancient Irish tradition. When a person believes an injustice has been done, they fast until the person they think guilty changes his mind."

Richard knew quite clearly that Eve would take such a fast seriously. She was stubborn enough to starve herself to death, of that he was certain. His anger at her set his jaw in a hard line. She thought to manipulate him into doing her will. If he gave in this time, she'd use the same weapon again. It was an effective means of blackmail, but he would not allow it. "I don't want you to tell my wife that I have aught to do with this. Let her think it is your idea, or Lor-can's."

Mother Ancilla's eyes widened. "Why on earth don't you want her to know?"

"In case you hadn't noticed, Eve and I seem to have a difficult time working out our differences. I don't want her to think she's forced me into this. She'll only do it again when we disagree, which I fear will be frequently."

"You're right about that, Richard de Clare. You and Eve will not have an easy time of it. Glorious mayhap, but not easy. Though I think you're wrong not to tell her. After all, you're doing a good thing by helping Brendan escape. I'll keep it to myself, though, if you think it necessary. Is there aught else I need to know?"

"No, I've told you all of it."

The abbess stepped nearer, and with her large, firm thumb traced a cross on Richard's forehead. "Go with God. And do try to talk some sense into your wife."

She swept out of the room, trailing a scent of soap and incense.

Morgan gave way to the laugh he had been holding back. "I swear, Richard, if more religious were like her, the world would be a sight better off than it is now."

"Without her intelligence and courage we'll never succeed."

"I'd say a good dose of guile and charm will be in her arsenal as well." Morgan clapped Richard on the shoulder.

Richard's features hardened with determination. "If all goes well, we can prevent a bloodbath."

Eve bunched her skirt beneath her knees, but the extra padding did not help the pain that came with long hours of kneeling. She finally gave up storming heaven. Her prayers were confused and wandering, though it helped to ease her despair. She had cried the tears of a lifetime since coming into sanctuary the night before. She wept for Maeve and Brendan and the cruelty of their loss. Mostly she wept at the unbearable grief caused by trying to kill the devastating love in her heart. No matter what she tried she could not keep Richard from her mind. She longed for him with a need that threatened to destroy her resolve.

She walked stiffly to a bench and sat down. Brendan glanced up at her from the seat he occupied along the opposite side of the altar. "You've not slept or eaten since you arrived," he said.

"I can't sleep, and I won't eat."

He shook his head. Brendan had said little since she arrived at dawn, and Eve did not pry. Whatever grief tore at Brendan's soul, he suffered it quietly. Just as she did.

The monks of Christ Church sang Vespers and Compline more than an hour ago and the church was quiet and dark. The Irish guard and the few knights Richard had positioned just within the cathedral entrance kept up a lively chatter. She heard the soft fall of footsteps and stood to see who approached. The man carried a lantern and as he came nearer she recognized Lorcan.

Brendan jumped from his seat and rushed toward the archbishop. "What news? Did de Clare find in my favor?"

Lorcan placed a calming hand on the young man's shoulder. "Be quiet. I don't want anyone overhearing what we say. Come around to the back side of the altar, where we'll not be seen. The meeting today in the king's hall was merely a way to gain time."

"Time for what?"

Lorcan smiled brightly. "For your escape."

Eve and Brendan stared openmouthed. Brendan was first to recover. "When? How?"

"Tonight, if all goes well."

Eve placed an affectionate kiss on her uncle's cheek. "I knew you would help us, when all others failed."

"Child, you give me credit I don't deserve, but we don't

have time to talk. We need to prepare for our visitors." He turned and called softly into the darkness, "Brother Patrik, Brother David."

Two elderly monks came out of the shadows. Eve watched, with growing curiosity, as they placed a large bowl and ewer on the altar, then a towel. On the towel they laid a razor and a bowl of soap. The two monks stepped aside and waited silently.

Lorcan picked up the razor. "Brendan, come here, lad. You're in need of a shave."

Brendan's hand went to his luxuriant brown beard and his eyes widened with disbelief. "You're going to shave my beard? No, I won't allow it. What possible reason——"

Lorcan sighed and placed the razor back on the towel. "Do you trust me?"

"Of course I do."

"Then trust me in this. By the time you leave this cathedral, you'll no longer be an Irishman."

Eve watched with fascination as Lorcan and the monks carefully cut the beard, then lathered Brendan's face with the soft, greasy soap, and shaved off what remained. They were careful to be neat, not letting the hair fall to the floor. As Lorcan worked, he explained what they were to do that night.

Poor Brendan, Eve thought. How humiliating for him. An Irishman without a beard. He must feel naked. She tried not to smile, but Lorcan's plan was clever and she believed it would work. Her part was simple enough. She would remain in sanctuary until Brendan was well away from Dublin. If she left, the Beaumont knights would wonder why. Though where she would go, she wasn't sure. Brendan would be safe, but Richard had naught to do with it. He had failed to rule by Irish law. He had broken his vow to her. *Merciful God, how am I to live without him? But if I go back he'll never take me seriously, he'll have no reason to keep his word. I must continue my fast and hope that forces him to see what he must do.*

She turned away as Brendan stripped off his clothes. When she turned back, the man was clad only in braies and shirt and boots. One of the monks, a man near Brendan's size but otherwise looking nothing like the younger man, now wore the fugitive's clothes.

"They'll be here soon. Does everyone understand the part they are to play?" Lorcan looked from one to the other as they nodded their agreement. "Good. Remember, stay calm, act as though nothing is amiss. Our lives could well depend on it. Brother David, get the shaving mess out of here, and be careful the guard at the door doesn't see you. Take the long way back into the cloister."

Brother David left on nearly soundless feet, a shadow slipping into the heavier shadows of the cathedral. Soon the church's main door opened and the faint light of a single lantern could be seen in the darkness.

"Be quiet and stay behind the altar," Lorcan whispered. He picked up his lantern and walked down the long aisle.

Eve sank to the floor behind the altar, Brendan and Brother Patrik on either side of her. She strained to hear the conversation at the door but could not make out the words. Richard's voice, so familiar to her she would know it out of a hundred others, came to her through the darkness. What was he doing here? Her stomach clenched, and she breathed deeply to calm herself. It wasn't the danger the next quarter hour promised, but the sound of his beloved voice that set her trembling. She leaned her head forward and let the tears fall to her lap.

Richard held his lantern high as he approached Christ Church, Mother Ancilla and three nuns behind him. The Beaumont brothers barred their way up the steps to the cathedral door. One of the nuns was unusually tall, and Richard made sure light from his lantern illuminated her face. The Beaumonts easily saw that the woman was middle-aged and plain. Nothing to draw their interest. One of the other nuns was young and very pretty and did not escape their notice. That little distraction had been Mother Ancilla's idea.

"What are you doing here, de Clare, in the middle of the night?" Alexander's voice was raw with suspicion.

Mother Ancilla anchored her bulk before the knight, who stepped back in surprise. "There's a pregnant woman in there who refuses to eat. I've come to talk sense into her."

Alexander eyed her, then turned his attention to the three nuns. "You need four women?"

"Ach. Men don't understand these things." The abbess planted her fists on her hips and took a step closer to the knight. "We've brought food and blankets and a change of clothing. The princess may be a stubborn fool, but I'll not in good conscience allow her to harm the babe she carries. Have you objections to an act of charity?"

Alexander would not budge. "Let me see what you carry."

"Are you questioning my word?" The abbess spoke with indignant outrage.

"If you've nothing to hide, why do you refuse me?"

"This is ridiculous. Sisters, show him what you have in your hands."

The tall nun uncovered the cauldron of soup she carried, and the rich aroma drifted enticingly into the cool air. Alexander sniffed at it appreciatively, but moved on to the pretty nun. She held out a yellow gown and multicolored cloak. The third nun carried a ewer of warm milk, a cup, and a spoon. Alexander showed little interest.

"See?" Mother Ancilla said, keeping her face stern. "We bring no weapons, no disguise, no gold to help the fugitive on his way."

Richard coughed to mask his surprise. They, in fact, brought all three.

"Be quick about it." Alexander turned his attention again to Richard. "I don't know what you're up to, de Clare, but I'll be watching."

"You do that, Alexander." Richard tried to make his voice casual, to cover his nervousness. If this turned dangerous, how was he to protect Eve and their child?

Lorcan stood in the doorway, blocking their entrance, his face stern. "What business have you here?"

"I've come to see O'Rourke," Richard answered. "I have questions I need to ask."

"These questions can't wait until morning? The man is asleep."

"Lorcan, you old fool, step aside." Mother Ancilla pushed her way forward, past the startled Beaumont knights. "I want to see for myself the princess is well. You and de Clare can argue the night away for all I care."

One of the knights chuckled. The abbess spoke in French, and that she did it so the knights would understand every word did not seem to cross their minds. Richard let out a breath he didn't realize he was holding.

With a heavy sigh and a shrug of his shoulder, Lorcan stepped aside to let the abbess and her nuns into the church. Richard moved to follow them.

Lorcan stepped into his path. "I've not given you permission, de Clare. I don't trust your coming in the night any more than your men do. Whatever you have in mind can wait until day, when we can gather credible witnesses to hear what you ask and what Brendan answers."

"I want to talk privately with the man."

"That I'll not allow. Only by doing this publicly will the Irish folk be satisfied with whatever judgment you render. They'll never believe you have their interests in mind if you go about it in secret."

"Ha. What now, Richard? Will you draw your sword on the priest, after you've forbidden us to do the same?" Alexander lounged against the wall of the church, a nasty grin baring his teeth.

Richard looked from Lorcan to Gui's brothers and tried to appear frustrated and angry. "What a mess." He turned back to Lorcan. "In the morning then, before noon."

"That may not—"

"That's all the time I'll give you, priest. I'll end this for good on the morrow." Richard turned and stalked away. Had they been convincing? Now he must wait for the others to do their part. He hurried to St. Brigid's Abbey, where the cart waited.

Eve peeked around the altar and saw Mother Ancilla and three nuns coming toward them. Where was Richard? She could hear him and Lorcan arguing, but she could not see him. No time for that now. She must do what Lorcan asked of her.

"There you are, child." Mother Ancilla's voice boomed in the quiet, and she wrapped Eve in a suffocating hug. "I'll not stand by and allow this nonsense. You must eat, and I'm not leaving until you do."

"I've vowed to keep a hunger fast. I'll not break that vow."

"Irish law does not allow you to endanger your unborn child."

Was that true? Surely the Lady Abbess wouldn't lie to her. They would have to discuss it later. For now, it was important that the abbess fuss over her loudly, to distract attention from the others. She had never seen the abbess so bossy, and dared not contradict her. If she didn't know better, she would think the nun was enjoying this dangerous game they played.

"You know you're wrong, don't you?" Ancilla's voice was without levity or teasing.

"Wrong about what?" Eve asked. She ate the soup they

brought, to make it look good, and found she was so hungry the kettle would not be enough.

"About Richard."

Eve's head jerked up, the spoon halfway to her mouth forgotten. "He broke his vow to me. I expect him to keep his word."

"Even as you keep yours?"

"Of course."

The abbess fisted her hands on her hips, in that familiar way. "Richard has not broken his vow to rule by Irish law. He hasn't had a chance to. You jumped so quickly to your conclusions that it was you who broke a promise."

Eve dropped the spoon back in the soup. Crossing her arms under her breasts, she glared at the other woman and said in her most imperious voice, "You don't know what you're talking about."

Mother Ancilla's head reared back in surprise, then a small smile quirked at the corner of her mouth. She quickly suppressed it, but not before Eve saw. "Think again, child. Did you not make Richard promise to rule Leinster equally with you? Did you not promise to advise him on matters of Irish law?"

"I told him what Irish law said should be done."

"And when did you become a *Brehon?* When did you go through the years of specialized schooling to become a master of Irish law? You are not qualified to tell your husband what to do. Your duty was to call for the nearest *Brehon* to travel to Dublin to judge the evidence. Richard did not know to do so. You left your poor husband to muddle about on his own."

Eve could not believe what she was hearing. Her poor husband? "That man is the most stubborn, arrogant, self-righteous hypocrite I have ever met. How can you defend him?"

"Richard is likely some of those things, though hypocrite

I doubt. You've given as good a description of yourself as you have him."

Eve felt as though she had been slapped. Why did the abbess say such cruel things to her?

"Mother, we are ready," one of the nuns whispered.

"You think about what I've said, Eve. I mean every word of it."

Eve turned her attention to Brendan. The man looked ridiculously uncomfortable. "Slump your shoulders a little, your carriage is too military, and remember to take small steps, stay behind Mother Ancilla. And stop scowling. The last thing you want is to draw attention to yourself."

"I feel an utter fool." Brendan scratched the veil covering his hair, and ran a finger around the wimple he wore. "This damned thing is too tight."

"It wasn't made for a man," Mother Ancilla said. "You'll be wearing it for a half hour at most. I don't want to hear any more whining, young man."

Brendan glanced to Eve and raised an eyebrow, but he had the sense to be quiet.

Eve smiled and gave him an affectionate tap on the arm. "I think you make a handsome nun, Brendan." She sobered and gazed into his grief-reddened eyes. "God speed you to a safe place."

Left with Eve at the altar was an old monk disguised as Brendan and an unusually tall nun who had given her habit to disguise the Irishman and now wore the gown and cloak shown to Alexander. Eve watched Mother Ancilla and her nuns leave, including one nun who had absolutely no qualifications for his vocation. She held her breath. The real danger was upon them. Brendan must slip unnoticed past the men at the cathedral door.

It seemed an eternity before Lorcan approached the altar. "He's safely gone. Now it's up to Richard."

"Richard? What does Richard have to do with this?"

Lorcan smiled and patted her cheek. "Get some sleep,

little one. There's no more for you to do tonight. You'll be free from here by noon tomorrow."

Lorcan left, and the men at the door quieted as the night wore on. Eve lay on the hard pallet that was her bed, a blanket pulled up around her shoulders. She felt alone in the world. More tears threatened but she angrily brushed them from her cheeks. They were tears of self-pity, and she'd not allow herself to begin down that useless road.

She could not sleep, despite Lorcan's decree. Mother Ancilla's words swirled about in her brain. Had she indeed been hasty in her judgment? Was she guilty of arrogance? The abbess thought so, and with great difficulty, Eve reluctantly came to the same conclusion. She did not like the taste it left in her mouth to look honestly at her faults and recognize where she was wrong. She had herself violated Irish law by not summoning a *Brehon*. Yet she berated Richard for his lack of decisiveness when he knew little of the law. It was her duty to help him understand the ways of her people. She had failed him. Just as she failed to admit Richard was given an impossible task. He must rule the Irish and the others with justice. How to do that must be worked out between them.

Eve sighed and turned onto her back. Everything was easy when it was seen in black and white, right and wrong, when one was unwilling to compromise or listen to another's reasoning. But the world was gray. She was learning that, slowly, one difficult lesson at a time. Gray and unpredictable and mysterious. Life could not be explained and tidied into neat little bundles. Loving a man she had been sure she would hate was the first lesson. Love could not be fitted to a stubborn ideal, any more than life.

By noon, a crowd of angry knights and Welshmen and wary Irishmen gathered before the doors of the cathedral. The crowd parted and quieted as Richard and Dermot made their way up the stairs, Morgan following to translate each man's words.

Richard raised his hands for silence. Had he done the right thing? It was too late to undo it. Now he must face the anger, perhaps the rebellion of his men. "This situation is more complex than Alexander and his brothers know. The man who sought sanctuary claims Gui Beaumont raped and killed his wife—"

"Christ, de Clare, where's the crime in that?" Alexander shouted. "The death of an Irishwoman is of no more concern than that of a cow. And rape? Why would Gui rape anyone when he could get any woman he wanted? It makes no sense. The death of my brother must not go unpunished."

Richard waited for the crowd to quiet. "Dermot and I have come to an agreement on this case. While Brendan O'Rourke most probably killed Sir Gui Beaumont—"

"That he did. Hang the bastard!"

"Give the man to us, Pembroke, we'll carry out your sentence."

Smiles broke out on his men's faces, thinking he was about to rule in their favor. Richard bit back his anger and raised his sword, a command all of them knew. They would be silent until he finished.

"O'Rourke was escorted out of sanctuary last night and is well away from Dublin."

"You treacherous bastard! You let my brother's murderer go free?" Alexander shouted.

Richard could almost sympathize with Alexander, except that Gui had committed so reprehensible a crime, there was no sorrow in his heart at his cousin's death. "Gui was not without blame. He killed an Irishwoman of noble rank. While I cannot condone either murder, neither will I allow a blood feud between the Beaumont family and the O'Rourkes. I mean to rule Leinster in peace, and to do that, it must be ruled by law."

Richard looked out again at the crowd. His men were

eyeing him with curiosity and disbelief, while the Irish seemed puzzled, though Morgan translated for them. He knew his decision was fair, but would either side be pleased? It was the best he could do. "The Irish people of Leinster will be ruled by Irish law in all things. The incomers will be under English law, except when what they are accused of involves an Irish man or woman. Then the foreigner will also be ruled under Irish law."

"God's blood, you can't be serious. I'll not submit to Irish law, Pembroke." Alexander moved toward Richard, his hand at the hilt of his sword. Several knights rushed forward to restrain him.

"The earl has ruled wisely, Beaumont," one of the knights said. "Be quiet and hear what he has to say."

Richard recognized the man and tucked away in his mind the reward he would give him for his loyalty. "Any of my men who cannot live with this decision are free to leave. You will not be allowed to stay in Ireland but must return to Wales or England. Only those who stay with me through this campaign can hope for a reward of Irish fiefs."

The grumbling was more subdued. The only men who stalked angrily from the field were the Beaumont brothers and half a dozen others. Richard had feared many more of his men would find the ruling untenable.

Dermot stepped forward, and Richard listened as Morgan translated the Irish king's words into French.

"My daughter I designate as my heir, in public and at this holy place, so there can be no question of my intent later. No other do I recognize. Since a woman cannot rule an Irish kingdom, her husband, Richard de Clare, will do so and with my blessing. I say he is an honorable man and you'd be foolhardy to abandon him."

Richard could hardly believe what he heard. Dermot seemed sincere for once, with no hint of duplicity. *Now what is churning in that man's brain?*

The crowd dispersed, the Irish going in one direction, his

men in the opposite, but it looked as though there would be no violence between the two groups. Still, Richard was cautious. "Morgan, I want a patrol of trustworthy men in Dublin the next week or two."

"I'll see to it." Morgan walked away, whistling a merry tune.

Dermot said something to him in Irish and Richard shrugged, not understanding. Dermot smiled and pointed toward the church, then went down the steps and headed toward the royal enclosure.

Richard turned to see Eve standing behind him. "How long have you been there?"

"Long enough to hear your decision."

She was calm and quiet, and Richard frowned. What had happened to the angry, wounded woman he had last seen? "Does my decree meet with your approval?" He kept his voice cool and distant.

As Eve turned her face up to him, he saw the tears shimmering in her green eyes. "I am so proud of you, Richard."

It was the last thing he expected to hear and the protective barrier he'd erected around his heart came crumbling down.

"I was wrong," Eve said. "I vowed to help you rule my people, but what I did was of no use to you or the Irish folk. I was angry and impulsive. I did not trust you to keep your word."

"As you told me once, trust must be earned. I begin to see what you mean. We can't succeed here if we don't work together. Nothing good comes of our battles."

A tentative smile touched the corner of her lips. "You are not without blame in this, de Clare. You too stubbornly resisted the idea of punishing one of your men."

"I see your vigil did not temper your tongue." He was startled to see her blush and lower her head. A single tear slid down her cheek. He reached out and gently raised her chin. "Did I say your tongue displeased me? How else am I to learn if you don't argue your side? This won't be the last time we must come to some compromise for the good of the people. Will you help me, my sweet Eve?"

She leaned into his hand as he pulled her to his chest. "With all my heart and strength."

He held her close. Looking up toward the cathedral, he blinked several times to clear his eyes. Only then did he trust himself to kiss his wife, tenderly, possessively, and with heartfelt thanks. She had come back to him. Never again would he let her go.

Twenty-one

"You are beautiful." Richard leaned indolently against the door frame between the outer chamber and the bed-chamber.

Eve blushed, but was pleased he noticed. She had taken special care dressing this morning. Her hair was neatly braided in two plaits with green silk ribbons woven through them, and a simple torc of twisted gold circled her neck. The bodice of her cream-colored gown felt tight, and she had to loosen her gold filigree belt to accommodate the gentle swelling of her belly, but to an unobservant eye she did not look pregnant.

"You're handsome yourself this morning." And it was true. For once Richard wore no chain mail under his gold and scarlet tunic. "Wait, I have just the thing." She ran to her clothes chest. Pulling the casket holding her jewels from it, she removed the heavy torc made to fit a man's larger neck. It was wonderfully whimsical, with two fierce dragon heads facing each other in the front. One dragon had eyes of emerald, the other of darkest garnet, and both were marvelously carved and beaded. This, too, had come from Lorcan, though he could tell her no more than that it was old. What king it had been made for was lost in the mystery of time. She walked over to him and held out the gift.

He took it reverently.

"Put it on."

It lay gleaming around his neck, bold and handsome, like

the man. Her hand came up to her breast as she studied him. He looked every inch a prince, and a powerful one at that.

Tonight the Irish lords of Leinster would gather in Dublin to swear oaths of support to Dermot. On this day Richard would begin the slow task of winning the loyalty of the Irish nobles he would one day rule. "Every man who gives his oath today will wish they were pledging themselves to you, rather than to my father. How can they look at you and not see a leader?"

"I'll be lucky to get more than a grudging promise of aid from any of them. For now it's their old loyalties to Leinster that will keep them from going over to O'Conor. It still amazes me your father is making so public my position as his heir. What do you suppose he is planning now?"

"Have you asked him?"

Richard laughed. "What a unique idea. Do you think he'll tell me the truth?"

"Mayhap it would be better if I talked to him." Eve frowned. "Father has looked unwell lately, have you noticed?"

"Now you mention it, he does seem thinner, diminished somehow. I've not paid close attention."

"Enough of such talk," Eve said. "This one day I want to enjoy without worrying about the future."

She finished dressing with a mounting sense of excitement. It had been a long time since she indulged in the pleasures of a fairing day. Somewhere in the glittering, exotic display of foreign wares she would find the perfect wedding gift for Caitlin and Morgan. She pinned her heavy wool cloak closed with a gold and garnet brooch.

"Where's your cloak? Oh, Richard, do hurry."

"I'd rather tear your clothes off and toss you into that bed."

His gray eyes smoldered with that private, intimate look he reserved solely for her, and she lifted a warning finger at him. "Don't you dare. I've been looking forward to this for weeks and I don't want to miss a minute of it."

"I have needs, woman. It's dangerous to deny a needy man."

"You're spoiled."

"And whose fault is that?"

It was true, they had done little else but eat, sleep, and make love in the last few weeks. The more they had of each other, the more they wanted. She was tempted for a moment to indulge him, and herself, then remembered Caitlin would be waiting for her near the cloth merchants' stalls. They had been teased enough by her cousin and Morgan over their recent unavailability. "The sooner we get to the fair, the sooner we'll be back here."

He crooked a smile at her even as he flung his cloak around his broad shoulders. "Come, Princess. We've a fairing to attend."

The autumn sky held a few clouds, and a strong breeze threatened to bring more. A solitary goldfinch, with his cherry-red face, balanced precariously on a dead thistle then lofted into dancing flight, his trilling song trailing after. Breathing deeply of the piercing air, Eve's heart filled with joy.

They left the king's enclosure and walked into the lanes of Dublin, which were crowded with people in a holiday mood. Men called greetings to friends as their wives scolded exuberant children, who ran about getting into mischief and tried to avoid their elders. Pigs, squealing in excitement or alarm, dodged the crowd to seek quieter feeding grounds in the cemeteries, gobbling up the oak mast that lay among the quiet graves and tall standing crosses.

The horse and chariot races would be run in a field outside the walls. The wicker chariots used by the Irish were light, fast, and dangerous when their teams of stallions galloped full out. It was a splendid sight when the chariots raced, with their silk banners whipping in the wind and the

harness bells crying. All true Irish warriors prided themselves on their skill in a chariot. It was a skill Richard's
men did not share, having never seen such vehicles before.
Eve wondered if any of the foreigners would be foolhardy
enough to try competing, then decided no Irishman would
risk his horses to an inexperienced driver.

Near the cathedral the traditional marriage bartering was
under way, young women and men standing shyly, or preen-
ing, smiling or made silent with dread, as their parents hag-
gled over dowries. The young people were a commodity.
Through them clan ties were reaffirmed or new loyalties
established. Poets and professional genealogists sat or stood
throughout the fair, and people gathered quietly around
them to hear the history of Ireland recited. When she was
very young, Eve spent countless hours at the fairs listening
to these revered men and women. She absorbed the legends
and traditions like the earth of Ireland absorbed the rain
that gave it life.

Ships from England, Norway, and ports farther away, too
exotic for Eve to imagine, crowded Dublin Harbor. Resplendent Constantinople had a ship in port, as well as bright,
indulgent Sicily. Knights in mail held themselves aloof from
the general revelry and kept a vigilant eye on everything,
alert to any trouble.

"I haven't seen so many people in Dublin since I was a
child." She marveled at the noise and movement, the swirl
of color, the strange mix of languages.

"We'll have our share of thieves and pick-purses and
whores, all trying for a silver penny. But the fair looks to
be a success. A ship carrying goods from Byzantium and
Baghdad arrived yesterday."

"You sound worried. Is something amiss?"

He shook his head, but a frown creased his forehead.
"I've been expecting a ship from Wales. The winds between
here and Pembroke can keep a ship in harbor for weeks.
I'll be more at ease when I hear from them."

"Why is this ship so important? Surely every imaginable trading good has arrived in time for the fair."

"It's not a merchant ship. I'm expecting news of how recruiting goes. I want another five hundred knights and a thousand men-at-arms here by spring, before I face Rory."

It was as though a cloud marred the perfection of the day. Spring would bring war. Somehow, before then, Egan must be released from Rory's custody.

A large field near the harbor had been set aside for the fair. Merchants in temporary stalls of wattle spread out the imported goods that made the town famous as a trading center. The Leinster lords who came to see for themselves what sort of man Richard de Clare was, also brought their wives and daughters and purses full of silver.

Merchants from Scandinavia had stalls laden with furs including the pure white bear of the Far North. They sold sea ivory made into combs and hairpins, manicure tools, and toothpicks. There was Frankish glassware, tinted rose and green and blue; amethyst from Egypt; bronze from Alexandria; port wine from Portugal. Soapstone, as easily carved as wood, was available as loom weights, lamps, querns, and bowls. Mixed in with the stalls were cook stands where everything from bread, still warm from the ovens, to ewe cheese, to pies of beef or cold smoked salmon could be purchased. There were crisp apples newly harvested, and cider and perry to quench a thirst, and the sweet indulgence of mead, sold beside the honey stands. Inevitably, in Dublin and every other trading port in the world, there was a brisk market in slaves.

Eve saw Caitlin in the area where the cloth merchants had established themselves, and waved a happy greeting. "I promised Caitlin I'd help her pick out cloth for her wedding gown."

Richard gave her a quick kiss on the cheek. "Morgan said he'd meet me at the falconer's mews. Can I trust you to stay out of trouble?"

She puffed up indignantly, then saw the gleam of humor in his eyes. "I still want to walk the rounds with you."

"I promise." He held his hand over his heart. "When the church bells ring for Tierce, I'll come find you."

She watched him walk away, and was amused to see the avid attention he drew from women in the crowd. Females old and young, married and maid, lords' proud wives and whores smiled, straightened their backs, thrust out their breasts, and hoped. He was oblivious to them all. *Does he still think of Rosamund?* She pushed the thought from her mind, and turned to join Caitlin.

Her cousin, radiant as only a woman transformed by love is beautiful, fairly danced with excitement. "Oh, Eve, look what I've found. It's perfect."

Spread out on the merchant's shelf was a brocade of the palest pink satin, and near it a bolt of heavy silk of a shimmering rose.

"M'lady has chosen well." The eager-eyed merchant ran his fingers sensuously over the materials. "The satin is Byzantine, of the finest quality, and the silk comes from the Far East, brought along the silk route to Constantinople. Empresses have worn these, but this fair Irish maid will put them all to shame."

He was a small man, with dark hair and dark eyes and he spoke the most strangely accented Latin Eve had ever heard. Greek probably, by the looks of him, with his connections to Constantinople. She reached out to touch the cloth, and his hands moved instinctively to prevent her. She smiled. So, he was a true lover of his trade, caring that she not spoil the perfection of the silk, not just a greedy merchant out to get his best price. She would enjoy the haggling she was about to indulge in. "How much do you want for it?"

He named a price Eve knew to be outrageously high. "That's far too much. Come, Cousin, there are other stalls."

Caitlin looked at her with horrified eyes, and, turning her

back on the merchant, Eve winked. Recovering smoothly, Caitlin said, "You're right, of course. I saw a scarlet samite a few stalls down. Perhaps pink isn't my best color."

"Ladies, please, let's not be hasty. Surely we can come to some agreement."

Eve turned triumphantly back to the merchant, and the fun began. He was apologetic; she was demanding; his feelings were hurt; she was adamant; he lowered his price fractionally; she would not budge; he lost his temper; she stared at him imperiously. After half an hour he agreed to deliver the cloth to the royal seamstresses for a little more than half his original asking price. They left the poor man to shout at his assistant.

"You're good at that," Caitlin said, admiration in her voice. "Where did you learn to bargain so well?"

"I've been married for four months."

Caitlin looked shocked, then began to giggle, and Eve joined her, their laughter ringing merrily through the crowd. People looked at them and smiled.

"I'm hungry," Caitlin said. "What about you?"

"Ravenous. Since the nausea went away, I've done nothing but eat."

They found a stall with hot food, and each bought a pie of beef and onions in a thick brown gravy. They settled on a bench beneath a tree, cups of warm mead between them. Caitlin poked at her pasty, reluctant to indulge in the good hot food. Eve dug into hers with undisguised relish.

"I have something to tell you." Caitlin stared at her hands.

Eve licked her fingers and waited. Why did Caitlin look so ill at ease?

"I'm no longer a virgin."

"What? You and Morgan? What am I saying, of course you and Morgan. Don't look so embarrassed Cait. I hardly expected you to wait until your marriage night, not the way you two care about each other."

"That's it'? No lecture? No profound disappointment?"

"I'm happy for you. There's nothing more precious than love. I say, seize it wherever you can find it."

"You mean you don't think there's anything wrong with doing—you know what—with a man?"

"I didn't say that. People can mate with no more care for each other than animals, out of purely physical desire, greedily, even selfishly. That isn't love. There are many forms of love, sweet Cait. With luck you'll discover them all with Morgan." Eve leaned back on the bench and smiled. "There is more than just the love between a man and a woman, as important as that is. I love this child I carry months before I'll be able to hold it in my arms, and pray each day that it will be born healthy. I love this land. I love being alive. I love you, more dear to me than any sister. So grab hard wherever you find love, Caitlin. It's what makes life bearable."

They finished their meal then returned their cups to the man at the mead barrel. "It's too cold to just sit. Let's go find our men," Eve said.

"They were going to look at hawks, Morgan said. I've heard them brag that no bird can beat a good Welsh falcon."

"Just as no archers are superior to Welshmen."

"And the finest horses come from Wales."

"And the handsomest, most virile men."

They went laughing, hand in hand, through the gay crowd. Today was for indulgence, and being young and carefree. They found Richard and Morgan arguing the finer points of hunting hawks with a master falconer from Norway. Hooded peregrines lined the perches in his makeshift mews.

"Did you find what you wanted?" Eve asked, linking her arm through Richard's.

"I don't have the time to spend working with a bird, but I do miss it. There's not much better in life than riding over the hills on the back of a good horse, with a falcon on your wrist."

"It's a shame," Morgan said, eyeing the raptors with disappointment. "Such beautiful creatures. A falcon on the wing, now there is a sight to lift a man's spirits."

"And do your spirits need lifting?" Caitlin asked.

He smiled down at her. "With you, my love, they are so high now I fear I would burst apart should any more happiness come to me."

The falconer looked disappointed, knowing he would make no sale as the four of them walked out into the sunshine. The day grew colder, and a few thick clouds, presaging a change in the weather, were drifting in from the west. Shivering, Eve crossed her arms beneath her cloak, her hands seeking warmth.

"I found something for you. The merchant is holding it for me." Richard steered her through the jostling crowds.

They passed the jewelers stalls, and she hid her disappointment. The perfumer waved and tried to draw them aside, but Richard kept going. The man with the sweets was not their destination, nor the woman with the embroidery threads of silk and gold, and the finest needles to go with them. She was sorely tempted to stop near the man with the wolfhound puppies, just to play with one of the darling things, but Richard marched resolutely on.

Finally, he brought her to a where a huge, redheaded Norseman stood beside piles of furs. The man smiled and disappeared into his stall, reappearing in a moment with a large cloth bundle.

"Richard, what have you done?" She tried to sound scolding, but it came out in a greedy little squeal, and he laughed.

Taking the bundle from the merchant, Richard unfurled it for her inspection with a dramatic flourish. It was a cloak of the softest, most tightly woven wool she had ever seen. The colors were subtle, muted, but all the hues worn by

Irish royalty were there. Then he turned it over and she gasped. It was lined with dark, opulent sable. She undid the brooch at her neck and handed her cloak to Caitlin.

"I take it that means you like it?" Richard asked.

"Just help me put it on before I freeze."

He draped it over her shoulders, and she pulled the sensuous fur up around her cheeks, marveling in the softness of it. It was so warm. She almost looked forward to winter, if she could wear this.

"There's more."

She turned to stare at him. The merchant was grinning and holding a pair of fur leggings in his large hands. Men's fur leggings.

"What am I to do with those?"

"Wear them. No one can see what you have on under your gown, and they'll keep your legs warm. There are fur-lined boots to go with them.

"I don't need boots."

"Yes you do. Whose legs do you think you warm your toes on at night? I say you need boots. And gloves."

Richard handed her a pair of gloves with long gauntlets, made of the softest, most supple leather. She slipped them on her hands and smiled. He was being outrageously extravagant. All of this must cost a small fortune. A lump formed in her throat and she ducked her head, pretending to examine the hem of her new cloak. No one had ever indulged her like this, or seen to her needs. She was prone to being affected by the cold, and he had noticed and done something about it.

"Don't I get a thanks?" Richard asked.

She threw herself at him, wrapping her arms around his neck. He crushed her to him and leaned down, claiming her mouth in a passionate, possessive kiss. How cherished and safe he made her feel, in a world filled with treachery and greed. When they finally parted, Morgan, Caitlin, and the fur trader were arguing over the price of gloves.

Eve wrapped an arm around Richard's waist and stood contentedly under the protection of his strong arm. She noticed a crowd gathering near a large oak tree, and there was shouting, loud, angry, and youthful. A fight was in progress. Before the crowd closed around the combatants, she saw a dark-haired youth, small and wiry, and a taller, heavier boy with fair hair.

"That's Tewdr!" she cried.

"Where?" Morgan whirled around, concern etched on his face.

"There, fighting that other boy." Eve pointed, but the crowd had closed around the boys.

"Dammit, I can't turn my back for an hour without him getting into trouble," Morgan said. "He's supposed to be Turlough O'Conor's escort."

"Rory's son?" Eve asked.

"I told Tewdr to guide him around the fair, since he knows some Irish. I thought if they spent some time together they might be friends."

The shouting from the crowd grew louder, and Eve could see men placing wagers on the outcome. She felt sure few of them were betting on Tewdr to win, he was so much smaller than the other boy. "Richard, you must stop them. Tewdr will be hurt."

"It's just a boys' battle. They'll bloody each other's noses and be best friends after."

No wonder men were barbarians, allowing, even encouraging, such behavior. "If you won't stop it, I shall." She marched toward the melee before he could prevent her. Pushing her way through the crowd, she could hardly believe what she saw. Both boys were pummeling each other into a bloody mess.

"Take it back!" Tewdr screamed. He shouted in an Irish so heavily accented it made his demand incomprehensible to the other boy, who saved his breath for the more serious business of murder. Eve looked about frantically. No one, it seemed, was willing to interfere, too busy enjoying the spectacle, much as they would a bear baiting or a cockfight.

Anger surged in her, and she rushed forward to pull the boys apart. A wildly swung fist hit her hard in the chest, and she stumbled back.

"Dammit, Eve, get out of there!" Richard pushed his way toward her.

The crowd quieted. Only the gasping and grunting and occasional contact of fist with flesh from the two boys broke the day's peace. Turning her back on her husband, she marched back into battle.

Two knights, who had been enjoying the spectacle as much as the next man, stepped forward. They pulled the boys apart, one holding a screaming Tewdr, the other grasping a deadly calm, angry young Irishman.

She rushed over to Tewdr. "Are you hurt? Look at you. I think your nose is broken."

"M'lady? What the holy hell are you doing here?"

"May you rot in hell, you damned whore!" The other boy looked at her with such hatred in his blue eyes, she took an involuntary step backward. He spat, hard, and the spittle ran down her new cloak.

"Shut up!" Tewdr shouted, thrashing wildly against his captor.

"Norman's whore! No Irishwoman would willingly give herself to one of them!"

"Is this what you were fighting over?" she asked Tewdr. He looked at her with angry, ashamed eyes, and nodded. Brave thing, to want to protect her honor. Such virulent hatred from Turlough O'Conor's son was an unexpected shock. It was as though someone hit her in the stomach, the sick feeling it caused. There were those in the crowd who agreed with the boy. She saw it in their eyes.

"What is he saying?" Richard asked, hooking a thumb at Turlough.

"Only what he's been taught. Help me get Tewdr to Morgan's bower. He's going to need my nursing, whether he likes it or not. I'll see to the other boy later, he doesn't look as badly hurt. Please, Richard, don't ask me any more. Just help me."

They escorted Tewdr through the crowd. The day was colder now, the clouds gathering fast, and it smelled of rain.

She tried not to think about what Turlough had said, but his words screamed in her brain. Whore. Traitor.

Twenty-two

The barracks were large, noisy, and overwhelmingly male. Eve stood in the doorway orienting herself to the scene. Men ate at long trestle tables, or slept in the crude cubicles built along the walls of the long, narrow hall, or gathered in boisterous clusters to gamble. A few sat in a corner listening to a harper, while others were gathered around a bitch and her litter. Amidst the chaos, in a corner by himself where no one intruded on his hostile privacy, sat Turlough O'Conor glaring at his surroundings out of blackened eyes.

Tewdr was close-lipped earlier, his pride wounded far more than his body. He refused to tell her what had passed between him and Turlough. She heard enough, at the end of their fight, to know the deadly hostility Rory's son held for her. In a strange way, she could not blame him. She had felt the same about the coming of the foreigners, until one gray-eyed man conquered her heart.

Making her way into the pungent room, she was amused to hear the cursing stop as the men became aware of her presence.

"M'lady, what are you doing here?" The Norman soldier looked decidedly uncomfortable at having this all-male preserve violated. Men around him quieted to hear her response.

"I've come to tend to O'Conor's wounds."

The man looked startled, and cut his glance nervously at

his nearest companions. "He's a hotheaded bastard. I can't let you near him without a guard, there's no telling what he might do."

"Then send a guard with me, but I need to see if he's hurt. We can't have it reported to his father that he is being mistreated. Not while my brother is held hostage in Rory's camp."

"M'lady, please," another man said, "let someone else tend to the boy. One of the slaves can see to his needs."

He was an older man, a grizzled veteran made uneasy by the idea of her being subjected to more unpleasantness. She smiled at his concern. "I'm well aware of what the lad thinks of me. There will always be Irishmen who think so, just as there will be those who think the earl of Pembroke has degraded himself by marrying an Irishwoman."

The man bristled at her words and looked about him with challenge in his blue eyes. "None of the earl's men would dare voice such an opinion, not in my hearing, I can assure you."

"Aye, Lady, none here think such a thing of you," another man said, and others took up the chorus, until there was a general acclamation that brought tears to her eyes. The loyalty of Richard's men eased the hurt of Turlough's words.

She tried not to show her trepidation as she approached the boy. He glowered at her, raking her up and down with a cold, calculating stare full of loathing.

"Stand up, ye great lout." The old soldier planted a toe roughly in the boy's ribs. "Show some respect to the countess." He spoke in French, which the boy could not understand, but the meaning of the kick was plain enough. With a grunt of pain, Turlough rose to his feet. The soldier smiled at the quick obedience of his captive.

Eve seethed with anger. This lad was only a few years older than Egan, and deserved no ill-treatment. "I will not allow you to abuse the king of Connaught's son." She rounded angrily on the Norman guard. "He will be treated with dignity and respect. The next man to lay a rough hand or foot to him will have to answer to the earl himself. Do I make myself clear?"

The men around her looked astonished and unsure of themselves. "M'lady, the boy is not ill-used. We keep him fed and he has a warm place to sleep. He don't understand gentle words or kindness."

"Aye, like an animal he is. A kick now and then does him good."

"He'd not hesitate to land us a good one, or worse, given the chance. Ye can't treat these barbarians like you would civilized folk."

There was a sudden embarrassed silence as Eve stared from one man to another. They declared their loyalty to her, because she was Richard's wife and their countess, at the same time holding her people in contempt. "I want Turlough moved to a private bower, near my own. He's to have a slave boy to see to his needs. One that speaks Irish."

"He's tried to escape more than once, Lady."

"Then place a sentry at his bower door, and keep him well guarded when he moves about, but I won't tolerate another hour of this mistreatment." She turned her attention to Turlough.

"What was that about?" His voice was surly, but eager as well to understand what was going on around him.

"I've ordered them to move you to a private room. Why didn't you let anyone know how they were treating you?"

"I'm a hostage. I expect no better."

His words sent a chill leaping down her spine. Was Egan being subjected to such harshness? "You're under the care of the Earl of Pembroke, and he will not allow a royal hostage to be so used."

The boy smirked at her, and winced at the pain it brought to his bruised and swollen face. "It's a foolish thing. It'll be easier for me to escape, if you free me from my vicious watchdogs."

"You won't be unguarded, just more comfortable."

He shook his head. "I will escape, that I vow. And when I do, be sure the life of your brother is as good as over."

His eyes were cold, hard and full of hatred when he said it, and Eve believed him. Was she making a mistake? But it was wrong to keep him isolated and abused. He could escape no better once gone from the barracks. His guards would be as vigilant as ever. He was making an idle boast, no more.

"I've come to tend to your wounds, not listen to your threats. Mark my words well, Turlough, should any harm come to my brother, the entire force of the earl of Pembroke's army will be used to revenge him. Now, tell me where you are hurt."

"Don't lay a finger on me, whore."

She stepped back as though slapped. The hate was like a living, writhing thing inside him, eating at his mind and heart. What hope was there for peace in Ireland when hatreds ran so inflexibly deep? Even she was not above threatening revenge should Egan come to harm, falling into the trap of revenge that kept Ireland at war.

She turned and walked away from him, past the silent soldiers, out into the cold, hard evening. The rain fell in heavy, oppressive torrents. It was as though the heavens themselves wept for Ireland.

The next few weeks passed in a flurry of preparation for Morgan and Caitlin's wedding. Eve had little time to worry about Turlough O'Conor and his threats. As far as she knew he made no attempt to escape from the bower she had him moved to, and she was content to leave him to his guards and his cold, righteous anger.

On Christmas morning all the bells of Dublin rang in a happy clamor. It was a day for rejoicing, when the world is made new and filled with hope. It was Caitlin's wedding day.

Eve finished lacing the sides of her cousin's gown, and turned Caitlin around to face her. The pink satin and rose silk had been made into a costume of stunning beauty, and the delicate colors complemented Caitlin's white-and-pink complexion. On this day her gold hair had been loosened from their braids and hung in heavy, shimmering waves down her back.

"There is one last thing." Eve picked up the gold coronet from where it lay on the table and placed it on her cousin's head. Tears glossed Caitlin's blue eyes.

"Why do you cry?"

Caitlin wiped the tears from her face, and gave a weak smile. "I am so happy. And so scared."

"Do you love Morgan?"

"With all my heart."

"Anyone who looks at the man can see he's besotted with you, as he should be. There is every reason to be happy."

"I'm afraid of losing him, of something awful happening. The joy is too great. It makes me wary of anything that might take it away."

Eve sighed and put an arm around her cousin's waist, drawing her close. "We can never know what the future holds, but if we hesitate to live each day fully, for fear of what might happen, we never know the greatest joys. Sorrow will come to you and Morgan, as it does to all of us. But you have your love to see you through the hard places."

Caitlin straightened her shoulders and nodded agreement. "There's a church full of people waiting for us. What are we doing standing here babbling?"

With joyful hearts they walked through the cold streets of Dublin to the cathedral. People who saw them cheered, and as they approached the church, someone in the round stone tower rang the bells in an exuberantly happy peal.

"Pray for me," Caitlin whispered, then turned and walked proudly into the church. Eve followed more slowly.

The cathedral church of the Holy Trinity was icy cold on this Christmas morning. Eve stood on the women's side and watched as her breath rose in a cloud of vapor. At the high altar, Lorcan, resplendent in vestments of green silk and gold embroidery, officiated at the office of Lauds, to be followed by Mass, and then the exchange of vows between Morgan and Caitlin.

The church was crowded with knights wearing the floor-length, formal tunics they favored in winter, while the Welsh and Irish soldiers dressed in Celtic costume, knees bare to the cold. Another test of manhood, Eve thought, who could best withstand the cold. She was dressed in a gown of dark-green velvet, her fur-lined cloak over it, for all the world could see an appropriately dressed noblewoman. But beneath the gown she wore the fur leggings Richard had bought for her, and was grateful for them.

The choir of monks, seated in their stalls beyond the rood screen, sang with undisguised joy at this happy feast. A few voices chanted the psalms with an ethereal sweetness, like angels loose on the earth. Some of the older monks, gone mostly deaf, made up for in exuberance what they lacked in harmony, until it was a cacophony of joyous noise. Eve smiled, thinking God well pleased with the spectacle. She glanced across the aisle to where the men stood, and caught Richard's attention. He winked at her and nodded, then turned his concentration back to the priests.

When the time came for her vows, Caitlin knelt beside Morgan before the altar. The church grew hushed with anticipation. Rarely had anyone seen such a lovely bride, or so affectionate a bridegroom. The love between the two was so obvious, like a luminous aura around their bowed heads, that hardened knights found themselves sniffling and wiping their noses on the backs of their velvet sleeves. The celibate monks were teary-eyed at the sight of such devotion and hope, and while some sighed with happiness for the bridal couple, a few of the younger monks knew a twinge of envy.

When the couple were pronounced irrevocably married, a great cheer rose from over a hundred throats, and the monks in their stalls jumped with surprise at so unseemly a display in God's house. Women smiled indulgently and wiped at their tears.

Morgan and Caitlin swept out into the churchyard with all the people trailing in their wake. There was the lightest skiff of snow on the ground, and the air was cold and pure and hard. Eve stayed back and watched as the others surged toward the hall, where the bride-ale would take place. Richard found her there.

"Are you not coming?" He placed a hand on her shoulder.

"In a moment. It's been so hectic these last few weeks, I wanted to savor the quiet. There's nothing more peaceful than a cold winter day, with the world hushed around you. Do you think they'll be happy together?"

"They've a better chance than most. They love each other."

She smiled and slipped her arm through his as they walked out into the cathedral yard. He was handsome today, in his strange Norman clothing. His long tunic was of a dark-blue velvet, trimmed with gray fur at collar and sleeves. The sword belt doubled at his waist accentuated how lean he was, and the jeweled hilt of his sword gleamed in the pale sunlight.

"There are those who say love is harmful in a marriage, that passion is a fickle and untamed beast," Eve said. "Marriage is a sober, solemn affair, to cement alliances, or join families for their mutual betterment." She glanced up at him, and noted the puzzled look in his gray eyes. "Do you think, my lord, that love is necessary to happiness?"

"Yes, I do. But like you I was raised not to expect to

find it in marriage. Love is supposed to be what a man reserves for his mistress, not his wife."

She felt a sharp pain near her heart. Did he still think of Rosamund? "Then a man who loves his wife is blessed—or a fool?"

He shook his head and, turning to face her, cupped her chin in the fingers of his hand. "What are you probing for, Princess? My heart is new at this and still unsure of itself, but I do know that I have been blessed more than I could have imagined possible by my marriage to you. I do love you, Eve. How can you doubt it?"

The lump in her throat made it impossible to speak. Instead, she buried her head in the soft velvet of his chest, and he wrapped her securely in his embrace, stroking her hair gently.

"You're trembling," he said. "Are you cold?"

"No, Husband, not cold. Your words are precious to me. More than I can tell you."

He tilted her head back to look into her eyes, and said very softly, "And do you love me, Eve?"

Reaching up with one hand, she placed it palm down on his cheek, and he leaned into it. She caressed him in that ageless lover's touch. "I would die if I could not love you. If I must some day choose between you and Ireland, I know I will choose you. You are my life, my soul, my happiness."

He turned his head and kissed the palm of her hand. "I'll never ask such a choice from you. You can have both me and Ireland. We'll make our happiness together, here in this land of yours."

She burrowed once more against his wide chest, and a wave of sadness washed through her joy. Whether he realized it or not, he had already asked her to choose, and she had chosen him. Ireland was like a lover she'd had in the past, leaving her with bittersweet memories, but it was no longer the passion that burned in her soul. Now only Richard fitted there, and the child she carried that was part of him.

"They'll wonder where we are if we stay out here much longer," she said, though she was reluctant to join the crowd in the hall, with the noise and heat. What she wanted was to spend the day with Richard, secure in his love, naked in his arms. The thought warmed her and brought a blush to her cheeks. What a wanton she had become, liking nothing so much as having her husband in her bed.

"We have to at least make an appearance," he said, as though reading her thoughts. "We'll leave early."

There was promise in his eyes, and she laughed, stretching up on tiptoe to plant a kiss on his warm lips. He would not let her escape with that simple token, but gathered her up against him, and kissed her hungrily, probing with his tongue until she opened her mouth to him. A soft moan escaped from her, and she pressed herself closer to him, until the layers of velvet were scant barrier to their desire.

Finally, he pulled away, and smiled down at her. "What you do to me, woman! Come into the feasting before I commit sacrilege by taking you back into the church and having my way with you."

They walked across the frozen mud, happy in each other's company. Just as they reached the hall, with the cheerful sound of revelry spilling out at the door, there was a strange noise, so loud the earth seemed to shake beneath it. They stopped, startled. There it was again, louder. The crowd in the hall quieted, and people came out of the building to stare at the sky. All listened intently, unable to believe what they heard.

There it came again. Crashing waves of thunder, rolling into each other. Thunder, at Christmas, out of a clear sky. The more superstitious crossed themselves.

It was mid-January when Redmon FitzWilliam, swathed in a heavy, hooded cloak against the pelting sleet, arrived in Dublin from his post at Waterford. He was escorted immediately to the earl's bower. Richard stared at the man filling his doorway, then, frowning, crossed the room to pull Redmon into the warmth of the bower. "Dammit, Redmon, why didn't you give us warning you were coming? What's wrong? Is it Waterford? Why do you come alone?"

"Give him a chance to sit first." Eve pulled a chair closer to the fire. "Redmon looks as though he's ridden straight through. Whatever news he bears can wait a few minutes before the telling." She fussed around him like a broody hen, taking his wet cloak, having him sit, propping his feet before the fire. The big knight relaxed into the chair gratefully, and grunted with pleasure when she handed him a tankard of warm mead.

Richard paced impatiently. The woman was as stubborn as they came, and he knew better than to interrupt her when she was being solicitous to a guest. It was an inviolable Irish custom, this hospitality they delivered with almost religious fervor. If it meant an entire Irish family went hungry, a stranger seeking shelter ate well while at their hearth.

What was so urgent Redmon traveled unescorted? Why had he come instead of sending a messenger? What news could not be trusted to another? Finally, Richard could stand no more of it. "Well?" he fairly shouted, startling the big man and Eve, so that they both stared at him as though he were crazed.

"My lord?"

"Damnation, man, why are you here? What news?"

The red-haired knight took another long drink from his tankard and wiped the foam from his mouth with the back of his big hand. "Not good, any of it. The king is not pleased with you, Richard."

"Henry? What does he have to be dissatisfied with? I'm doing his dirty work for him in Ireland, just as he solicited me to do."

Redmon burped and sighed loudly with content. "Henry's decided to look at it a bit differently. Instead of remember-

ing he asked you to come to Ireland, he claims you're here
on your own, with your personal ambition in mind. He's
ordered a blockade of English and Welsh ports. We'll be
receiving no supplies, no more men will be joining us. In
short, Henry's jealous of the power and wealth you stand
to accumulate for yourself."

Richard clasped his hands behind his back to keep himself from hitting something, anything, in his frustration.
"Power and wealth he wants in his own hands, no doubt."

"Aye, well, the pope's edict did name Henry Lord of Ireland, not you."

"What does he mean to do about it?"

This time Redmon looked away, and cleared his throat
nervously before continuing. "He wants you out of Ireland."

"Now? But I haven't finished what I've begun. It would
be a monumental waste of time and money if we left now.
I've already paid to have five hundred knights join me before spring. I can't very well take my coin back from them."

"Henry's forbidden anyone giving them passage to Ireland. In fact, he's raising his own army to invade Ireland if
necessary, to stop you."

The silence in the room was stiff and careful. Richard
felt the sudden, overwhelming desire to get very, very
drunk.

"You cannot leave," Eve said, her eyes round with fear.

"No, nor will I. The Irish Sea is nearly impassable this
time of year. Henry can't expect me to comply with his
'request' before spring. Damn. I'd hoped to take the field
against Rory with an army he couldn't defeat. Now my task
is much more difficult, thanks to Henry Plantagenet's jealousy. He was ever too careful of his pride, and why? The
man is immeasurably wealthy, and owns more land than he
can account for. You'd think he has enough to worry about
without concerning himself with Ireland."

"Then you haven't heard?" Redmon said, glancing from one to the other.

"Heard what? There hasn't been a ship in Dublin Harbor since before Christmas. News from outside Ireland is slow in reaching us."

"The archbishop of Canterbury is dead."

"Thomas Becket?" Richard asked. "Now, there was a thorn in Henry's side. Good old Thomas gave him a long ride and much trouble. I always liked Thomas for that. But how dead? He was yet a young man."

Redmon looked uncomfortable and reluctant now to tell what he knew. "Murdered."

"Did you say murdered?" Eve asked, her voice high with the absurdity of it. "Surely I didn't hear you correctly. Who would dare murder an archbishop?"

"The pope blames King Henry. Henry blames himself, though he was in Normandy at the time. He complained too loudly once too often about the trouble Becket gave him. Seems four of his more loyal and less intelligent knights took the king at his word, and got rid of the troublesome priest for him."

"When?" Richard asked.

"It was strange. On Christmas Day we heard thunder at Waterford, I swear it. Folk say it was heard in England as well, and many wondered what such an omen foretold. Becket was killed a few days after Christmas, on the very steps of the cathedral altar as he prepared to say Mass. Some already call him Saint."

Richard's stomach clenched at the sacrilege, the barbarity of it. The quarrel between Becket and the king, long-standing and acrimonious, had merit on both sides. This could only inflame the issue of who had the right to invest men in church offices, the King or the Church. It could serve Henry no good. The king must be writhing with guilt.

"The pope wants the king to do public penance for Becket's murder," Redmon said.

"That's to be expected." Richard shook his head and turned toward the fire, his anger at Henry warring with compassion for the man. "How it must gall Henry's pride. He was never one to admit a mistake, especially not publicly." Richard took up a tankard and drank deeply from it, but the mead did little to soften his anger, or his disgust.

At one time Becket had been a close friend of Henry's, before the king made him archbishop. Before the archbishop discovered God . . . or God found him. It seemed now God loved Thomas too well and Henry not enough.

"If Henry wants to escape the pope's wrath, Ireland is a good enough excuse to keep him occupied," Eve said. "He'll be too busy to do penance if he's planning a campaign in Ireland."

She sat in her usual place beside the fire, but her face was pale, with a shocked look, and Richard noticed that her hands were clenched tightly together in her lap.

"She's right," Redmon said.

"God curse that man! Nothing I've ever done has satisfied Henry Plantagenet. So be it. If Henry wants me out of Ireland, he damned well must come and get me. I'm not going anywhere."

"He's still our liege lord," Redmon said, his voice full of worry.

"I'll not ask you to break your vows to the king. You've been too loyal a friend for that. Any of my men who wish to leave are free to do so."

Redmon grunted, and poured himself another tankard full of mead. "I'm not going anywhere anytime soon. Even if Henry comes to Ireland he can't put an army together before next summer. Who knows what the situation here will be by then?"

Richard was grateful for the man's loyalty. So much so that he had to hide his emotions by going over to the fire and violently tossing a turf of peat onto it. The flames sprang up, and a shower of sparks escaped onto the hearth stones. He stomped them absently.

"How goes it in Waterford?" Richard asked.

"Quiet enough, though there are always rumors Hasculf is preparing to attack, to take back what we've taken from him." Redmon shook his head. "Seems he's a nasty bastard, mean as they come. I'd not want to bargain with him. What's O'Conor like? You've met him?"

"In November, when we exchanged Dermot's son for Rory's in a winter truce," Richard said.

Redmon whistled in surprise. "That's risky at best. Is the prince safe with O'Conor?"

"Probably safer than Rory's son is under my father's tender care," Eve said, her eyes flashing.

"O'Conor seems an honorable man," Richard said. "At least as honorable as can be expected in this tangle of old feuds. Rory and his followers have good cause to hate Dermot. In truth, if I had known more about the man, I'd never have agreed to be his ally."

"Then why stay? Why fight for Dermot, if you can't trust or respect him, especially now with Henry angry with you as well?"

Richard stood behind Eve, and placed his hands on her shoulders. She reached up to touch him. "I've too much at stake in Ireland to leave now."

Even Redmon, who did not have a romantic thought in his head, seemed to understand. "Then it's true, what we've heard? There's to be an heir to Pembroke come summer?"

"An heir to Pembroke, and to Leinster," Eve said, one hand going instinctively to the small mound of her belly.

"Reason enough," Redmon said. "You've planted your seed in Ireland, my lord. It needs time to take root. God willing, Henry will be delayed in his coming and you'll get the time you need."

Twenty-three

Winter settled in like an unwelcome guest, with interminable days of rain and fog. The end of February brought the first tentative hints of spring, a warming in the daytime under a pale sun, a hopeful greening around the edges of fields. By Saint Walburga's feast day, Dervorgilla knew two things: spring was near, and Dermot was dying. He couldn't die soon enough to please her.

With the coming of spring her fear mounted, until it would not let her sleep, hounding her relentlessly. Her mind focused on one overriding fear. The longer Egan was held hostage by Rory, the more danger he was in. Pacing back and forth in the king's bower, she twisted the rings on her fingers and fought to control her frustration and anger. Dermot sat listlessly in front of the fire, a heavy fur robe over his lap. He had lost weight and was often beset by nausea and vomiting and intense pains in his gut. Lately he fatigued easily, and he found it hard to eat, so tender was his ulcerated mouth. He grew weaker each day. When he would die Dervorgilla did not know, but she enjoyed watching death come creeping after him. Strangely, Dermot himself had not yet come to the realization that his days on earth were numbered.

Since the day Egan left, she had dosed Dermot with small amounts of deadly autumn crocus. The herb was quickly lethal given in a large enough dose, but she wanted no one to suspect her hand in his death. Once Dermot was gone, she would rid herself of Eve. Then Richard would be free to rule with her, as Egan's guardian.

Dermot spoke of little now except the campaign he planned against O'Conor. As soon as the fighting began, her son's life would be at greater risk. Should Rory find himself in a losing position, Egan's life could well be forfeit.

You old fool, she thought, glaring at him from across the room. *You put my son in mortal danger. For that alone you deserve to die.* She turned again to her nervous pacing. The bower was oppressively hot, to please Dermot, and sweat ran in rivulets down her sides, soaking her gown. Four futile months of pleading and arguing could not persuade Dermot to liberate Egan. What could she do to free her son?

She could not go to Rory to plead her cause. Tiernan would be there, as he ever was, close by Rory's side. How she hated cruel, one-eyed Tiernan, who was still her husband for all her years with Dermot. Forced to wed him when she was little more than a child, she remembered with disgust his hard use of her, thinking only of his own pleasure. Then came Dermot, and she had set out to snare his heart so that he risked everything to steal her away from Tiernan. Now Dermot betrayed her.

She needed Egan. He was her future, not that pitiful shell of a man huddled at the hearth. As mother of the next king of Leinster, she could expect years of unquestioned rule. To have that ambition threatened was beyond imagining. She would not tolerate such a fate.

Marching over to stand beside Dermot, she demanded, "When will you have my son returned to me?"

Dermot did not trouble to glance up at her. "Not again, woman. I'm in no mood for your tantrums. The boy is safe enough where he is."

"He is not! How can you allow this? I still can't believe you were fool enough to make him a hostage. What could you have been thinking?"

"I don't need to explain myself to you."

She wanted to slap him, to vent her anger fully, to make him suffer even as she suffered. "How can you be so unconcerned toward your own son?"

He did look at her then, and his eyes were cold and unmerciful. "I have only your word to go on for the boy's parentage. For all I know he's the son of a stable slave."

It was as though he hit her in the gut, so unexpected was the accusation. Never had he voiced such a suspicion, but it explained his actions. With growing dread, she realized he would not care if Egan died, that her son was an expendable pawn in Dermot's vicious game. "You are a greater fool than I ever imagined, old man. If you will not free your son, I shall."

"Do whatever you want. Just leave me alone. Your constant voice in my ear grows tiresome." He turned back to the fire, seeking the warmth there.

Grabbing her cloak from its peg by the door, she marched out into the wind-scoured day and crossed the muddy yard to the royal stable. The grooms and stable boys were so startled to see her, none thought to run from her extravagant wrath. She grabbed the nearest boy roughly. "I want two of your fastest horses saddled. Now! I'll be back for them soon."

They jumped to do her bidding, and the quick triumph of power that surged through her at having her command obeyed without question was like the best wine laughing in her blood. She picked up her skirts in both hands and trudged on, toward the bower where Turlough O'Conor was kept under close guard.

The two guards at the door came to attention as she approached. "Get O'Conor out here, and see he's dressed for a long ride."

"Lady, we have orders from the king, the boy is not to leave the royal enclave."

"God's blood, who do you think you're talking to? Do

as I say, or the king shall hear of your disobedience. It's not your place to question me. Do as I command!"

They looked nervously at each other. "He's our responsibility—"

"I'll take full responsibility, you fool. Just do it!"

The men finally judged it prudent to do as she demanded. It was not long before Turlough appeared, bundled into a warm cloak, gloves on his hands. Sullen-faced but curious, he came toward her.

"Where are we going?"

"Don't ask questions, boy. Just follow me." Turning back toward the stable, she did not check to see if he followed. She smiled to herself. This was so simple, why hadn't she thought of it before? Egan would be back in her arms within days. She walked faster toward the waiting horses.

"M'lady, wait."

Turning once again, she saw the two Irish guards running to catch up with her. What patience she had left was sorely tested. These insignificant men were interfering with her purpose. She turned her back on them and continued toward the horses.

Just as she mounted, the guards reached her and stood on either side of her stirrups. "Lady, wait but a minute and we'll join you. We can't let you ride unescorted. The boy may try to overpower you and escape."

"No. What I want to say to O'Conor is for his ears only."

"Then let us bind the boy so he can't ride off on his own.

They were not worth arguing with. All she wanted now was to be clear of Dublin. "Do what you must."

They tied a stout rope around Turlough's hands, then secured his hands to the pommel of his saddle. They bound his feet to his stirrups, then handed her the reins of his horse. She smiled at them sweetly, thanking them for their concern, and assured them she would return within the hour. The gate was opened to her reluctantly, but it was opened.

They rode through slowly and in silence. When they were out of hearing, without turning her head to look at him, she spoke to the boy. "Don't think of escaping. Once we're out of sight of Dublin, I'm setting you free."

"Why?" His voice was sharp, edged with suspicion.

"There's no ambush waiting, if that's what worries you. I'm acting on my own. Call it a mission of mercy."

The laugh that escaped him was full of mockery. "Do you expect me to believe you give a dog's fart for my welfare?"

She looked at him then, and he grew somber under her cool gaze. "You're not stupid, boy. If you were, I'd let you rot. I want one thing from you." He waited expectantly, but said nothing. "When you return to your father, I want my son released and returned to me. Unharmed."

"What makes you think my father will agree to such a thing?"

"I know Rory well enough to know he's hounded by an overactive sense of honor. There's no reason for him to hold Egan, once you are safely in his camp."

They rode several miles in silence, until she was sure they had not been followed. Stopping the horses, she turned in her saddle to look at the boy. "Swear to me, Turlough, on all you hold holy, that you will do as I bid you."

He hesitated a moment. "I swear it, Lady. Justice will be done."

Satisfied, she cut the ropes from his hands and feet and handed him the reins of his horse. She watched until he galloped into the concealing Irish mist.

"She did what?" Richard looked from the distraught knight to Morgan, and back again.

"Dervorgilla helped O'Conor's son escape," the knight said.

"I heard what you said, I just don't understand it. How

could she have done such a thing? Why? Does Dermot know?"

Morgan shook his head. "That was strange, if what I heard is true. Dermot laughed himself sick when she told him."

Eve stood beside Richard, her hand on his forearm. "Surely she didn't believe Egan would be released?"

"It would seem that is exactly what she believes." Morgan looked at Richard and shrugged. "She's a mother. She was distraught over the danger her child is in and acted foolishly."

"You're more understanding than I can afford to be," Richard said. "Dervorgilla has broken the truce and removed O'Conor's reason to hold back. He may attack before I can convince Henry to release my troops."

"Then Henry is still adamant? No more men will be coming from England or Wales?" Morgan asked.

"Last I heard he was busy trying to appease the pope for Becket's death, but he still had enough excess energy to rave about my unbridled ambition." Richard shook his head. "For now it's Rory who worries me. Until I know what he'll do, I can't worry about Henry's jealousy."

Morgan placed a hand on Richard's shoulder. "God grant Rory will be merciful with the boy."

Richard could only nod, and plan for war.

Twenty-four

There was a hint of warmth in the March air, with a mild breeze blowing inland from the sea. Eve touched her heels to her mare's flanks, smiling with joy as the animal broke into a smooth gallop. It was two days since Dervorgilla had helped Turlough escape, and there was no sign of Egan, no message from Rory's camp. She was going mad with worry and had convinced Richard they needed time alone, if only for a morning, away from the cares that burdened them.

Richard followed on his stallion, Emys. Both animals were excited after long confinement, and eager to run. Eve let the mare have her head, and bent lower over the animal's neck, settling into the rhythm of the ride like a dancer with a well-suited partner.

It was the first time in weeks she had been riding, and the greening fields of Ireland flew beneath her. A song thrush stood in a meadow, head tilted, listening for worms. From the trees the high-pitched call of a goldcrest followed them over the hills and toward the river. Eve slowed the mare to an easy canter, then to a walk.

"Is it safe for you to be riding like that?" Richard's eyes squinted with worry and focused on her belly, which was now too rounded with the child to keep hidden beneath loose gowns and winter cloaks.

"I feel wonderful. How can it be wrong? Surely the child is healthy and strong, if I am."

"I worry you'll fall."

"I never fall." She saw the concern in his face, and sighed. "I'll stop when it grows uncomfortable, when I'm too ungainly to mount on my own. That will be soon enough. For now, let's enjoy the day, and our hours together."

He looked up at the sky, with its high, scattered clouds and patches of clear blue. "We may be safe from rain for a few hours. Where is that place you told me of? Are we near?"

"Just there, beyond that great oak tree."

They rode toward the tree, and Eve's excitement heightened. She had discovered this cloistered place years ago, and often came here to be alone when the world crowded in on her. Here, in her private world, she could escape for a few hours. Now she was going to share it with Richard. Slowly she was learning to share all the little corners of her life with him. Soon there would be no secrets left.

In the lee of a hill a secluded meadow grew, ringed with rowan which were just beginning to bud. In another month they would be in bloom and the meadow would be covered with soft grass, ferny bracken, and bluebells. Now it was a pale, new green, just coming back from sodden winter.

"It's not at its best this early in the year," she said, letting him help her down from the saddle. "We'll come back this summer, after the baby is born. It's glorious then."

"It's not bad now," he said, holding her close. They stood quietly, enjoying the view, and the sweet, clean scent of early spring. The horses lowered their heads to the tender grass and began to feed.

Was it only eight months since this man rode into her life? She felt she had known him forever, as though they were linked in eternity and her life before him had been a time of waiting. Now life and love grew in her, and she felt an overwhelming urge to revel in it, here in this secret place.

"Did you bring the blanket?" she asked.

"It's in my saddlebag, with the food." He released her to fetch their meal.

"I need to relieve myself—"

"When don't you these days?"

"Just set the food out, de Clare. I'm hungry."

He bowed to her in mocking subservience and she pushed at his hard chest. Laughing, he toppled over into the grass as though her touch felled him. He would have pulled her down on top of him, but she stepped aside and skittered away. Walking into the surrounding shrubs and behind some rocks, where he could not see, she quickly slipped out of her clothing. Shivering, she put the warm cloak back on, careful to hold it closed in front. Plastering an innocent look on her face, she walked back to where he sat waiting, food spread out around him on the blue wool blanket.

"I hope you're hungry," he said. "Look at all the food the kitchen sent. There's cheese and cold salmon and young onions and cider. Too bad it's Lent, or we could have had some lamb with that mint sauce Cook is so good at making. Well, what are you waiting for?"

She waited until he looked up at her, then slowly, gracefully, she raised her hand to the brooch that held her cloak clasped at her neck. The fur-lined garment fell from her shoulders to reveal her nakedness, and she noted the quick, hungry look in his gray eyes.

Raising her arms above her head, she began to sway to a slow, gentle music that played in her head. She danced on the cool, wet grass, until her feet sparkled with drops of dew like quicksilver. Turning slowly one way, then the other, she moved in ancient abandon, wild as the ponies that wander the hills, gentle as the spring sun, pagan as the voice of the water rushing over rocks in the river. Her belly thrust out proudly in front, her breasts, heavy and blue-veined with her pregnancy, bounced as she moved, and the nipples hardened in the cool air. She was humming under her breath, and her eyes were partially closed.

She felt like a goddess of the old religion, pregnant with the world, fertile, life-giving, bountiful. Her hands went to her hair and began to unweave the braids, until the abundant veil of it flowed unrestrained behind her. The hair tickled her back, her thighs, her breasts, and she laughed.

The groan, deep and wild, from Richard made her smile wider. She glanced at him from under her lashes, looking over her shoulder. He was naked. And magnificent. She held out a hand to him.

They were savage and pure and timeless together, under the racing clouds, with the ancient hills to bear witness. When they were done, they lay exhausted and content and fed each other bits of cheese, and drank the cider until their blood cooled. Then they slept, their cloaks over their nakedness, curled into each other, her buttocks against his hips, his hand draped over her belly, with the child kicking softly.

She came awake suddenly and sat up, listening.

"What is it?" His hand reached for his sword.

"I'm not sure. I thought I heard something, but now I don't know what it was."

They listened intently, but only the subtle sounds of spring whispered near them. "Mayhap it was a dream," he said. "It's getting late, and those clouds look ominous. We'd better get back to Dublin before the rain comes."

She frowned, wishing she could identify the noise. It seemed so familiar, and so urgent. They dressed, cold now, but a lingering tenderness, the remembrance of pleasure, lay between them and made them reluctant to hurry.

Then the noise came again, clear and unmistakable—and unbelievable—down the river valley toward them. It was close, and, gathering her skirt, Eve broke into a run, Richard following. She crested the nearest hill and saw the big white wolfhound racing toward her.

"Ban!"

The dog barked again, and the sound was like joy, golden

and rare, echoing around the hills and into her heart. She knelt in the grass, and the dog came into her arms, pushing and dancing with excitement, licking her face and whining, his tail wagging so hard it seemed it would come off.

Laughing, she pounded on his chest and rubbed her hands through his damp, smelly fur. "You great ugly beast, what are you doing here? Did you bring Egan with you?"

Richard stood over them, scanning the horizon in the direction the dog came from. "I don't see anyone."

"But Egan must be coming. Why else would Ban be here?"

Richard looked down at the dog. "What's that around his neck?"

For the first time she saw it. "Ban, sit." The dog obeyed, sitting quietly, and she knelt in front of him. Her hands trembled as she undid the chain of gold around his neck. At the end of the chain hung the cross she had given to Egan before he left.

"It's some sort of message." She stared at the gold in her hand. "But what can it mean? Is Egan in trouble?"

"I don't know. Mayhap he's come with the dog after all, and has ridden on to Dublin. Ban caught your scent in the wind and came here."

He is trying to reassure me, she thought, and clutched the chain in her cold hand. "Yes, Egan is waiting for us in Dublin. Hurry, Richard, we must hurry."

Egan was not in Dublin, just as Richard feared he would not be. He tried to hide his concern from Eve, knowing she worried. "The boy is intelligent and strong. If he finds a way, he'll escape."

"Is there nothing we can do, Richard? Can't you go to Rory, ask for the boy back?"

They were in their bower, and it was late. They had argued this back and forth for hours. Richard struggled with what he said next. "If I thought it would help I'd go there on my knees. You know I never wanted Egan held hostage, but what good will it do? It gives Rory that much more power if he sees us desperate or fearful. Chances are he'll release the boy himself in a day or two, now that Turlough is back."

"You don't know that." There was anger and fear in her voice.

"What would you have me do? Do you think O'Conor would allow me to ride unchallenged into his camp and ride back out with the boy? Stop thinking with your heart and use your head. Dervorgilla has handed Rory a powerful weapon to use against us. How are we to attack O'Conor, knowing it would be a death sentence for Egan?"

"I never knew you to be a cold-hearted bastard." She stalked the bower, back and forth. "The longer you leave Egan in Rory's camp, the more danger he is in, why won't you see that? You forget, I know Rory. He will honor a truce flag. You can at least make the effort. For God's sake, Richard, he's my brother. We must do something."

He tried not to let his anger flare at her words. Eve placed too much trust in her past association with O'Conor. Could he trust the High King to honor a truce flag? If he could be sure of that, he would ride to Rory's camp in the morning and ask for the boy's release. But how could he be sure of the man? His own anger and uncertainty made his words harsher than he meant them to be. "Rory would think it a sign of weakness if I went begging for the boy's life. The other alternative is to demand his release, and such a demand would have to be backed up by the threat of force. With the reinforcements I'd counted on no longer available, I'm in no position to back up demands with arms. There is nothing we can do for Egan."

She rounded on him in fury. "Are you so blinded by ambition you'll sacrifice my brother to it? Is Egan expendable, as long as you get what you came to Ireland for? I can almost believe you want Egan's death. There would be no one to contest your claim to Leinster if he were dead."

Her words were like a fist in his gut. "You dare say such a thing to me? We won't discuss this further."

"Don't you order me to be quiet, damn you! If you won't do anything to help Egan, I shall. Rory will listen to me."

"I forbid it! You're not to go anywhere near O'Conor, do you hear me?" He had never shouted at her with such anger before, and he saw her flinch under it, her green eyes brimming with tears she refused to shed.

She had never made him so furious before, or filled him with such fear. "I'll triple the guard at the gates, if necessary, but I won't allow you to leave Dublin." He grabbed his cloak from the wall peg and headed toward the door.

"Where are you going?"

"I'm sleeping in the barracks tonight." He slammed out of the bower. The night was cold, and hinted of rain. Damned Irish rain. He was sick of it. Everything was a mess. He was stuck in Ireland with a large portion of his army stranded in Wales because of Henry's stupidity. The longer he was forced to wait, the more men O'Conor gathered, but with Egan held hostage how could he attack? His one refuge from it all was Eve. He had come to depend on the deep, rich love she offered him. It was his solace and his strength. The rain started. He cursed as he marched toward the barracks.

Eve stared at the door for a long time. She felt abandoned. His anger, like a dark presence, lingered in the room and chilled her heart. She had said horrible things and wished she could recall them. At the same time she felt he had not listened to her, had discounted her as an emotional woman who needed to be quieted. Anger and regret seethed in her in equal measure. She wrapped her arms around her breasts to try to control the trembling that shook her body.

What was she without Richard's love to shelter her? But he was wrong about Rory.

With all her heart Eve wanted to believe Rory would not hurt her brother. Rory had been kind to her, the summer she spent with him. That was before war made them enemies. War, she knew, could make a man do things he would not do in time of peace. It forced horrific decisions on them.

There was a sharp fear deep in her gut that Richard's reassurances could not touch. Egan was in danger. There were others besides Rory who could harm the boy, including Turlough. Although Dervorgilla had been careful not to allow her son much contact with Eve, she had fond memories of her brother, and a strong affection for him. She had changed his soiled swaddling, heard his first chattered words, watched as he learned to walk, to run, to ride.

Perhaps it was true, what Richard said. Perhaps Rory would release the boy. Could she gamble Egan's life on that possibility? Since Rory had not let Egan go he could no longer be considered a hostage. Egan was now a prisoner. No one, not even an honorable man such as Rory, treated a captive well for long.

Ban lay before the hearth, snoring and twitching, as though he had never been away. The dog would not have come back if Egan had not sent him, of that she had no doubt at all. Ban had fulfilled his mission by letting her know Egan needed help. Now what could she do? The idea that formed in her mind frightened her. If she told Richard, he would forbid such a reckless scheme. She saw no other way and knew she'd have to deal with her husband's anger when she returned.

Rory's army was at Drogheda, in Tiernan's territory. If she started now she could be there by midday tomorrow. It was past midnight when the rain stopped, and she slipped out of the bower. A few stars could be seen between the fleeing clouds. The world was foreign to her in the darkness. Familiar shapes took on strange and menacing forms, and shadows played in the imagination. There would be moonlight for another hour or two. She could not risk using the lantern she carried until she was out of sight of the extra sentries Richard had posted on Dublin's walls. Nor could she retrieve her mare from the stable; there were too many grooms and squires asleep in the straw. If they woke, they would be sure to ask questions.

It was easy enough to slip unseen past the guards. She was as familiar with Dublin as she was with her own body, and knew just where a gap in the wall was large enough for a small woman to fit through. She had used it since childhood, whenever she wanted to roam unnoticed outside the walls. It took a minute to find the breach again, it was so overgrown with ivy, and she had to pull at the thick, strong arms of the plant to make her way through. She almost did not fit through the space, having forgotten that she had never been six months pregnant before.

The fields were wet, and she hiked her skirts up above her knees, pulling the back hem between her legs and securing it in front with her girdle. Pale lumps of sheep, with tiny new lambs, slumbered and chewed as she passed. An owl, hunting in the night, flew by on velvety wings.

She walked fast, every now and then stopping to catch her breath. The baby slowed her, and she could not go far without tiring. It was several hours past noon when she came to the edge of Rory's camp, near the river Boyne. She stopped to let down her skirts and tidy her hair, then walked as regally as her aching legs and sore feet would allow to confront the nearest guards.

"Ay? Who's that? What's yer business, lassie?"

"Ain't no lass that one, Malcolm. She's breeding big."

"Ye're right about that, ye are, Colin. Mistress then, stead o' maid, all the same, it's not a place for no decent matron. So what be yer business?"

The one called Colin was tall, thin, and bald, while his companion was shorter and very blond. Both were in their middle years, simple farmers by the looks and sound of them, set to guard the periphery of Rory's camp. Other groups of men scattered along a line seemed stationed to the same purpose. There was little chance Egan could slip through this tight a net.

"I've come to see the High King."

The tall man gave a rude snort of a laugh. "Did ye hear that, Malcolm? She's come to see Rory hisself. And why should Rory be wanting to see ye, save for the obvious reasons?" The man leered at her, and Eve resisted the urge to slap his insolent face.

"Tell him the princess of Leinster has come to talk to him."

The men looked startled, the taller one squinting at her as though unsure to believe her.

"Well, she don't look much like a peasant, now do she," Malcolm said.

"She's playing us fer fools, I tell ye. What business would Dermot's daughter have with Rory?"

"I've come about my brother." Eve hoped they did not notice the nervousness in her voice.

Malcolm poked the taller man in the ribs. "Makes sense to me. Now Turlough is back, they'd be after wanting their own lad." He turned back to Eve and frowned. "But have ye come alone, lassie, on foot, and in your condition?"

She smiled at his solicitous tone. Compassion was never far below the surface in an Irishman. Placing the back of her hand to her forehead, as though she were exhausted and near collapse, she said, "I've walked all night to see my poor brother. I can't rest until I've seen for myself he's safe."

"God's toes, there speaks a true Irishwoman," Malcolm fairly bellowed. "Would to God they were all as loyal as ye, lassie. Come, my dear, I'll show ye direct to the king."

Malcolm brought her to a large tent in the midst of a sprawling encampment. Wildflowers bloomed in the fields in clusters of pink and yellow. She waited outside while her guide announced her. A new fear twisted in her. Rory's army was huge. Men, as far as she could see, were camped in tents or had plaids spread on the ground for beds. Richard was right. Rory had spent the winter, not in idleness but in gathering men to his banner.

She could not help thinking how different her life would be if her father had been content to be one of Rory's under-kings, instead of lusting after the High Kingship for himself. There would have been peace in Leinster. There would be no foreigners in their land now, nor rumor of war.

Richard disagreed with her, believing Henry Plantagenet would have come soon anyway. She was beginning to think he was right. The pope had given King Henry a mandate to rule in Ireland, to convert the Irish to a stricter conformity with Rome, to quash once and for all the unsettling customs of the Celtic Church. It was hard for her to believe the pope so ignorant a man he thought the Irish unorthodox. She despaired of understanding the minds and hearts of ambitious men.

Nervously, Malcolm ushered her to the tent, then hurried away as soon as she was through the entrance. The interior was dark, and it took a moment for her eyes to adjust. There were three men standing inside, with the leavings of a large meal on a table. Her stomach growled at the sight of food, then she focused her attention back on the men.

Rory she recognized. One of the other men, older, small and thin with a sharp, ugly face, wore a patch over one eye. This must be Tiernan O'Rourke, Dervorgilla's estranged husband. Being in the same room with the man made her skin crawl. The third man, hugely tall, with reddish blond hair braided into long plaits and a deadly Norse ax stuffed into his belt, glared at her with undisguised anger. Who he was she could not be sure, but instinctively she moved closer to Rory.

"What a piece of luck this is," the big man said in Irish

heavily accented by the cadences of Norway. "Now we have Dermot's daughter as well as his son. The entire Leinster dynasty in our hands."

She turned her attention to Rory. "My lord, I've come to petition you for the release of my brother. Your son has been returned to you. There is no longer any reason to hold Egan hostage."

Rory placed a finger at his lips and studied Eve carefully. "You are either very brave or very foolish to come here. Would I be correct in assuming your husband does not know of your whereabouts?"

"He'll come for me at sunset if I haven't returned by then."

The smallest of smiles curved along Rory's mouth, and he flicked her a look that told her he did not believe a word of it. The smile was gone when he turned to his companions. "I have no wish to have Richard de Clare come calling this day, gentlemen. What say we grant the lady's request?"

The Norseman shouted his outrage. "Have you lost your mind? Or have you forgotten what that bastard Dermot did not more than eight months ago? Seventy of my best men killed!"

"Shut up, Hasculf. Of course I remember. It doesn't change our situation now. I do not want de Clare here." Rory's voice was strong and commanding. Only a fool would question his authority. The other man was quiet, but she could see anger still raged in him.

So this was Hasculf. It was his men her father had slaughtered at Waterford, throwing them into the river to drown. She could understand the man's wrath, losing his companions in so vile and treacherous a way.

When Tiernan spoke, it was in a voice as smooth as silk, a peculiarly seductive voice coming from so unappealing a man. It was like listening to a snake with poetry on its tongue. "Let the princess have her brother. Surely we have no use for the boy, and really, Hasculf, the idea of harassing a pregnant woman and a boy to satisfy your overwrought sense of vengeance is just too barbaric. You abandoned your men to their fate. You're as much to blame as Dermot."

She thought Hasculf would kill him, but something deadly glittered in Tiernan's eye, and Hasculf backed down.

"Tiernan, bring Egan here," Rory said. The man left quickly to do as he was bid. "Are you hungry? There is some cider and bread left."

She shook her head. How could he expect her to eat? She would see her brother in a few minutes, and they would go home together. Her plan had worked. Richard would be so proud of her. Still, she was nervous and wanted to put her arms around her brother and march him out of here. She would not feel safe until they were in Dublin.

Just when she thought she could endure it no longer, Egan stumbled into the tent. He was dirty and looked like he had just wakened, blinking in the darkness.

"Egan."

"Eve? Is that you?" His face lit up with delight, and she moved toward him, only to find herself roughly pushed aside by Hasculf.

Falling to her knees, she looked up to see the huge Norseman holding Egan by his long red hair. The boy looked startled, but not frightened. She started to rise, then stopped, seeing the flash of metal in the dim light.

The blade fell in its deadly arc, and Egan's body crumpled and fell to the floor. Why had he fallen? Something was wrong.

"Jesu!" Tiernan shouted. "Look at the mess you've made."

Rory reached down and pulled her up, just as she was about to crawl over to Egan's body.

"Something is wrong with my brother. I have to go to him."

"God's blood, Hasculf, I should have you hanged for this!" Rory shouted, still holding her in his strong arms.

What was he talking about? She looked up. Hasculf was holding something. It was Egan's head.

"Take this message to your father. May he rot in hell!" He flung the head at her.

Rory tried to turn her aside, but he was not quick enough. Egan's severed head hit her in the chest, leaving a sticky smear, then rolled to the floor. She stared at it.

That is Egan's head! No. That's impossible. Something is wrong, why won't he get up? Hasculf cut his head off. I saw the ax. No. No!

If I start screaming, I won't stop. God in heaven, there's an eternal scream in me. He killed my brother. I will not faint. I will not. Holy Mother of God, help me. He killed my brother. He'll kill my baby, if I faint. I can't be weak, not now, not in front of that man. I have to save my baby. Don't let me faint. Let me go home to Dublin. I can scream when I get home. Richard will hold me.

"Eve!"

Someone was shouting her name. She was cold, so cold she could not stop shaking.

"Eve, stop this now."

It was Rory, holding her, shouting at her through the red, bloody fog that surrounded her.

"You killed my brother. God in heaven, why?"

"I didn't order it, you have to believe me. I don't kill children." Rory's face was hard, and his eyes were full of disgust.

She believed him. He had meant to have Egan go home with her. It was Hasculf, who hated her father, who was obsessed with vengeance, who killed Egan. Who would kill *her,* if Rory were not there to protect her.

"I must take Egan back to Dublin." Her voice was oddly flat, as though someone else spoke the words.

"I'll have horses saddled. I'll escort you as far as I dare." Rory still held her up. "You do understand, Eve, how I regret this? You will explain what happened to de Clare?"

What did he want of her? That Richard know it was not Rory who had done this thing? She nodded, too exhausted to wonder why he cared so much what her husband thought of him.

What did he want of her? That he cared she was unharmed was obvious enough. She wished more this time... She realized she was exhausted. She wondered why she had to drink in her thirst in her thoughts.

Twenty-five

"There she is, and thanks be to God, looks unharmed," Morgan said.

Richard's relief was tempered by anger. After finding her gone that morning, he had been in a blind fury of anger and fear since then, coursing the countryside with a dozen of his men. To disobey him was one thing. To endanger herself and the child another. Where had she gone, and why? What must he do to convince that woman to listen to reason?

Who was the man riding with Eve? Richard touched his spurs to his stallion and galloped toward the pair, Morgan and a dozen knights on his heels. The man with Eve saw them, and, turning his gray Irish pony, galloped back the way he had come, leaving Eve to travel on alone.

"Do you want us to go after him?" one of the men asked.

"No, not until I've heard an explanation from my wife." The look on his face kept them from questioning him further.

Eve stopped, but she did not seem to see them. She sat her horse, her head bowed, as though oblivious to the world, though how she could miss the men and horses thundering down upon her he could not understand. A thread of worry wove itself into his anger.

Another horse, with some sort of bundle slung across its back, stood beside her, cropping lazily in the new grass.

He slowed his men to a trot, then a walk. He was afraid

to startle her, she had such a peculiar expression on her face. Like men after battle, trying to cope with what they had seen and heard. By God, if that man had hurt her in some way, he would pay with his life.

"Eve?" He slid from his saddle and came to stand beside her. She did not seem to hear him.

Morgan went to the second horse to see what the dull brown blanket covered.

"Eve, sweetling, talk to me." Richard touched her leg, and she turned to look at him.

"Richard?"

"Aye, love, it's me." He held out his arms and she fell into them, and clung to him so tightly he knew something terrible had happened. She was trembling all over, and was cold to his touch.

"Sweet merciful God!" Morgan cried.

Richard looked to where Morgan stood, white-faced, staring at a large sack of coarse brown hemp he held as though something unspeakable were inside it. The other men came, curious, and checked under the blanket, and looked into the sack Morgan held.

"Shit!"

"Who is it?"

"The prince, her brother." The men looked toward Eve, then quickly away.

Morgan came over to Richard, his face was drained of color. If Richard did not know him better, he would think the Welshman was about to faint.

"It's Egan." Morgan's voice was little more than a whisper. His throat worked as though he were trying to keep the bile down. "His body is on the horse. His head is in the sack."

"Jesu. Who did this?" Richard took Eve by the shoulders and forced her to look at him. "Who was the man you were riding with? Who killed Egan?"

Her eyes were huge in her pale face, desolate with shock.

She did not look as though she had cried. It would be better if she did, better than this wordless, devastating grief. He shook her gently, and that seemed to help her focus on what he was saying.

"Rory," she whispered.

"Rory killed Egan? Why?"

"Hasculf killed Egan. Rory rode with me, until he saw you and knew I would be safe."

"She's not making sense," Morgan said.

Richard wrapped an arm around her shoulder. "We'd better get her back to Dublin."

"Dermot must be told," Morgan said. "And Dervorgilla."

Shaking his head, Richard glanced at the bundle hidden by its blanket. As much as he disliked the Irish king and his concubine, they did not deserve this kind of pain. What could be worse than the loss of a child? "Let's try to keep Dervorgilla from seeing the body. Take Egan straight to the cathedral. Perhaps the monks can have him decently coffined before she knows of his death."

Sending two knights ahead, leading the horse with its horrible cargo, he started back toward Dublin, riding behind the others with Eve curled tightly in his lap. His anger at her going to Rory dissipated at sight of how fragile she was now. How could he berate her when she was so sunk in grief he was not sure she knew what was going on around her? There was still much he did not understand about this, but it would have to wait. Eve was too shaken for questions and recriminations. All he could do for her now was offer his comfort and protection, and hope it was enough.

As they entered Dublin, Lorcan came striding toward them, his face wreathed in sympathy and sorrow.

"Good Father, I need your help," Richard said. He lifted Eve down into her uncle's arms, then dismounted.

"I could hardly believe my eyes when they brought Egan to me," Lorcan said. "And I've seen more than one bloody battlefield in my day. I have the brother infirmarian building a coffin now. With luck, Dervorgilla won't know how her son died. How is Eve?"

"Not good. I'm worried, Lorcan. Crying, raving, screaming I'd expect, even welcome, because it's a release, but she's said hardly a word."

Lorcan supported his niece, and one elegant hand stoked her bright hair. "I've known her since she was born. There is great strength in her soul. She's seen a horrible thing, but she'll recover. Give it time, Richard."

Richard pushed his hair back with both hands, wishing he could get his hands around Hasculf's cowardly neck. What Dermot had done, treacherously killing men under a safe conduct, was reprehensible, but it had been an act of war. Hasculf murdered a child. Richard found that unforgivable.

It was inevitably the innocent who suffered most, though he tried to protect them, forbidding the killing of women and children, or the rape after a battle the average soldier counted his due reward for surviving. His men thought him crazed, but they obeyed him. They learned early the consequences of disobedience. The worst of it was watching Eve and not knowing how to relieve her suffering. Every warrior instinct in him goaded him to go after Hasculf. Every bit of his love warned him to stay with her.

There was a loud shout, and a tumult of people rushed from the king's hall, headed toward the cathedral. Dermot and a host of Irish men and women bore down on them.

"Not now," Richard said wearily.

"Take Eve away from here," Morgan said. "Lorcan and I can deal with Dermot."

"It's not just Dermot. He has Dervorgilla with him," Richard said.

"All the more reason to get Eve away from here. She doesn't need to see or hear this." Morgan's voice was soft with compassion.

"Too late," Lorcan said, and gently handed Eve over to her husband.

Dermot descended on Lorcan in a whirlwind of fury. Richard understood more of the Irish words than anyone would have supposed, but he kept quiet, holding Eve in his arms, trying to shield her by hiding her beneath his cloak. Lorcan's voice was low, calm, but it could not mitigate Dermot's wrath.

Dervorgilla stood silently, her hand to her mouth, her eyes huge with disbelief. "No!" Her scream silenced all others. "You're lying, my son can't be dead."

Dermot moved toward her, sympathy apparent on his face. "Dear woman, there's no reason for Lorcan to lie." He moved to put an arm around Dervorgilla's shoulder, but she pushed him away roughly.

"Don't touch me, you filthy bastard! You had Egan killed. I see it now, what a fool I've been. You knew Egan wasn't your son. You hated him."

"You don't know what you're saying." Dermot reached out, and again she refused his touch.

"You think you've won, don't you?" Dervorgilla stared wild-eyed at the silent crowd, then an ugly, vicious smile deformed her face. She turned again to Dermot. "Egan was to be king when you died."

"Be quiet, woman." Dermot no longer tried to approach the screaming woman. "I've suspected the boy wasn't mine, but I didn't know until now. I did not hate the lad and I don't kill children. I never named him my heir, he could never be king . . . how you could think otherwise I can't fathom. It's grief that makes you say such things."

"That's where you're wrong," Dervorgilla hissed. "How do you feel, Dermot? Weak lately? Had trouble eating, does your skin itch, your legs burn? You've been avoiding thinking about it, but death has hold of you."

"It's nothing, it will pass," Dermot said, but fear clouded his eyes.

"Nay, it will not. I've given you enough of the poison that you'll soon die. Then all I needed was to be rid of your daughter and that bastard she carries. The idiot I sent when she first married didn't do what I paid him for. An accident is so easy to arrange. Then Egan would be your only heir. It was Egan who was to be High King." Dervorgilla collapsed to her knees and wailed her pain to the heavens. "It was all for Egan, my little fire."

A horrified Morgan translated for Richard. Everything was clear now. It was Dervorgilla who sent the killer, and Eve had been her target.

Eve turned her face into Richard's chest, like a frightened child trying to hide from an imaginary phantom. Only hers were very real.

Lorcan gently helped Dervorgilla to her feet. "Come, Lady, let me help you."

"Just where do you think you're taking that traitorous slut?" Dermot's voice was glacial.

"Her son is dead. No matter what she's done, she has the right to spend a night in vigil before he's buried. I'm taking her to the cathedral."

"I want her under guard, locked in the deepest hellhole I can find," Dermot raved.

Richard placed a hand on Dermot's shoulder. "She's not going anywhere, I'll see to that."

Dermot nodded once. "You take care of it then, de Clare. If I get near the woman, I'll strangle her myself." The king turned and walked slowly away, his shoulders stooped.

Lorcan led Dervorgilla into the church where Egan lay, awaiting his final journey. Soon only Richard, Morgan, and Eve were left standing in the brittle spring sun.

"Come, love, I'll take you home." Richard's tone was low and soothing.

"It was my fault, Richard. I shouldn't have gone. I should have known who Hasculf was." The words came in an urgent rush and she began to shake violently, as though she could no longer contain the horror.

Richard held her more tightly. "Morgan, help me get her to the bower. I want to get her into bed, where she'll be safe."

"If she'll ever feel safe again," Morgan said.

A scream shattered the quiet, startling birds into flight. It was a scream of such primal anguish that all who heard it stopped to cross themselves and whisper a quick prayer for a soul in such obvious agony. It was Dervorgilla, screaming the scream of all mothers through the ages over the bodies of their children.

Richard saw then that Eve was crying, silently, and with such hopeless despair he wanted to raise his own voice in a shout against heaven.

Dervorgilla stumbled into her bower and closed the door behind her, leaning heavily against the rough wood. She could not pull a deep breath into her lungs, and her whole body trembled with the rage that still rode her like a demon. She had failed.

The monks had opened the coffin. She wanted to see Egan, to know beyond doubt he was truly dead. After screaming her rage to heaven, she finally walked out of the church and rushed to her bower, where she could be alone. Three armed guards escorted her, and now stood sentry outside her door, but they were not needed. She would not be going anywhere.

One of her maids approached her and said in a small, frightened voice, "Do you need help, m'lady?"

She stared at the insipid, cow-eyed woman, and the three others standing in a clot near the hearth. It was one of the banes of her existence, this lack of privacy. There was invariably someone about even when she was in most need of being alone. Her breathing was more normal now, and she straightened, forcing herself not to scream at them and send them all away.

"I'm expecting a visitor soon. I need to bathe and dress to prepare for him."

"Is the king coming?"

She nearly laughed at that. No, it was not Dermot who would be judging and condemning her tonight.

The bath was hot and soothing. When she finished, she sat before a blazing fire as one of her women combed her brilliantly red hair and another rubbed rose-scented oil into her smooth skin. She chose a gown of regal purple velvet, dark and dignified, and an undertunic of scarlet silk. Around her throat she fastened a necklace of pearls and amethysts, and on her fingers she wore gold rings encrusted with jewels. Her thick hair was plaited with ribbons of gold and strands of small pearls, and from her ears dangled delicate gold bobs that made a tiny musical noise when she moved.

"Leave now," she said to her women. They stared at her, unsure how to obey this strange command. "Leave!" she shouted, and they jumped to do as she bid. Soon she was alone in the bower. Sitting in the cushioned, high-backed chair before the fire, she artfully arranged the heavy folds of her skirts and waited.

Within the hour the door was thrust open. Turning her head slowly, she looked at Richard and the three knights, swords drawn, who stood behind him. A small, weary smile curved her lips.

"Wait outside," Richard said to his men. He closed the door and crossed the room until he stood near her, but not too near.

She did not rise from her chair. Now that it was here, she was surprised at how calm she felt. Her heart beat in a slow, steady rhythm, her breathing was normal, her hands did not tremble. Indeed, she felt little except an immense weariness. Whatever he chose to do with her no longer mattered. Nothing did. Egan was dead, and with him all her dreams. This powerful, handsome man who haunted her would soon rule Leinster. There was nothing left for her.

"I should kill you now and be done with it."

She smiled at him more fully. "Then do it. It would serve me well."

"I'll not have your murder on my soul, woman, no matter how I'm tempted. But you'll never be a threat to me and mine again, of that I can be very sure."

Trembling, she forced herself to hide the unexpected fear. Death was preferable to imprisonment. Death would bring surcease from the unbearable pain of living. It was living she no longer had the strength for, now that everything was lost to her. "You mean to have me rot in some dark dungeon, de Clare? I'll not give you the satisfaction."

He understood the threat, she saw it in his eyes, and she saw also that he would not mourn should she choose to end her life with her own hand. It was another betrayal, that cold, hard look in his gray eyes. How she wanted to reach out and touch him, with the touch of a woman, and have him respond to her. How she ached to have him in her bed, to hear him laugh, to hear him cry her name in the throes of passion. Looking into his eyes, she knew it would never be, and another part of her died. She turned her head aside to stare into the bright world of flame dancing on her hearth.

"I can't stop you from destroying yourself. I'm not sure I would try if I could. Irish law does not allow for the execution of an insane person, and only madness can explain what you've done."

"I'm no more insane than you, Richard. In a man ambition is rewarded. It was my misfortune to be born a woman."

"I'm not a cruel man, Dervorgilla. Imprison you I must, but not in any dungeon. The monastery at Drogheda will be your place of exile, for the rest of your life."

She nearly cried then. Not from relief at being spared a harsher confinement, but at the absurdity of it. A monastery, of all things. To spend the remainder of her days surrounded by prune-faced, pious women, her hours regulated by the incessant bells, her food plain and sparse. A life of austerity after one of luxury and indulgence did not appeal to her. The stark simplicity of life—the dreary sameness of one day after another, the dull companions, the unnatural silence, the enforced celibacy—would drive her slowly mad.

She had not thought Richard a particularly clever man. But he could not have chosen a worse fate for her than this one. It would be a living hell. "Why Drogheda? You know I've built the nuns' church at Clonmacnoise. Why not send me there?"

"I met the Lady Abbess at Drogheda, when I first besieged Rory. She is more than a match for you. I couldn't ask for a better jailer, and it would be unwise to send you to a place where the nuns sympathize with you. It's to Drogheda you'll go. You may learn to appreciate the life there, in time."

Staring into the fire, she did not answer him, nor turn to look until she heard the door close. The bower was empty, with an emptiness that felt like dark eternity, endless and cold. She did laugh then, a low, bitter sound. How strange that he did not see himself as a cruel man.

Twenty-six

Eve heard noises in the outer chamber of the bower. Voices, low and full of worry. Pulling the blue wool blanket tighter around her chest, she stared at the ceiling of the brightly lighted bedchamber. She had insisted on the lanterns, set about the room, to keep the darkness out. It still was not bright enough. The shivering would not go away, no matter how many blankets she piled on, and the heavy fur robe on top of them. Ban lay beside her, pressed up against her. Occasionally she would absently pat the dog, or pull on his ear.

She could still hear the screams, though she knew those terrible cries had long since ceased. She would forever hear them, as long as she lived.

Dear God, what have I done? Egan is dead because of me. The more she tried to shut the horrible truth out of her brain, the more fevered the images became, the more harrowed by guilt she grew as she lay, motionless and staring. She noticed a spider in a corner of the room. It waited patiently in its web. She felt enmeshed by guilt, as surely as any small, helpless creature caught in a web. But guilt served no purpose. It could not bring life to her brother, nor comfort to Dervorgilla for the loss of her son, for the loss of a part of her soul.

Mother Ancilla told her earlier guilt was to be repented as a sin of disbelief. Only those who did not believe in God's mercy and forgiveness indulged in guilt. She tried to listen, but could not hear God's mercy, nor feel forgiven, and her faith was at its weakest.

What she wanted was to sleep, perhaps forever, and erase the confusion and pain. Sleep would not come. Her mind filled with Hasculf. Once more she saw the blond giant with the cruel eyes; saw the Viking war-ax swing in its irrevocable arc. Hasculf murdered her brother. Hasculf, whose anger was directed at her father. Then she thought of Dermot. His ambitious, vengeful rule led them to war and death. If she could accuse herself of Egan's death, because in her naiveté she should have known or suspected who Hasculf was when she saw him, should have known the degree of his hatred and need for revenge, then Hasculf and her father were the real culprits, the agents of evil.

The baby kicked and she rubbed the side of her abdomen. How close had she come to getting this little one killed as well? She had been powerless, helpless. Only Rory's intervention saved her. Sudden anger rose in her, hot and bitter. She would not be a helpless, whimpering woman, dependent on the nearest man for her protection. She could not find herself in so precarious a position again, not if she were to protect her children from harm.

With difficulty she pushed the blankets aside and climbed from the bed, surprised to find herself dizzy when she stood. When had she last eaten? For the child's sake she could not wallow in self-pity and grief. Mourn Egan, cry her anguish, but get on with living.

Richard looked up, startled, as Eve walked into the outer chamber, her hair tangled about her pale face. She looked haggard, the skin around her eyes bruised dark with fatigue. In the three days since Egan's death, he had watched helplessly as she did not eat, or sleep, or talk.

He walked over to her, then stopped without touching

her. She looked so fragile. "I'm glad to see you up. We've been worried about you."

"That we have, child," Lorcan said, from his chair near the fire.

"Are you hungry?" Caitlin asked.

"Yes, a little."

Caitlin grabbed her cloak and flung it around her shoulders. "I'll see what I can get from the kitchens at this hour."

"I'll help," Morgan said, and held the door for his small wife.

Richard noted the relieved looks in their faces, the eagerness to be of some use after days of fierce worry. He had nearly gone mad with it himself. But Eve looked strange, as though still not fully aware of what was happening around her.

"I am sorry, Richard, for being so much trouble to you."

He led her to a chair near the warmth and saw her settled there. Then he knelt before her and took her small, cold hands in his own large ones. "Sweet love, look at me, Eve." Her weary eyes came up to meet his, and he cringed at the pain there. "Whatever you need, I am here to give. Tell me what I can do to help you."

"When is my brother to be buried?"

He glanced at Lorcan. The archbishop sighed and said gently, with a note of sorrow edging his musical voice, "We buried Egan yesterday. Don't you remember?"

Eve shook her head, and tears welled in her green eyes. "There is something you can do for me, Richard."

"Anything."

"Teach me how to use a weapon."

Whatever he might have been expecting, it was not that. "Why do you want to learn such a thing as that, sweet? When we married, I vowed on sacred relics to protect you."

"You weren't there when Hasculf . . ." Her voice trailed into nothing. "Please, Richard, I need to be able to protect myself when you aren't there. You can't always be with me.

You don't know what it's like, to be so helpless, to be able to do nothing when someone you love is in danger."

He did not argue with her. It was the first thing she had shown any interest in since Egan's death and he hesitated to deny her request, no matter how incomprehensible to him her motives might be.

"But what weapon could you learn, Eve? A sword is too heavy, the same is true of an ax. A knife you already know how to use, though in truth you'd not be strong enough against a man in hand-to-hand combat. What weapon can I train you in?"

Her face brightened, and a small, tenuous smile lifted the corners of her mouth. "They call you Strongbow. Teach me to use a bow. I have the knife for close range where I'm as effective as any man if I have surprise on my side. With a bow I can protect our home and children when you are gone. Surely I'm strong enough for that."

He was not convinced it was a good idea, but neither could he find any real argument against it. It would at least get her out of hiding. "Would tomorrow be too early for you?"

"Tomorrow is a good day to begin."

Twenty-seven

"The center boss," Eve said, sighting down the ash arrow at the shield propped against a tree.

Richard squinted at the target. "You hit that and I'll buy a red bridle with silver bells on it for your mare."

Eve smiled and drew the bowstring to her cheek, then let the arrow fly with a smooth, practiced grace. "You owe me one bridle, de Clare."

"That I do, Princess. Try not to stay out too long. You know how you complain when your ankles swell." With a quick swat at her rear end, he went to join Morgan and others of his knights at their archery practice.

"I don't complain," she said to his rapidly retreating back.

"Talking to yourself, Coz?"

"Nay, Caitlin, to that beast of a man I married. And you shouldn't sneak up on people like that."

"I wasn't sneaking, you were just preoccupied. How goes your practice?"

"I'm getting stronger and more accurate every day. See, I hit the very center of that target." She pointed with pride, but Caitlin only squinted nearsightedly. "It's a shame you can't see clearly beyond the length of your arm, Cait, or you could practice with me. It's such a feeling of achievement, to set out to learn something and master it."

"I have other things besides bow and arrows to fulfill me." Caitlin sat in the sweet April grass and pulled a blade to chew on. She smiled up at her cousin. After four months of marriage, Cait still glowed with happiness, and looked sweetly feminine in her lavender linen gown. Eve, seven months pregnant, wore a shapeless tent of a gown which was soiled with sweat from her archery efforts. Her ankles were swollen from too much standing.

"Give me your feet," Caitlin said.

Awkwardly, Eve sat and placed her swollen feet in her cousin's lap. Caitlin slipped off the loose leather shoes. Her strong fingers massaged Eve's feet and ankles. "That's heavenly," Eve said. "Don't ever stop."

There was a festival quality to the day, one of the first truly warm, sunny days of spring. Richard had brought his men out to the hills beyond Dublin to practice their archery, swordplay, and riding skills. Many of the women of Dublin watched, cheering on their favorites, and the men preened handsomely for them. Romance was woven into the happy noises, but there was a seriousness to it all as well.

Richard's men were scattered over the green hills where the wildflowers were blooming in a riot of blue and yellow. How different they were from Irish warriors, Eve thought. Her father's men, and Rory's as well, she was sure spent the winter before their hearths, singing or listening to the harpers play, eating, getting drunk, arguing, laying with their women, dandling children on their burly knees. What they did not do was what Richard's men did. Train for war.

Through the winter Richard marched and worked his men, not allowing them to remain idle or grow soft. Today, most of them were stripped to the waist in the warmth, and she noted how hard and muscular they were from hours of practice with sword or bow. She watched their archery practice especially. In the month Richard had been training her to use the small, lightweight short bow, she learned an awed appreciation for the Welsh weapon of choice, the longbow.

She was not strong enough to pull the huge longbow to her body, as the Welsh did, and so learned to shoot the smaller bow, which was the same bow the Irish warriors still used. When she thought of an army of Irishmen armed with the smaller bows against Richard's archers, she knew the superior weaponry could make the difference in a battle.

This was how Richard earned his name of Strongbow, this nearly maniacal insistence that his men learn and practice the use of the longbow. Even his knights, who would normally think of a bow as beneath their dignity, a weapon for a common man, were expected to be proficient in its use. Any who grumbled about it were told to leave Richard's service. Few found reason to complain. It was Richard who set the example for his men, who was the best at the bow's use, who could fire six arrows in the time other men let fly four, and with deadly accuracy. The longer the bow, the more force it built up and the farther the arrow would fly. Richard's was the longest bow of all, standing over six feet from tip to tip.

Tewdr, his dark head tilted up to catch every word that dropped from Richard's lips, was practicing farther down the line, and she smiled to see his dark intensity. The lad had grown in the months since coming to Ireland, and had less of that scrawny look to him. In fact, he gave promise of growing to a tall, strong, handsome youth. A sudden lump came to her throat looking at him. Egan should be here, with Tewdr and the other squires, happily learning to be men in the company of the huge knights and the silver-tongued Welshmen.

"You have that sad look again," Caitlin said.

"I was thinking of Egan. It's been a month now, and the pain is a little less. It no longer seems as though my heart is being ripped out. But the anger grows larger everyday."

"Anger is a useless emotion."

"Not if it's focused, if it has a purpose."

Caitlin sighed. "What purpose can it serve, Eve?"

"Hasculf will pay for what he's done. I swear it." Her voice was low, hard, and edged with hatred. "He thinks I'm a helpless woman, that I can't exact revenge for Egan's murder, but he's mistaken. One day he will know the strength of my anger."

"Eve, let it go! Lorcan would tell you the same."

"Lorcan is a holy man, God help him, probably even a saint. I am not."

"Don't be blasphemous. Vengeance is a powerful master. It can destroy your soul. Look at the mess we're in now, all for the sake of vengeance. Your father kills Hasculf's men, and the Norseman vows vengeance. Hasculf kills Egan, and you vow revenge. If you kill Hasculf, do you think that is the end of it? Will not his sons vow vengeance against you, against Richard, against your child?"

"I don't want to hear this," Eve said, struggling to put her shoes on. She could not quite manage to reach her feet. With a grunt of disgust, she slowly rose to her feet, leaving her shoes in the grass. Stalking away from Caitlin, she was angry that her cousin could not see the need that grew in her every day, just as the child grew, until it consumed her thoughts. Hasculf must die for what he had done.

Caitlin ran after her, carrying the red shoes. "Damn you, Eve, don't you walk away from me."

Eve turned to face her cousin, whose flushed and angry face belied her usually peaceful nature.

"It's been a month," Caitlin said, "and we've all been careful what we say, what we do, to spare your feelings while you grieve, but this notion you have of killing Hasculf is dangerous. Someone needs to tell you the truth. Does Richard know that is the reason you're learning to use the bow?"

"No. Besides, that's not the only reason."

"You're lying to me and to yourself."

"I don't lie. How dare you say such a thing?"

"I dare because I love you, and because I'm worried about you. Look at you, out here every day, hour after hour, with that damned bow. You're going to have a baby in June.

You should be thinking about that, preparing for that. You should be planning for that happy day, not plotting a man's death."

"Why, because it's not my place as a woman? I should let Richard fight my battles, expect him to punish Hasculf?"

"Yes. That's the way it is done, and with good reason. We're meant to give birth, to raise our children, not put our hands to death."

Eve bit back the angry words. Caitlin could not understand. She had not been there, she had not seen Egan die, had not seen the body twitch, or the blood flow from the ghastly headless neck. Nor had she seen the look of cold indifference on Hasculf's face. Not for an instant did the man think that Eve was any threat to him, or any deterrent to what he did. She had been as unimportant as a gnat one crushed between the fingers.

Never again would she be that helpless. Her hand tightened on the grip of her bow, but her anger weakened. How could she stay angry at Caitlin, who even now was on the verge of tears over their quarrel?

"I'm tired, Cait. Tired of the anger and the grief. You're right, I should be planning for the baby. Walk with me to Dublin. There's something I need do that I've been neglecting."

They walked in companionable silence, arms linked. Eve knew without looking behind her that Tewdr followed, Ban by his side. Since Egan's death Tewdr had become her shadow, never far, but never intrusive. When she told Richard she no longer needed a watchdog and he could call the boy off, Richard informed her it was all Tewdr's doing, and none of his. The boy felt protective of her and had become close friends with the big white wolfhound. She let the boy play his role.

Entering Dublin through the gate nearest the Cathedral of the Holy Trinity, they slipped into the quiet church. Eve laid her weapon at the door. It was the first time she had been here since before Egan's death. She walked down the silent nave toward the altar, and there she knelt at the rood screen. Burying her head in her hands, she prayed. Having forgiven God his cruelty, she now had the peace of heart to talk to Him, rather than cry recriminations. The building was imbued with the peace only lifetimes of prayer wrought, and like a benediction it settled around her. Caitlin and Tewdr allowed her some privacy, standing back in the shadows, waiting.

Faintly, she became aware of a door opening in the sacristy, behind the altar, and heard hushed voices. Footsteps approached through the choir, coming toward the carved wooden screen that separated the monks' part of the church from the public portion. The footsteps stopped and there was a deep silence. She lifted her head and saw Dermot, looking weary and old. Beside him was Lorcan.

Eve rose slowly from the kneeler, shocked by the naked despair in her father's eyes. Dermot slowly walked through the gate in the rood screen, but Lorcan did not follow. Her father looked so frail, and he seemed confused, as though he did not know what to say.

"We must talk," Dermot said. "I am dying, Dervorgilla did not lie about that."

She did not argue with him, the signs were too many, too obvious. "I know."

He rubbed his arms, as though cold. "We all die. I'd forgotten that somehow. If we resist it, we make ourselves mad with pain and longing. After a certain point, it's useless to fight. I'm leaving Dublin. What little time I have left I'll pass at the monastery at Ferns."

"Father, please, I can care for you here." Unexpected tears stung her eyes. For all he had done, he was her father.

"Sweet child, it's no longer my body I care about. I've need of penance before the end, mayhap more than most men. But that's true of all kings, I fear. Your husband is a good man, and powerful. If things go as he hopes here, he'll rule well, if not, he'll keep you safe in England or Wales."

He reached out and took her hand, gently, and held it. "There is something I want you to understand. Even if Egan had been my son I would not have named him my heir."

His hand was cold and it trembled slightly. He had been so strong. As a child she thought him invincible. "You don't need to explain anything to me."

"I do, and I need your forgiveness. I've been so blinded by vengeance I've not taken the care of you I should have. God forgive me, you are so like your mother it tore my heart to look at you."

He had never spoken of her mother before. A tear slid down her cheek, but she kept her hands around his.

"Your mother was my soulmate, my very life. When she died, I thought I'd go mad. And I blamed O'Conor for her death."

"What did Rory have to do with it?"

"Nothing. But I learned that too late. Dervorgilla was clever when she manipulated me into thinking O'Conor guilty of murder."

"Why would she do such a thing?"

He sighed and looked toward the altar, as though seeking strength. "Because it was Dervorgilla who killed her."

A new grief pierced Eve's heart. Grief for her mother and her father. She leaned over and placed a kiss on her father's shrunken cheek. He looked startled, and tears filled his eyes. Wrapping his arms around his daughter, he hugged her close. Eve cried for all the wasted years, all the hardness between them. He asked her to forgive him. Could she? Some of the things he had done were terrible, dishonorable acts. Then she knew if she were to find peace when her time came to die, she must forgive him.

"Don't cry, child, I'm not worth your tears."

She stepped back and gathered both his hands in hers.

"My tears will pass. You asked for my forgiveness and I give it freely."

He smiled sadly. "I can make peace with God now. If I'm still in this world when my grandchild is born, I want to be introduced to him. I always loved you, Eve. I want you to remember that." He chucked her affectionately under the chin. "No more tears."

She nodded and watched him slowly walk away, but the tears would not stop.

Twenty-eight

Eve woke just as dawn began to poke in at the window of the bedchamber and lay for a long moment, savoring the warmth of Richard along her back. One of his arms was wrapped around her big belly, his hand spread protectively over the baby. The hand she played with was strong enough to crush the life out of her, gentle enough to stroke her to the heights of passion. What a marvel the man was, made of such contradictory strength and gentleness.

Richard stirred in his sleep, snuggling closer, his manhood swelling along her back, and she smiled. Even in sleep desire played him. He was a lusty man and she had discovered an answering earthiness in herself, enjoying their lovemaking with an exuberance that surprised her. No one had told her it was so much fun, or so heart-wrenchingly tender, or that rough could be exciting. He taught her many things, and together they discovered joy.

She pulled at the hairs on his fingers. No response. She pulled harder. There was a low, playful growl in her ear, then his tongue traced a line along her neck. With a little squeal, she turned toward him. His gray eyes, half hooded with sleep, flared with hot need. "Are you rested enough, m'lady?"

"Aye, m'lord, well rested. What had you in mind? A game of chess mayhap?"

"I'll play you a game," he said, his fingers tracing down her arm, over the curve of her hips, around the fullness of her belly, to her heavy, tender breasts. "You are so beautiful, you hurt my heart."

"I am fat and awkward and can hardly wait for this babe to be born. But you are kind to say so."

"You have never been more beautiful to me than you are now, huge with my child, your breasts blue-veined, your feet swollen, your constant need to pee, your—"

She put a hand over his smiling mouth. "Hush, sweet, such words of devotion will drive me wild."

He kissed the palm of her hand, and she moved it to stroke his beard, full and beginning to grow long. It was redder than his hair, and promised to be truly luxurious in another year or so. She found him all the more attractive for it.

"In truth, Eve, all jesting aside, you are beautiful to me, now more than ever."

"More beautiful than Rosamund?" She could not help herself.

"Rosamund was different from you. As different as spring and summer. Both have their beauty."

It was not exactly what she wanted to hear. She felt ugly, big, an alien in her own body. She wanted him to have forgotten about Rosamund. She wondered if he thought of her as spring or summer? She felt decidedly wintry, and abruptly turned her back to him and struggled to sit up.

"Where are you going?"

"I have to use the privy."

He sighed, and his hand reached out to hold her where she was. "Rosamund is past, and forgotten. It is you I love, you I want. You are my life. How can you doubt it?"

How indeed? What had she done to deserve him? She placed his hand against her cheek, then turned her face and kissed his palm lightly. "And I love you, Richard de Clare, with all my soul, for all eternity."

She stood up, gathering her sleeping robe around her shoulders.

"Where are you going?"

"I still have to use the privy."

He chuckled and sprawled back onto the pillows. "Be quick about it then."

"Yes, m'lord." The urgency of her need rushed her out into the dawn. She hated using a pot in the chamber, much preferring the walk in the soft air to the nearby stall with its wooden seat.

She finished quickly, then opened the door of the shack and stepped back out. Someone hurried toward the bower. "Morgan?"

"Eve, is that you?"

Stepping nearer, she saw more clearly the grim look on Morgan's face. "What's happened?"

"A rider arrived from Ferns a few minutes ago."

"My father?"

"Yes, Lady. He died yesterday."

It was only two weeks since Dermot left. She had not expected him to die so soon. He would not, after all, meet his first grandchild. She did not cry, though grief wrapped her heart with pain. "We must tell Richard. He's ruler of Leinster now. There are things he'll need to discuss with you."

"You took your time, woman." Richard stepped naked into the outer chamber when Eve returned, but found a solemn Morgan standing beside her.

"My father is dead."

Richard crossed the room and gathered Eve into his arms. Of all his cruelties, perhaps this was Dermot's worst. At the last he told his daughter what she ached a lifetime to hear, and when he died she grieved.

"I'll be fine, Richard," Eve said. "It's not that unexpected after all. Let me sit by the hearth a while."

He led her to a chair, covering her lap tenderly with a blanket, then knelt to stir the fire to new life.

"Richard, you're naked." She looked at him and smiled.

"You've seen me undressed enough times, and so has Morgan." He retreated into the bedchamber. When he returned, he was pulling a tunic over his head.

"You and Morgan need to make plans. Go on, Richard, I'll be fine, I'm not as fragile as you think. I did my mourning earlier."

Richard hated to leave her, but she did seem to be in control of herself. "I'll be back as soon as I can, love."

She smiled at him and nodded, then turned back to stare into the fire.

When they were outside, Richard stood for a moment, marveling at the soft loveliness of the May morning. How beautiful Ireland could be, all tender and green and gracious. They walked toward the stables.

"You're king of Leinster, if you claim the title."

"That, my friend, is the one thing Henry Plantagenet will never allow." Richard nodded to the men they passed, but the look on his face forbore any interruption of his conversation with Morgan. "Henry worries I grow too ambitious and prevents me from building my forces to full strength. I had hoped to persuade him to change his mind. I even sent a messenger to England requesting that we meet to discuss our differences."

"Any reply?"

Richard kicked a pebble in his path, putting more strength behind the small act than it strictly warranted. "Not a word, and I'm unprepared for battle. I don't have enough men to go against the vast army Rory has gathered."

"You think O'Conor will force you to battle?"

"What is there to prevent him? Now is his best chance for victory, while we are weakened by Henry's refusal to allow my men into Ireland." They came to the corral, where the knights' war-horses were kept, and the two men leaned against the fence to watch the animals.

"What are your plans?" Morgan asked.

"I'm sending you to Waterford, to fetch Redmon and his men. We'll need every warrior we can get if we're to hold Dublin until the rest of my army arrives. From there, you're going to Pembroke. Henry is there, gathering an army to stop me."

"Wales? Now, when everything is happening here?"

"I need a man I can trust with this mission. I want you to find Henry Plantagenet and plead my case. We need those troops he's holding back. If he isn't made to see reason, all will be lost here." The truth of it sank in, and Richard felt a great sadness. If he must give up Ireland, he was not sure Eve would survive the heartbreak.

"How soon do you want me gone?"

"Now. Travel lightly and in secret until you reach Pembroke. With Henry blockading the Welsh ports, it'll take all your charm and cleverness to slip through."

"A little silver wouldn't hurt."

"I'll see you have a purse."

Richard's bay stallion trotted over to the fence and looked down at them, his soft lips nibbling at Richard's hair. He reached up to stroke the animal's neck. How he longed to ride unfettered by responsibility or fear, with Eve at his side. Ride until they came to some far, sheltered place and there stayed, letting the world spin its destiny without them.

"I'll say my farewell to Caitlin and be gone within the hour. It will turn out well in the end. I do believe in you, Richard. I'm proud to serve you and no other."

Richard found he could not look at the Welshman, and merely nodded.

By the time Richard returned to the bower, Eve was dry-eyed. He quickly told her his plans. She quirked an eyebrow at him. "Do you think even Morgan, for all his charm, can change that king's mind?"

Buckling his sword belt around his slim waist, Richard shook his head. "No, truth be told, I have little hope of help from Henry."

"Then we are on our own."

He looked at her, something close to fear in his gray eyes. Fear for her and the baby, not for himself, she knew that. Would he ask her to leave Ireland, to seek safety somewhere far from here until the conflict with Rory was decided? It was too late for that. The babe was due within weeks, she was too far advanced in her pregnancy to travel. There was no choice but to stay in Dublin, with Richard. She wanted to be nowhere else.

"I don't mean to frighten you," he said. "It's the sheer numbers of men Rory can command that worries me. Man for man my army can beat any on earth. But not outnumbered forty to one, fifty to one, as I fear we shall be."

"It will be as God wills." She tried to keep the fear from her voice.

He crushed her to him, big belly and all, and she leaned her head into his hard chest. A profound peace filled her and she knew no matter what came she would find the courage to face it, as long as they were together.

A fortnight later, Redmon arrived in Dublin with twenty knights and almost a hundred Welsh archers. Richard watched from the ramparts. He climbed down as the big red-haired knight rode through the gate to the royal enclosure, and went to greet his captain.

"Did Morgan get away to Wales?"

Redmon dismounted from his huge chestnut stallion. "That he did, on a stinking fishing boat that appeared as though it wouldn't stay afloat. He looked the part, too,

dressed in wadmal, and happy for the transport. Within the
month we should know how Henry stands."

"For all the good it'll do," Richard said. "It'll take weeks,
mayhap months to get an army that size organized for transport. We can't fight O'Conor until then."

"Then it's a siege you're preparing for? I wouldn't have
thought it of you, Richard. You were ever the first to charge
headfirst into an enemy line, the last to stand and watch
instead of taking action. What's happened to you?"

Richard did not want to admit the change, but it was
true. Where once he would have ridden hotheaded against
Rory, simply because that was what he was trained to do
and because he enjoyed the thrill of danger, he had a family
to think of now. It surprised him how vulnerable a man
became when he had the welfare of his loved ones to consider. "I'm older is all, and I hope wiser. We don't stand a
chance against Rory's thousands, not without Henry's help."

Redmon was grim-faced as they walked the stallion toward the stables. "You place a greater faith in Henry than
I, m'lord. I'd say we're on our own here."

Richard agreed with the knight, but was reluctant to admit to it. He needed the big man's loyalty and help. He was
a popular commander among Richard's men, and his courage was unquestionable. The knight's bluntness was refreshing, after the intrigues of Dermot's court.

As Richard had foreseen, there were only a handful of
Irishmen left in Dublin willing to fight with him. The rest
had slipped away, with their families, into the countryside.
Not all would fight with Rory. Some left knowing a town
under siege was a hungry place, believing the countryside
would feed them through the summer.

Richard was relieved to see them go. The fewer people
he had to feed, the longer Dublin could stand, but what if
Henry did not come? No, even that stubborn king would
not allow an army of his countrymen to starve. It would

violate his sense of pride and honor, and for all his faults, Henry was a meticulously honorable man.

"I hear you're to be a father soon."

"Any day now," Richard said, but there was no joy in his voice.

"It doesn't please you?"

"The child, yes. The timing is anything but good. I thought to send Eve away, to a safer place, but she wouldn't hear of it."

"Willful, is she? You should have sent her anyway. Dublin will be no place for a woman this summer."

Richard chuckled. "You're not a married man, Redmon. I can no more command Eve than I can tell the tide to turn."

Twenty-nine

The dull ache in her back had kept her awake most of the last two nights, and Eve woke tired and restless. She reached across the bed, but the hard, masculine body she was accustomed to was not there. Where could Richard have gone at so early an hour?

It was a week since Redmon arrived in Dublin, and the preparations for a siege were nonstop. The cattle and sheep had been driven in from their rich summer pastures to be confined within the walls of the town. The geese of Dublin were nearly naked, their feathers plucked to fletch the thousands of arrows needed by Richard's archers. Whatever folk could find an excuse to leave had done so, including the foreign merchants. The only ships left in Dublin Harbor were those of her husband's fleet. The people who gave life and color and its routine rhythm of living abandoned Dublin, to be replaced by hard-faced knights and soldiers. There was little laughter in Dublin.

Eve groaned as she swung her legs over the side of the bed. The pain in her back was sharper, more constant, and she knew her labor was beginning. *Soon, little one, I'll be able to hold you in my arms. How I have longed to do so. But what a world you come to.* Still, it would be better when the child was born. She was too clumsy with the weight of her pregnancy to do anything but watch the busy preparations. The enforced laziness frustrated her. It would take a week or so to recover from childbirth, then she could be useful again, working in the infirmary. If Dublin were truly besieged sometime this summer, as Richard feared it would be, there were bound to be fevers and other ills brought on by poor food and close confinement.

Pain drove her from the bed. She did not bother to change out of the plain linen chemise she slept in, just flung a lightweight summer cloak about her shoulders, slipped her feet into a pair of soft leather slippers, and went out to find Richard. What she saw filled her with dread.

Dublin's walls were built of stone, and on top of that was built a palisade of stout timber. A walkway ran the length of the timber wall, and on this walkway hundreds of Richard's men stood, in near silence. It was eerie, so many men and so little noise. It was as though a heavy pall had fallen over Dublin, choking out all sound of living.

With a chill of foreboding, she knew what they stared at. She was far too clumsy to climb a ladder to the walkway. Instead, she made her way to the nearest gate, where a nervous cluster of monks and women gathered. She pushed her way to the front, then stood to stare with all the others.

On the hills surrounding Dublin, Rory's army was camped. Thousands upon thousands of Irishmen, an endless sea of them, colorful spots in the green summer grass. The numbers inspired terror, so vast was the army. How could they possibly resist such a force? Richard had been right not to seek battle. The Normans would have been annihilated.

"So, it has begun," Eve said.

"M'lady?"

"The siege." She turned to the sweet-faced old monk who stood beside her. His eyes were calm with a lifetime of faith and prayer, and she envied him. She had so much to lose, and her fear was great.

Caitlin found her there and slipped an arm around her shoulders. "You should have gone with Morgan when you had the chance," Eve said.

"My place is here, with you. Where else would I be with your babe so near."

Eve squeezed her cousin's hand. How Caitlin had matured in the last year, from frightened girl to strong woman. She would have need of her strength ere this day was done. Already the first hard cramps were starting, her belly tightening, the ache in her back intensifying. "Do you know what today is?"

"What?" Caitlin asked.

"The solstice, the first day of summer. They say a child born on this day is protected by the little people."

"So it's said. Holy Mary, are you in labor?"

Eve nodded, choked for a moment with the overwhelming realization that a new life would soon be in her arms.

"What are we doing standing here?" Caitlin asked. "I'll get Richard, he'll want to know."

"No, he has other things to contend with. There's no hurry. It'll be many hours yet before the babe is born. It may not happen today. Before anything else I want to go to the nuns' abbey and pray. I have special need of grace."

She looked a moment longer at the mass of Irishmen swarming the hills. It had come, what she feared all these months. Her beloved husband, the man who had captured her heart and soul, would be the instrument of destroying her countrymen. Or her countrymen would destroy Richard, and how could she go on living without him? The child, impatient now to be born, was neither Irish nor Norman. What was its destiny in this world?

She sought Richard with her eyes and found him on the wall beside Redmon. So tall and proud he looked, but she knew the worry of the last month had etched lines around his eyes and disquieted his soul. Richard had no stomach for war, did not relish the idea of good men dying, on either side, and was torn apart by the situation. Perhaps she should have agreed to leave with him, to turn her back on her native land. How could one ever know if a decision was right? All she knew was that by deciding to stay, a different fate had been put into motion than would have been otherwise. A choice in one direction made other, contradictory choices impossible. The best she could do was find the strength to live with the decisions made.

"Come with me to church, Caitlin. It will give us strength."

Together they turned from the sight and sounds of waiting war, and walked slowly through the silent crowd toward the nuns' abbey, where the bells rang for Lauds as they did every morning at this time, war or peace. God and prayer were constant, when all else turned to chaos.

The contraction came hard and long, and Eve leaned forward on the birthing stool. The day had slipped past sundown an hour ago, and in the cool of the summer night her laboring filled the chamber. There was no midwife left in Dublin, and she was grateful when Mother Ancilla insisted on helping. Poor Caitlin nearly fainted with relief, afraid she would have to deliver the child herself. Caitlin and Mother Ancilla were busy now that the child was almost here. Such a long journey, Eve thought, and such a short distance, but half the length of a woman's body.

The pain stopped momentarily and she leaned back, pulling damp curls of hair away from her sweaty shoulders. Mother Ancilla squatted down between Eve's widespread knees, and her beaming round face reappeared. "Not long now."

The abbess had reassured her the labor progressed normally, but the last several hours, as the contractions came harder with barely time between to relax and prepare for the next one, Eve wondered if she could endure to the end. She had not expected the pain to be so intense, or so unrelenting, as though some alien force inhabited her body, and she must simply survive. If she started screaming, she was afraid she would not stop. There would be a babe soon, and that reality kept her from giving in to the pain. The reward for her trouble would be remarkable. Soon she would hold Richard's child in her arms.

The door to the bower slammed open, and Richard stood, staring openmouthed at the spectacle. "Merciful heavens, Richard, get out of here," Caitlin commanded, planting her tiny self squarely before him.

"Sweet Jesu, why didn't anyone tell me?"

"There is nothing for you to do Richard. This is the one thing that is woman's work. Now go back out until we call you." Caitlin tried to shoo him away, but he stood, stubborn and incredulous.

Eve, her face purple with effort, drenched in sweat, was as bizarre to him as some creature out of a dark dream. No wonder women banished men from the birth chamber. It was enough to scare a man to death. She did not scream exactly, but made strange animal noises, grunting and panting and gasping for breath.

He knelt beside her, taking a hot hand into his own. "How are you my sweet wife?"

She growled at him, her eyes slitted with pain, her teeth bared in a grimace. He turned startled eyes on the abbess.

"She's fine. There are no complications, she's young and strong. Another hour should see your child born. Now, do as Lady Caitlin says and we'll call you in when it's over and the mess is cleaned up."

"I'm staying."

"It isn't seemly. There are things a woman might say or do in labor that her husband would take amiss."

"The baby," Eve gasped, freeing her hand from Richard's to grab the arms of the birthing stool.

"Soon now, the babe is well on—"

"Now!" Eve shouted, and began to push.

Mother Ancilla squatted to her task. "At last, here it

comes. Caitlin, bring the towels and the scissors. Richard, get out. Now!"

Richard retreated. Perhaps this was better left to women. They seemed competent and he didn't know a damned thing about childbirth. He opened the door and stepped out, relieved he did not need to help.

"That's it, Eve, rest a little, and when the next pain comes, push like hell," Mother Ancilla coached.

The pain came quick and hard.

"Push, Eve," Caitlin encouraged. "The babe is near. It will all be over soon."

The baby slid into Mother Ancilla's broad hands, and Eve stared down her child. It was a bloody mess. "What's wrong with it?"

"There's not a thing wrong. She's a perfectly formed wee girl you have." She laid the baby on Eve's breast, the cord that still attached them pulsing.

Caitlin tied red yarn in two places on the cord, then with sharp scissors cut the link between mother and child. When mother and child were cleaned, Mother Ancilla opened the door.

"You may come in now, Richard."

"How is she?"

"Tired but very well. You have a daughter."

Smiling, he picked the abbess up and twirled her around, planting a kiss on her forehead as he set her down. She blushed and pushed him gently toward his family.

Richard knelt beside his wife and daughter. "You were magnificent," he told her, the pride in his breast nearly choking him.

"Are you disappointed she's a girl?"

"Nay, Princess, never. I hope she grows to be as beautiful and strong as her mother. I never knew what birth was, until now. Why do you women keep it secret from us?"

She smiled weakly and cuddled the baby closer to her breast. "Sometimes, Richard, there should be a few mysteries in life."

They named the baby Isabella, after Richard's maternal grandmother, Isabella d'Vermandois, who was the granddaughter of a French king and had been born a countess, just as this Isabella would be, if no brother came along to displace her. Isabella d'Vermandois was a formidable old woman when Richard knew her, but his awe was tempered with a real love, for the countess was generous and patient with her numerous grandchildren, instilling in them an unshakable sense of honor.

He held his daughter against his chest, marveling at the tiny perfection of her hands. Eve slept deeply, and the bower was dark and quiet, except for the small gurgling noises the baby made and her mother's even breathing. Richard could not sleep. Not this night, the first night of his daughter's life. He picked her up and sat in a chair before the hearth, where the embers had been banked and covered by a clay fire-keeper.

Carefully, he covered Isabella with a soft blanket, and she slept. His big hand more than covered her body. Richard stared into the dark hearth, trying to understand the overwhelming ache of sweet and fiery love this tiny creature evoked. His daughter. Isabella was heiress to all his lands, and to Eve's as well. And beyond the walls of Dublin camped an immense army. This tiny child posed a danger to Rory O'Conor. She was a rallying point for the men of Leinster. Half Irish, she was an acceptable heiress to them.

He had to protect her, to ensure she grew to enjoy her inheritance, to know her destiny. How was he to do that, with Henry Plantagenet still forbidding him additional men? Dublin, like any other fortress, could withstand a siege for only so long.

A fierce protectiveness came to resonant life within him. He would do anything to safeguard his child. This was what he struggled for in this foreign land, what his dreams focused on. His children. In them lay the hope for a peaceful Norman settlement in Ireland. He knew in the depths of his soul that only if the two peoples intermarried would they learn to tolerate each other. Only by becoming one kin would their loyalties be undivided. If they remained stubbornly apart, there would be strife and hatred for generations, just as there was in England, between Saxon and Norman, more than a hundred years after the coming of the Conqueror.

Slowly, he walked back into the bedchamber and laid the baby in her soft pile of blankets beside Eve. He knew sleep would evade him, and slipping his sword and belt around his waist, he quietly left the bower.

Walking across the nearly deserted yard, he felt an eerie sense of oppression. He climbed a ladder to the rampart atop the high walls of Dublin, and stared into the darkness. Rory was out there, with his thousands of men, but the darkness hid them from his view. Only the light of campfires dotted the darkness, like watchful eyes. What destiny waited them in the next few weeks? Victory or defeat, there was no middle road. And without help from the English King, victory was a remote possibility at best.

Thirty

"You can't be serious." Redmon's face was red with angry disbelief. "You talk to him. He'll not listen to me."

Eve could hardly believe what Richard was planning to do, and was as incredulous as the big knight, but feared her arguments would be no more useful than Redmon's had been. "Is it truly the only way?"

Richard ran his fingers through his hair. "I don't look forward to meeting with O'Conor, but we're at a stalemate. It's been six weeks since the siege began, our supplies are running low and there has been no word from Morgan. We can't expect any help from England."

"You don't know that," Redmon shouted, slamming his fist into a nearby door frame. "Henry could well be on his way here with an army. I say we wait. The food supply in Dublin is not yet critical, and negotiating with Rory now will make him suspicious. It will make him think we are in a weakened position."

"Which we are," Richard said, his voice calm.

"But do we need to let Rory know that?"

"I'm not surrendering to him, Redmon, only negotiating for the release of the women and children."

Eve shifted Isabella from one arm to the other. The baby's eyes, fast turning a deep green, followed her mother's fingers as Eve absently played with her daughter's tiny hands. The depth of the love she felt for Isabella never ceased to astonish her. She knew now why women died protecting their children. It was as natural as breathing.

During the days, Eve kept busy enough to tamp the fear down into some dark, secret place, but in the quiet of the nights it came to her in all its malevolent fury. The fear was not for herself so much as for Richard and the baby. How could she go on living if something happened to either of them? Though she desperately wanted Isabella safe, how could she leave Richard when he was in such danger?

Curse Henry Plantagenet to hell. Why would he not release the rest of Richard's men? Surely they were not to be sacrificed to Henry's stubborn pride? Dying was a real possibility, and death by starvation in the course of a siege was a miserable fate. "What if some compromise could be worked out?"

Richard and Redmon both stared at her. "What sort of compromise?" Richard asked.

"You accept Rory as your overlord, as High King of Ireland, in return for ruling in Leinster. That would leave his kingdom intact, and you've said before your ambition doesn't include all of Ireland. Rory has no way of knowing that."

"Good God, woman, you don't know what you're asking," Redmon said. "Richard has vowed himself to his sovereign lord, and he's the king of England, not some petty Irish princeling."

Eve bristled at the knight's tone and his words. "That petty Irish princeling has you and your powerful Norman army closed up so tight you've no room to move. This is no time for arrogance. Richard is right, something must be done before the people begin to starve. Talking with Rory can hurt nothing."

"Except our pride," Redmon said.

Richard clapped his hand on the big knight's shoulder. "Pride won't feed the children, old friend."

"God's feet, Richard, marriage and fatherhood have made

you soft. There are always deaths in war, you know that. It's to be expected."

"And you know I've never been one to take innocent lives in battle. My sword I use on warriors. The deaths of women and children I'd not have on my conscience, if I have any choice in the matter."

"It's too dangerous," Redmon said. "It would be easy for O'Conor to take you hostage, or kill you, then where would we be? God, you hardly speak the language, and Morgan's not here to translate for you. How do you propose to understand what Rory says to you?"

By the look on Richard's face, Eve realized he had not thought of that particular problem. He would need a translator, someone he could trust implicitly. "I will translate for my husband."

"No. I'll not put you in such danger," Richard said.

"I'll be in no more danger there, with you, than we all are here, waiting. And in truth, Richard, if something should happen to you, I want to know of it. I want to be there with you."

He came to stand before her, his hand reaching out to cradle the baby's downy head. "Do you think I could ever risk you in that way? I say no."

His gray eyes were filled with such a raw pain and helplessness, it was all she could do not to give in to him.

"She may be your best choice, Richard. Who else can you trust to understand everything Rory says, and give it back to you true? She knows both languages equally well. Eve is the logical choice."

"Logic be damned. She's my wife!"

Eve laid a hand on Richard's arm, and peered up into his tormented eyes. "As your wife, my place is beside you, and I do this willingly. Do you forget it is Isabella's life, and that of all the children of Dublin, that we will bargain for? I know Rory O'Conor to be an honorable man. He'll listen to us and give us safe passage back to Dublin.

Whether he will agree to our terms I can't predict, but hear them he will."

"How can you say that, after what happened to Egan?" Redmon asked.

Memory of Egan's death, still so vivid in her mind, caused a swift wave of nausea to pass through her. "That was Hasculf, not Rory." She shuddered at thought of seeing the Norse murderer in Rory's train, but even that she would endure if she could bargain Isabella's safety. She would beg if need be, though she hesitated to tell Richard that. His pride was already severely tested, forced to wait helplessly in Dublin while part of his army sat in Wales, unable to cross to Ireland.

She was so proud of the calm way her husband carried himself through the siege. His steadfastness had gone a great way in keeping the people from panic or despair. Though in truth, the only people left in Dublin were soldiers and monks, slaves, and the women and their few children who had aligned themselves with Richard's men. Other than Richard's army there were less than two hundred people in Dublin. It was for this remnant Richard worried, and schemed to find a way to get them to safety.

His men were warriors, trained for whatever would happen, and hardened to it. An armed enemy he knew how to meet. It was the enemies of fear and worry and hopelessness he battled now, and she could do little to help him with the struggle except remain by his side.

It was the sense of hopelessness that began to pervade Richard's army that was the most frightening. In the weeks Rory had been encamped in the green countryside, more Irish had joined him, until his army spread for miles along the river valley west of Dublin. It was the vastness of those numbers, against Richard's knights and archers, that drained their spirits. Each day that passed with no sign of ships from England saw Richard's men more disheartened. They could not hope to win on a battlefield. And Rory was not likely to show mercy to the men. No commander was that foolish in time of war.

If Rory did agree to allow the women and children to leave, he would force an untenable decision on Eve. Everything in her fought against leaving Richard, knowing the fate of the men left behind in Dublin was all but written in blood on the pages of eternity. And every protective instinct in her would fight to keep her child alive. She could not do both, save Isabella and remain in Dublin. Of course, it was possible Rory would not grant the women and children safe conduct, thus condemning them to die with their men. Shuddering at the thought, she held Isabella closer. Surely Rory could not be so cruel?

It was the longest ride of her life, from the gates of Dublin to Rory's camp, less than two miles away. Leaving Isabella in Caitlin's loving arms, she rode now with Richard and Lorcan on either side of her gray mare, Richard on his huge war-horse, Lorcan on a sedate white mule. She had dressed carefully, in green silk, and the gold of her jeweled torc at her throat, the coronet on her head, gave her an aura of dignity she barely felt. She would approach Rory as an equal, as a princess of Ireland, of Brian Boru's blood.

Richard rode unarmored, with only his sword at his waist. Even his long bow he left behind in Dublin, to show Rory he came with good intent.

Lorcan wore the simple habit of a monk, and was weaponless. Of them all Lorcan was the safest. No Irishman who cared for the fate of his eternal soul would raise his hand against the archbishop. Or so Eve devoutly prayed, remembering what had happened last winter to Thomas Becket at Canterbury.

Eve's mare tossed her head playfully, after a month without being ridden, and the bells on the red leather bridle tinkled merrily. It was a disconcerting sound, under the circumstances, reminiscent of happier times. The August day was hot and bright, and so green it brought tears to her eyes to see the beauty of it. Ireland. What value was there to life if there was not something, or someone, you were willing to die for? They came to a halt half a mile from Rory's men and waited.

"Will he come?" Eve asked.

Richard gazed at her with worried gray eyes, but he smiled. "He'll come. His curiosity alone will drive him here."

He was right. Within five minutes Rory and two men came thundering across the high grass on their sturdy Irish ponies. Eve squinted against the sun, and saw that Rory's companions were one-eyed Tiernan and Hasculf. Her hands tightened on the reins. If she had her bow she could easily kill Hasculf as he rode toward them. Vengeance, hot and blind, reared its deceitful head until all she saw was Hasculf and her desire to see him dead. She vowed it would happen, if not here, not today, soon.

The Irish king drew rein within a few feet of them. "De Clare. So we meet again. Have you come to surrender?"

Unobtrusively, Eve translated back and forth between the men.

"Never that, O'Conor."

"I thought not. Good morrow, Lorcan. You're here to keep us all honest, are you?" Rory chuckled, his blue eyes lively with triumph. "Tell me then what you've come for, if not surrender."

"I want safe conduct for the women and children of Dublin, to see them unharmed from this place."

A loud roar of laughter greeted Richard's words, and all eyes turned to Hasculf. "The great Norman warlord comes crawling, begging for the lives of his loved ones." The laughter was gone as suddenly as it had appeared, and murderous hatred transformed the Norseman's face into a mask of contempt. "Send them back, Rory. It can't be long now before they starve like dogs in the streets, and Dublin will be ours without a man lost in battle."

Tiernan eyed the Norseman with open amusement, his mouth set at a crooked smirk in his thin face. "Our Norse friend is crude as ever, though he does have a point, Rory. They'd not be here if the situation weren't becoming desperate."

Rory was silent, and Eve prayed her trust in him was not misplaced. He had helped her once, but was that enough, now, to risk her life on and the life of her child? Her future and her happiness lay in his hands.

"At least let the children go," she said, trying to keep the pleading from her voice.

"Was it a son you bore the Norman?" Rory asked, a surprising note of tenderness in his voice.

She shook her head. "A girl. Her name is Isabella."

Rory looked as though he wished to be anywhere but here, and would not meet her eye. Then his shoulders squared, and he looked at Richard, never letting his gaze come her way. "You came to this island an invader, at the invitation of a man deposed from his kingdom because of his cruelty and ambition. You are not Irish, de Clare, no matter that you marry a princess of our blood. Your children by her are not Irish and have no right to rule here.

"I am High King of Ireland. She will have an Irish king, or no king at all. Go back to Dublin and take your wife with you. She cast her fate when she married you, and your fate is not to rule here, ever.

"Surrender, go back to Wales, and I will give safe passage to all the women and children, except your family. That is all I will offer."

"And if I do, what will become of Eve and my daughter?"

"They will die with you. It is too dangerous for me to allow any of you to live."

"Henry Plantagenet would never allow the murder of one of his barons without severe reprisals."

Rory shook his head. "Where is this King Henry of yours? He seems reluctant to come to your aid, de Clare, for whatever reason. If he will not come when you are alive, why should he come if you are dead? My offer does not change. You may save the lives of all your men, and the people of Dublin, by your surrender. But only at the forfeit of your life and that of your family."

"Then you give me no choice," Richard said. "I'll never willingly give my wife and child up to slaughter."

Rory stared into the distance, at Dublin lying so quietly, awaiting her fate. "No. Sadly, there was never any choice."

Eve watched as Rory rode away, taking all her hope with him. One way or the other he had condemned them to death. Starvation in Dublin, or surrender and execution.

For the first time since the siege began, she was overwhelmed with despair. That it had come to this, all the bright promise of her life with Richard, all the years they should have together, and the children, sacrificed because she would not leave Ireland when he first asked her to. But even now she would make the same choice. Richard and Isabella were her heart and soul. She could not leave.

"There is still hope," Lorcan said.

"How can you say that?" She was tired and frightened and wanted nothing more than to hide in the safety of Richard's embrace.

"Where there's life there's hope. You're a healer, Eve, you know that better than most."

"We're outnumbered fifty to one, and O'Conor is right, there will be no ships from England or Wales to rescue us," Richard said, his face pale and grim. "It will take a miracle, Lorcan."

"Then we must pray a miracle into existence." The archbishop turned and started back to Dublin with such calm assurance, Eve felt some of the grinding fear lift.

"Prayer does not win battles," Richard said.

"Who are you to say so?" Eve asked. "And what do you mean by battle?"

"I'll not sit in Dublin and starve. We'll do battle with Rory."

"That is suicidal!"

"It is also our one hope."

She rode beside him because it was her destiny to be there. Lifting her head proudly, she turned her back on Rory and his army of Irishmen.

Thirty-one

In the small hours of the night, between midnight and dawn, Eve sat propped against pillows as she nursed the baby. It was extraordinarily sensual, the warm, eager little mouth suckling at her nipple. The relief it brought, releasing the pressure of the milk in her breasts, was blessed. Isabella's delicate skull was covered with a new crop of fine pale hair and Eve stroked it gently with her finger, crooning wordlessly.

Richard shifted in the bed and she gazed over at him. He was watching her.

"I didn't mean to wake you."

"I enjoy watching. She's grown." He turned silent. His mind twisted around and around, but he inevitably came back to the same place. Their only hope for survival was to go to battle against O'Conor. As Eve had said, the idea was suicidal, since they were so greatly outnumbered. But he could not sit in Dublin and watch his wife and child starve.

In the week since talking with Rory, his preparations for battle had been uninterrupted. They were as ready as they would ever be. At dawn he would lead his men out of Dublin. He hoped to surprise the Irish army camped to the west of the town walls. Today their fate would be sealed, in victory or defeat. There was no middle ground, no room for mistakes. A small miracle or two would not be amiss, but he held little hope for that. His pragmatic Norman heart left the miracle-seeking to Lorcan and his dreaming Celtic monks in their prayer-shrouded church.

He had not told Eve today was the day of battle, and knew himself a coward, but he wanted to spare her as long as possible. Dear God, what would he do if he lost her? He could not even think of such a thing.

Watching as she put the baby back to rest, a surge of hot, sweet desire washed over him. It might be their last chance to be together, and when Eve came back to bed, he gathered her into his arms.

"My sweet love," he whispered against her silky hair. Leaning back against the pillows, he cupped her face in his hands, and saw desire, devotion, and strength in the green eyes staring back at him. His thumbs brushed her cheeks, gently, and she leaned into his hand, turning her face to kiss his palm with light, warm kisses.

"I need you, Richard." Her lips trembled, and she curled against his broad chest, her hands caressing his shoulders and arms, then moving lower, finding the hard, swollen part of him, and stroking him there, too. "Just for a while make me forget there's an army outside our door, make me feel young and carefree again."

He knew what she meant, knew their loving could do that, could take them to a fair, wide place full of sunshine and joy. He rolled her onto her back, and covered her with his hard, bold body, his mouth and hands rousing the passion that lay just beneath the dignified exterior she wore.

She responded to him eagerly, clinging hard, trying to shut out the world in the passionate gift of his body. He ran his tongue lightly along her warm lips, then down her throat, to her breasts, where the baby had been. Her eyes grew luminous with desire, green as summer behind their lashes.

The soft, sweet flesh, the silky skin he ran his hands over, responded to his touch with a fiery need. His own desire was feverish, wild as it had never been before, as though their loving could stave off the fear of death that hung over them so thickly it was choking them. Their union was hard and desperate, and it left him shaking, his breath shuddering, his heart pounding as she lay curled into him.

Eve started to cry, silently, the tears rolling down her cheeks and onto his chest. "Hush, Princess." He caressed her glorious silvery hair, aware of its faint heather scent.

"It's today." Not a question, but she spoke it softly, as though not wanting to hear the answer.

"Yes."

Slowly her tears quieted, and they lay together, neither wanting to break the embrace, until the bells for Vigils rang in the Irish cathedral, and Richard knew he must leave the bed, and her arms, and prepare for the most significant battle of his life.

It was an hour before dawn as Eve knelt in the hushed church. A heavy weight of dread filled her heart, and she could not form coherent thoughts, her prayers were disjointed and desolate. Fear filled her throat like vomit, and she swallowed hard to force it down. Slowly, the quiet shadow of grace that permeated the church began to calm her. The smell of incense and honey from the fine wax candles lingered in the dark air, though the only light was a single votive near the tabernacle.

The monks of Holy Trinity sat quietly in their choir stalls, their singing of Vigils ended, the psalms of Lauds not yet begun. She knew they prayed, but she wondered *what* they prayed. They were Irish. Did they ask for victory for Richard, or for Rory? Or did they rather ask simply to accept whatever happened? She knew acceptance was the higher, more spiritual place, but found she could not go there. All her heart and soul cried out for one thing; that Richard live, that victory be his.

Caitlin knelt beside her, outwardly calm, lost in the customary solace of her prayers. Eve felt no comfort, only a red, feverish fear, like some malevolent beast gnawing at her mind, gripping her soul. She spent an agonizing hour pleading her cause, beseeching God for mercy. Just before dawn she rose stiffly, no less fearful than when she began.

"Eve, don't." Caitlin's eyes were sober with concern.

"I have to see it. I can't kneel here and wait to hear what has happened. I have to see him."

"I'm coming with you."

They left the church together, two frightened, proud women, and crossed the town to where Richard and his knights were mounted, waiting for the gate to open. Some of the archers were stationed along the walls, but the majority would fight with the knights. Her eyes met his across the distance, and it was all she could do to keep her composure. He slowly turned from her and ordered the gate opened.

The war cry of "Strongbow" broke the calm of the morning as Richard and his knights surged forward, hoping to take Rory's men by surprise in this dawn attack.

"Richard, my love." She felt as though her heart were being ripped apart. "God keep you safe."

Thundering of horses hooves, swords, bows rubbing against chain mail, rattle of bridles and spurs, the hard breathing of the horses and shouts of men encircled Richard. The sounds of battle were as familiar to him as his own name. Ahead lay Rory's camp. Men leapt from sleep with terror in their eyes and scrambled for weapons. Surprise was on Richard's side, but nothing more.

Richard's archers came within range and stood in their practiced formation, a wall of shields protecting each phalanx. A barrage of arrows descended on Rory's men, then another and another, spreading panic among the men still scrambling from sleep. Richard swerved to one side, leading his knights away from the deadly assault. His stomach churned with fear, as it inevitably did when he rode into battle, and his mind focused, cold and resolute, on what he had to do. Distraction would be fatal.

Pulling his sword from its scabbard, with a cry of battle rage, he bore down on the nearest Irishman, who turned, his own sword upraised, to meet him. The man was no match for Richard's skill and soon fell beneath the blows, but there were a dozen Irish warriors to take his place. With knees and thighs and heels he guided his war-horse, and Emys responded instantly to his years of training, pivoting, leaping, charging and retreating on command. It left Richard's hands free to use his shield and sword, and mounted on the big animal, with chain mail to protect him, Richard was a formidable foe. The Irish wore no body armor, their horses were small and ill-trained, their weapons inferior to those used by Richard's army.

Five Irish warriors bore down on him, swords raised, faces contorted with battle fury. The blows came from several directions. Like a wolf pack the ring of snarling men advanced and retreated, seeking a weak spot. One finally drew close enough to attack Emys, and, screaming in pain and terror, the big war-horse collapsed. Richard sprang free from the saddle. Emys struggled up and staggered away, too injured to be of use. Smiles of triumph lighted the faces of the mounted Irishmen. Richard twirled about, sword slashing. They kept their distance for now, but he knew it was hopeless. Within minutes they would overpower him.

He thought of Eve, and tiny Isabella, and fierce determination raged through him. He would not die on this bloody field at Dublin!

With renewed strength, he began to beat back his attackers, who, surprised, moved more cautiously against him. First one man, then another came forward to fight him. He grew exhausted while they stayed fresh.

He knew they were toying with him and would soon close

in for the kill. He had failed. He had promised to protect Eve and the baby, and he could not. Tears of anger and grief stung his eyes.

Sweat ran down his face beneath the conical helmet, his breath came hard and sharp into his burning lungs, his sword arm screamed with each effort he made to keep fighting, but fight on he did. They were not far from the walls of Dublin, having doubled back. With an unmistakable thud, an arrow rammed into the back of one of his attackers. The man had time to look startled before falling dead from his horse.

More arrows rained down from the walls, and as the Irishmen sought to escape the barrage, Richard attacked with fresh strength pulled from the depths of his tired body. One died by Richard's sword, another by the arrows. The others turned and galloped away.

Glancing up at the high walls, Richard saw Eve, bow in hand, signaling down to him. She was shouting something which he was too far away to hear. If he did not know better, he would say the woman was smiling. He squinted through the sweat and fatigue. She *was* smiling.

He looked up then, ready for the next attack, and to his utter astonishment found himself alone on a field that was nearly deserted. His knights milled around in a sort of daze, turning their horses this way and that, seeking an enemy that no longer existed. Redmon came galloping toward him, a huge grin on his face.

"By God, Richard, we did it! The bastards turned tail and ran!"

Richard pulled the helmet from his head. Rory, with all his thousands, had been no match for his archers and their deadly longbows, and his mounted knights.

Even as his men shouted their victory cries, something nagged at Richard. It was too easy. Too easy by far. Though he could see Irishmen fleeing in all directions, disappearing into the hills, his unease increased. Then he saw the tall

Norseman, Hasculf, and a band of several hundred men riding toward Dublin. Dublin, which had been left with no more than a token guard. Dublin, where Eve and Isabella waited.

Fear curled into a tight knot around his heart. He mounted the horse one of his men offered, and with a touch of his spurs the animal leapt forward.

Eve watched from the rampart that ran along the walls of Dublin. Relief, as giddy as any wine, flooded her when she saw Richard was safe. Her arrows had been true as one Irish warrior after another fell. She still could not believe Rory's great army had run away. Here and there small skirmishes were fought, but it was obvious Richard was wildly, miraculously victorious.

The archers along the walls raised their voices in a cheer of triumph, eager to join their fellows on the battlefield. She watched as they clambered down the ladders and ran for the gates, and she smiled to see their youthful exuberance. She let herself laugh a little, but was afraid to give in to the overwhelming emotions that washed over her, afraid she would become hysterical if she let herself go. Caitlin was with Isabella in the sanctuary of the nuns' cloister. Eve must tell her cousin the news. Just as she turned to climb down the ladder, something caught her eye.

She went back to the wall and looked over. There were horsemen galloping toward Dublin. Sudden terror seized her. The gate! In their excitement the archers had surged out through the nearest gate, leaving it wide open and unprotected. There was nothing to prevent the Irish warriors she saw from riding into Dublin. She must get to Isabella. Gathering her skirts, she ran along the wall, hoping to get nearer the nuns' abbey before descending.

It was too late. She heard the sound of horses coming through the gate at a dead gallop, and the war cries of men

determined to have blood. At the head of the band rode
Hasculf. A sudden dark and furious rage overwhelmed her
at sight of her brother's murderer. Checking the leather
quiver at her hip, she fingered the arrows that still lay there.
Only three left, but all it would take was one. Hasculf was
within reach, and if she were to die this summer morning,
that bastard would go with her. She prayed Richard would
come, but knew she could not wait. If Hasculf made it to
the abbey, all was lost.

"Hasculf!" She shouted his name as loudly as she could.
He turned startled eyes on her. "This is for Egan," she whispered as she nocked an arrow into place and, with all her
strength, drew the bowstring toward her. She saw disbelief
light the Norseman's eyes. Too late he sought to protect
himself. By the time he reacted to the threat, the arrow was
flying to its target. He fell from his horse at the impact,
the arrow going in his chest and protruding through his
back.

Her fierce satisfaction was followed by a swift wave of
fear as Hasculf's men, pointing and shouting, focused on
her. More than one archer had her in his sights.

A baby cried, far away, through a haze of pain. Eve struggled to wake, aching to comfort the child and hold it safe.
Finally, she managed to opened her eyes and tried to focus
on the tall man with his back turned toward her. She must
have made a sound, because he turned, and, seeing her
awake, came to the bed.

"Thank God," Richard said, dropping wearily into a chair
beside her. His hand caressed her cheek, his thumb brushed
aside a wisp of hair.

"Where is Isabella?" Her voice sounded strange to her
ears, hoarse and low.

"With Caitlin. She's safe."

"I heard her crying."

"No, she's asleep." He raised her hand to his lips, and kissed it with a desperate need. "Caitlin removed the arrow from your leg. The wound was not deep, and should heal completely in a few weeks."

She remembered the battle then, and Hasculf. "Did we win?"

"That we did. Rory isn't broken by any means, but he'll not be able to put together another army of any size for a while. We're safe for now, and many of the Irish lords have promised me their loyalty. It seems they're not adverse to casting their lot with the victor, though I doubt not should I lose to Rory in the future their loyalty would swing as easily and swiftly back to him."

He was a powerful man, she realized, both in body and soul. A man others would follow, a man they would look to for leadership. She had every hope he would prove a wise ruler for her people. The idea struck her as ironic, remembering how she despised the idea of him a year ago, sure no man but an Irishman could rule Leinster. Yet her father had proved a cruel and greedy ruler, unable to keep his people from warring with each other, unable to make peace with the other kings of Ireland.

"You are king of Leinster now, Richard."

He gave her a strange, self-mocking smile. "Never a king, and in truth my ambition never went so high as that. Henry Plantagenet will never allow me the title, let alone the reality of so powerful a position. In Henry's mind there is one king."

"The Devil take the man. What business is it of his?"

He laughed outright. "That's the wife I know and love, all fire and indignation. He makes it his business, and believe me, his army is much larger than any I could hope to raise. The best way to ensure an all-out invasion of Ireland is to defy Henry further."

"How do you mean to avert such an invasion? Henry doesn't know you have no intention of setting yourself up

as his rival. The only word he will receive is of your great
victory, of the Irish lords who vow themselves to you now.
Henry may yet invade us, and then where shall we be? He'll
bring war such as we've never seen in Ireland. I can't bear
to think of it."

"Morgan arrived in Dublin last night. He brings word
from Henry."

She eyed him suspiciously. He had known all along what
he was going to do, he'd had all night to think about it.
"What does Henry want?"

"He's agreed to talk."

"He's coming here?" Her voice rose on a note of alarm.

"No, we go to him. As soon as you're able to travel, we
sail for Pembroke."

Thirty-two

Pembroke. Eve gazed out of the small window of her chamber, high in the stone keep that was Richard's seat of power in south Wales. They had sailed past soaring cliffs, wilder and more rugged than any she was accustomed to in Ireland, before putting into the wide harbor and tidal river. The walled town was built along a prominent ridge, with the castle in the west end and Monkton priory nearby. She gazed now over undulating, fertile country, with the Cambrian mountains, blue and mysterious, to the north. Wales was a beautiful land.

She wondered if she could ever be at home here, should Henry refuse them leave to return to Ireland. Gazing downward, she saw the English king's army camped in tents all around the castle. Not only was Henry angry enough to forbid Richard's men from sailing to Ireland, he had spent much of the last year collecting an army to invade that island. It was worse than they feared. Somehow they must convince Henry not to come warring to Ireland.

She turned from the window. Isabella had been bathed and fed and the nurse had taken her off for a nap. Richard was dressing for their meeting with the king, and she felt a surge of pride at sight of him. He was achingly handsome, his hair freshly washed and combed, his beard neatly trimmed. It was to be a formal occasion, a banquet in the great hall of the keep, and so Richard wore a long tunic of dark-brown velvet, in keeping with the Norman style. But around his neck he wore the pagan torc, its gold gleaming faintly with reflected light. It was his one ornament, but he needed no other, so strongly did he exude an aura of power and vitality.

Her own gown of yellow silk was unadorned, but she wore over it a cloak with the many colors of Irish royalty, woven together so skillfully that none of the colors clashed, nor were they merged together, so losing their impact. They were a handsome couple, she knew, and she was glad of it, for tonight she was to meet not just Henry, king of England, but Rosamund Clifford.

"You are handsome tonight, my lord."

His gray eyes showed his pride. "And you, Princess, are the most ravishingly beautiful creature I've ever set eyes on. There are times I can hardly believe my good fortune, that you are mine." He gathered her into his arms, caressing her rounded cheek, and leaned down to kiss her sweetly eager mouth.

"We'll be late," she whispered.

"Henry can wait."

She gave him a little shove, and he stepped back in mock distress. "Don't antagonize the man, Richard."

"There is near an hour before the meal. We have plenty of time."

She smiled at him mischievously. "A lifetime, my lord, surely." She held out her hand to him, and when he took it led him to the wide bed. For the next hour no thought of the fair Rosamund crossed her mind.

"God's blood, Richard, you've taken your time. Busy with that pretty wife of yours I'd wager, by the looks of her. And look at you. Turning yourself into an Irishman?" Henry Plantagenet fairly bellowed his amusement, and those near him laughed, as was politic to do when the king deemed it so.

Eve blushed. She had not expected the English king to be quite so loud, nor so crude. At her one earlier meeting with him, when she had translated for her father when he went begging to Henry for help, the man had been weighted with dignity. Who was the real Henry?

Richard bowed to his sovereign, just enough not to raise the king's eyebrow, and said, "I am here now."

Those near the king quieted, waiting to see if Henry took the terse answer as an insult. If he had been expecting an apology or explanation, it was plain it would not be forthcoming. The rivalry between the two men was evident to all. Eve held her breath, aware of the tenseness with which Richard held himself.

The king nodded his head just enough to let them know he was not angry, but with a look that warned he would not be mocked or disobeyed. It was then Eve saw the small, delicate woman standing near the king. She had gold hair, and her pale-blue eyes were set in a face of perfect beauty.

"Countess, may I present to you the Lady Rosamund Clifford."

Eve realized some reaction was expected to the king's introduction, but did one curtsy to the king's mistress? Surely not. She bowed her head politely. She knew she appeared stiff and formal, but she could not help it. Rosamund was the most beautiful woman she had ever seen. How could Richard look at her and not remember what had been between them? How could he not think of what Henry had taken from him?

"Rosamund, this is Eve, countess of Pembroke. Our dear Richard's wife."

The woman smiled at her sweetly. "You must tell me all about Ireland." Rosamund took her by the arm and led her into the hall, leaving the men to follow.

The stone hall was huge, with a dozen long tables set up on trestles, and important men waiting impatiently for the king to appear. Barons and earls would dine with them tonight, as well as Welsh princes. Morgan and Caitlin waited near the high table, subdued and cautious in this crowd of bold, greedy men. Scanning the crowd, she saw Tewdr at the far end of the hall. The boy had uncles in attendance tonight, and Eve wondered when the time came to return to Ireland, if they were allowed to do so, if Tewdr would follow. The pull of one's native land was strong.

Richard's return had forestalled an invasion, for the time. How long he could keep Henry here, or persuade the English king to turn back into England, she could only guess. But looking at the men gathered in the great hall she did not believe they would be easily dissuaded. They had come expecting adventure and profit and would be angry if disappointed.

Torches blazed in their sockets along the walls, and tapestries of hunting scenes hung all about. The men brought their hounds and their hawks into the hall with them, settling the hooded birds on whatever perches they could find. Ban, walking beside Eve, fairly twitched with excitement, and she lay a restraining hand on his head. Richard had not dared to argue when she insisted on bringing the big wolfhound with her.

Rosamund led her to the table at the head of the hall. It was set crosswise to the two long rows of tables spread out below, and was the only board covered with linen and set with plates of silver rather than wooden trenchers. Eve settled onto a cushioned bench, where Rosamund indicated, and found she was sitting next to the king, with Rosamund on his other side, and Richard next to Rosamund.

"You seem ill at ease, Lady Pembroke," Henry said, as he poured wine into her goblet.

She took a sip of the wine, to calm herself. She had to get her mind off whatever Richard and Rosamund talked about, beyond where she could hear. There were more important things to be concerned with. "Forgive me, my lord. I'm unaccustomed to such luxury as this."

"You'll get used to it soon enough, I should think. Pembroke is a pleasant place, though a bit primitive. You should be comfortable here."

If he thought this stone keep primitive, whatever would he think of the simple wooden buildings of Ireland? Then the impact of his words hit her. "Pembroke is not our home. We will be returning to Ireland soon."

Henry's eyes were hazel, she saw. They studied her now, and she was relieved to see neither anger nor impatience in them. For all his volatility it seemed Henry was also a careful man. "Do you think it wise, Lady?"

"Wise or not, it is our destiny."

A small smile touched his mouth, a very sensual mouth, she noticed. Henry was yet a young man, and handsome, with ruddy coloring, though he was not tall and was given to a certain heaviness. He seemed more alive than most men, more virile, and it was not just the allure kingship and power could give any man, even the most ugly and vicious. It was the man himself, and Eve surprised herself by relaxing.

"I have never seen Richard so happy," the king said.

She was startled by the change of subject, but was careful not to appear so. "He is most unhappy at the discord between you, my lord. It was never his wish to usurp your place in Ireland. He would gladly give up all he has won there to keep your good opinion of him."

"If he opposed me, I'd destroy him."

Of that she had no doubt. "Richard is loyal to you. Command him to remain in Pembroke and he will do so."

Henry pursed his lips, then took a long draught of wine. "No doubt he would, and hate me for it. De Clare is one of my most powerful earls, not a man I'd wish as an enemy. He's much more valuable to me as an ally. I've made the mistake of thinking a friend my enemy. I'll not do it again."

The king spoke this last very softly, and a pained, distant look came into this eyes. *He is speaking of Thomas Becket.*

She placed a comforting hand on his arm. "Richard will never betray you, but his heart is in Ireland. He is a good, compassionate man. My land has been torn by war for so long, it has need of a competent ruler. You cannot be there, but Richard, as your representative, can rule in your name."

The king seemed to ponder this, though it could not be the first time such thoughts had occurred to him. He placed his hand over Eve's, where it still rested on his arm. "I begin to see why Ireland has captured his heart, Lady. If I forbade his return there, would you stay with him?"

"Of course I would," she said without hesitation. "Though I love my land and my people, it is Richard who is my life."

"Then you have something more precious than any kingdom." He raised his hand to gently forestall her next words. "Enough for now, Eve. I'll think on what you've said. And tell my friend de Clare that I have never met a more charming or beautiful ambassador. With you pleading his cause, he is a lucky man indeed."

They talked of pleasantries, inconsequential polite conversation, and Eve found her attention wandering. The king spoke of hawking, which was a passion with him, and she smiled and nodded, and leaned back so that the burly earl of Chester, seated to her right, could join the king in comparing the quality of one species of bird against the other.

On the other side of the king she saw Rosamund lean in toward Richard, touching his arm with a familiarity that sent a surge of anger through Eve. The other woman laughed, a sweet, melodious sound, and Richard smiled. Eve sipped at her wine, all the while watching from the corner of her eye. What was the strange emotion swirling about in the pit of her stomach? Jealousy? It seemed a ridiculous response. She knew without doubt that Richard loved her, and therefore she trusted him. What was jealousy but a lack of trust? With an effort she tore her eyes away. She trusted his fidelity. There was no need to focus her attention on him, as though he were a child at his lessons and needed her supervision.

The meal ended, the last course was cleared from the littered tables, and what was left carried out to be distributed among the poor who gathered at the gates of Pembroke Castle. Soon the harpers would come to sing for them. Eve watched as people rose from the benches to visit among their fellows. There were few women in the crowded hall. Most of the men gathered this summer evening were the knights and barons of Henry's army. They did not bring their wives with them.

"Come, Lady Pembroke, walk with me," Henry said, standing and holding his hand out to her.

She smiled and accepted. How did one say no to such a man?

"You really must refrain from staring at your husband. He is quite safe with Rosamund."

Was that a note of teasing in Henry's voice? "I didn't know I was obvious, I do apologize."

"Sweet lady, there's no need. I only meant to reassure you. Richard loves you, any fool can see that, and Rosamund is devoted to me, as I am to her."

Eve blushed, not knowing what to say, but a quiet peace settled around her heart. She believed Henry. Rosamund was no threat to her. They walked through the hall, the king calling greetings, exchanging jokes with his men.

The hall was crowded and hot and she wished to escape it, but knew she must stay, for Richard's sake. As Henry guided her through the maze of men Eve overheard the whispers and saw the too-bold glances from men, which implied the reason Richard had wed her was for the pleasure she gave him in his bed. She endured the slights, for Richard's sake, but her hand tightened on the king's arm. No doubt every man there thought Rosamund to be a more suitable match for the powerful earl of Pembroke. For the first time since her arrival in Wales, she wondered if it would not have been better for her to stay in Ireland and wait. But wait for what? There was no guarantee Richard would be allowed to return, and she would not be separated from him when things were so uncertain.

"Do you find Wales to your liking?" Henry asked.

If Henry heard the whispered insults, he gave no sign of it. She tried to answer calmly. "The land is beautiful. Pembroke is much like Dublin, with the sea so near and the hills in the distance. I wish I knew more about the people."

Most of the barons Henry introduced her to were polite, exquisitely so, when she was within hearing. But they talked about her openly enough when they thought she could not hear, and the general consensus seemed to be that Richard had married beneath himself. Eve found herself disquieted by the hostility concealed beneath the correct words and careful gestures.

The king himself had displayed no such intolerance, yet it was Henry who would bring this army into Ireland. One look at the English king's force and the Irish lords would capitulate without a fight. All that was left was to see what Henry would decide to do with Richard, either punish or reward him.

"You look unwell, Lady Pembroke," Henry said, his face softened with genuine concern.

"I am a bit tired, my lord."

"Then I shall return you to your husband. No doubt that beautiful babe of yours will be missing you."

As they passed one group of knights, they were so loud Eve unmistakably heard what they said.

"Look at the piece de Clare married. You'd think he'd know better than to bring such trash with him."

The sudden tenseness of the king's hand over hers told Eve he had heard the remark as well. Slowly Henry turned and retraced his steps, pulling Eve with him. The knights rose at his approach. One saluted his king with a goblet of wine. "To Ireland and the wealth to be ours." The others cheered.

Henry did not return the greeting, and the knights grew uneasy at his silence. It was plain to Eve the king was struggling to restrain his anger. When he spoke, his tone was dangerous.

"You were ever a tedious ass, Gilbert. You will apologize to Lady Pembroke for your foul remark."

The knight tried to smile, but the effort only made his mouth twitch nervously. "I do apologize, my lord."

"Not to me, you imbecile."

"But my lord, I speak no Irish."

"You don't need to. Lady Pembroke understands you perfectly."

The knight cut a quick glance at Eve and blushed. "I am sorry, Lady de Clare, for any insult I may have given."

Eve nodded her acceptance, fearing if she spoke she would say something appalling.

Henry's voice was still stiff with anger. "Now you will gather your things, Gilbert, and return to England. Tonight."

The knight had sense enough not to argue.

Henry spoke softly to her. "Do you wish to leave, my dear?"

"Yes, if you will grant me permission."

"In truth, I wish I could join you." Henry smiled and released her hand. "They do try my patience at times."

Eve maneuvered her way through the throng of people. No one tried to converse with her, and for once she was grateful for their indifference. She feared few in this crowd of men, greedy for Irish land and the rewards Henry would grant to them, would do as Richard had and marry Irish women. They would keep themselves separate from her people. Eve felt close to tears. Ireland, her beloved island, would never be the same after Henry Plantagenet claimed her as his own.

She finally found her way out through the single door

and down the steps into the bailey. The September air was sweet and heavy, with just enough of a cool breeze to warn of autumn. She felt better away from the undercurrent of emotions she could only guess at, the atmosphere of ambition and intrigue that inevitably attended a king.

The stable paddock was overcrowded with the large mounts of the Norman knights. Splendid horses, big-hearted, glorious beasts. Better than the men who owned them, most of them, she thought, and reached through the railing to stroke one of the animals. Richard's stallion Emys was recovering from his wounds back in Dublin. Eve had nursed the horse as tenderly as any of her human patients, and though he was ruined for war, and would never be as swift as he once was, he was still a magnificent creature. She was thankful she had been able to save him, and though Richard said little, she knew he was grateful as well.

Beside her, Ban scratched and yawned, then went exploring and seemed more interested in the smells of the stable yard than any other concern. She kept a watchful eye on him, knowing he would find something dreadful to roll in if she were not vigilant, but glad for the moment that her most pressing duty was to keep the dog out of trouble.

Recognizing his walk, she did not turn at the sound of Richard's approach. He stood behind her, not touching, but his presence was comforting. The stars were beginning to pierce the darkening sky. "Wales is a beautiful land," she said.

He put his arms around her then, and she leaned back against the hard, warm security of his chest. "We're going back to Ireland, I swear it to you. If I have to forfeit everything else in fines to Henry, we're going home."

Home. The tears came to her eyes then, and spilled slowly down her cheeks. Richard thought of Ireland as their home. If she had harbored any small doubt regarding his love for her, she knew now she had been foolish. Never again would she question his devotion, to her and to Ireland.

Thirty-three

The mare skittered nervously, and Eve soothed her with a touch and a soft word. The castle bailey was crowded with mounted knights, eager for a day's hawking with the king. Rosamund was the only other woman in the crowd. Eve noted the other woman had a tense seat and tended to jerk her horse's reins, signs that she was not her most comfortable when mounted. Eve knew herself to be relaxed and competent. It was like second nature to her, the ease with which she rode, and she was excited by the promise of a long, hard ride.

Richard brought his mount next to her. "The king is eager to fly a young goshawk he's been training. I thought we'd ride to the north. There's a good forest that should prove full of small game."

"Have you had a chance to talk to Henry yet?"

His gray eyes were dark, and he shook his head. "When Henry is ready he'll let me know what he's decided. It would be foolish of me to press him."

She knew it was hard for him, the uncertainty. That Henry held their destiny in his hands, could decide on a whim what direction their lives would take, sat uneasily with her as well. Looking around, she spied the king near the gate, the master falconer beside him with several hawks on his cadge. The king was holding an earnest conversation with the man, and Eve was once more beguiled by Henry's contradictory nature. He was powerful enough to decide the fate of a people and simple enough to debate with a servant the qualities of one bird against another.

The king's laughter rang out in the yard. He laughed with his head thrown back, full of life and enjoyment. She smiled to see it, and for all that her fate lay with the man, she found she could not dislike or resent him. Moving their horses carefully through the crowd, she and Richard made their way toward the king. Henry glanced at them and his smile broadened.

"This man tells me no English goshawk is a match for a Welsh peregrine falcon. Can you credit it, Richard? Do you have such a bird in your mews so that we may settle the question?"

"Alas, my lord, I've been so seldom in Pembroke the last several years, I keep few birds, and no peregrines at the moment. What Rhodri says is true. There is no match for a falcon on the wing."

"Are you saying the Welsh bird is superior to the English?" The king spoke in a light tone, but Eve wondered if something more lay behind the seemingly innocent question.

"Not better, except in her own environment," Richard said. "They hunt differently, the hawk and the falcon."

"Though the result is the same." Henry was sober now, and he seemed to study Richard closely for a moment. "Much as you and I come to the same end, through different routes. We're both destined to play a part in Ireland."

Eve forced herself to relax her grip on the reins, not wanting to pass her nervousness to her mount. What did Henry mean? Was he going to allow them to return to Ireland? Before she could question him, he called to the guards to open the gates, and the whole company galloped out into the hills.

Falling back from the press of people nearest the king, she followed at the end of the long procession. It was a glorious late-summer day, warm and fragrant, and she breathed deeply of the gold-washed air. It was the first time she had ridden like this since Isabella's birth, and she reveled in the strength and grace of her body and the quick, strong mare between her thighs.

They rode for a quarter hour, into the dense wood of oak and beech, where the last wild roses of the season clung in pale-pink clumps on spreading bushes. The hunt moved nosily ahead of her, but she was content to wander through the countryside, curious about this land where Richard had spent his boyhood. She stopped beside a small rill of a stream, letting her mare drink, listening to the men and horses moving noisily through the green darkness of the forest. What sort of hunting would they find if they scared away every living creature? It seemed as with most things men did, the companionship and camaraderie of being together in a group was as much the object of the day as any game the king's goshawk might bring down.

It was then she became aware of the voices, a man and a woman, not far from where she stood, though she could not see them. The man she recognized as Richard. The woman could only be Rosamund. A chill of apprehension touched her. She could not hear their words and there was an intensity to the exchange that frightened her. Without hesitation she moved closer, knowing she must hear this, and dreading what she would find. From her hiding place behind an oak tree, she watched and listened.

"I must know if you are happy, Rose."

"Richard, you were ever too intense." She reached up and smoothed the frown from his forehead. "You must believe me when I tell you I am content with Henry. He is kind to me, you need not worry."

"That is the reason you stay, he is kind?"

Rosamund laughed, a soft, gentle sound. "Stop playing my protector, Cousin, we've both outgrown the role. Many women would be pleased with kindness from their men. But it is more than that. If I wished, I could leave Henry to marry. I have no desire to leave. Henry needs me."

Richard crossed his arms and shook his head. "In what way does Henry need you?"

"Have you ever met his queen?"

"Eleanor? A few times."

"What is she like?"

"She's strong, determined, intelligent—"

Rosamund laughed again. "She's stubborn and troublesome and makes Henry's life hell. Don't you see? I want nothing in this world but to please him. I become whatever he needs. I'm not a strong woman, not like Eleanor or your wife. I need a safe place to hide."

"Henry provides that place?"

"He does. What of you, Richard? If Henry does not allow you to return to Ireland, can you be content with your life?"

"The king has the power to do many things, but the one thing he cannot do is separate me from Eve. I will gladly go to the ends of the earth to be with her, far from Henry Plantagenet's reach if it should come to that."

Eve watched and listened, and a smile of pure joy made her face radiant.

Richard led Rosamund toward her horse and gave her a hand up.

"You must not worry about me." She reached down and laid her hand on Richard's cheek. "Be happy, Richard."

"I am. I wish the same for you, sweet cousin."

Rosamund gathered her reins and rode from the meadow without another word and without looking back.

Eve stepped from behind the oak tree and Richard walked over to her. He touched her gently, his fingers caressing the curve of her cheek. "How much did you hear, Princess?"

"I was curious."

"I can see that. There is no reason to concern yourself about Rosamund. My heart has been conquered, as you well know, and is so armored with love for you, nothing will ever tempt it away." He gathered her close, and all the doubt drained from her as she wound her arms around his waist and laid her head on his chest. His heart beat strong, steady, just beneath her ear. With great gentleness she placed a kiss there. When she looked into his face, she saw a shimmer of tears in his gray eyes.

"You are my life, Eve. Nothing Henry or anyone else does can change that."

"There, do you see?" The king pointed to a high, rocky ledge, and the others squinted, shading their eyes with their hands to see what drew his attention.

Richard saw the peregrine falcon on the high, rocky ledge, her gold eyes focused on the men and horses milling around far below. She was an adult and glorious as her proud head reared back in offense at the intrusion.

"Bring my goshawk," the king shouted. His falconer hurried to do as he was bid, taking the bird from its perch on the four-sided cadge and handing it up to the king. Henry's gauntleted fist held the bird steady as he deftly removed the goshawk's hood with his other hand. A piercing cry of anger came from the high nest, and the goshawk swiveled his head toward the noise. *"Oui, away my sweet,"* Henry crooned, and launched the bird skyward.

"What is he doing?" Eve pulled her mare close to the side of Richard's horse.

Richard felt an ugly queasiness in the pit of his stomach. "He's set his hawk on the falcon." The look of disgust on her face matched his mood exactly. It was a wasteful thing to do. One of the birds must die.

They stared skyward where the peregrine soared, high above the pursuing hawk. Richard knew how it would end and wondered that Henry could be so foolish. There was no match for a peregrine on the wing. Even as he thought it, the falcon stooped, folded her wings and plunged with increasing speed toward her prey. The hawk was dead before hitting the ground. All around him men were nervously silent, uncomfortably aware that the king's bird was dead.

Henry rode over to Richard, his expression a mixture of incredulity and self-mocking humor. "God's feet, they breed them brave in Wales, eh, de Clare?"

There was more to the question than the courage of a wild falcon, but Richard found the king's hazel eyes inscrutable. "My lord's hawk was hindered by jesses, while the wild bird had none. And she was protecting her territory."

"A strong instinct, that one, to defend one's home and kin. Strong enough to lead men to war. Ireland is mine, Richard. I'll not share it with any man." It was said softly, with a hint of humor in the voice, but no answering mirth in those Plantagenet eyes. Richard knew the whole force of a kingdom and the strong will of the king, as well as the sanction of the pope stood surety to those words.

"As you say, a man's home and kin are worth fighting for." The king gazed skyward, where the peregrine still rode the currents. "The question is, do you consider Wales your home, or Ireland?"

His fate, and that of Eve and their children, hung on Richard's response. It would be safe and simple to answer Wales. They could, in time, hope to reconcile themselves to life here, but it would be second best. It would be a lie. "Ireland is where my destiny lies."

Henry was silent in his appraisal, his eyes going slowly from Richard to Eve and back again. "Do you know you reminded me of my friend Becket when you said that? He was a man of unbending honesty. It was his greatest fault."

A sharp chill shivered down Richard's spine. Thomas Becket had been the man's friend, and it had not saved him. How much less chance did Richard have of coming out of this as he wished?

"You can't have Dublin." The king no longer looked at him, but back over his shoulder, as though growing bored with the conversation.

"My lord?"

"Dublin is mine, but Leinster I can grant you." He turned again to face Richard, and this time raised an admonishing finger. "But as my vassal, not as some independent princeling. You'll do homage for your lands just as you do for the other fiefs I allow you. And only if you help me bring this Rory O'Conor to heel. He's the only one worth worrying about, from what I gather. That damned falcon ruined one of my best birds. Bloody hell. It's time I sailed for Ireland, I've spent too much time dallying here as it is. We leave before week's end." He turned his horse about and trotted away.

"Did he just grant us permission to return to Ireland?" Eve asked.

Richard's face split into a wide grin, and he laughed as he looked down at his wife. "That he did. We're going home, Princess."

Home. She had thought it was a place. Now she knew it was this man.

Author's Note

I hope you enjoyed reading about Richard de Clare and Eve MacMurrough as much as I enjoyed writing their love story. I "discovered" Richard and Eve while researching a genealogy project. As with most fiction, this story began with a question. What was it like for a woman in twelfth-century Ireland, forced to marry a man she considered her enemy?

Writing an historical novel based on people long dead is a challenge because history is fluid and seldom recorded in an unbiased way. Much of what we know is not clear and therefore open to different interpretations. While I found useful information on Richard Strongbow de Clare, King Henry II, Dermot MacMurrough, and Rory O'Connor, the information for the female characters was much harder to find. The historical events are as accurate as I could make them with the information I had, however I did change the chronology slightly to keep the story compact.

No one knows if the marriage of Richard, Earl of Pembroke, and Eve, Princess of Leinster, was happy or disastrous. I choose to believe they loved each other.

I love to hear from readers. You can write to me at P.O. Box 1066, Highlands Ranch, CO 80126-1066.